ACCLAIM FOR SUSAN CRANDALL'S PREVIOUS NOVELS

MAGNOLIA SKY

"A terrific story . . . features two of the best characters ever written."
—*Romance Reviews*

"An emotionally charged tale of love, responsibility, and sacrifice. This story brings tears and laughter."
—*Romantic Times Bookclub Magazine*

THE ROAD HOME

"Crandall weaves a tale that is both creative and enthralling."
—*Romantic Times*

"The characters pull you into the story and stay with you long after the last page is read."
—*Bookloons.com*

"Susan Crandall writes an extremely poignant story of young love gone astray. Her attention to detail makes it a story that is easy to become deeply involved in."
—*TheRomanceReadersConnection.com*

"Ms. Crandall has again written a book that makes readers yearn for the small-town lifestyle."
—*ARomanceReview.com*

Promises
To Keep

Also by Susan Crandall

Back Roads
The Road Home
Magnolia Sky

SUSAN CRANDALL

PROMISES TO KEEP

WARNER
FOREVER

NEW YORK   BOSTON

Warner Forever is a registered trademark of Warner Books.

Cover design by Diane Luger
Cover illustration by Rick Johnson
Hand lettering by David Gatti
Book design by Giorgetta Bell McRee

Warner Books

Time Warner Book Group
1271 Avenue of the Americas
New York, NY 10020
Visit our Web site at www.twbookmark.com

Printed in the United States of America

First Paperback Printing: March 2005

10 9 8 7 6 5 4 3 2 1

*For my sister, Sally Hoffman,
who brought writing into my life.*

Acknowledgments

As always I'd like to thank editor extraordinaire, Karen Kosztolnyik, for her expertise in forming this book. Thanks to my agent, Linda Kruger, for being such a great source of support and enthusiasm. And I never would be able to pull it all together without my fabulous critique group, Indy Witts, Alicia, Brenda, Garthia, Laurie, Pam and Sherry. Appreciation to Karen White, whose sharp eye and great writing instincts repeatedly prevent me from making serious blunders.

Most of all, I'm greatly thankful for the love and support of my family, who make everything worthwhile.

PROMISES TO KEEP

Chapter 1

The revelation struck Molly Boudreau without warning, like a giant crashing wave of frigid water. The fierce power of it sucked the breath from her lungs and the determination from her heart. It was as if she'd stood deaf while the thunderous surge behind her had gathered power, numb while the ground had trembled in warning beneath her feet.

Deaf and numb and utterly unsuspecting.

Her entire life had been centered upon becoming a doctor. Perhaps she'd emerged from the womb possessing a single-minded determination. It hadn't been a distant wishing as most childhood fantasies, but a ruby red laser beam, so focused and intense in its being that nothing distracted her from it. Not slumber parties, or big games, or boyfriends. Not financial obstacles—of which there were many for a poor girl from a small midwestern town. She hadn't wavered once in her resolve, not from grade school through the endless fatigue-strained hours of residency.

But suddenly she realized her focus had been the

journey, the fight, with little concentration on what was to come after. She felt as if she'd been engaged in a frenzied uphill battle, wresting free of enemies that struggled against her, finding herself at the summit, breathless and bewildered by the lack of opposition.

A sense of disconnection settled heavily in the center of her chest as she stood in her beloved free clinic—which was in its unfortunate last days because of a lack of funding. This was her most recent, and most disappointing battle. And, as hard as it was to admit, this was the first time she'd met an obstacle she'd been unable to overcome. The clinic had been the sole reason she'd put up with the infuriating internal politics of her paying job at Boston General's emergency room.

For a long moment, she remained still, waiting for the unsettling feeling to pass. She shoved her hands into her lab coat pockets, staring beyond the clinic's crowded waiting area, out the large storefront window. Wind-whipped sleet was icing over everything with dangerous swiftness. The unseasonably early arrival of this winterlike storm just compounded her sense of floundering.

Seeking that inner spark that had always propelled her forward, she closed her eyes. She felt the swirl of motion around her, as if the rest of the world kicked into fast forward while she remained stuck in pause. She heard the crying babies, the quiet comforting murmurs of mothers, the motor noises made by a little boy near the front window pushing his matchbox car on the scarred, dark pine table.

"Dr. Boudreau!" A shout yanked her away from her battle with self-doubt.

Carmen, the girl working the sign-in desk, had jumped

from her chair to support Sarah Morgan, one of the few patients Molly saw here on a regular basis. Sarah had come to the clinic over six months ago for prenatal care. Molly had seen right away that she was different from the free clinic's usual maternity cases. For one thing, she wasn't a teen mother, or on her fifth pregnancy before her thirtieth birthday. She was expecting her first child and was just about Molly's age. She appeared well educated and was well dressed, yet utterly guarded about the details of her life—Molly had quickly deduced a woman in hiding.

Sarah had seemed as isolated and lonely as Molly. Molly's isolation was a by-product of her impossible schedule; she quickly learned that Sarah's was strictly self-imposed. Still, Molly saw a kindred spirit in Sarah's determination and independence.

Upon Sarah's invitation after her second visit to the clinic, they had forged a fragile friendship over coffee and conversation after clinic hours. Molly liked Sarah's quick wit and indomitable spirit. They had grown as close as two women could in their unusual situation. Sarah had been completely secretive about her past, the baby's father, or anything else that might have given Molly a clue to the reason she was living as she was. Even so, Molly felt they were friends; she might not know about the woman's past, but she knew what kind of person Sarah was inside.

Now, as Sarah's step faltered through the clinic door, she was clearly in labor.

Wrapping her arm around Sarah's back, Molly helped

move her as quickly as possible toward the examination rooms. "I thought I told you to go straight to the hospital!"

Sarah's knees wobbled and she groaned with a contraction.

"Has your water broken?" Molly asked.

Sarah nodded once, her pale blond hair falling over her face. Then in a breathy whisper she said, "About two o'clock this morning."

"Jesus." It was nearly noon. Molly knew that Sarah had a serious aversion to hospitals, but she had no idea it was so severe it would eclipse her common sense. "You should have called 911—how in the hell did you get *here*?"

"Taxi." Perspiration beaded on Sarah's brow as they settled her onto an examination table.

Molly turned to Carmen and said quietly, "Get an EMS unit here now!"

Carmen hustled from the room.

"All right now, Sarah, let's take a look and see where we are." Molly quickly swept her dark hair up into a pony tail to keep it out of the way. When she examined Sarah, she was stunned to see the baby was crowning. Even if the EMS was in the bay and ready to respond, it was doubtful that they could transport Sarah to the hospital before delivery.

Sarah started to push.

"Don't push yet. Take deep breaths." Molly took a couple herself to calm her voice before she spoke again. "Looks like we're going to have this baby right here."

Through pinched lips, Sarah said, "Good."

Molly's mouth went dry. Sarah didn't understand the risks. Molly had specialized in pediatrics. Under normal circumstances, with the proper medicine and equipment available she would feel confident in treating the baby once delivered. In this financially strapped clinic she had neither. Plus she'd never done a delivery alone, only assisted a couple of times during her rotation in OB/GYN. What if there were complications? At least with the head visible, the baby wasn't breech. Should she do an episiotomy? Was it too late for that?

She wanted to chastise Sarah for not going to the hospital where emergency equipment and obstetric specialists were plentiful. She wanted someone to stand over her shoulder and tell her she was doing everything right. But deep down, she couldn't deny the little rush that was building. This baby was coming—and Sarah depended upon Molly to keep both her and her child safe. It was all in Molly's well-trained, if ill-equipped, hands.

Inclining the head of the table and placing a couple of pillows under Sarah's shoulders, Molly pulled on gloves and said, "All right, next contraction, push."

She positioned herself to deliver the baby, listening for the scream of an approaching siren.

Sarah bore down with the next contraction. The baby's head pushed forward, then retreated slightly when the contraction was over.

Without a fetal monitor, Molly couldn't begin to tell if this baby was in distress. What if Sarah bled out? A thousand possible complications raced through her mind.

Come on, she thought, *babies were born for thousands of years without modern medicine.*

And lots of them died.

Molly shook off the thought. She coached Sarah through three more contractions.

Where was that damn EMS?

"Carmen!"

The girl came rushing back in with the cordless phone still in her hand. She looked as panicked as Molly felt. "They've got one unit in a ditch. And all others are dispatched—the storm. . . ."

"Try Mass General."

"I already have. They said they're having to prioritize. They're working a bus accident on I-93 right now."

Molly gave her a quick nod. "Keep after them." Then to Sarah, "You're doing great. We should have this little one here very shortly." Sarah had already told Molly that she had no family and the father didn't know of the baby's existence. Perhaps she'd reconsider telling him. "Isn't there someone we can call for you?"

Sarah was between contractions. Her voice quivered as she said, "No one. Promise me—" Her voice strangled to a groan as she bore down with a contraction.

The baby's head slid into Molly's hands; she rotated it slightly to the side, allowing the fluid to run from its mouth. Immediately she saw there was trouble.

"I need you to stop pushing. Breathe through the next contraction."

"What's wrong?" Panic gave Sarah's voice new strength. "What's wrong with my baby?"

Molly didn't answer, she had to concentrate on what she was doing. The cord was wrapped around the baby's neck. Everything was so slippery, the baby's neck so short, she couldn't get her finger under the cord.

Sarah started to groan.

"Don't push, Sarah. Breathe!" If the baby moved farther down the birth canal, the cord was going to cut off oxygen. Statistics of previously normal babies handicapped because of oxygen deprivation at birth whirled in Molly's head. Seconds mattered.

Sarah huffed exaggerated breaths, fighting the urge to push.

The contraction lessened.

Sarah blew out a long shuddering breath.

"Good girl!" Molly made another try at getting her finger between the baby's neck and the cord. This time she was successful, but her grip was tenuous. With the slightest movement, she could lose it.

She was ready to try and slide the cord over the baby's head when Sarah had another contraction.

"Breathe! Don't push." She didn't think Sarah was pushing, but the cord tightened around her finger anyway. "Carmen!"

The girl ran into the room.

In a calm voice Molly said, "Be ready to hand me that bulb syringe."

Carmen quickly pulled on gloves and picked up the syringe. Molly hoped Sarah didn't see the wild-eyed fear in the girl's face.

The contraction relaxed. Molly's brow beaded with perspiration and she held her breath as she attempted to slide the cord over the baby's head. If the cord slipped from her grasp, she'd have to wait through another contraction. More risk.

Quickly, Molly moved the cord over the baby's head. In a rush of relief, she finally took a breath.

Carmen put the bulb syringe into Molly's outstretched hand. She suctioned the mouth and nose. "Okay, push

with the next one. We're ready for the shoulders." To
Carmen she said, "Get several towels ready."

In three minutes, the baby was delivered.

"A boy!" Carmen shouted excitedly. "A baby boy!"

Silence followed.

Molly laid the baby face down across her forearm and
slapped the bottom of his feet.

Nothing.

She again suctioned the blue-tinged mouth, then
rubbed his back vigorously with a towel.

Carmen stood watching with huge eyes and open
mouth.

Sarah started to cry, a pitiful, helpless thin whine of
fear.

"Come on. Breathe," Molly whispered as she slapped
his feet again. The baby sucked in its first breath and
began to cry like a hungry kitten.

"That's it!" Molly wrapped him in a towel and laid
him, squalling, on Sarah's chest.

Sarah repeated over and over, as if to reassure herself,
"He's okay. He's okay."

"He's better than okay. He's great," Molly said, cutting
the cord and watching the baby's color improve by the
second. She looked to Carmen. "Get back on the phone.
We need the neonatal unit to check him out and give him
his walking papers. And Sarah needs a once over by an
OB/GYN."

"How much do you think he weighs?" Sarah asked.

"I'd guess at least seven and a half pounds—a good,
healthy size." She massaged Sarah's abdomen to deliver
the placenta. The danger to the baby was past, but until
she was certain there wasn't going to be any immediate

bleeding problem, Molly kept her attention close on the mother.

"Look at all that black hair," Sarah said with wonder in her voice. "I expected him to be bald as a billiard ball. I didn't have enough hair to hold a barrette until I was three."

Molly, preoccupied with her work, responded absently, "Must take after his father." It wasn't until she realized Sarah hadn't responded that she grasped what she'd said. "Sorry."

"His father was a redhead."

Surprised, Molly looked at Sarah's face. This was the very first thing she'd ever said about the father. Sarah had acted as if there *was* no father. "Oh."

"You think I'm terrible. But his father is . . . dangerous . . . *evil*. I can't ever, ever let him near Nicholas. I won't put him on the birth certificate. I don't want there to be *any* link to that man." There was a certain panicked vehemence in Sarah's voice that Molly thought bordered on hysteria.

For a moment, Molly held her words. Circumstances had led her to believe that Sarah had been a victim of domestic violence, hiding away from an abusive husband or lover. Sarah herself had been as secretive as a mummy, not divulging the slightest detail of her past. But she had that haunted look about her, a humming tension, a jittery fear that never quite left her eyes. Molly had seen it dozens of times. But she had never heard even the most battered of women refer to her child's father as "evil." Surely Sarah's emotions were talking, the primal combination of protective new motherhood and raging hormones.

"You've named him Nicholas, then?"

"Yes. Nicholas James."

"After anyone in particular?" Molly fished.

Sarah shook her head, but kept her gaze on her baby's face. "He's a person unto himself, a new start. He won't take after *anyone*."

There was a certain stony conviction in her words that made Molly reconsider. Maybe the father *was* truly bad.

The siren she'd been straining to hear finally pulled up outside.

"Sounds like your chariot has arrived."

"I don't really have to go to the hospital, do I? I'm fine. Nicholas is fine."

"I think you're both fine. But it's always a good idea to have a newborn under close observation for the first few hours. Besides, unless you have someone who can stay with you, I don't want you to go home yet. But if there's someone I can call. . . ."

Something shifted behind Sarah's innocent blue eyes. Suddenly she looked much younger than twenty-nine. "No. I'm alone." Then she smiled warmly and cuddled the baby closer. "Or at least I was until now."

Molly looked on, wondering what that connection must be like, having a human being completely created within your own body. And now that human being was a life force of its own, yet relying on you for every need. The awesome responsibility. The love.

Eighteen months ago, she'd had surgery to remove a tumor from her cervix. It had been more extensive than the surgical team had anticipated. The prognosis for Molly's carrying a child to term wasn't good.

As she gave Sarah's hand one last squeeze before the

paramedics rolled her out of the clinic, she wondered if this would be as close as she'd ever get to the birth experience.

Molly finished out her day with a satisfied buzz in her veins. Holding new life in her hands had helped eclipse the bleakness that had threatened to swamp her earlier—had pushed the dissatisfaction back behind the black curtain.

Finally, the last patient was out the door and she was free to go to the hospital and see Sarah and the baby. She was as excited as she'd been when she'd gone to see her nephew, Riley, for the first time. Having coaxed Sarah's baby's first breath, it was hard not to think of Nicholas as family.

The weather hadn't improved over the past hours. The instant Molly stepped out the door, sleet pelted her like tiny needles, stinging her cheeks and bare hands. She had to squint into the wind to protect her eyes. Despite Carmen's frequent applications of ice-melt on the walk outside the clinic, Molly didn't dare lift her feet off the slick concrete; she did a shuffle-skate toward the parking lot at the side of the building. The sleet made a silvery halo around the streetlight that sat at the edge of the lot.

The lock was iced over on her car door. She gave it a couple of thumps with her fist to break the icy film so she could insert the key. Luckily all of the freezing had been on the outside of the lock and it opened fine. The cold interior creaked and crackled as she settled in the driver's seat.

"Why didn't I go to med school in California or Arizona?" she asked, her breath forming a cloud in front of her face. She could easily have relocated after graduation, but she'd stayed here in Boston, where she felt like she'd laid the groundwork for her career. What a misconception that had turned out to be.

Once the defroster had cleared the windshield enough to see, she pulled out of the nearly deserted parking lot. The tires spun before they finally gripped the road; she inched along, testing her brakes every so often to see how slippery the pavement was. Even though it was only seven o'clock, she found herself virtually alone on the streets. She should just drive home, forget the stop at the hospital. Even as she thought it, she turned right at the stoplight, toward the hospital, instead of making the left that would take her home. She came up behind a salt truck and poked along behind him, hoping for a marginally safer road.

It took her twice as long to reach the hospital parking garage as normal. She was glad to drive inside the structure and onto the first dry pavement she'd seen all day.

She stopped in the gift shop and bought flowers; every new mother should have flowers. The thought of Sarah alone with her baby, not having anyone to share this moment, broke Molly's heart.

Stopping at the nurses' station in maternity, she asked for Sarah's room number. The duty nurse looked up from the medication cart, then shook her head as she double checked her roster. "No Sarah Morgan registered."

"Maybe they haven't moved her up here yet." Even as Molly said it a chill crept over her heart. "She delivered at my clinic today. EMS brought her here."

"You want me to call down and check?"

"No, thanks." The nurse was clearly in the middle of

getting meds ready to dispense. If Sarah was downstairs, she'd have to go down there to see her anyway.

Worry kept Molly's stomach in her throat as the elevator slowly descended to the first floor. She followed the familiar corridor to the ER. Walking past the registration desk, Gladys Kopenski called, "Dr. Boudreau! You're on duty tonight?" She looked quickly at her schedule. Gladys had manned this desk for more years than Molly had been alive. The woman ran a tight ship. It really threw her to have an unexpected face show up. Molly smiled. "No. Looking for a patient. What on earth are you doing here at this hour?"

Gladys's lips pursed and she shifted in her chair. "*That* Cindi didn't show up again. I'm pulling a double."

Molly nodded in sympathy. Gladys had advised—to put it in mild, professional terms—against hiring Cindi Forbes in the first place. Hadn't called her anything but "that Cindi" since the first day. Gladys took a no-nonsense approach to her job, and Cindi's most remarkable credentials were an impressive set of hooters—which, ironically, was the name of the location of her last job. Dr. Michaels, director of emergency medicine, who was smack-dab in the middle of a midlife crisis, complete with red Porsche and new gym membership, felt Cindi had been the "most qualified candidate." But Cindi had missed at least half of her work days since she'd been hired three weeks ago.

Molly said, "I'm looking for a patient brought in by the EMS around one-thirty this afternoon. Sarah Morgan, she'd just delivered a baby."

Gladys frowned. "I remember when she came in. She should be up in maternity by now."

"She's not."

Gladys started shuffling paperwork. "Things did get pretty crazy this afternoon. I hope they didn't leave that poor woman parked in a cubicle all this time." She got up and headed through the double doors, looking like she was going to extract a pound of flesh from whoever had thrown a wrench into her well-oiled machine.

Molly followed, flowers clutched in her hand. Occasionally, she'd been the recipient of Gladys's ire; it was much more entertaining when the woman had another target.

Molly's amusement quickly disappeared. Sarah wasn't in the ER. Apparently, she'd disappeared at some point in the afternoon when the victims of the bus accident, the overflow from Mass General, had flooded this facility. No one had seen her leave.

Had Sarah simply gotten up and carried her child out into this storm?

Molly picked up the chart from the foot of the gurney. The clipboard was empty. Apparently, Sarah had had the presence of mind to take the paperwork with her. The woman really didn't trust to leave a trace of herself, even a confidential hospital record.

"Do you have an address in the computer for her?" Molly asked Gladys. She could go back to the clinic and look it up herself. But that would take another thirty minutes.

"Yes. But that's about all."

They returned to Gladys's desk. Molly laid down the flowers to make a quick notation of the address. Then she snatched them back up in a tight fist and headed to the garage. About halfway there, she realized she was swinging the bouquet at her side as she steamrolled her way toward her car, knocking the heads of the flowers against her coat, leaving a shower of petals in her wake. She felt just like Gladys had looked just minutes ago—ready to rip someone's head off. Why in the hell would Sarah put herself and her baby at risk like this?

It took Molly forty minutes on the slick streets to get to the address on Sarah's chart. When she pulled up and stopped, she slammed her fist against the steering wheel. This was no residence. It was just one of those mailbox places. She sat there for a few minutes, listening to the sleet clatter against the car and the windshield wipers thump back and forth. Had Sarah made it safely to wherever she was going? A shiver coursed down Molly's body. Somewhere in this big city, a new mother huddled with her child against loneliness and the storm. Molly prayed to God they were all right. It was the only thing she could do.

That sense of sad isolation, of cold detachment, once again covered her like an unhealthy skin. Finally, she turned around and headed home, to her own fight against loneliness.

The next day the sun shone brightly, glinting off the icy tree branches like diamonds. The cheerfulness of it didn't begin to penetrate Molly's mood. Worry had kept her awake most of the night. This morning's roads had been reduced to nasty, yet relatively safe, slush. She concentrated on its gray ugliness instead of the fairyland created by the sparkling ice coating everything else as she drove to work at the ER.

Throughout the day she hoped against hope that Sarah and Nicholas would appear. Three different times she called the clinic to see if they'd shown up there—or at least called to tell Molly they were all right. Carmen assured her that she'd call the instant she heard anything.

She never called.

By the end of her shift, it was beginning to sink in that Molly might never see either one of them again. She left work with a growing sense of loss. By the time she was warming up a can of soup for her solitary dinner, she'd managed to fall into a perfectly disgusting quagmire of self-pity.

It wasn't that she didn't love medicine. She did. But living like this wasn't enough anymore. The past day's events had shone a bright light on the fact that her personal life consisted of no more than a visit home at Christmas and a single, watered-down friendship with a woman she barely knew. She really needed to rethink her life, reassess what she really wanted.

As she was going to bed, she decided tomorrow she would decide. She would have the whole day to herself. She'd take stock, then take hold of her life and set it on a course that would deliver the fulfillment she was currently lacking. Her decision delivered a measure of calm. She went to sleep certain that when she awoke her future would begin to take shape.

Just as Molly was stepping out of her morning shower, frantic knocking sounded at her apartment door. She grabbed her robe and tied it around her as she hurried to answer it, wondering if the building was on fire. Instead of a fireman with an ax waiting for her when she opened the door, she was stunned to see a nervous-looking Sarah holding Nicholas.

Sarah didn't hesitate, but stepped right in. "Close the door."

Molly did. "What's wrong? I've been so worried about you two." She looked at Sarah. Even with cheeks reddened by the chill air, the girl looked like the walking dead, exhausted beyond normal new-mother exhaustion. "Sit down." Molly pointed to the only piece of furniture in her living room, a futon.

Sarah sat and laid the baby next to her on the futon. She unwrapped him from thick blankets. Molly looked closely at the child to assess his health. His appearance was the opposite of Sarah's: good color and alert, bright eyes.

Sarah didn't look at Molly as she said, "I need your help." She raised her blue eyes then, and the deep purple smudges beneath them were even more evident. "I need you to keep Nicholas for a day or so."

Molly drew a deep breath, then sat down on the floor next to Sarah's feet and said, "Tell me what's happening."

"I just have to take care of a few things—and I *can't* have the baby with me." Again, Sarah's gaze skittered away from Molly's probing expression.

"This has to do with Nicholas's father?"

Sarah nodded and ran a pale finger along the baby's cheek. Then she looked Molly in the eye. "He can't know about Nicholas. That's the only way I can protect him."

"Sarah, don't you have someone—"

Jumping to her feet, Sarah threw her arms in the air. "Don't you think if I did . . ." She stopped herself and took a breath. "I understand how much I'm asking. I don't have much time—and I don't have anywhere else to turn. Once I get this taken care of, Nicholas and I can start over . . . safe."

"My God, what kind of man is this?"

"Dangerous."

The way she said it made Molly's blood run cold. She decided if she was going to do this, she deserved more of an answer. "How could you have gotten involved with—"

"He's not what he appears. He's very convincing in his lies. The ugly truth is buried so deep . . . When I found out, it was too late. All I could do was run to protect the baby. But I can't run anymore." There was a chilling finality in her last statement.

Molly had the odd feeling she was caught up in a weeknight television drama. "Why not? If you've stayed away from him this long, why can't you just leave it this way?"

"Because I'm a liability. He can't afford liabilities. It's just a matter of time."

"You make it sound like he'll kill you."

"He will." Her voice was flat, as if fear had ground away all emotion until there was nothing left.

"If he's dangerous, you should go to the police." Molly grasped Sarah's hand; her flesh was as cold as a corpse.

Sarah looked down at her and ignored the statement. There were tears in her eyes. "Will you take him? I don't have a lot of time."

"What if I can't?"

Sarah's eyes closed briefly and she drew a breath. "Then I'll have to leave him somewhere else."

"With someone else?" Even as Molly said it, she knew that wasn't what Sarah meant.

"No. Abandon him somewhere where they'll take care of him—like the hospital . . . or a church."

Molly shot to her feet. "You've got to be kidding! You'll never get him back."

Sarah blinked and a tear rolled down her cheek. "But he'll be safe."

Somehow Molly kept herself from saying, *Don't bet on it.* She had seen plenty of kids from foster care end up in the ER. It had happened again just this week. "I've got two days off. Can you be back here before my shift on Friday at three?"

Sarah grabbed her into a quick, fierce hug. "Thank you." Then she stepped an arm's length away. "Promise me you'll protect him . . . no matter what. Keep him from his father."

Molly looked at her sternly. "If I knew who his father was, that'd be a whole lot easier to do."

Sarah stared hard into Molly's eyes. "No. Just the opposite."

Molly tore her uneasy gaze from Sarah to look at the baby, who'd fallen asleep on the futon. She could not let this child get swallowed up in the system.

"You're sure the father doesn't know?" Molly asked.

"Absolutely."

"I still think you should go to the police."

Sarah gave Molly a quick hug. "Everything he needs is in the case. I'll be back before your shift on Friday."

"I'm worried about you," Molly said gravely.

"Don't worry about me. Nicholas is the one who matters."

Putting her hand on the doorknob, Sarah paused and looked back at the baby one last time. Molly couldn't help but think she looked like a sad fairy princess; fair and beautiful, yet caught in a nightmarish tragedy.

Sarah said, "Thank you," once again, and slipped out the door.

Molly stood for a long moment, just staring at the closed door, an impotent fear filling her throat.

As Molly gave Nicholas his 5 A.M. bottle the next morning, she turned on the television news and discovered that Sarah was dead.

Chapter 2

Dean Coletta drew himself up to his knees on the floor of his room in the Al Bahara Hotel. This was the third night in a row that he'd been rocked out of bed by one form of explosion or another. It seemed journalists had become the newest preferred target in this wartorn Middle Eastern city. His magazine had ordered him to evacuate the country last week, an order he'd been compelled to ignore. The locals had no choice but to stay and suffer the swings in political control, the ravages of conflict, and if all of the journalists left, who would tell the world what was going on here? Unlike so many others working here, he had no wife and children back in the States depending upon him. His only family consisted of a sister he saw on holidays. He'd hardly be missed.

He ran his hands over his face, then checked his fingers for blood. It was a drill he was becoming accustomed to. The room's large window had been shattered two nights ago; at least the danger of flying glass had been reduced.

Plaster dust, shaken loose from the building by the explosion, clung to his sweaty skin. He rubbed his hair roughly to get the debris out. He saw, but could not hear, the sprinkling shower as dirt rained down and hit the floor; his hearing was too dulled by the blast for such a gentle noise. From experience he knew it would be at least an hour before he had a full range of hearing again. He shook his head, then coughed and snorted to clear his nose.

"You all right in there, chap?" Nigel Clifford, from the BBC, yelled through Dean's open doorway. The latch had long since broken on the door. In a city where grenades and bullets were frequent, hotel robbery was the least of anyone's concerns. An emergency light in the hallway backlit Clifford and a cloud of gray dust.

"Still in one piece." Dean got to his feet. At that same moment, he saw the tiny red dot of a laser sight track across the far wall of his room. "Down!" He threw himself on the bed as shots whistled through the air and pinged against the building. A searing heat cut across his neck.

He heard Clifford grunt and lifted his gaze just in time to see the man's silhouette crumple in the hall.

A rapid succession of automatic rifle fire erupted again. Shouts rose in the street. Dean rolled off the bed and belly-crawled over to Clifford. The man was face-down.

Remaining out of rifle range on his stomach, Dean struggled to roll him over. "Cliff! You okay?"

Clifford didn't answer. It was easy to see why: there was a neat round bullet hole in his forehead.

Damn. Why hadn't the man left last week? Dean knew

he had twin five-year-old sons and another child on the way. Telling the story was important, he thoroughly believed that, but not at the expense of leaving your own children fatherless.

As he closed his friend's eyes, he noticed his own hands were covered with blood. The hot poker remained in his neck. A quick glance at the floor confirmed the blood was indeed his own; a puddle had begun to form beneath his chin. It was a big puddle. Rapid blood loss.

Shit.

There was no one else in the hall, no one else left living on this floor. It could take at least an hour for a floor-by-floor search to reach him. His blood was coming fast. He'd have to get to the lobby if he was going to find help in time. He put pressure on the wound in his neck, but had no idea if he was doing any good. There was already so much blood; there was no way to gauge if he'd staunched the flow.

His head spun as he struggled to his feet. The walls appeared to undulate before him. The floor felt as if it tilted with the shift in his weight. He stumbled down the hallway, supporting himself against the wall. The warm trickle of blood slid down his chest.

Grayness forced its way into his vision. He had to keep moving.

Where were the stairs? He should have reached the stairs by now. Looking around, he couldn't focus his eyes, couldn't get his bearings.

I'm fucked.

It was his last thought before his knees buckled and he fell facedown on the floor.

* * *

Molly listened as the newscaster explained that Sarah had been murdered in an execution-style killing. Her body had been found on the banks of the Fort Point Channel under the Summer Street Bridge. No robbery. No sexual assault. No witnesses. No suspects. She'd been identified by her Massachusetts driver's license—which the police reported to have been forged. They asked for anyone who could verify this person's identification to please contact the police.

Sarah's ID photo filled the screen. She wasn't smiling; she looked small and delicate—and afraid.

A strangled sob escaped Molly's throat. She would have cried out, but she couldn't draw a breath. With a heart that continued to accelerate, she stared blankly at the television. Then she began to tremble.

The baby started to cry, almost as if he'd heard and understood the news.

In an effort to calm Nicholas, Molly got up and paced the room, heart pounding, tears streaming, hugging him tightly to her chest.

"Oh, my God. Oh, my God," she muttered.

You make it sound like he'll kill you.

He will. Sarah's chilling words echoed in Molly's brain.

The Summer Street Bridge was in the vicinity of both the Amtrak and the Greyhound terminals. Had Sarah been trying to get out of town?

Molly had to go to the police.

She had her clothes on, the baby wrapped up, and her keys in her hand before she realized the full impact of what she was about to do. She stopped cold halfway out the door.

What could she tell them that would help? With the forged license, Sarah Morgan most likely wasn't even her real name. Her suspicion that Nicholas's father had killed Sarah would be worthless; she had absolutely no idea who the man was. The only thing she could tell them was that she *thought* he had red hair.

The only certainty in that course of action was that Nicholas would be endangered. She couldn't go to the police and hide the fact that he was Sarah's baby. Nicholas would instantly become a ward of the state. Once his existence became public knowledge, the father would know. If he came forward, there would be no keeping the child from him.

Sarah's only concern had been for her child's safety. No matter whoever had actually put the bullet in Sarah's brain, Molly had no doubt the father had been behind it. The man was every bit the monster that Sarah had said he was.

Molly had made a promise.

For the briefest moment, she wished she had not; that she could grieve for Sarah as a friend and not have to assume the awesome responsibility of protecting this child.

But as she felt the baby's gentle breath on her neck, she realized, promise or not, she could not let this innocent child suffer more than the loss of its mother. She could not turn him over to a state agency—or worse, to the cold-blooded killer who had fathered him.

How would she protect him? Her mind began to frantically search for the answer. Panic started to take hold, creating a helter-skelter of thoughts. She stopped in midmotion, closed her eyes and ordered herself to think. She was a smart and resourceful person, she told herself. *Slow down and think*.

No one knew she had Nicholas.

Sooner or later there would be an autopsy that would show Sarah had recently given birth. But there was no birth record—Molly, as physician attending the birth, had yet to fill one out. There was no way to trace where the baby was, or even if he was alive. Perhaps the police would assume whoever killed Sarah had taken the baby. With no grieving family to pressure them, this case would quickly slide down the priority ladder. Chances were there would be little effort made to locate the child.

A plan began to form. It seemed ridiculously simple— but, she thought, that could be the key to its success. The simpler she kept it, the less likely it was that she'd draw unwanted attention.

First she called Boston General and asked for an extended leave—a family emergency, starting immediately. She was certain her voice sounded upset enough to be convincing. Besides, several people knew her father had had episodes of heart trouble. No one would question her. Quitting her job outright would rouse suspicion; plus she wasn't certain where her life was going to go from here. For now she was living minute to minute. Best to keep all of her bridges intact.

As the free clinic was closing permanently on Saturday at five P.M., she had already worked her last shift there.

She attended to all of the things a person normally does when leaving town, careful to make her departure appear logical. She had the mail held, stopped her newspaper, turned down the thermostat. She packed a suitcase and shut off the water. An hour and a half later, she was ready to go.

She had her suitcase in hand, ready to leave, when she took one last glance around her apartment. There wasn't much she was leaving behind. She'd never accumulated much beyond medical books; they were her most valuable possessions. As she took a cursory glance over them, realizing she'd have to leave them behind or spend half the day loading her car, a flash of turquoise caught her eye. Sitting on top of a stack of books on the shelf was the only thing she'd carried with her from childhood; a small, glass-domed clock with Tinkerbell in flight on its pendulum.

It had been a gift from her father—who really wasn't very good at picking out gifts, but this one had thrilled Molly the moment she'd opened it. She'd been five the Christmas he'd given it to her. He'd been nearly as excited to give it as she'd been when she opened it. Inexpensive, probably from the dime store on the square, but it held a place in her heart that couldn't have been equaled if it had been a Fabergé egg.

Pausing for only the briefest moment, she threw down her suitcase and opened it back up. Carefully, she wrapped the clock in a sweater, then closed the case again.

After she shuttled her suitcases to the car, she brought Nicholas, snuggled in a blanket inside an open cardboard box lined with towels. She put him on the floor of the back seat of her Volkswagen Jetta, wedging the box securely between the front and back seats. She drove to the closest discount store and paid cash for a car seat.

By the time she had it installed in the car, it was time

to feed Nicholas again. She did it right there in the parking lot, constantly anticipating trouble, continually scanning for approaching danger. She assured herself it was ridiculous. They looked like any mother and baby on a morning shopping errand. No one knew she had Sarah's child. The clinic was the only real link between her and Sarah, and no one could have made that discovery yet. Still, the fear built with each second she remained stationary. Over and over in her mind, a redheaded giant crept up beside the car, tore open the door and yanked Nicholas from her arms.

My God, what am I doing?

Even as she asked herself this question, a fierce protectiveness welled in her soul. She'd coaxed this child's first breath. She'd been given a mother's trust. How could she do any less than keep him safe?

It seemed to take forever for Nicholas to take the three ounces of formula. Once he was burped and changed, she strapped him in the new car seat, then drove through a McDonald's for a Coke. There was no way she could eat anything; her stomach felt like it was in a paint shaker.

Merging onto the interstate, she looked at the clock: ten o'clock. It normally took fifteen hours to drive to Glens Crossing. With the baby, she'd be lucky to make it in twenty. Going home made the most sense, she reassured herself. Where else could she go with a newborn baby and limited resources? As it was, if anyone from the hospital tried to contact her, that's where she'd said she would be. Simplicity was the key.

She headed southwest, looking frequently in the rearview mirror, alert for anyone who could possibly be following. Just to ensure no one was, she pulled off at each rest stop, mindful of those cars that followed her in. She was all the way to the Pennsylvania state line before she'd convinced herself she hadn't been tailed out of Boston.

Fortunately, Molly was accustomed to functioning with little sleep. The drive was broken up frequently enough with feedings and diaper changes to maintain her alertness. The final miles were on a two-lane highway that had enough curves and hills to keep anyone on their toes, exhausted or not. She pulled into Glens Crossing just as the eastern sky was showing signs of dawn.

Slowing as she drove into downtown, she realized that this was the first time since she'd started med school that she'd come to town and the square wasn't decorated for Christmas. Over the past few years, there hadn't been a lot of money, or time, for trips back home. Somehow it looked unnaturally bare without the colored lights, giant red bows, and evergreen roping.

The sun edged over the horizon, igniting the brilliant fall colors of the maples on the courthouse lawn. For a moment she sat at the stoplight, ignoring the fact that it had turned green, reacquainting herself with the once familiar downtown.

Duckwall's Hardware looked just like it had when she was in grade school, including the rip in the screen door. Molly always thought the ripped screen was poor advertising for the store, especially since it offered screen and glass pane replacement as one of its services. Hayman's Drug had a new dark red awning. Its windows were painted with spirit slogans in royal blue and gold for the high school's homecoming. The courthouse itself and the square upon which it sat never changed. The ancient cannons, monuments to wars past, sat sentinel. The hands on the clock in the tower were frozen at eleven-fifteen, just as they'd been for the past three years. Dad had said the county couldn't find funds in the budget for something as unnecessary as a clock. But Molly thought it was sad. Throughout her childhood, she'd heard that clock strike every hour. To this day, a chiming clock always made her think of home. Now the kids were growing up without it—one less link to anchor them to this place.

Her gaze moved to the Dew Drop Inn, the little café on the square. It was much too early to knock on her father's door, as he normally worked into the morning hours at his bar. Today was Friday; he would be working very late tonight, so she didn't want to interrupt his sleep. She considered heading straight to her sister's, but wasn't up to explaining the past four days to Lily on an empty stomach. She'd spent the past twenty hours in a panic. She needed a bit to gather herself. So she pulled into a parking place in front of the Dew Drop.

This was where she'd shared her last late-Sunday breakfast with her dad before she'd left for college. Dad had been his usual good-humored self that morning. Yet Molly had seen the sadness and longing in the depths of his dark eyes. She was his baby. And since Lily had married and moved to Chicago when Molly was in eighth grade, it had been just her and her dad.

Her mother had been gone so long, Molly only remembered what she looked like from pictures. The last lingering hope that she would return had finally disappeared on high school graduation day. Until then, Molly had held the secret dream that she'd look out from under her mortarboard to see her mother's proud face among the crowd in Glens Crossing High's gymnasium. Of course, her mother wasn't there, just as she hadn't been for any other important occasion in Molly's life. By the time she was packed and ready to leave for Boston, she'd vanquished all fanciful ideas concerning her mother.

Benny Boudreau had raised all three of his children to be independent and self-reliant—and yet that last morning, Molly had seen a part of him reach out and try to clasp her close to his heart, keep her here, keep her safe.

She had ignored it then, fearing that if she acknowledged it, she'd be too afraid to leave.

She remembered the look in his eyes as she'd driven away from the Crossing House, where they lived in a small apartment over the bar. Her car had been packed to the gills with clothes, bedding, and the new mini-fridge he'd bought for her dorm room. It was that image of him she held close when she was homesick—knowing he would be there, in that same place, whenever she returned.

Now, unlikely as it had seemed only weeks ago, she *was* returning. And she hoped that loving look would still be in her dad's eyes after he heard what she'd done.

Behind her in the back seat, the baby made a soft sound in his sleep. She was beginning to develop an understanding of that protectiveness she'd always seen in her dad—that need to do what was right, what was best for his children.

She got out and put a quarter in the parking meter. After she unfastened the pumpkin seat from the car seat base, she carried it and the diaper bag with her.

It was a chilly morning; the windows and glass door of

the Dew Drop were steamed over on the inside, reducing what she could see beyond the glass to a warm, yellow glow. Inviting.

She was struggling to open the door while managing the car seat when a hand shot from behind her and grabbed the door, opening it for her.

She smiled and said "Thanks," to a lanky middle-aged man who looked familiar, yet his name eluded her.

"Hey, aren't you Benny's little girl?" He smiled, crinkling the corners of his eyes. "I used to fix that old Ford of yours."

His identity clicked into place. Hank Brown, owner of the garage on Maple. "Brownie! Hello." She shifted the unfamiliar weight of baby carrier to her other hand.

"Still driving the old Purple Dragon?" he asked with a wink.

She'd nearly forgotten the nickname she'd given that beastly car—which was mostly purple like a grape Popsicle, except for the passenger door and half of the rear quarter panel, which made a distinctive style statement in gray primer. How on earth had he remembered? "No," she smiled. "It was slain by a white knight in Boston during my junior year in college." The days when she'd had the time and energy to do whimsical things like name cars seemed long, long ago.

He looked pointedly at the baby carrier. "So, who's this?"

Molly's mouth went dry. How little could she get away with telling? "This is Nicholas."

"Can I have a peek?" Brownie's kind eyes twinkled and he leaned down.

Molly wanted to refuse. How irrational would that appear? Babies drew attention. She could hardly walk around town and act like she didn't have Nicholas with her. She removed the blanket that she'd put over the top of the seat to ward off the damp morning air.

"Why, he's a dandy. Got your dark hair, I see." He tilted his head to the side, considering for a moment. "I think he looks a little like Benny! The chin."

Like Dad! Really? Molly made a noncommittal noise in her throat and moved toward a booth that had just opened up. "It was good to see you again."

She hung her coat on the tall chrome hook mounted between the booths, then slid in next to the baby. She was just unbundling him when the waitress arrived. Looking up, she saw it was Mildred, who didn't look a day older than she had when Molly was five: same gray hair, same shade of red lipstick, same oversized glasses.

"Why, Molly Boudreau!" She leaned a little closer and cocked her head. "Or should I call you *Doctor* Boudreau?" She chuckled warmly.

"Don't be silly, I'll always be Molly around here. How are you, Mildred?"

She waved her pencil in the air. "Oh, couldn't be better." She looked at Nicholas. "And you've got a baby!" Her smile broadened. "What a little heartbreaker. I didn't even know you'd gotten married."

Molly reminded herself: *simplicity*. The fewer lies, the less likely to be tripped up by them. She maintained a bland expression and said, "I didn't."

"Oh." Mildred's smile slipped slightly. She quickly recovered. "I guess it doesn't matter these days. Don't know why I assumed. . . ." Her gaze drifted away as her voice trailed off.

Molly changed the subject. "I'll have two eggs, over easy, and wheat toast, please."

Mildred seemed glad to be freed of the uncomfortable turn in their meeting. "Coffee?"

"Please. Cream." She turned back to adjust the baby in his seat and heard Mildred's rubber-soled shoes squeak slightly as she turned and walked away. No matter how much time she had spent thinking about what she'd do once she got here during the drive, she now recognized she was ill-prepared to deal with even the simplest of situations. She should not have come to a public place first. She should have gone to talk to her dad and devised a clearheaded plan before exposing herself to others.

God, she realized belatedly, her thinking had been fuzzy over the past hours. Fatigue. Fear. Uncertainty. She had to get herself together. Everyone assumed Nicholas was her child—and she wasn't sure what she should do about it.

Molly kept her head down as she quickly ate her breakfast. She didn't need any more conversations with people she hadn't seen in nine years. Not yet.

Dean drifted in darkness, his body weightless. He tried to fight his way to the surface of consciousness, but it was like quicksand: the more he struggled, the farther he was sucked into the black void. After a moment he no longer cared if he reached the surface again. He let himself go; gave himself over to the strange and obscure warmth of the dark.

The next moment, he was twelve again and on the Wild Mouse. It was his favorite ride at Thunder Hill, the small amusement park he went to as a child. His mom and dad took him and his sister, Julie, there once every summer.

Dean never thought of the Wild Mouse without thinking of Julie.

Suddenly the ride jerked and bucked and dropped without warning, slamming his shoulders first against one side of the tiny car, then the other. But this time it was different. The movement shot pain through him. Each time the mouse made a hard turn, Dean's neck felt like it was breaking. With each jolt, his shoulders felt as if ice picks jabbed to the bone.

It wasn't right. The pain. No Julie screaming behind him. He struggled to make sense.

That's right. Thunder Hill had been closed for years, the Wild Mouse's cars removed and the tracks disassembled. A Wal-Mart now stood where the park had been. He'd bought an artificial flower arrangement to place on his parents' grave at that Wal-Mart the last time he'd been home.

The irregular jolting movement and the sharp pain persisted.

Where was he, if not on the ride?

Then he remembered. Clifford. Clifford was dead. *I'm hurt.*

He tried to open his eyes. He couldn't, yet he came to himself enough to realize he was being carried over someone's shoulder, someone who was hurrying along double-time. That made sense of the jerking motion—it wasn't the Wild Mouse after all.

The rocking movement stopped. There was an explosion of pain. A truck engine ground to a start. Then, unconsciousness engulfed him again and the pain miraculously ebbed away.

He drifted in darkness for a bit. Then he found himself standing next to his parents' grave, looking at the gray granite tombstone. The bright red silk arrangement he'd left so long ago had faded to pale pink, its fabric petals frayed by years of wind.

When he looked more closely at the engraving, it wasn't his parents. It was him: James Dean Coletta.

He heard a footfall behind him and he turned. His mother stood there, the bright sun behind her. She smiled and reached out to him. She was strong and healthy, like she had been when she taught at the university; not the gaunt woman whose body had been consumed by cancer.

Warmth washed over him as he raised his hand to take hers.

For the past hour, Molly had driven the road around Forrester Lake—the old road, the curvy one with deep potholes and no shoulder. She stopped briefly at the spillway, got Nicholas out of his car seat and walked along the edge of the lake. Being late in the season yet before the heavy fall rains, the lake's level was below the dam, the spillway bone dry. It was there, looking out over the greenish water, smelling the hint of a wood fire in the air, holding a child that depended solely upon her, that she made her decision. She'd embarked on a path to protect this child and there could be no half measures.

As she'd done with everything in her life, once the decision was made, Molly didn't look back, didn't torment herself with what-ifs. She had thought this through, carefully, logically. She drove straight from there to her father. He still lived in the apartment over his tavern where she'd spent most of her childhood.

The crunch of the car tires sounded unnaturally loud in the empty crushed-stone parking lot of the Crossing House. Loud . . . and guilty. Just like it had when Molly had been out after her curfew in high school. The times had been few, that was probably why the sound had stuck so in her mind. If she'd been like her brother Luke, sneaking out all of the time, she was certain the guilt would have worn right off that sound.

She put the car in park. It was time to get the worst over with.

Drawing her shoulders square, she reminded herself that she was a grown woman. She'd been living on her own for years. She was a *doctor*, for God's sake. There was no need to be as nervous as an errant teen. But the fact was, she was going to lie to her father—which was probably a much larger cause of her sound-associated guilt than ancient teenage secrets.

She decided to carry Nicholas in her arms, not in the baby seat. The outside stairs to the apartment seemed much longer than they had the last time she'd climbed them. Once she reached the top, she could hear a television on inside. She rapped on the door without hesitation. After all, she had decided.

When her dad opened the door, he stood quietly for a moment, giving her the same expectant look he'd give a stranger. Then his black brows shot up and his eyes widened.

"Dad." Molly's heart seemed to be inching up her throat.

He flung the door open wider. "Molly! What's

wrong?" His gaze then shifted to the bundle in her arms and he frowned.

"I'm coming home," was all she could say.

He took a step out onto the landing and wrapped an arm around her shoulders, drawing her inside with him. "Leaving Boston? What's going on? Why didn't you let me know you were coming?"

She stood just inside the door, amazed as she always was upon arriving, that the apartment was so much smaller than in her childhood memories. The cramped living room was completely filled by a single recliner, a TV, and sofa. The kitchen had an efficiency-size stove, a refrigerator shorter than Molly, and a round table crowded into the corner. She and Lily had shared a bedroom, her dad had a tiny bedroom toward the front, not much bigger than a walk-in closet, and Luke had slept on the same foldout sofa that still sat in the living room.

For a single second, she had to blink away tears. "I didn't know myself until today."

Tension lined his face. "Whose baby?" he asked.

Simplicity. She drew a breath. "Mine."

Chapter 3

Benny felt as if a trap door had fallen away beneath his feet. Heat shot throughout his body.

"What do you mean, yours? You adopted him? How could you do something like that and not tell me? How do you expect to raise a child without a father? What about your career? Did you even think this through?" Benny couldn't stop the rush of questions. And as long as he kept asking, he didn't have to listen to his daughter's answers. After all of her struggles to become a doctor, establish herself at the hospital in Boston . . . how could she do something so irresponsible?

He stared hard at her, his jaw tense.

"I mean he's mine. My son." She swallowed hard, but lifted her chin in determined defiance, just as she'd done as a child when told something she wanted was impossible.

Well, hadn't he been the one to teach her that nothing was impossible if you wanted it enough? *But this. This was different.*

"And the father? I don't suppose you got married and didn't tell me, too?" he said harshly.

"No. I'm not married." She paused, but didn't look away. "His father isn't involved."

Benny sputtered and shot to his feet. He rounded on his youngest child, more angry than he could ever remember being. "Not *involved*? Just how does that work? You slept with a man who has no more responsibility than that?"

"Dad—"

"You're not a teenager, for God's sake. You're a grown woman. You're a *doctor*! How in the hell did you end up pregnant?" His ears felt as if they were on fire.

"The same way anyone else ends up pregnant." She held his gaze, but he could see the tears shining in her eyes, the only hint that she was less than solid in her confidence.

"Who's the father? Is he another doctor? Married?" The idea that Molly had allowed herself to be used by a married man was almost too awful to consider. "You can't just let him shirk his responsibility. If you don't want to marry him, at least make him financially responsible for this child! What kind of man doesn't take care of his own child? This boy will need things—and you'll have to be home with him, not at some hospital working all hours. . . ." Benny knew he was yelling. He never yelled. He'd never had to. His children usually understood reason.

"Plenty of single mothers work and take care of a baby." The challenge was stronger in her posture now, her back straighter, her chin higher.

"Is that what you want for your son—a home that's not a home, a mother who's never there?"

"My mother was never here—and I turned out fine!"

"Yes. Just look at you." He turned his back on her and scrubbed his hands over his face. That was the crux of the matter, really . . . Molly's mother. She'd humiliated his children by leaving them as if they were unwanted kittens. They'd had to grow up in this town with that shame hanging over their heads. And ever since that day, Benny had modeled his life, guarded his words, insisted that his children always stand on high moral ground, in an effort to reestablish respect for this family.

He heard Molly take a deep breath behind him. His heart was breaking. He'd wanted so much for his bright and talented daughter. A career. A loving husband. A good home. A happy family. Security. Now, there was nothing easy about the road ahead of her.

"Listen." He heard her get up from the couch. "Dad, all of this argument is too late. I have him. Nothing's going to change that."

Turning to face her, he found himself unsettled that she was so close. He drew a ragged breath himself. He adopted her rigid stance. "Why didn't you tell me before now? All of these months . . . all of those phone conversations . . . and you never once hinted at this!"

She bit her lower lip for a minute. After glancing at the floor, she said, "Because I wasn't going to keep him. I was going to give him up for adoption. I didn't want to upset you. I didn't decide until the last minute. . . ."

Benny felt as if a hot poker seared his heart. "You were going to give away your own child!" He closed his eyes and shook his head. *Was* she like her mother, then? Had he been blinded to her deeper moral flaws by her brilliant mind and dedication to her goals? It killed him to think so.

When he opened his eyes, he said, "I don't know what makes me more disappointed in you—that you got yourself into this situation in the first place, or that you were going to hand your baby off to strangers . . . so it would be more *convenient* for you."

At that, he moved himself a little farther away, giving her only his brooding silence. It was all he had left. He could see the pain in his daughter's eyes. Yes, the words he'd just said were cruel. But they demanded to be said.

After a moment in which she looked like she might shatter if touched, she turned around and picked the baby up off the couch. As she walked to the door, she said, "Right now, I'm pretty disappointed in you, too, Dad."

He watched her walk out the door, knowing he should stop her. They shouldn't leave things like this. But shock and anger kept his feet from moving.

Molly held herself together until she got Nicholas in his car seat and herself behind the wheel. Then the shaking started. It began in her knees and quickly radiated to encompass her entire body. Within seconds she heard her own teeth chattering. In all of her harried thinking and planning, she'd never once imagined this—that her father would react so coldly, so furiously. Throughout her entire life, he'd always been logical, pragmatic. When she was faced with a difficult situation, she could always count on her dad to take the cool approach and talk her through.

She remained in the parking lot of the Crossing House,

trying to calm herself enough to drive. It wasn't until she caught herself looking up at the apartment door for the third time that she realized she was waiting—waiting for him to come after her.

He didn't.

She had intended to stay with her dad for at least a few days, until she had a solid plan for her future. So much for that. Starting the car, she took one last lingering look. Then she put the car in drive and pulled out of the lot.

Well, she thought, *I have to alight somewhere.* Glens Crossing didn't have a motel. And she still put stock in this being the best place for her and the baby to be—even without her father's support.

Nicholas started making the soft little noises that preceded a newborn cry. She only had enough formula to get her through this afternoon, which meant she also had to do some shopping.

"Shhhhh," she said softly. "Just hang on a few more minutes, little guy."

There was only one other place she could go: Lily's. She wondered if she'd get the same unexpected reaction from her big sister as she had from her dad.

I'd better not. I might have been young when Riley was born, but I knew how to count.

Lily and Peter's son, Riley, had been born six and a half months after they eloped. Molly didn't remember her dad blowing a gasket then. However, Lily had *married* Peter. Molly wondered if she'd shown up with a diamond on her finger and a prospective husband in tow if Dad would have reacted differently.

Well, she thought, Lily and Peter had ended up divorced. Was it any less emotionally disturbing for a child to have to go through his parents splitting up than being raised by a single parent in a stable environment?

This whole disappointment thing stung more than she cared to admit. *If he knew the real story. . . .* Molly quickly dashed that thought. There was a risk involved that she hadn't previously considered. Taking a baby that wasn't hers, even for its own protection, could have serious legal ramifications. Anyone she told could be held in some way accountable. Thank God she'd kept the truth to herself.

Even so, the child in her felt betrayed by her father's reaction. If he couldn't support her in her adult decisions, then maybe their relationship had been no more substantial than toilet paper out in a spring storm, losing all of its integrity as soon as the rain began to fall.

She took the road toward the lake. Lily and her new husband, Clay, lived in an old farmhouse not far from the marina where Clay worked. That relationship was something of a puzzlement to Molly. While growing up, Lily and their brother, Luke, used to pal around with Lily's first husband Peter and his buddy Clay. Molly, of course, had been excluded from the circle of friends because of her age. The guys were all about the same age; Lily had barely been old enough to fit in. Even though they had all been friends, it had seemed to Molly that Lily and Clay were closest. That's why Lily's elopement with Peter had come as such a surprise to her.

Molly remembered the way Lily would dodge her probing questions on the telephone. When fourteen-year-old Molly had said she had always thought Lily had been in love with Clay, Lily had laughed. But to Molly it had sounded wrong, like the laugh had been forced and laced with more nervousness than humor. As things had turned out in the long run, maybe Molly hadn't been so far off the mark. But Lily had never wanted to discuss her love life with Molly—come to think of it, Lily never shared *any* of her inner secrets or problems.

By the time Molly pulled her Jetta into Lily's long driveway, Nicholas was crying.

"All right, sweetie. Just a few more minutes."

After one fortifying breath, she got out, then lifted the baby and the diaper bag out of the car. As she had at her dad's, Molly carried Nicholas in her arms, not the baby seat—a show of solidarity, commitment, of unity between spirits.

He quieted with the closeness and Molly felt the magic she'd always assumed came with motherhood—like breast milk and recognizing your own baby's cry—the power to calm. That feeling spread over her, erasing her doubts, soothing her fears, allowing her to set one foot in front of the other toward an unknown destiny.

She held him tighter for a moment, her own heartbeat echoing throughout her body, offering up a prayer that she was doing the right thing for this child.

Glancing at the barn, she wondered if Lily would be out there in her pottery workshop or in the house.

Molly decided to try the house first. She climbed the wide steps to the wraparound front porch. A swing and four rocking chairs sat intermingled with Lily's huge pottery containers filled with flowers—mums and pansies for the late season. For a brief moment, a pang of regret struck Molly's heart. She'd never really thought she wanted the weight of a home and a family, preferring to concentrate fully on her work. But suddenly there was something infinitely appealing about this rural setting, this warm and welcoming home. She realized Lily had created just the kind of home she and Lily had always dreamed of when they were kids living without a mother over their dad's bar.

Molly just hoped the welcoming atmosphere continued after Lily had heard her story.

She raised her hand to knock at the same moment the door swung open. Lily stood there in denim coveralls smeared with red-brown clay, her hair up in a pony tail. She looked ridiculously young for the mother of a sixteen-year-old; suddenly Molly felt like the aging older sister.

"Molly! What are you doing here?" Her shocked expression said she expected something terrible. "What's happened?" The color was rapidly draining from her face.

"Nothing—everything." When Lily remained motionless, Molly asked, "Can we come in?"

At the word "we," Lily's worried gaze flicked from Molly's face to the bundle in her arms. Her alarm didn't appear to ease, but she did open the screen and stepped back to let Molly in. "Are you all right?"

"Yes," Molly said as she stepped inside. But her answer was masked by Nicholas's full-fledged howl. It was such a distinctive newborn cry that Lily's eyes widened further.

Then her eyes narrowed as she honed in on Molly. "Why aren't you in Boston?"

"I'm coming home." Molly jiggled the baby, trying to quiet him. "I'll explain everything, but first this guy needs to be fed."

"Just who is 'this guy'?"

Nicholas squalled, his face a rumpled beet red.

"I don't want to yell over him. Let me feed him and I'll explain."

Lily took the diaper bag and helped Molly out of her jacket. "In here?" she asked, motioning to the living room.

"I have to warm his bottle." Molly headed toward the kitchen, patting Nicholas's bottom—not that he noticed the comfort. His little body was rigid with fury. He'd lapsed into the breath-holding stage of his crying, which was broken occasionally by a healthy wail until the bottle was warmed and the nipple plugged into his mouth.

Molly sat in a kitchen chair. The quiet that descended on the room was only interrupted by the little hiccuping breaths the baby took as he calmed. The silence wrapped around Molly and all of her intentions, making her pause with second thoughts.

It seemed wrong to foster a lie, but if she was going to succeed in keeping Nicholas safe, there didn't seem any way around it. If she told her sister the truth, she'd have to tell her dad; it just wasn't in her to force Lily into lying to their father, too.

If her family knew the truth, chances were it would inadvertently slip at some point. This was a small town—everybody would soon know. And just maybe the slip wouldn't be *completely* inadvertent. Her dad had always taken a great deal of public pride in her; exposure of the truth could quickly change *Molly the Fallen Woman*, who filled him with disappointment, to *Molly the Self-sacrificing Saint*.

No. Until she had her plan completely figured out, she

was going to stick to the story that Nicholas was hers—which, in a way he was. His mother had entrusted him to her, and now his mother was dead. He had no one else. Ridiculous justifications for her actions, but her immediate choices were extremely limited. Sarah's death had thoroughly and shockingly proved the truth of her accusation that the baby's father was viciously dangerous.

Lily allowed Molly to process her thoughts, waiting on the other side of the table with her hands in her lap, letting the silence spin. The worried look remained on her face; Molly knew without seeing that her sister's fingers fidgeted under the table top.

Finally Lily said, "That baby can't be over a week old."

Molly stopped herself from blurting out that he'd been born four days ago—what new mother would drive cross-country alone four days after giving birth? "He's two-and-a-half weeks."

Lily tilted her head, wordlessly inviting Molly to elaborate.

Molly drew a deep breath and began. "This is Nicholas . . . my son."

For the longest moment, Lily looked as if she'd been slapped; stunned into immobility. Then she regained herself and nearly shouted, "Are you kidding? Why didn't you tell us you were considering this?"

"I didn't tell *anyone*." The lie was falling easier from her lips each time. "I had planned on giving him up for adoption—"

"What!" Lily jumped to her feet. "You *had* him; he's not adopted? You were *pregnant* for nine months and didn't tell us!"

Molly nodded, finding it easier than speaking the lie.

Lily's hand went to her forehead. "Jesus, Molly!" She walked in a tight little circle. "Who's the father?"

"No one you'll ever meet." *Please God, let this part remain true.*

"Oh, Molly." The words were no more than a sympathetic breathy sigh. Finally, after standing there looking down at Molly with nearly the same disappointment that Molly had seen on her father's face earlier, Lily finally sat down. "What about your career?"

"I'm moving it to Glens Crossing. I'm not as stupid as you think; I know I can't raise this child completely without support. I need my family—I need you."

A light dawned in Lily's eyes, as if a thought just popped into her mind. "Dad?" she breathed. "Oh God, what will Dad say?"

Molly forced herself to look into her sister's eyes. "He's already said it." The tears that had threatened earlier now broke free. She spoke around the lump in her throat, tucking her chin in order to get the words out. "He's 'disappointed.'"

After a second, Lily asked, "What else did he say?"

"That was pretty much it. He hardly even looked at the baby."

Lily's mouth screwed slightly to the side, looking just like it had when they were kids and she was contemplating something. "You have to admit, you did drop a bomb." Then her face hardened and her back stiffened. "How could you have done this—after all you've worked for? And why didn't you tell us? My God, Molly, how could you *not* have told us?"

"It seemed best, as long as I was giving him up." She

took herself along the imaginary path of her newly invented past. The emotion in her voice was real enough, even though the true motivation was masked. "The decision was hard enough without having everyone in the family putting in an opinion. I was trying to do the right thing for the baby." *At least that much was true.*

"I see." Lily's voice had taken on a surprising edge. In all of Molly's memory, she could never recall Lily using this kind of tone with her. "We would have been troublesome in the decision making, but now that you have a baby and no way to take care of it, you need us?"

Molly didn't even try to conceal her shock. "That's not what I meant! You're not being fair."

"And you're being *fair* to this baby? You bring him to a town like this without a father and expect things to go smoothly for him?"

"You think I should have given him away?" That Lily, a woman who had devoted her life to her son, could think such a thing had never crossed Molly's mind.

"I don't know how you could have *considered* giving away your own child. But coming here—"

Molly's jaw clenched and her body flashed hot. She would have shot to her feet if she hadn't been feeding the baby. "Listen to me." She leaned slightly forward to emphasize her words. "Every choice I've made has been based on what's best for this child! If I had chosen adoption, it would have been because it was best for *his* future. Dad already threw that 'convenience' card in my face. It has nothing to do with *my* convenience." She sucked in a trembling breath. "And don't make it sound like every mother who gives her child over to someone in a better position to care for him is a monster."

Lily's tone softened when she said, "I couldn't imagine not seeing Riley grow up—to wonder every day what was going on in his life."

Molly looked at the baby in her arms—another woman's baby. Lily had had the option of marrying Peter—a loving man who cared for both her and their child. Poor Sarah had had no such option. Molly wanted to explain, to defend Sarah—but that was both impossible and useless. She said in a soft voice, "Sometimes a mother doesn't have any other choice."

Lily sat for a long moment in silence. Her posture told Molly that she was still upset.

"So both you and Dad are going to pass judgment," Molly said. "I just don't understand it. It's not the fifties. I'm not a kid. My God, Dad was the one who talked Missy Jackson's parents out of sending her away when she got pregnant in the tenth grade. How could he *not* lend me just a little support?"

With a sad shake of her head that said Molly didn't understand anything, Lily said, "You don't know what it's going to be like here—you don't remember how awful it was when Mom left. You didn't see how Dad's pride suffered."

"How can you even compare the two situations!"

"How can *you* not see how people in this town will react? I know you've been in the city for a long time, but my God, Molly, think! Yes, Missy Jackson stayed in town and had her baby. But as soon as she graduated, she moved away. It's hard to raise a fatherless child in a place like this."

"You're overreacting."

"Maybe. I hope so." Lily was ever the peacemaker in

their family—the one who always smoothed out the wrinkles. "How are you financially? Is the father helping out at all?"

It was a step toward peace, and yet, Molly sensed a certain amount of strain remaining.

"I'm okay." At least she would be as long as she could get up and running in a job within a month or so. As with most young doctors, she had a boatload of loans to pay off. "The father doesn't know and I plan to keep it that way."

Suddenly that defensive stiffness was back in Lily's posture and her eyes sharpened with something that bordered on suspicion. "Do you think that's fair to the father? Doesn't he have the right to know?"

Even as Lily voiced the question, there was a certain hesitancy that made Molly wonder exactly what *Lily* thought about the father's rights.

Molly thought of Sarah's quiet nature and her shining innocence, all destroyed by the man who gave her this child. Her voice was cold when she said, "Some people, by their very actions, forfeit that right. I've made up my mind and I won't discuss it anymore."

With Molly's tone, Lily's eyes narrowed in censure. Then she settled back in her chair and said, "All right. I'll respect that."

She may have said the words, but there was disapproval in her eyes.

Molly had come to her sister expecting a life raft in the storm and all she'd found was more rain.

Through the thick fog of pain that played with him— winding tighter, robbing him of breath, then without reason, slipping away momentarily, only to return with a piercing vengeance—Dean Coletta heard voices. No longer the sweet voice of his mother calling his name. Mother had vanished in a brilliant white flash the instant these new voices began their discordant squawking, like a flock of big black crows pecking at a harvested cornfield.

Dean recoiled from the harsh voices, reaching out, grasping at that flash. He called for his mother to return, needing her beautiful comfort. Except for the faint aroma of freshly-baked chocolate chip cookies—the warm, chewy ones she often surprised him and his sister with when they arrived home from school—it was as if she'd never been there at all. The scent lingered, teasing his senses, assuring him that she had indeed been there, within an arm's reach. So close.

Now gone. Leaving Dean alone with his cold, dark pain.

The crows grew louder. Harsh. Quarrelsome.

They were arguing about him. Dean tried to gather his scattered thoughts. He knew he'd been dreaming. But was what was happening now real? The pain was back, so it must be. He tried to grasp that thought, but it slid quickly away, hiding once again in the darkness.

The voices slipped into the distance. The pain dimmed. Warmth began to caress his cold limbs.

He heard his mother again. And this time another voice joined hers. He strained to hear it. Then his sister, Julie, appeared from nowhere and took his hand. Her touch was warm and welcome. It had been so long since he'd seen her; they'd been close as children, but as adults had taken very different roads. She tugged on his hand, pulling him toward his mother's calling voice.

"Come on," she said, with a smile that made him long for youth and carefree summer days. "Mother's waiting."

He was too tired to move.

"We're late," Julie said. There was just enough edge in her voice to tell him they were going to be in trouble.

They were *never* allowed to be late. That was rudeness in the extreme, according to Mother. With his sister's urging, he gathered his strength and started to get up.

Suddenly, someone slapped him on the cheek.

"Don't you dare die on me!" The shouted words crashed through the confusion.

Die? Reality struck like an ice spear through his chest. *No, he wouldn't die!*

The same woman's voice yelled, "I need another unit of blood. Now, dammit!"

Julie was gone. He was alone again in the dark, falling through silent, black space. He didn't want to be alone. For the first time in his memory, he was afraid of being alone.

The next thing Dean heard was the droning of an aircraft engine. The crows were gone. He had no idea how much time had passed. He tried to open his eyes, but his lids refused to obey. He tried to speak, but his throat was too dry. The slightest movement of his neck muscles shot an electric pain down through his shoulder and up to the top of his head.

He remembered the laser dot on the hotel room wall. The poker-hot pain. Clifford falling. The blood.

Was it just seconds ago?

If he was going to survive, he had to get up. Get help. If he didn't get to the lobby, it would be too late.

Something held his body down. He strained against the band of pressure on his chest, tried to move arms that seemed strapped in place. With the restriction, he fought harder.

"Easy there!" a voice shouted over the noise of the engine. "I'm giving you something to relax you. We'll be in Germany soon."

Even as the warmth of the drug moved through Dean's veins he thought, *I hate Germany.*

Lily finally crawled into bed next to her sleeping husband. She tried to tamp down the resentment that had been fighting against her sisterly concern since Molly's arrival. How could her sister throw away a career in Boston? The entire family had worked so long for her to achieve her dream. Lily certainly might have made different choices if it hadn't been for her desire to protect Molly from scandal. It wasn't fair to punish Molly for sacrifices she herself had made years ago on Molly's behalf—sacrifices that Molly knew nothing of. Logic told Lily that. And yet, her sister's situation made mockery of that sacrifice. Lily couldn't help but be hurt.

The entire day had passed in an emotional blur. From the moment Molly had shown up on her doorstep, everything seemed to shift into fast forward. Lily had had to make some quick decisions—decisions that would affect everyone in the house. However, in reality, she knew there wasn't any debate over the outcome. Molly was family. She needed a place to stay. In spite of her disappointment, Lily would never turn her sister away.

But it was going to be difficult, her feelings about Molly's choices aside. Her own marriage was only a year old. She and Clay and Riley were still learning to live like a family. At times they sailed along as if they'd lived together forever. Other times the tension between Clay and Riley was nearly enough to make her doubt her decision to get married before Riley left for college. Still, Clay had been gracious when he arrived home from work to discover that his sister-in-law was moving in, along with a newborn baby.

Lily had watched Clay all evening. His quiet, measuring gaze continually went to Nicholas, whether the child was awake or sleeping. She'd wondered if he was thinking of all he'd missed in not being a father to an infant. Or maybe he was just dreading the crying and the dirty diapers and the disruption to their already active household. It was impossible to tell.

She hadn't had the opportunity to question him before he went to bed at eleven; work at the marina started early. Lily had stayed up with Molly until after the baby's one o'clock feeding.

Clay rolled onto his back. Lily slid close to his side. Automatically, his arm went around her. She didn't think he was awake enough to realize he was doing it. That was one of the things she loved about him. Even when he wasn't conscious of it, he acted in ways that told her he loved her. How close they'd come to missing this. Having fallen in love as teenagers, fate had cheated them out of their early years. But in the end, they'd found one another again.

There were still hurdles to cross. They were very close to taking the biggest leap—in fact had planned on doing it this weekend. Now with Molly's unexpected arrival, it would have to wait. There was only so much upheaval a family could tolerate at once.

The truth had waited sixteen years; a few weeks more weren't going to make that much difference—she hoped. Down deep, she knew they'd made a mistake in not dealing with it before they married. But things had been going along so well, Lily had talked Clay into waiting. It was selfish of her, she knew. But she'd waited half her life to marry Clay, she didn't want to risk having everything fall apart.

As she drifted to sleep, measuring her own breathing against Clay's, she thanked her lucky stars that he had come back into her life—new complications and all.

It was still dark when she heard the baby cry. Instinctively, she started to get up. Clay put a hand on her arm.

"You were up late. I'll go see if there's anything I can do." He got up and pulled on his jeans before he went out into the hall.

Just after he disappeared through their bedroom door, she heard Riley's quiet voice in the hall. She listened carefully.

Clay whispered, even though everyone in the house was awake. "What are you doing up?"

Riley was equally quiet when he answered, "I wanted to see if Aunt Molly needed anything."

Lily's heart turned into a melted lump of butter. Riley was showing more signs of maturity every day—even though they were still quite liberally interspersed with skewed teenage perceptions and unthinking behavior.

She heard a noise, as if Clay were patting Riley on the

shoulder. "You're a good boy." Then he told Riley to go
back to bed, he'd look in on Molly.

Lily wriggled deeper under the comforter, feeling both
content and blessed. She ignored the part of her that
warned of rough days ahead.

It took all of four days for Molly to realize that living
in her sister's house was not going to work—even for the
short term. The house had three bedrooms. Molly and
Nicholas were in the guest room, which was situated between the master bedroom and Riley's room. Every time
the baby woke up in the night, Lily, Clay, or Riley—
sometimes all three—would stick their heads in and,
with sluggish speech and bleary eyes, offer help. By the
end of the fourth night, they all had bags under their eyes.

And, as hospitable as Lily had been, there was undoubtedly a strain between her and Molly. Lily said all of
the right things, but she acted as if there was a taut rubber band inside her that was ready to break. Her answers
were just a little too brusque; her movements too rigid;
her avoidance of conversation with Molly too obvious to
ignore.

Although she had planned to stay at Lily's until she
managed to join a medical practice in town, she decided,
for all of their sakes, she had to move now. Of course,
Lily—again saying the *right* thing—maintained they'd
all adjust in no time; Molly should stay.

After a frenzied three-hour search with a Realtor,
Molly signed a lease on a small house a few blocks from
downtown on Grant Street. The landlord was a little skittish about leasing to someone without a job, but the fact
that Molly was a physician seemed to override that

worry. In a town this size, doctors had a certain amount of clout, warranted or not.

Molly discovered that McDougall's Furniture had moved from downtown to a larger showroom on the outskirts of town, near the 4-H grounds. They accepted major credit cards, so by six o'clock that evening, Molly had a house, a bed, one nightstand and a lamp, a kitchen table and chairs, and a crib.

Over dinner at Lily's kitchen table, she informed Lily and her family that she was moving and it was a done deal. Through Lily's protest, Molly could see the yearning realization in her sister's eyes that a full night's sleep was just around the corner.

Riley, who had vacillated between sixteen-year-old curiosity and teenage oblivion when it came to Nicholas, said, "Are you sure the house is baby-proofed?"

Taken aback at his concern over such a matter, Molly said, "It'll be a few months before Nicholas starts moving around. I'm sure I can have things safe by then." The words were out before she realized their full implication—she was planning a future with Nicholas.

Riley gave a stiff, manly nod. "Good. I can help put locks on the cabinets and stuff. Mason Henry's little brother had to go to the emergency room last year and have his stomach pumped."

"I'd appreciate the help." Molly noticed the look of pride in Clay's eyes as he looked at Riley. She thought it was particularly sweet, considering Clay was Riley's stepfather. Of course with her own recent experience, she could easily understand bonding with a child that wasn't biologically your own. It was just that Clay and Lily had gotten together at a particularly rocky time in Riley's adolescence. Often that proved to be a recipe for disaster.

"Oh, Molly, I nearly forgot. You got a telephone call this afternoon." Lily got up and went to the counter and picked up a slip of paper.

"Nobody knows I'm here," Molly said, suspicion creeping up her spine.

"They called Dad's first."

Instantly, suspicion mixed with regret. She hadn't heard from her dad since she left his apartment four days ago. Lily had encouraged her to contact him, but Molly had avoided it. If Dad was going to be forgiving and supportive, he'd be calling her; she had enough anxiety and strain at the moment without adding fresh conflict to the mix.

Lily handed the note to Molly. It was no more than a phone number with a Boston area code. She didn't recognize it. Molly's tongue felt thick as she asked, "Did they give a name or say what it was about?"

"No. Just asked for you to call that number. It sounded official, like the hospital or something."

She *had* left her dad's phone number with the hospital; it had to be someone from there. No one else knew where she was. If Dr. Hannigan was going to give her trouble over her emergency leave. . . .

"Excuse me," Molly pushed back from the table. "I'm going to try this number. Don't start the dishes without me." She went to the living room to use the phone.

After she punched in the number and it started ringing, she had the irrational urge to hang up.

As soon as the woman answered, "Detective McMurray here," she wished she had.

Chapter 4

The telephone rang, startling Dean out of a disorienting doze. His response was that of a man used to living in a war zone: he immediately dove over the side of the hospital bed and covered his head. When he hit the cold tile floor, his wits returned and he realized just how affected he had been by his recent experience.

Thank God they'd removed the IV this morning. He hated needles. The thought of one ripped out of his vein by his duck-and-cover gave him a nasty shiver.

He pushed himself to his knees and reached for the phone.

"Yeah?" he croaked out in a voice raspy from lack of use. The swelling in his neck compounded his difficulty speaking.

"You all right?"

At the sound of Vincent Smith's voice, Dean stiffened, ready for the confrontation he knew was coming.

Dean's boss went on, "This is the first day they'd connect my call to your room. I was beginning to get suspicious that you weren't there at all. I was gonna book a flight and come there myself if they didn't let me talk to you today."

Dean got to his feet. "Not supposed to talk—" He couldn't force more than a rough whisper. He swallowed painfully, "—before today." He now understood why; it hurt like hell. He sounded like he was a hundred years old, with a voice that reminded him of the whispering rattle of dry cornhusks. Maybe he'd give up talking altogether. He was a writer after all; who needed to talk?

"Well, you sound like hell." Smitty's tone held more reproach than sympathy. "How soon can you travel?"

Dean didn't have to be told the man meant travel *home*.

He decided to meet this head on, like the stubborn bullheaded man he knew himself to be. He'd never left a story unfinished—and wasn't about to start now just because of some extremist's lucky shot in the dark. The fact that Nigel Clifford wouldn't see his children to adulthood seemed to make following this through to the end all that much more important. If the assignment wasn't worth some risk, the man's death was utterly pointless.

He said, "Doctor'll release me tomorrow or the next day. I figured I'd go back next week."

"You're not going back."

"But—"

"But nothing. All you're doing is making yourself a target for a political statement. Next time they might have a better shot—or kidnap you and try to use you for leverage. Our magazine won't have it."

Since Daniel Pearl had been kidnapped and executed

in Afghanistan, the executives in journalism had become skittish about reporters working in hostile territory.

"I have to go back. My laptop and my notes are still in that hotel. The information on it could be damaging to—"

"Nice try. I know you too well. You're too smart to leave your sources' names on anything so dangerously permanent. You're done. If you want to do a final piece when you get back here, fine. But you're coming home." Before Dean could get his voice up and working again, Smitty went on. "You've got three cartons of mail waiting here. We haven't been able to forward anything for two months. Probably something important in there."

Dean took a sip of water, hoping to ease his throat. It burned like he'd swallowed turpentine. He sat on the bed and broke out in a sweat. When he had his breath again he said, "Send it to Riyadh. I'll work from there for a while."

"No."

"Cairo, then."

"No."

"Jesus." He drew a deep breath and backed himself another step further from the hot zone. "Italy."

"Home. You're coming home. You've been out too long. You need a dose of home cooking, civil liberties, and the bright lights of Broadway. We have plenty of work for you stateside. It'll just be for a few weeks— until you're completely recovered."

Home cooking, my ass. What Smitty thought Dean needed was a dose of up-close-and-personal *"Who's Boss."* After he'd blatantly refused the order to evacuate—then gone and gotten himself shot on top of it—

he'd be lucky if Smitty would let him cover anything more foreign than the St. Patrick's Day parade.

Dean made one more attempt at delaying his removal from this side of the globe. "How about we think it over and talk again after I'm released?"

"I've already made arrangements for your return flight on Saturday—so it's good you're going to be discharged." Smitty's voice told Dean he'd been outmaneuvered; he'd already admitted he was as good as out of the hospital. Smitty went on in a self-satisfied tone, "Stephen Bristol, our correspondent in Munich, will drive you to the airport. In fact, I'll have him come by when you're dismissed to take you to a hotel. He'll hold your passport for safekeeping until you get to the airport."

A babysitter. "You certainly have little faith." Even as Dean said it, he inwardly admitted the man had reason to be concerned; Dean's past record having given just cause. Plus, given the slightest opportunity, he *would* head straight back to the same city he'd just been med-evaced out of.

Smitty only gave a dry bark of disbelieving laughter.

Dean sighed. It burned so much, he could swear the air whistled through the hole in his neck. "Guess I have no choice."

"None. We'll find something interesting for you when you get back."

"Yeah." Dean hung up the phone with little hope of such a thing. After living the way he'd been living—constantly on edge, life-and-death scenarios all around him—nothing was going to be interesting. Besides, given Smitty's past dealings with wayward reporters, himself included, Dean was certain he'd be forced to give a pound of flesh for his transgressions against authority.

Unless he could think of something quick, he'd be back in New York by Monday finding out in excruciatingly boring detail what awaited him. If *The Report* wasn't the absolute top of the heap as far as magazines went, he'd just quit. He would find a way back into that country and finish the job he'd started.

Leaning back on his pillows, he closed his eyes and nearly chuckled at himself. Who was he kidding? He'd never leave the magazine. Smitty might be a bastard, but Dean knew he'd never find another editor who listened to Dean's journalistic instincts like Smitty did.

As he lay there in bed, contemplating his future, a tightness formed in his chest. He yearned for family, the invisible shoring up of being surrounded by those who'd loved him since birth. The weight of being alone seemed too much to bear.

He straightened up and rubbed his hands over his stubbly face. Ridiculous. He was alone by choice. He'd never needed someone else to stabilize his self-confidence. His own parents, both professors of psychology, had structured his entire upbringing to breed independence. Since the age of twelve, he'd essentially made his own choices and lived with the consequences, be what they may. He didn't require a loving hand to assure him in his decisions, to remain steady on his back to keep him from falling down.

But suddenly, that was exactly how he felt. Falling without anyone who cared enough to catch him.

It was a feeling totally alien to him. For the first time

in his memory, he couldn't hammer his emotions to bend to his will.

It had to be the drugs. Once I'm out of here, I'll be back to my old self.

Molly's stomach dropped to her toes.

The detective repeated, "Hello? McMurray here."

It took the stretch of several heartbeats for Molly to find her voice. When she did, it quivered as if she were shivering with cold. "Detective McMurray," she paused and cleared her throat, "this is Dr. Boudreau returning your call."

"Ah, Dr. Boudreau. Thanks for the prompt callback." Molly could hear the shuffle of papers over the line. "We understand you worked at the free clinic on Franklin."

Molly closed her eyes and took a breath. "Yes. I did, before it closed last week." *There, that sounded pretty calm—normal.*

"We're trying to find some information on a homicide victim. Boston General's emergency room said you transferred a young woman from your clinic last Monday shortly after she gave birth. In our questioning, the staff there ID'd the woman as our victim."

"Oh, dear. How awful." Molly closed her eyes and saw the photo that was flashed on the television Thursday morning. Her heart fluttered in her chest like a moth against glass. She tried to sound sympathetic yet unemotional when she said, "I'm so sorry to hear that, but I don't know what I can tell you that would be of help."

Her knees felt like rubber. Lying didn't come naturally to her; she was going to have to watch herself. Keep to the true facts as much as possible. Don't elaborate. "We did have an emergency birth. EMS transported mother and infant to Boston General immediately after delivery."

"Did you see this woman after that?"

"I tried to see her at the hospital, but she was already gone." That answer kept the lie minimal. She mentally batted away the image of Sarah, small and so obviously frightened, casting one last look at her son before slipping out Molly's apartment door.

"What name was she using at your clinic?" McMurray asked.

"Um. Sarah . . . Morgan, that's it, Morgan. I really don't know much else about her. Sorry I can't be of more help." *How quickly can I get off this call without looking suspicious?*

"Hmm." McMurray sounded disappointed, yet not surprised. "We think this is an assumed name. Do you have any idea what her real name might be? Where she's from? If she has family?"

"No. We saw a lot of people at that clinic. I was lucky to remember the name she gave us." *Stop elaborating! Yes. No. Just answer the damn questions.*

"Of course. When do you think you'll be returning to Boston? In case we have more questions."

"I really don't know." Her heart sped up again. "I've taken emergency leave—my father has cardiac problems."

"Will we be able to reach you at this number?"

"Yes, but I don't know what more I can add."

McMurray chuckled under her breath. "You'd be surprised what comes to mind when you least expect it. You have our number if anything surfaces in your memory." Before Molly could once again deny that there was anything else, McMurray said, "Thank you, Doctor." Then the line went dead.

As she hung up the receiver, Molly realized McMurray hadn't mentioned anything about the baby. Weren't they trying to find Nicholas?

That thought bred another, more disturbing, question. Why hadn't *she* asked the detective about the baby? It would have been the logical thing to do. Would that set off alarm bells in McMurray's mind? Well, it was too late now. She'd just have to wait and see—and make sure she was more careful in the future.

Molly sat on the hardwood floor of the empty, echoing house, waiting for the furniture delivery. The sun of early morning had been eclipsed by low-slung gray clouds that tumbled and swirled as they were pushed along on a brisk wind. She watched through the living room window as the big maple tree showered its orange leaves onto the small front lawn. The air had turned chilly and damp; she'd turned on the furnace when she arrived and it was finally beginning to edge out the cold. She held Nicholas—tiny, helpless Nicholas—in her arms keeping him close for warmth.

Looking into his face, she tried to find some resemblance to his mother. But he was neither fine-boned nor fair-haired. Unable to help herself, she wondered where he'd gotten his dark hair, his deep blue eyes and his dimpled chin. Questions that would never be answered—neither to satisfy her own curiosity, nor Nicholas's own queries as he grew.

The magnitude of what she'd done finally sank in. The irony of the situation seemed almost too much to believe.

The protection of children had always been the focus of her passion, the reason she'd become a doctor. And now a child had become the thread that threatened to unravel her entire medical career. As she sat motionless for the first time in days, it became blazingly clear; she'd crossed the line and there would be no going back. The reality was, she had as much as kidnapped this child. If anyone ever discovered that, it would be the end of her career—and maybe even her freedom.

Over the past days, she'd been too frantic, too preoccupied with fear that a red-haired stranger was going to step out of the shadows, tear this baby from her and perhaps end her life as well, to think on the particulars. When she'd fled with Nicholas, it had seemed the only reasonable action. In fact, it still did. Yet the law would certainly see otherwise.

She *could* go back, return to Boston and explain to the authorities why she'd felt she had no other choice. And then she'd have to hand Nicholas over to an uncertain future. His fate would lie either with a murdering father, or the social services system she'd seen fail so many times before.

Once the report that Sarah had recently given birth hit the papers—as it surely would as the police searched for her true identity and the details of her life and death—the father would certainly start looking for the baby. Even if he didn't, who knew how long it would be before the legalities would allow the adoption of a child in Nicholas's position. Crucial developmental months of his life would slip by. Maybe he'd get lucky and have loving foster care. And maybe he wouldn't. The risk was just too big to take.

Besides, if the father did claim him, the man had

already proven himself cruel and manipulative and without morals; charges would most certainly be brought against Molly for abduction. It was one hell of a mess.

A knock on the front door made Molly nearly jump out of her skin. Her gaze shot to the door, which had a glass-paned upper half. Relief prickled her skin when she saw it wasn't the police, or the red-haired killer. It was a thin, blond girl of about fifteen.

After taking a breath to slow her racing heart, Molly got up and answered the door.

The girl said, "Hi, I'm Mickey Fulton." She tilted her head to the side. "I live next door." Holding out a paper plate of chocolate chip cookies, she said, "Welcome to the neighborhood."

Molly adjusted the baby in her arms and took the plate. "Thank you. I'm Molly." She motioned the plate toward the living room. "Do you want to come in? Sorry, I don't have any furniture yet."

Mickey shifted her weight and stuck her hands in her jacket pockets. She had warm brown eyes and a wide smile. She looked . . . wholesome. Such a contrast to the new teen norm of forcing maturity before its time. Molly immediately liked her—it would be hard for anyone *not* to.

"No, thanks," Mickey said. "I have to get back home. I saw the baby when you came in . . ." She paused in a shy way. "I'm a good babysitter if you ever need one."

All of her warm thoughts of Mickey being a nice girl were snatched from her mind. Molly held the baby tighter, fighting the instinct to shove the girl backward, away from the house—away from Nicholas. Another reality smacked her in the face. How was she going to protect him from his father if she couldn't be with him every minute? What if the man waited until there was a sitter here . . . then. . . She shook her head. She had to remind herself: Simplicity. One step at a time.

Her fear must have shown on her face, because Mickey blushed and said, "You can talk to my mom first. I have references." She hesitated. "Don't feel obligated just 'cause I'm next door."

Molly forced a smile. "It's not that. Not at all. I just haven't thought about leaving him yet. Of course you'll be the first one I call." There, that was pretty normal-sounding. Rational. Most new mothers didn't like to leave their babies the first time.

Mickey just nodded, her silky blond hair falling over her blushing cheeks. As she started to turn around, she paused. "You're Riley Holt's aunt, aren't you?"

Molly smiled and gave a nod. "Are you friends with Riley?"

The girl hesitated, a pained expression crossed her face. "I used to be." Then she hurried down the porch steps and headed toward her own house.

The hurt in the girl's eyes was genuine, but Molly didn't have long to wonder over what had passed between her nephew and Mickey because the delivery truck pulled up.

Two hours later, Nicholas was asleep in his newly assembled crib. Molly took the quiet time to unpack her few belongings. She took her Tinkerbell clock and placed it on the fireplace mantel in the living room. Molly realized how silly it appeared, this starkly bare living room with its one accessory a juvenile memento. But she didn't care. Looking at that clock gave her the sense that time would move on and things would work out. The flow of her life, although diverted, would soon find a normal channel in which to run. She took the key and wound up the clock, then nudged Tinkerbell into her back and forth motion, ticking away the seconds.

Dean arrived back in the United States on Sunday. He didn't want to admit it, but the trans-Atlantic trip had just about sucked the life out of him. He took a taxi home, and endured the enthusiastic greeting of his landlady. Then he staggered into his rented room, dropped his suitcase, and collapsed on the bed with his clothes still on.

On Monday he defied yet another boss's order and returned to work. He sat in Smitty's office, letting the man vent, tuning out all but the most abrasive of comments. He knew from experience it was best to just let the old man wind down on his own. Any attempt at defense or argument only prolonged the verbal lashing.

Finally Smitty got to the meat of the matter. "Of course you'll take a few weeks off."

"I've already taken over a week off."

"You can't think I'm going to send you back over there."

He tried to appear indifferent, but inside his relief was undeniable. Time and clearheadedness had given him the opportunity to realize just how lucky he'd been. He wasn't quite ready to be shot at again. Lifting a shoulder he said, "You're the boss."

"Damn right. And you're not going on assignment for a lo-ong time. Maybe I'll let you cover Macy's Thanksgiving Day parade." He honed his dark eyes in on Dean, most likely in an attempt to appear menacing.

Dean tried to oblige and *appear* contrite. "Of course."

"Get on out of here and clean up that pigsty you call a desk. The mail alone should occupy you for a week."

Dean walked to his work station. His heart sank when he saw the cartons of mail. His voice mailbox was undoubtedly full too, as he hadn't been able to check it for over two months. He picked up the mail cartons and dropped them on the floor. Then he sat in his chair and took in the view. Jesus, it had been a long time since he'd looked at life from this perspective: fabric-covered modular walls, tidy shelves of reference books, beige file cabinets, paperclips in a magnetic holder. He could hardly breathe. Now he was going to be stuck here for who knew how long.

He picked up the telephone and dialed his sister. He hadn't called her since before they met for Christmas; he had to dig the scrap of paper with her number on it from his wallet.

Man, was she going to be surprised to hear he was home. Maybe they'd go out to dinner tonight; someplace nice and quiet so they could catch up. There used to be this little place over on 52nd Street. He wondered if it was still there.

On the second ring he got a recorded message saying the number had been disconnected.

Puzzled, he rechecked the number and dialed again.

Same recording.

He then tried her work number. A man answered her extension.

"Hello, this is Dean Coletta, Julie's brother. May I speak to her, please?"

The man cleared his throat. "I'm sorry. Ms. Coletta is no longer with us." His tone said Dean should be well aware of this fact.

"Can you tell me where I might reach her?"

"Mr. Coletta, let me give you to my supervisor."

Before Dean could ask anything else, he was shifted to Muzak. Shortly thereafter, a woman came on the line.

"I understand you're Julie Coletta's brother?"

"Yes. What's going on?"

"Mr. Coletta, I'm going to have to refer you to NYPD." She read a number to him.

He didn't even have anything to write with. He flung open a desk drawer and rifled through with shaking fingers. "What has happened to my sister?"

After a pause, the woman said, "We've been instructed to have everyone call that number." She took a breath, as if deciding whether or not to break the rules. Then she said, "I really don't have much to offer you. She simply stopped coming to work."

"Like she quit?"

"No, just stopped showing up. No one knows why."

"When?" His mouth went dry as perspiration broke out on his forehead.

"It's been over six months now."

"Six months!" Dean's gut felt like a writhing snake. Sweat trickled down his sides.

"Yes."

"What's that NYPD number again?"

She gave it to him. "Mr. Coletta, I do hope you find her."

With his head spinning, but unwilling to wait another second, he called. It took six transfers to finally find the detective assigned to his sister's case. Each time he was put on hold seemed endless. He ended up with Missing Persons. *Jesus*. Then a practical little voice buried deep in his head said, *at least it's not homicide*.

He couldn't even swallow.

It took the detective five minutes to track down the file. It obviously was not on the top of his to-do stack.

The entire conversation was completely unsatisfactory. According to the PD, Julie had closed her bank accounts, sold her car, and walked away from her life. Nothing criminal in that. She'd left her apartment full of furniture. After investigating the scene, they had allowed the super to have her things put in storage. They had interviewed her fellow workers, her neighbors and acquaintances and not come up with a clue.

It all seemed totally impossible. Julie—responsible, pragmatic, intelligent, courteous Julie—would not simply have picked up and walked away from her job—her life—without telling someone.

The detective assured Dean that the case was still open. Whatever the hell that meant. The more Dean pushed, the more disinterested the detective sounded. It was clear he had concluded Julie had left the city of her own free will.

Well, Dean was an investigative reporter. He'd damn well see it done right himself.

First, he had to know if Julie had tried to contact him. If she was making a change like this, of course she would have. Anything else screamed foul play in Dean's mind.

He questioned Smitty. Julie had been instructed

always to contact Smitty if she needed him. If she had and the old man hadn't gotten word through to him . . . but Smitty swore he hadn't heard a peep from Julie.

It took seventy minutes for Dean to go through his voice mails. None were from Julie. There was one from the detective he'd just spoken to at NYPD—the fact that the man never followed up spoke volumes to him about the thoroughness of this investigation.

Then Dean went into the men's room and locked himself in a stall. Silent tears of frustration and fear forced themselves beyond his control. A stony resolve settled in his heart. It was up to him. He was going to find his sister.

That lightness he'd felt when anticipating a rare impromptu dinner with his sister transformed into a lead band constricting his heart. He didn't have a good feeling about this at all.

On the eighth day of his quest, Dean hung up from yet another fruitless phone call. He'd studied a copy of the police report. He'd interviewed everyone he could think of. He'd looked through her things, which were now boxed and stored in the basement of her apartment building. He'd even gone to the head of the department at Juile's workplace and threatened that if she'd been working on something that had resulted in her disappearance, he was going to use all of his journalistic power to bring it to light. Now he was making stabs in the dark. He hadn't slept more than catnaps in days.

He had been using his desk at the *The Report* because he couldn't stand the nerve-wracking quiet of his tiny rented room. He concentrated better with the buzz of people around him. Also, from here it was easier to put the considerable resources of the magazine to work for him. For all the good it was doing; he'd sent out missing persons reports by the boatload, checked to see if a new bank account or credit card had been opened in Julie's name or social security number, and spoken to everyone he could find who knew his sister, but hadn't come up with a single lead.

Before he could get up and refill his coffee, the phone rang.

He snatched it up, his nerves raw from frustration. "Coletta."

"Mr. Coletta, this is Detective McMurray with Boston PD. I think I may have a Jane Doe who matches the description of your missing person, Julie Coletta."

Dean's chest grew tight. He'd been through this three times before. Three times he'd marched into a morgue to view a body. Three times his insides turned liquid as the moment approached. Three times, it hadn't been Julie.

Still, the crushing weight of dread robbed him of his breath. He managed to say, "In the morgue?"

"Yes. Do you want us to send a fax for a preliminary ID?"

"No." He knew the only thing worse than finding his sister in a morgue would be to preview a photo of her dead body, *then* go to make the identification in person. "I'll come up." He looked at his watch. It was only nine-thirty. "I'll be there this afternoon."

It was four-thirty when Dean was escorted to the morgue. The sound of his footfalls competed with Detective McMurray's as they echoed off the concrete block walls of the hallway. They passed a man in his mid-sixties walking in the other direction. His head was bowed and he pressed a handkerchief to his face.

Dean's gut reacted, threatening revolt.

This routine didn't get any easier. In fact, it grew harder each time. With every step Dean took, his mind calculated how much greater the odds were that it could be Julie.

In the three previous instances, he hadn't experienced the rush of relief he'd expected when the body hadn't been Julie's. On the contrary, he felt depressed and a little guilty for the hope he still held as he stood next to someone else's dead kin.

Detective McMurray explained where this body had been found, then said, "Cause of death was a gunshot to the head, small caliber, no exit wound."

That was her nice clinical way of saying the victim's face hadn't been blown off.

Dean's stomach did a double flip before the knot tightened further in his abdomen.

McMurray said, "This Jane Doe had given birth shortly before her death. Was your sister pregnant?"

He wished he could say no and turn around and walk out of here. "I don't know. I don't think so."

She pulled a door open and held it for Dean to enter the viewing area.

As he stepped inside, he felt the walls close in on him. He tried to take a steadying breath, but it only served to make him nauseous.

"Ready?"

He nodded.

Julie looked as if she'd been carved out of wax—a ghoulish reproduction of his beautiful sister.

Dean tried to swallow, but found he couldn't. He also couldn't speak. He turned away, unable to give voice to defeat.

"Mr. Coletta. I need you to affirm that this is your sister." She paused. "A nod will suffice."

He felt like a coward—a shameful, disgusting coward. He turned around and looked at the ashen skin and matted hair. He needed to give his sister the respect she deserved. "Yes," he said. "That is Julie Coletta."

In that second, the most selfish, most pitiless thought entered his mind. *He* was alone. His family was gone.

It was horrible. His sister had died alone, been dumped like garbage under a bridge, and he could only think about how abandoned *he* felt.

Chapter 5

At four-thirty Hank Brown sat alone at the bar in the Crossing House. The way he stared into the bubbles in his beer and absently turned the base of his glass in slow, quiet circles told Benny the man had something on his mind. It was rare that Brownie came in and sat in quiet introspection. He was generally a man with an easy manner and quick smile. He also didn't normally show up until after six in the evening. All together, this set Benny's radar off.

"So," Benny asked as he continued to dry glasses, getting ready for the evening rush, "how are things at the shop?"

Brownie owned the best garage in Glens Crossing, ran it the old fashioned way, with attention to detail and customer service. Benny couldn't imagine the man's troubles had anything to do with his business. Same for his marriage. He and his wife, the most placid and amicable woman Benny had ever met, had been married for thirty years without so much as a ripple to disturb their domestic peace. He didn't have children to torment him. What could have him so bothered?

Brownie nodded slightly, keeping his gaze on his beer. "Garage is fine."

"Good. Good." Benny kept his hands busy, his eyes averted—best not to look like he was nosing in Brownie's business. But his demeanor was so out of character, Benny worried about him. Brownie was first and foremost a friend.

As Benny searched for possible reasons for Brownie's upset, a thought occurred to him. Brownie's Aunt Rose ran the office at the garage. She was an amazingly straightforward dynamo, topped with dandelion fuzz that fooled most people into thinking an old woman lived in that body. She and Brownie were especially close. Maybe there was something with her health.

He asked, "Aunt Rose okay?"

"Fine."

Benny tried to prod the conversation forward. "She's one amazing woman. How old is she now? Eighty?"

In the same distracted tone, Brownie answered, "Eighty-five."

Benny whistled. "Sure hope I'm in that kind of shape at her age."

Brownie nodded and shifted in his seat. Then he raised his eyes to look at Benny for the first time since the beer had landed in front of him. It was clear he had something that he felt needed saying.

"Something on your mind?" Benny asked, setting the glass and towel on the bar, showing Brownie he had his undivided attention.

Brownie rolled his lips inward, seeming to choose his

words carefully. "I feel a little funny talking about this . . . but Aunt Rose . . . she's dinged and donged at me all week long. I finally couldn't take it anymore."

"We've known each other most of our lives. Speak up."

Brownie shifted uncomfortably. "Well, Aunt Rose is worried . . . I mean she thinks . . . aw, hell." He ran his calloused hand over his short bristly hair. He finally let the words come in a rush, as if suddenly anxious to be rid of them. "Have you seen Molly lately?"

Benny straightened, drawing back slightly. He picked the towel back up. "Been a few days."

"A few days?" Brownie's voice was skeptical.

"Okay. Weeks. What's the problem?"

"Rose says nobody's seen her. She's been back in town for a month—"

"She's busy," Benny said brusquely.

Brownie slid off his stool. "And you know this because . . . ?"

Faye, Benny's companion who worked in the bar and continually vacillated between being his comfort and his frustration, appeared behind his shoulder, her hair a russet cloud around her face and her green eyes snapping with fire. "He don't know anything." She jabbed a red polished nail into Benny's shoulder. "And that's because he's as stubborn as my granddaddy's plow mule."

Benny suddenly envied Brownie with his placid wife—Faye was a firecracker. He usually liked that about her, the fact that she constantly challenged him. But not when it came to this particular subject.

"She's busy," Benny said again, then turned around and walked back toward the kitchen. It was none of anyone's goddamn business if he'd seen his daughter or not—not even Faye's.

As he walked away, he heard Faye and Brownie discussing him in hushed tones. That just burned his balls. Faye had been playing the same song for weeks: *You're missing your grandson's infancy. Punishing Molly like this is a little like shutting the barn door after the cow's gone a runnin' into the storm. That baby's here now, he's not going away. Both he and his mother could use your support.* She whined around day after day like a broken record. Well, he hadn't seen Riley much as a baby, and that never hurt anything. They had a great relationship— went fishing every couple of weeks.

This deal with Molly—that was different. How could he condone what she'd done? She had worked so hard; they'd all made sacrifices so she could be a doctor, have an easy future . . . respect—something he'd wanted for her more than anything. Every time he thought about how she'd thrown her life away—a single mother, that's what they called it these days. Well, that wasn't what they'd called it when he was young. They had another name entirely. People were going to have a hey-day with this one, just like they did when Molly's mother took off.

He rubbed his hand over his face. His heart ached. He'd wanted so much more for his children. After listening to people whisper behind their backs as kids, he'd wanted the rest of their lives to be humiliation-free. Molly had thrown it all away, without a word to the rest of her family.

Against his will, worry sprouted in his mind. What if something *was* wrong? He'd assumed, after their uneasy parting, that Molly was simply avoiding him.

Maybe he'd call Lily later and see if she knew what was going on.

He poked around in the storeroom until he was pretty sure Brownie had gone on his way. When he returned to the bar, Faye was leaning against the counter talking to a man Benny didn't recognize. Faye was laughing; must be a friendly guy. Friendly or not, at least his presence would put off Faye from coming after him about Molly.

Faye motioned Benny to them. "Benny, this is Dean Coletta. He works for that magazine you like . . . the . . . the—"

"*Report,*" the man said, rising from his bar stool to shake Benny's hand.

Benny shook his hand. "Benny Boudreau." He eyed the new-looking scar on the reporter's neck. "I remember seeing your name. You've been doing the stuff on the Middle East, right?"

In fact, Benny was very familiar with Coletta's work. Benny had gotten into the habit of keeping track of what was happening around the world while his son, Luke, had been an army Ranger. Coletta always seemed to be smack-dab in the middle of the most volatile location on the planet. Which was also the most likely spot for Luke to be deployed. Benny always felt a little closer to his son when reading Coletta's articles.

Dean gave a half-smile and a curt nod. "I'm working on something different right now." He rubbed his chin. "Boudreau? Now that's an unusual name. Are there a lot of Boudreaus in this neck of the woods?"

Faye answered for Benny. "Just Benny and his young 'uns. Course everybody's married or moved off."

Benny didn't bother to correct her; Molly was back—and wasn't married, a fact which pained him daily.

Dean smiled and leaned back on his stool. He directed his next question to Benny. "How many children? Faye here makes it sound like you have a tribe." He chuckled.

Benny shook his head. "Nope. Lily lives here. Luke is living in Mississippi. He used to be an army Ranger. You two would probably have a lot to talk about."

"A Ranger. Really? When?" Dean asked.

Benny was glad to talk about Luke. "Well, he went to the army when he was nineteen. Rangers came 'bout a year later. Last year he was injured in a chopper crash—I suppose he Rangered for around fifteen years. I wonder if you two were ever in the same place at the same time."

"It's likely." Then Dean said, "So just a daughter and a son, then?"

Benny nodded and mopped an imaginary spill on the bar.

Faye cleared her throat.

Benny ignored her.

Faye said, "Benny's forgettin' that his baby just moved back here from Boston."

Benny clenched the towel in his fist to keep from smacking her. This stranger didn't need to hear how his brilliant daughter had thrown away her respectability.

"Boston! Bet you're glad to have her back."

Benny stopped wiping the bar. "How'd you know my baby is a girl?"

Dean sat straighter and tilted his head, looking slightly curious himself. "I didn't. I guess it's just when someone refers to an adult as 'baby' I think of a woman." He paused. When Benny didn't offer more, he said, "Is 'baby' a *he* or a *she*?"

Faye chirped, "Oh, baby's a girl all right. In fact—"

Benny interrupted her before she had all of the dirty laundry out in the front yard. "I heard the delivery truck in back. Go take care of it for me, will you?"

Faye pressed her lips together and snorted. "All right."

He felt her angry glare on him as she walked to the kitchen.

Dean asked, "Why did your daughter decide to move back?"

Benny lifted a shoulder. "Who knows why kids do anything?"

"Oh, I didn't realize she was still a kid. How old is she?"

"Twenty-nine." Benny turned to check the stock in the cooler behind him.

Coletta didn't take the hint; he asked, "What does she do?"

"Doctor."

"Really! You must be proud."

"I'm proud she stayed with it—glad she's a doctor." Benny didn't look at Coletta.

"What brought her back here?" Coletta asked.

"Benny! You must be hearin' things. There's no truck back there." Faye bustled back behind the bar.

Benny grunted. Maybe he'd turn the tables on this nosey reporter. He had a few questions that could be asked; like what in the hell was Coletta doing here on the outside of nowhere? Did he get injured while over there working among those fanatical extremists that acted like the Middle East was the Wild West? That scar on the man's neck sure looked like a gunshot wound. If Coletta was going to start digging around in Benny's sandbox, two could play at that game.

He was actually a little disappointed when Faye took the conversation in a different direction. But at least it wasn't about "baby." "Dean said he's looking for a place to stay for a few weeks. I told him that a lot of the lake cottages are empty this time of year—be better than driving all the way to the interstate to stay in a motel."

Benny couldn't help himself. He asked in a suspicious tone, "Why would a man like you want to hang around here?"

Dean didn't seem to notice the tone. He answered as easy as you please. "I'm working on a piece of Americana right now. I'm spending time in various small towns around the country, trying to get a feel for real life—you know, more in depth than just driving through, asking a few questions and taking a few pictures."

Faye was nearly hopping up and down. "Isn't it exciting?" She splayed her well-manicured hand over her heart and sounded breathless. "Our little town in that famous magazine?"

Benny wanted to tell her all of that red-headed enthusiasm would be better spent checking the stockroom than thinking this was going to make her some sort of celebrity. But he held his tongue.

She went on in a rush, "Earlier, I was telling Dean he should check with Brian Mitchell. Sometimes he lets folks use his lake house." She faced Coletta again. "He's got a real estate business right on the square—you can't miss it. If he doesn't want to rent his house, he'll be the one to find you someplace else."

"That sounds like a plan." Dean pushed himself away from the bar. "I appreciate the information."

Faye was grinning like an idiot as the man headed toward the door. "Come back sometime. We serve the best steaks in town." Then she added, "Everybody comes here. It'd be a good place to do interviews."

He paused before going out and looked over his shoulder. Benny thought he saw something bordering on unfriendliness in his previously guileless eyes. But it could have been Benny's own aggravation with Faye coloring his perception.

Coletta said, "I'm sure I'll be back real soon." Then he was gone.

Benny ignored Faye's excited chatter after the man left. It just didn't make sense to him that a man with a journalistic reputation like Dean Coletta was going to spend weeks sitting around a bunch of nowhere towns— even if he had been shot in the neck.

As Dean left the Crossing House, he had the distinct impression that Benny Boudreau had a problem with his youngest child. Well, Dean had a couple of issues to clear up with the woman, too. He just wasn't sure how to best go about it yet. He couldn't jump the gun and scare her off. Dr. Boudreau's flight from Boston had shown just how big of a risk that was. Maybe Daddy knew more about why she'd come home than he'd let on; there was definitely something about her that he didn't want anyone to know. Did that something have to do with Julie's death?

But, Dean thought, she hadn't been "Julie" in Boston. She'd been Sarah, Sarah Morgan. Why? Why had she disappeared from her life in New York and invented a new identity for herself? Had she been hiding from someone? If so, Dean hadn't been able to unearth who that someone could have been. Her life in New York, by all accounts, had been independent, productive, and well-balanced. She had a small circle of friends, who appeared baffled by her disappearance.

But that disappearance had been months before she'd been killed, making an abduction unlikely. Paired with the false ID and the fact that she seemed to have been moving freely around Boston, kidnapping seemed totally out of the realm of possibility.

All signs pointed to the fact that the baby she'd delivered shortly before her death was the key. But how? She had been a professional woman, working in a benign research laboratory that specialized in commercial foods. She'd been far from destitute, and certainly of an age that a pregnancy wouldn't have to be hidden—not from a progressive-thinking family like theirs.

That thought stopped him cold. There was no family. He and Julie had been all there was left. And now it was just him.

He'd never seen shortcomings in the way they had been raised. But now he'd begun to trip in the pitfalls. Both he and Julie had been brought up to be self-sufficient, to make their mistakes and learn from them. They'd been close growing up, but as adults, even though he still thought of them as close, the reality was they rarely communicated. They were both busy with their lives, satisfied with the occasional telephone conversation and the sporadic holiday spent in the same city.

Now he realized he didn't know the woman his sister had become at all.

Had Julie decided to give her baby up for adoption, then changed her mind? He knew there were women desperate enough to commit murder for a child. Or had she been the victim of a black market baby organization?

Molly Boudreau could be the missing link in either case. He was an investigative reporter; and he was going to put his talents to work in a way he'd never imagined in his wildest dreams.

It had taken four long weeks before Molly was able to close her eyes at night without the unremitting fear that someone was going to crash through her door, murder her, and take Nicholas. The first night she'd spent in her new house, she hadn't slept at all. Every windblown leaf, every scrape of a branch on that blustery night had sent shivers down her spine and a cold stab of panic into her heart. During the subsequent nights, she'd been able to doze, but had been plagued with nightmares in which Nicholas was raised in an environment of lawlessness and cruelty. Over and over she saw the sweet infant mature to be a merciless killer like his father.

She had done all that was physically possible to foster a sense of safety and security in her new home. All of the bedrooms in the house were on the first floor, the gabled second story given over to one huge dormered room that hadn't been used in decades, judging from the finish-worn floor and fifties-era wallpaper. In her more optimistic moments, she thought that it would one day make a good playroom. But these days her optimism came only in microscopic doses. More often she stayed inside, double checked window latches and door locks, kept an eye on dark windows at night, and slept with a baseball bat she'd borrowed from her nephew, Riley, under her bed. Nicholas's crib remained in her bedroom where she could hear any noise he—or any intruder near him—might make.

On the morning that marked the beginning of her fifth week in Glens Crossing, she awakened realizing she'd slept the night through. As she opened her eyes and saw the sun had risen, she bolted out of bed, certain that she'd slept through Nicholas's cry.

But Nicholas slept peacefully, his precious pink mouth blowing tiny bubbles with every exhaled breath.

As the tension left her body, she looked upon the baby and realized how much he'd grown. It made her see just how quickly time was passing. Day after day went by, dominated by dread and fear, her life drifting in limbo. It had to stop—or they would both become emotionally crippled.

After so many weeks, odds were that if the father was going to hunt her down, he'd have done so by now. With that thought, the fear that had been ever present but diminishing, shrank to a manageable size. It was time to forge ahead. She needed work. Nicholas needed to be around other people. She'd been in hiding long enough. No one had come after her. She hadn't heard from Detective McMurray after that first unsettling conversation.

It was time to stick her head back out of her burrow and begin to build a life. A *family* life for Nicholas.

He was hers, now and forever. She wanted him to grow up with the security of community as well as in the comfort of her love.

That thought stopped her midbreath. She *did* love Nicholas. No longer did her feelings revolve around a promise, an obligation. She loved this child, would fight tooth and nail if anyone tried to take him away, would be devastated if she lost him.

Well, if that's the case, you'd damn well better get yourself in a position to support him.

At ten o'clock, she called Boston General and told them she was resigning. Her conversation with her boss, Dr. Hannigan, was anything but what she expected.

He said, "I'm not surprised."

"Really?" How could he not be surprised? *She* certainly was.

"I know you've kept an Indiana license."

Molly didn't think he ever paid that much attention to her personal details. "Well, I applied when I took the boards," she explained. "It was to make my Dad happy. I never really thought I'd come back." She realized she needed this to sound like a logical move. "But with Dad's health, I just can't be that far away."

"Molly, you never belonged in the ER. It was just a matter of time before you saw it. You should be in a community where you can develop long-term relationships with your patients—use your specialty. You've got too much heart for this kind of work."

"You never mentioned that to me before." In fact, he never said much to her at all.

He gave a dry chuckle. "Think I'm crazy? I didn't want to lose one of the best doctors I've got on staff."

Best doctors? He had never found fault with her work; but she'd never had any indication he thought she was performing exceptionally well, either. "Thank you, Dr.

Hannigan. Just have custodial services box up the things in my locker."

"Will do. I'll just have the boxes put in my office for now." Then he added, "You *are* setting up a pediatric practice."

"Not right away. I'm going to do some hospital work until I get settled here—and see how Dad's health is going."

"Damn shame. You belong in Peds. Don't waste your talents, don't get caught up in the routine."

"I'll keep your advice in mind, doctor."

"Good luck."

As Molly hung up the phone, she felt a kind of restlessness she hadn't experienced since arriving home; a need to work, to doctor. She had been so preoccupied with her predicament that she hadn't noticed the longing that was growing in her heart.

Now it was time to face the outside world. The only place she'd been since moving into her house was Lily's. She didn't like the idea of coming home to a house that had been unattended, allowing someone to slip inside and wait for her, any more than she liked the idea of parading around town setting gossiping tongues to wagging. She'd become quite skilled at avoiding going out. She'd repeatedly managed to finagle having Lily doing the little bit of shopping she needed by using one excuse or another; it was too cold to get Nicholas out, or "as long as you're going to Kingston's could you pick up . . . ?" Once she'd even stooped so low as to feign illness herself.

Her relationship with her sister remained puzzling. Lily was cordial enough, but there was something bothering her that no amount of questioning could bring to the surface. And, to be perfectly honest, Molly had enough to deal with without coddling her sister out of a mood. If Lily had a problem with her, she'd better just come out and tell her what it was—or get over it.

As Molly put Nicholas in the car, she took a deep breath of crisp autumn air. The sun was shining; the sky was a clear, deep blue. The morning frost was gone in all but the shadiest of areas. It was a glorious day. A day of pumpkins and hayrides. Of hot apple cider and wiener roasts. It brought back simple pleasures that she didn't even know she'd missed after leaving this small town. On a day like this, it was easy to leave her darkest fears behind her. A perfect day for a new start.

As she'd arranged by phone, she stopped at Lily's to drop Nicholas off before her appointment with human resources at Henderson County Hospital. After she'd shuttled the baby and all of his paraphernalia inside, she was surprised how difficult it was to leave him. In fact, at the last second, she turned back around in the doorway. Lily stood with Nicholas in her arms and a pottery dust smear on her cheek.

Suddenly the beautiful day wasn't enough to banish Molly's fears. This farm was pretty isolated. Someone could easily sneak up the lane. They could snatch Nicholas and be gone, without anyone seeing. A cold fear gripped Molly's stomach.

She wanted to tell Lily to keep the doors locked and not answer if anyone knocked. But she could hardly say something like that without explanation. She'd sound as crazy as she felt at the moment.

Instead, she said, "If you lay him down, be sure and prop him on his side."

"Right."

"His diaper probably needs changing."

"Okay."

"He wiggles out from under his blanket, so be sure and wrap him up when he naps."

Lily shook her head and rolled her eyes. "Really, Molly, I *have* done this before. And you're only going to be gone an hour."

"Maybe I'll just take him with me."

Lily raised a brow. "Don't think I can handle it?"

"No, of course not. It's just . . . it's the initial interview; I'll only be in there a few minutes."

"Mol. I know it's hard, but we'll be okay. In fact, you should take a little time for yourself—get coffee, run errands. You haven't had a break in weeks. Trust me; it'll be good for both of you."

Molly doubted that. How could it be good for her to have her insides twisted with worry? Besides, Lily didn't know the danger. This suddenly seemed like a very bad idea.

Lily said, "Go. You're going to be late."

Molly stood there for another minute. If leaving him for an hour was this hard, how was she going to manage a job? A new knot formed in her gut. She didn't have a choice. The money was fast running out and she had bills to pay. She made herself turn around and walk out the door.

Her interview went like clockwork—which was a miracle considering how distracted she was with worry. When she left, she had an offer for a part-time position in the emergency room starting in two weeks. That gave her true mixed feelings: It removed the financial ax that was about to drop on her neck, but it made it completely necessary to arrange care for the baby. If only this hospital had a daycare center for its staff. Then he'd be close; it'd be easy to check in on him periodically.

She tried to rationalize to herself that mothers had to do this every day. Before she could take comfort in that thought, or maybe it was more in line with "misery loves company," a little voice of dissent rose, saying, *most mothers don't have to worry about an armed killer hunting down their child.*

Starting her car in the hospital lot, she shook her head in an effort to dislodge negative thoughts. If she was going to keep her sanity, she had to stop thinking like that. If she wanted a normal life for Nicholas, she had to start behaving *normally.*

With that in mind, she willed herself not to beat her way back to Lily's, breaking speed limits and running stop signs. Instead, she drove to the square. Lily was right, she should do some shopping. Her cupboards were beyond bare and there were a thousand things she needed for the house. It would be so much quicker and easier to run errands without Nicholas.

For the first time in her life, she missed having a cell phone. While in Boston, her social life had been nonexistent and the hospital used pagers, so she never needed a cell. But, as she looked for a pay phone in the old-fashioned downtown area to call and check on Nicholas, she felt the lack. There wouldn't be pay phones inside the hardware store or JC Penney. She almost decided just to go on back to Lily's when she remembered the pull-up pay phone at the gas station two blocks off the square.

The town had recently decided to make the traffic around the square one-way—a very bad move in her estimation. She didn't want to circle the courthouse again, so she turned into the alley to cut across to the next block. The alley was so narrow she held her breath as she drove between the old brick walls, as if that would somehow make her car narrower.

When she reached the other side of the block, the buildings sat right next to the sidewalk, making it difficult to see. She edged out, then saw a break in the traffic and accelerated into a left turn.

A sickening thud made her slam on the brakes. Her gaze jerked to her right. Two people from across the street were hurrying toward her car.

Had she hit a dog?

She jumped out and ran around the front bumper.

There, half in the alley and half on the sidewalk, lay a man.

"Oh, my God!" Molly knelt beside him. "I didn't even see you!"

"Good," he said with a grimace. "Hate to think you ran me down on purpose."

He started to move, trying to raise himself up on one elbow. Molly gently forced him back down. "Lie down."

"I'm okay."

"Let me be the judge of that, I'm a doctor." Lucky for her this was a young, healthy-looking man, not an octogenarian with fragile hip joints.

He looked at her for the first time. His blue eyes narrowed against the bright sunlight. "First good luck I've had in a while—being run over by a doctor."

One of the people who'd come to help, a woman with graying hair and tinted glasses, said, "Should I call an ambulance?"

Molly said, "Yes." At exactly the same time the man said, "No."

"I'm the expert," Molly said. "Call them."

"Waste of time. I won't go. I'm fine; I've spent enough time in the hospital recently to know."

For the first time, Molly noticed the fresh scar on his neck. Instead of asking about it, she kept to the business at hand. "Where did you hit hardest?"

"My ass."

A nervous laugh blipped out. Molly quickly squashed it. "Anywhere else?"

"Right elbow smarts a little. Can I get up now?"

"No. Did you hit your head?"

"No, just my ass and my elbow." He started to move. "I'm getting up." Then he pointed a finger at the middle-aged woman who was pulling a cell phone out of her purse. "Don't make that call. If I already have a doctor here, why would I need an ambulance?"

Against Molly's continued protest, he got to his feet. He looked around where he'd fallen. "I had a key in my hand. See it anywhere?"

Molly reached out and took his right arm. "Let me check your elbow."

He didn't protest, but his gaze locked on her face as he slid his jacket off the right shoulder. He smiled when he said, "Want me to take my shirt off, too?" There was enough suggestion in his voice to make Molly roll her eyes.

She thinned her lips to keep from laughing. "Just give me your arm."

He did; his smile lingered. She ran her hand over the elbow joint, her fingers gently probing for splintered bone or misalignment. Then she worked her way toward his wrist. She could feel his gaze fixed on her face, not his own injury. When she glanced up, it struck her just how good looking he was. Intense blue eyes in a rugged outdoorsy face, the kind of face that made cologne commercials. There was something else shining there too, an open kindness that kept his looks from being harsh. It made it difficult for her to tear her own gaze away.

"Should I call, or not?" The woman was growing impatient.

Molly kept her eyes fixed on his. "I'd feel a lot better if you'd go."

His voice was teasing when he said, "How about if I sign an affidavit promising I won't sue?"

Molly let go of his arm. "That was *not* my concern."

He slid his arm back into his jacket and shrugged it back on.

"Oh, no! Your jacket's torn, too."

He lifted his elbow and looked. Then he shrugged. "It's old. No big deal."

"Here—" Molly opened the passenger door and pulled out a pen and paper from her purse "—this is my name and number. Get the jacket fixed, or if they can't repair it, buy a new one. I'll take care of the cost." She pressed the paper into his hand. When it looked like he was going to protest, she said, "It's either this or the ambulance. And I want your name and address, in case you *forget* our deal."

"It's not necessary—"

She raised a brow and glanced toward the woman with the cell phone.

He shook his head and waved the woman away. "Dean Coletta." He finally looked at the paper and his brow creased. A flash of what looked like recognition passed in his eyes. After a moment, he said, "I just got to town, actually. I've rented Brian Mitchell's cottage out on Forrester Lake for the month. That's the key I dropped."

Molly's heart nearly stopped. "You're not from here?" She wanted to snatch the paper back, but he'd already put it in his pocket.

"No. New York. I'm here to do some research for a magazine article."

What could possibly interest a New York magazine in Glens Crossing? This was too much of a coincidence. She took a small step away from him and glanced at her car, gauging how quickly she could get back inside and drive away. A silver key with its plastic Realtor tag lay on the hood.

"Here's your key." She reached out and picked it up. She tried not to touch his skin when she handed it to him. "If you're all right . . . I'm late." She was already around the front fender.

He said something as she slammed the door, but she couldn't make out the words. As she pulled out of the alley, she looked in her rearview mirror. He stood stock still, staring after her.

Now she did feel like running stop signs. Her mind tumbled and tossed the image of Dean Coletta. Was there any resemblance to Nicholas? Blue eyes. A slight dimple in the chin. Nothing beyond that. No red hair—but hair could be dyed.

Sarah's voice echoed in her mind. "He's not what he appears. He's very convincing in his lies."

Magazine article—here in the middle of nowhere. Jesus, did he really expect anyone to believe that?

Chapter 6

Brian Mitchell stood before the wooden steps that led to the porch of the yellow and white cottage. He held an empty cardboard box in his hands. A sense of inevitability settled in his bones. He'd finally accepted that his marriage was over. All of the dreams he'd had of bringing his children to this lake house, teaching them to fish off the dock, to skip stones on the smooth surface of the water, to swim along the shallow shore, were forever beyond his reach. There would be no children—and soon no lake cottage.

When Kate first moved away and filed for divorce, Brian had thought he might be able to hang onto this place; he wanted it more than anything. He'd much rather live here than in the big echoing house on the edge of town.

But the house in town wasn't selling. Even though he was a Realtor, he hadn't been able to entice a buyer. The old Tudor with its tennis court and swimming pool were something of a white elephant in the local market. The kind of money it took to buy and maintain the place just didn't live in Glens Crossing anymore. The few people who could afford it preferred to build something new and showy.

So the lake house had to go. But winter was not the ideal time to sell lake property. Spring would be a much better climate. He'd been scraping money together month to month to keep Kate satisfied and hold onto the cottage until he could get top dollar. He'd been thrilled when Dean Coletta showed up needing a place to rent. That would help make ends meet for the next month at least.

Brian made a mental note to stop by the Crossing House and thank Benny personally for sending Coletta his way.

Turning slowly, Brian took a long look at the property, the lake, the tiny boat house, the dock. Things appeared in order. Then he climbed the steps and unlocked the front door.

There were personal items he felt he should remove before his tenant moved in. As he stood inside the cold interior of the house, looking at the white painted beadboard walls, sadness gripped him. He hated to part with the place, creaky floors, warped ceilings and all.

He picked up a framed photograph from the end table: He and Kate, dressed in bulky sweaters with autumn leaves scattered at their feet, were huddled together on the front step of the cottage porch. Those had been better days—at least marginally better, he begrudgingly admitted. He and Kate hadn't seen good days in a long, long time. They'd hung on to the pretense of marriage, with both of them living distinctly separate lives for years.

The pretense ended when Brian lost his bid for a congressional seat. He'd embarked on the prospect with high—and he now saw, unrealistic—ideals. Kate had hung onto their marriage with the prospect of a move to Washington and what she imagined to be the glitz of being a politician's wife.

By the time he'd had enough experience with the system to see that once elected his main focus would be on getting *re*-elected, not striving to change the things he thought needed changing, Kate and the campaign had been in full swing. And so many local people had climbed on board to support him that he decided he would do his best to win, then his best to make changes; re-election be damned. But he'd lost—and he'd been relieved.

Then Kate had packed up and left town. And, in a way, that felt like a relief, too. The fact that he felt that way made him ashamed.

He dropped the photograph in the empty box. The dull thud as it hit bottom resonated through his empty heart. He picked up the next photo, this one of his sister Leigh, his only family. He smiled and laid this one gently inside the box.

With all of the recent changes, he was feeling loneliness more acutely than he'd ever imagined.

Which led to the other reason Brian was glad to see Dean Coletta arrive in town. He could tell, even in their short meeting, that he liked the guy. In fact, they planned to meet for dinner tonight. It would be good to have someone new to talk to, especially someone as well-traveled as Coletta.

There could be a side benefit to the magazine article Coletta was working on. With the additional exposure, "the yearning of the urbanite to return to simpler times," as Coletta had put it, property around here might start appreciating. That would be good for Brian, and good for the community as a whole. These days small towns were choked out by the hundreds, water-starved flowers on the landscape of this country. It wouldn't be until all of the flowers had died, replaced by cracked earth and high-tech plastic, that people would see what they had lost. The progression seemed unstoppable, and it broke his heart. He'd lived here all of his life. It would kill him to see Glens Crossing shrivel and die one block at a time.

Brian just hoped the exposure wouldn't lead to *too much* change around here. There were things he liked just as they were. It was a fine line to maintain. He'd have to ask Coletta in more depth what angle he planned on taking with this article.

With his mind focused on the future, he quickly finished going through the cottage, emptying personal items from the tiny bathroom and checking to make sure there wasn't any moldering food in the fridge. By the time he locked the cottage door behind him, he was feeling much more in charge of himself. Safeguarding his town against the wrong kind of publicity was just the kind of thing he could sink his teeth into.

As Molly passed through the last stoplight on her way out of town, her mouth remained dry and tasted nasty, but her heart had begun to settle back into a reasonable rhythm. If the man she'd run over was Nicholas's father, it was too bad she hadn't killed him.

She reined in her racing thoughts. *Logic. Use your logic.* There was nothing that said the man *was* the baby's father. Nothing at all. She had jumped to that conclusion in an irrational heartbeat.

Yeah well, logic said no national magazine would be interested in a town where the most exciting thing that happened was a high school football game.

Then again, if he was the father and had followed her to Glens Crossing, why wouldn't he just have slipped into town and grabbed the baby? Why would he let so many people know he was here? It didn't make any sense. She wasn't that difficult to find in this small town; he wouldn't need to concoct the magazine story at all.

Maybe Coletta had been hired by the baby's father: a private investigator. Which only made marginally more sense than him being the actual father. She couldn't imagine the man who killed Sarah would do anything to draw attention to himself—if he wanted the baby, he'd sneak in and grab it.

She drew a deep breath and let it out. She'd keep an eye out and her ears open. Forewarned was forearmed. If Dean Coletta had anything to do with Nicholas's father, his element of surprise had just evaporated.

Driving into the country, she forced herself to obey speed limits. If Coletta was a threat, he was well behind her at the moment. Nicholas was safe.

She entered Lily's house and heard her singing. Molly followed the sound to the rear of the house.

Lily and Clay had added a cozy sitting area and fireplace to the kitchen when they first moved here. Lily was sitting in an overstuffed floral-print chair with Nicholas dozing in her arms.

Molly paused in the doorway. Looking at the tranquil scene, she could almost believe Nicholas was a regular baby living a normal life; that his very future didn't depend upon the success of her lies and deception.

She said softly, "How'd it go?"

Lily smiled. "He was an angel. I just fed him." Then she looked at Molly with that disapproving sisterly eye. "You must not have done much shopping."

Molly waved the comment away, asking with a raised brow, "You don't remember the first time you left Riley?"

Lily gave her sister a conciliatory look. "All right. Enough said." She got up and put Nicholas on the couch. "I'm just glad you finally got out of that house. You were beginning to worry me."

Molly lifted a shoulder, deciding not to make any more excuses.

When Lily straightened up, she asked, "Lunch?"

"Don't you have pots to toss or something?"

Lily laughed. "*Throw*. You throw a pot." She started pulling stuff out of the refrigerator. "I have to eat before I go back out to the workshop anyway. Besides, you don't want to wake a sleeping baby."

"That's a lesson I've certainly learned." Molly stuck her nose in the fridge. "Do you have any pickles?"

"My God girl, you don't still eat those jumbo dills like they're candy bars, do you?"

"It's a perfectly good snack. Low in fat. No carbs."

Lily added, "Enough sodium to pickle *you*."

Molly shrugged. "Hey, a woman has to have at least one vice."

As they worked side by side making sandwiches, Molly thought of all of the dinners that Lily had made when they were children.

Their family had moved over the Crossing House

when their mother left. Molly had been so young, she didn't remember living anywhere else. Their dad had to work evenings in the bar, so Lily made dinner—or at least served what their father had prepared ahead. She, Luke, and Molly ate alone. But Molly never felt lacking. Lily and Luke provided her with a strong sense of security, of family. And Dad had just been downstairs. The fact was, Molly had been in first grade, eating dinner at a friend's house, before she even noticed that their family was different from others.

But Lily had always known. She'd felt the sting of desertion, the shame of small-town gossip. Therefore, Lily had always been a little touchy when it came to conversations about their mother; had always been quick to react when people outside the family mentioned her. Molly had never felt that way. Maybe it was because she didn't possess more than a few incomplete scraps of memory about the woman.

Molly stopped what she was doing and wrapped an arm around her sister, leaning her head until it touched Lily's.

Lily's hands stilled over the sandwiches. "What's that for?"

"I love you."

Lily chuckled. "You used to say that when you were about to ask for cookies before dinner."

Inadvertently, Molly had opened the door to something she'd been trying to put off. She said, "Well, I didn't intend it to be a softening tool—but actually, I do need a favor."

Lily set the plates with sandwiches on the table. "What?"

As they sat down, Molly said, "I got a job at the hospital."

"That's great! Now maybe you'll start living like a normal person."

Her sister echoing her own thoughts of this morning took her off guard. Would she ever feel normal again? From her overreaction at finding out the man she'd run down wasn't a born and bred Hoosier, signs pointed to no.

"It is great. Part time, but enough hours to provide benefits." Molly paused. "But it brings up another problem—I need someone to watch Nicholas."

Lily pressed her lips together. "So since you preceded this with 'I love you,' I suppose you want that someone to be me?"

Molly fiddled with the crust on her bread. "Could you? I don't know anyone else. He's so young, I can't leave him with just anyone."

Lily sighed. "Gosh, Mol. I could help out sometimes, as a backup maybe. But I really can't commit to all of the time. I've gotten orders and contracts for my pottery. Things are just getting off the ground; it takes a lot of time."

Molly sat in silence for a moment. Lily was home every day, her only child was in high school, driving himself wherever he needed to go; it had never occurred to Molly that she wouldn't say yes.

"It's only four days at a time with five days in between. Maybe you could do it for the first few months, until he's a little bigger." Even as she said it, she felt guilty. Although only four years older, Lily had acted as Molly's mother as they had grown up; she'd already given more than anyone should have to. But Molly squashed that guilt. There were circumstances here that were far beyond the ordinary.

Lily shook her head slowly. "I wish I could. But," she hesitated, "right after Clay and I got married, we made the decision *not* to have a baby. There were lots of reasons, but one of the big ones was because I was beginning to have some success with my pottery. He made the sacrifice for me. I can hardly stop working to take care of *your* baby."

Molly sat for a second, then said, "But it'd just be for awhile. I have to go back to work—money's getting tight."

"I'll help you find someone." Lily leaned across the table and took Molly's hand.

Molly said, "I'll pay you." She had to have Nicholas someplace she could feel safe leaving him. And this seemed the only option, at least until he was older—and the threat of his father appearing diminished even further.

Lily shook her head. "I just can't." After a second she said, "I understand your reservations about a stranger, but sooner or later you have to take that step. I have friends who might recommend somebody." She looked Molly in the eye. "If money's tight, why not look to the father? He should be made to be financially responsible. You owe it to Nicholas."

Molly pulled her hand away and didn't say anything. A cold ball of dread formed in her stomach.

Lily pressed on, "I assume the father isn't destitute."

"I've already told you, the father isn't in the picture. He doesn't know, and he's not going to know."

"Be realistic, Molly! There's no reason for you to

shoulder the financial responsibility alone. Even if you don't want him to have contact with the baby, you can surely work out something for support." A look of dawning understanding crossed Lily's face. "Do you think he would try for custody?"

"Probably." *Custody or kidnapping, what difference did it make? The end result would be the same.*

"Is he married?" There was a brittle tone to Lily's voice that Molly hadn't heard from her sister since they were children and someone brought up their mother.

Molly wanted to shout, *Afraid I'm following in* her *footsteps?* But she needed Lily's help, not her animosity. So she took a deep breath and said, "I really don't know."

Lily's eyes widened.

"Let's get this out there once and for all," Molly said, matching her sister's angry tone. "I don't know anything about him. He might be married. He might be destitute. He might be a goddamn millionaire. I didn't plan this. I didn't check his credentials. I don't even know where he lives. And I *don't* ever want to see him again."

"Oh my God." There was true horror in Lily's voice. It was as if all of her fears had materialized right before her eyes.

"Don't look at me like that! I'm not married and I have this baby. What difference does it make who fathered him? If he *was* a millionaire, would that have made it more acceptable to you?"

There was a sharp bitterness in Lily's eyes that Molly couldn't recall ever seeing. "Love." She paused and shook her head. "If you'd loved him it would have made a difference. This . . . this just sounds—"

"Like Mom?" Molly finished for her. "Is that what

you're so worked up over?" She stood. "For God's sake, Lily, I'm an adult, not a child that you can frown upon because I'm not performing up to snuff. You and Dad, you're just alike; everything's all right as long as Molly doesn't disappoint!

"For your information, it wasn't like Mom at all. No one got hurt—I didn't leave a husband and three kids behind." Molly left her lunch untouched and walked over to gather up Nicholas.

Lily said, "Mol—"

The shrill ring of the telephone cut off her words. She reached for it and snatched it up.

"Hello." The sharpness lingered in her tone, telling Molly that Lily was as angry as she was. Then she lowered her voice. "Hi, Dad."

Molly kept moving, pretending not to be in the least interested.

Lily said, "Yes, I've seen her . . . She's fine . . . Well, she's right here. Why don't you ask her yourself?"

Molly was ready to refuse to talk to him—only because she was so angry right now. But, if Dad was ready to talk, maybe she should take the opportunity.

Her decision became unnecessary when Lily said, "All right. Bye."

So that's the way he wants to play it. Punish me with silence. By the time Lily had disconnected, Molly had Nicholas and was heading toward the door.

"Molly, please. Dad called because he's worried about you."

"If he's so damn worried, maybe he should call *me*!"

Things were not working out as she'd imagined. She came here because she needed help, needed her family.

First her dad had pulled the rug out from under her; she'd never known him to be so narrow-minded and judgmental. And Lily had some stick up her butt that Molly felt responsible for putting there, but apparently had no power to remove. She would have been as well off had she gone someplace where she didn't know anyone.

Lily said in a half-exasperated plea, half-big sister order, "Come back and eat lunch."

"I'm not hungry." She realized she sounded like a pouting child, but that's just the way this family was treating her—like a child. "Thanks for watching the baby." She pulled the door closed behind her.

Chapter 7

Looking through her cabinets, Molly regretted her hasty decisions of the day. If she'd taken Lily's advice and gone shopping, she would have food in the fridge. If she'd eaten lunch before she left Lily's, she wouldn't be starving at four-thirty in the afternoon. And, if she hadn't stormed out like an angry child, she could call Lily and see if she was going to the store.

But as things stood, until Nicholas woke up from his nap, she was hungry and stranded in a house with two saltines and a peanut butter jar scraped so clean there wasn't enough to cover even one of those crackers.

On the counter lay a coupon that had been stuck in her door earlier this week. *Papa's Pizza 212 N. Ralston Avenue Free delivery 555-8890.* It was four blocks from her house—but delivery removed any obstacle of distance or naptime. She picked up the phone and dialed.

"Papa's. What's your pleasure?" It was a flat teenage voice that sounded like it truly pained him to spit out the restaurant's greeting.

"I'd like a small, thin crust with everything except onions—" she paused, "—what the heck, make it everything." There wasn't anyone she'd offend with her onion breath. Nicholas might mind, but he was too young to make a big deal out of it.

"Delivery or pick up?" There was a loud clatter in the background, followed by a "dammit!" The boy on the phone chortled under his adolescent breath.

"Delivery." She gave him her phone number and address.

"Small, thin crust, everything. Delivered. That'll be ninety minutes."

"Ninety minutes! You've got to be kidding."

"No, ma'am."

"Is that your regular delivery time?"

"No."

She waited for him to explain.

He didn't.

"What's taking so long? It's only five o'clock."

"Friday night football game. Everybody gets pizza."

Molly heard Nicholas begin to cry in the other room.

"Forget the delivery," she said. "I'll pick it up."

"Thirty minutes." The phone went dead.

"Thank you for your order," she said mockingly to the phone. "Please call Papa's again soon." She had always attributed rudeness in Boston teenagers to living in the city, where anonymity hid them from recrimination . . . *where nobody knows your name*. She had to chuckle at her own play on the "Cheers" theme. However, rudeness was apparently a worldwide epidemic.

She changed and fed Nicholas. As she was putting him in his pumpkin seat, she had second thoughts. If the pizza place was that busy, she probably wouldn't be able to park very close. It'd be easier to walk the four blocks.

Wrestling the folded stroller Lily had bought as a gift for Nicholas out of the front closet, Molly gave it a wary eye. It looked complicated. There were levers and pouches and clips and buttons and a cup holder. Surely in there somewhere was a place to put a baby. After she tried a couple of different buttons, the stroller finally sprang into a functional form. When she laid Nicholas inside it, he was dwarfed by the sheer bulk of the thing.

Wrapping them both against the chill and locking the door behind her, Molly set out with a rumbling stomach to retrieve her pizza. Step two in beginning a normal life—a public appearance at a busy pizza parlor. She was on a roll now, baby.

As she walked, she sifted through her feelings. It surprised her that she was actually looking forward to seeing people for the first time in a month. The familiarity of her surroundings had stirred her curiosity about those she used to know. Some of these folks were practically institutions in Glens Crossing. Did old Mr. Grissom still think aliens were messing with his cows? Had anyone ever figured out that Mrs. White was sneaking cigars behind her barn? (Molly had seen it first hand while riding her bike past the Whites' farm when she was thirteen; ruining forever the southern belle image that Alma Lynn White liked to foster. But her secret was safe with Molly; to expose the woman seemed just too mean.)

Molly walked past Brian Mitchell's real estate office and felt a flash of guilt. When she'd been looking to rent a house, she had consciously avoided Brian. It was easier to work with someone she didn't know. Even though a stranger still asked all of the same questions, Molly felt less deceitful answering them. She'd known Brian all of her life—everybody knew Brian.

Another of her Glens Crossing questions surfaced in her mind; she wondered if he was still the most handsome man in town. Since he was several years older than she, he'd always seemed like a legend . . . handsome, athletic, so unbelievably cool that, when she was growing up, she'd always found herself tongue-tied when he was around. She, like every other girl in town, had had a major crush on him.

A flash of a new face entered her mind. If Dean Coletta hung around, Brian's place as "most handsome" was sure to be challenged. But Coletta wasn't hanging around. He was just here *snooping,* for one reason or another.

That thought brought back the question: Did he pose a danger to Nicholas? Reason told her no. He was making himself too well known to have kidnapping in mind. Panic had released its icy grasp. She knew Coletta was here; even if he had some secret link to Nicholas's father, there would be no sneak attack.

Even with a thousand unanswered questions on her mind, strolling along peaceful streets and enjoying the fresh stillness of early autumn dusk, it was easier than she'd imagined to push aside wayward fears, to pretend she was that normal person she was trying so hard to portray.

As she approached the pizza place, her decision to walk proved to be the right one; there wasn't a parking place for a block and a half in any direction. When she opened the door, she realized there wasn't any way that she was going to maneuver the bulky stroller through the crush of people. She backed out and picked Nicholas up to carry him in. She only gave the briefest thought to thievery as she left the stroller on the sidewalk. In this town, nobody would steal from a baby.

After squeezing through the crowd that was waiting to be seated, Molly stopped at the end of the long line at the pick-up window. It quickly became clear that Nicholas, dressed as he was for the brisk outdoors, was going to overheat long before they got their pizza. As she took off his hat and attempted to unwind a layer of blanket, her purse fell off her shoulder and knocked the hat out of her hand. She shifted Nicholas a bit so she could stoop and pick up the hat without dropping her purse, but a man appeared next to her and beat her to it.

"Here." He held the tiny knit cap out to her. "Looks like you've got your hands full."

When Molly looked into his face, the warmth of familiarity spread over her. "Brian Mitchell. How are you?"

He tilted his head slightly, then recognition shone in his eyes and he smiled. "Little Molly Boudreau? I heard you were back in town."

Nicholas started to fuss. She gave him a little jiggle. "Oh, I bet you did."

His gaze cut to the baby. "We're all not so provincial around here. Why, a couple of us actually subscribe to the *New Yorker* and *Rolling Stone*." He leaned closer, smiling as he looked closely at the baby's face. "What's his name?"

She was grateful for his straightforwardness. "Nicholas."

A waitress bumped against Brian's back as she

squeezed through with a tray of drinks, making Molly aware that they were blocking the way. She took a small step closer to the person ahead of her in line and asked, "Would you mind holding my purse for just a second so I can get him unwrapped? He's going to roast before we can pick up the pizza."

"I've got a better idea. I have a table. Why don't you join us? We can tell the waitress to bring your pizza to our table and you can eat with us."

She glanced back at the line. It wasn't moving very quickly.

"Come on," he urged, turning his golden boy smile on her once again.

She fumbled for an excuse. "The baby—"

"They've got one of those sling baby seats. I'll go get it." He was already walking away. He called over his shoulder. "Our table's back here."

It was easy to see why he was so successful in his real estate business. With very little obvious effort, he'd made her feel welcome and had effectively taken away her ability to argue—all with such charm and ease that she didn't feel like she'd been railroaded.

It might actually be nice to share a meal with someone. She didn't know Brian's wife, Kate, very well. But if the woman had such good taste in men, she couldn't be all bad. The guy even knew about baby seats. "All right, Nicholas, your first dinner out is about to begin."

She followed Brian toward the back of the dining room. As she did, she studied the place, mostly so she didn't have to study the people and notice if they were staring at her or not. Papa, whose real name was Harold Jorgensen and who was Swedish to the roots of his blond hair, had remodeled the place. The old plaster had been scraped from the walls, exposing the rough, red brick. Wall sconces kept the lighting from being harsh and the stamped-tin ceiling had been painted dark brown, she supposed to reduce the feeling that it was so high. Unlike some of the changes that had happened in Glens Crossing during her absence, she approved of Papa's updating.

When she caught up with Brian, he was sliding the baby chair up to a table with a man sitting with his back to her. Guess dinner wasn't with Kate after all.

Before she could even wonder if she knew their dining partner, he stood and pulled a chair out for her.

Her stomach fell to her feet. Apparently she should have clarified who "us" was. But she could hardly bolt and run at this point.

Clay sat at the kitchen table as Lily made a salad for dinner. He'd been listening patiently to her without saying much for the past fifteen minutes.

After Molly had left, Lily's mood had grown more sour by the hour. She'd been tempted to follow Molly home and get everything out in the open. But she knew Molly had a stubborn streak even wider than their father's. Nothing good was going to come out of talking to her anymore today.

Which didn't set at all well with Lily. She hated turmoil; she always felt responsible for getting things ironed out—especially when the turmoil had to do with family. Boiling conflict sat like an undigested meal in her stomach. The need for resolution gnawed at her relentlessly until it became a reality. Too bad conflict never seemed to eat at her sister the same way. Molly seemed to be able to close that area of her mind, until the time came when she was ready to settle the problem.

She took the chef's knife and hacked a carrot into pieces. Out of the corner of her eye, she saw Clay flinch.

"Careful. You're going to lose a finger."

She shot him a nasty look—mostly because he was right.

Riley came clomping in the back door.

"Stop right there and take those muddy sneakers off!"

He tossed a plastic bag onto the counter. "Here's your butter." Then he toed off his shoes.

Lily heard the dried mud crumble and fall on the floor. "Get a damp paper towel and wipe that up."

"I was *going to*—but I had to get my shoes off first! Sheesh."

"Do not 'sheesh' me. And tell me why it took you forty minutes to go get a pound of butter?"

Riley rolled his eyes at Clay. Her husband had enough of a sense of self-preservation to look away and pretend he didn't see it.

"I saw Codi at the store. I talked to her for a minute."

"A minute?"

Now Riley's glance at Clay had a trapped rabbit quality to it. "Yeah, I didn't know I wasn't allowed to talk to anyone while I was on my *mission*. What's the big deal, anyway? Dinner's not ready yet."

"It's not ready because I needed the butter to mash the potatoes."

Clay stood. "I'll mash them. Riley, get that mud up, then go wash your hands."

Riley got the paper towel and ran it under the faucet. He mumbled, "Just 'cause she's pissed at Aunt Molly—"

"*Excuse* me, mister!"

"Watch the language around your mother." Clay turned his back so Lily couldn't see his face, but she heard his whisper. "Get out while you still have your legs. I'll hold her off as long as I can."

Riley snickered; luckily for him he had the grace to do it quietly as he hurried out of the room.

As soon as he was gone, Lily felt Clay's hands on her shoulders. He turned her to face him and pulled her against his chest. She didn't know whether to laugh or cry. She ended up doing a little of both.

He waited, rubbing her back softly. When she sniffled and looked up at him, he cupped her face. "Molly's a grown woman. She's made her choices, now you're going to have to let her live with them."

She blew out a breath that carried away a little of the tension in her body. "I know, but—"

He put a finger on her lips. "There are no buts. This is Molly's life."

She started on her "how could she throw it all away" tirade, when she realized there was something deeper bothering her. "There are things that are just . . . odd. Do you know she doesn't have a hospital first photo of Nicholas?"

"And that's clearly a sign of . . . ?"

"I know I sound nuts. But it's not just that. She's a pediatrician—and she's bottle-feeding her baby. Is there something wrong with her? Is she one of those women who can't bond?"

Clay said, "That doesn't make sense; you said she was a basket case about leaving him."

"And she's cut the father completely out. He doesn't even know about the baby."

Clay's pointed look cut her straight to her heart.

"This is different," she said quickly.

"Is it?"

He held her with that sharp gaze and it was hard for her to breathe. But she stood and faced it, because deep down, she thought she deserved it.

"I'm worried about her," Lily said. "Coming back to this town is going to be hard on Nicholas in the long run."

"He has family here. What can be bad about that? I think she made a smart choice there."

"Come on, Clay, you know how this town is."

"Sure people are going to talk for a while. Then things will calm down. By the time he's old enough to know, it'll all be forgotten."

Her lips pressed together for a moment. "*Someone* always remembers—after you think it's over, someone always brings it up."

He kissed her forehead. "We're talking about a baby, an innocent baby. In this day and age single mothers are as common as ants at a picnic. It's going to be good that she came here."

"I hope you're right."

"No matter what, keep in mind, this is Molly's business. It's her choice."

"I just don't want those choices to hurt Nicholas."

He stared deep into her eyes and her heart squeezed in her chest. "What child doesn't get hurt by his parent's choices at one time or another? You can't fix everything for everyone."

True enough. In fact, she had her hands full fixing problems of her own making at the moment.

Brian cheerfully introduced them. "Molly, this is Dean Coletta." He took the baby's hand between his index finger and thumb. "And her son, Nicholas." Brian shifted his gaze to Dean. "Dean, Molly Boudreau." Then he turned back to Molly. "Dean's here working on a magazine story."

Dean grinned, keeping his gaze on Molly as he said, "Actually, Molly and I ran into each other this morning."

Molly gave a *harrumph*. Her distress over seeing Dean spun on a dime. She was going to use this meeting to her advantage. They were in a crowded room, sitting with an upstanding and respected citizen. She could probe and prod under the guise of interested conversation. Dean Coletta was now under *her* microscope.

She put on a convivial face. "Oh, come on now, tell the guy the truth. He'll hear it eventually anyway. No secrets in a small town." As soon as the words were out of her mouth she thought, she'd better hope *some* secrets remained buried.

Dean pressed his lips together and shook his head. "No ma'am. I won't tell." He looked at her with laughing sincerity in his eyes. "Have to maintain my integrity. As a journalist, people have to trust me not to blab confidential information."

With that, he put out his hands, offering to take the baby while she took off her coat. She ignored him and settled Nicholas in the baby seat herself. She didn't like handing the baby over to *anyone*. She was working on getting over it, one baby step at a time. Baby steps did *not* include putting Nicholas in the arms of a stranger whose purpose for being in town she had yet to determine.

As she took off her coat and hung it on the back of her chair, she said, "I'd hardly call what happened in broad daylight with multiple witnesses confidential."

When Brian raised a brow, looking intrigued, she said, "I ran over him in the alley beside Hildie's Day Spa."

Brian choked on his laughter. "You're kidding."

Molly shook her head.

"Like, ran over him with your car?"

"Yep, just like that."

Brian's gaze cut to Dean. "Well, you don't look any worse for the wear."

"Almost lost the key to the cottage, though," Dean's teasing gaze cut to Molly. "Knocked it right out of my hand."

"You're lucky you weren't knocked out of your shoes!" Brian chuckled.

Molly tried to stay in the conversation as she studied the man beside her. "So, any new aches and pains?" she prompted. It was difficult to gaze into his honest-looking face and have thoughts of treachery cross her mind. *That's probably how Sarah ended up in the mess she was—trusting someone who looked honest and forthright.*

Dean looked steadily back at her, a hint of calculation in his eye, as if he were sizing her up the same as she was him. "You asking as a doctor?"

She shook her head. "No. As an apologetic assailant with a motor vehicle. Or am I considered a vehicular batterer?" Looking to Brian, wanting to keep him in the conversation, she asked, "What do you think my crime would be?"

Before Brian could say anything, Dean threw up his hands. "Hey! I'm not making charges. I already told you, this signals a real change in my luck." Then he said to Brian, "For the better."

Brian looked skeptical. "Getting run down in an alley is an *improvement* for you?"

Dean looked thoughtful and took a sip of his beer. "Actually, it is." Then his gaze shifted back to Molly. "But the part that I considered lucky was *who* ran me down."

If she weren't looking at him with such a suspicious eye, she might have passed it off as flirtation. But she sensed a darker undercurrent—or maybe her imagination was galloping off with her good sense again. She didn't want to react irrationally as she had in the alley; she held his gaze, probing without speaking. For the first time, she noticed that his eyes were a blue-green that reminded her of an unsettled South Pacific sea she'd seen on the Discovery Channel. Her breath tightened in her chest with the intensity of what she saw there. Curiosity. Kindness. Humor.

If she truly were that normal person she pretended to be, she might be swept away by such soulful eyes. In another place, another time, she might want to explore the depths of that kindness and humor—for reasons other than self-preservation.

Dean finally released her from his gaze and turned to Brian. "She's a doctor, you know." His light tone signaled his awareness that Brian was well aware of Molly's profession.

"That I do know." Brian lifted his beer in salute to Molly. "We're glad to have her back."

Dean raised a brow. "Back? From where?"

Before Molly could gather herself and respond with a properly evasive answer, Brian said, "Boston. Left big city medicine to return here, where the heart is. Right, Molly?"

When Dean focused his questioning gaze back upon her, Molly said, "Yes. I decided I didn't want to raise my son in a city. I wanted him to be close to his family." She lifted a shoulder in what she hoped appeared to be non-chalance. "So here we are."

Dean looked from her to the baby and back again. "I guess children make everything different."

"You have no idea," Molly said reflectively before she could censor herself.

Luckily, the sentiment must have seemed normal to the men. Neither one reacted. Brian smiled fondly at the baby. Dean took another drink of beer.

"How old is he?" Dean asked.

"Seven weeks." The lie was quickly becoming the truth.

"Bet his dad's proud." Although it was a statement, there was something questioning in Dean's voice.

Molly straightened. "His father and I aren't together."

"All the more reason to be near family and friends," Brian offered, cheerfully. "You did the right thing in coming home. Kids need family." He fiddled with a straw that was on the table. He stared at that straw when he said, "I always thought this would be a great place to raise kids— I suppose you know I'm divorced. . . ."

Molly heard the sadness in his voice. Certain things began to fall into place: his awareness of her struggle while standing in line; his knowledge of baby seats; the fond way he looked at Nicholas. He obviously wanted children—made a habit of watching them.

There was a short lull in conversation.

Then Dean started to open his mouth.

Before he could hone in on her again, Molly said, "Mr. Coletta, what kind of story are you looking for here in our quiet little town?"

"I'm doing an in-depth piece on small town America. I want to take a look at it from the *inside*. In order to do that, I need to spend several weeks living in a few towns."

"So," Molly said, "earlier today, you said you're from New York City. Did you grow up there?"

"Yeah. My parents were professors at Columbia. They're both gone now."

He went on, "I guess *technically* I still live there. That's where I pay my taxes. I have an apartment—well, it's just a rented room in a big old house. Although up until about four weeks ago, I hadn't been there for more than a day or so at a time. For the past five years, I've been spending almost all of my time overseas."

Brian set his forearms on the table and leaned forward, as if sharing confidential information. "Dean writes for *The Report*. He covers the Middle East. Great in-depth articles that center on the human story. Always fascinating." He looked at Dean. "Before you joined us, he was just about to tell me why the abrupt change in topics."

Molly was very interested in that question herself. She leaned an elbow on the table and settled her chin on her palm, trying to look offhandedly interested. "Yes, why would you leave your area of expertise to write about—" she motioned around the tiny pizza parlor "—this?"

Dean scrubbed a hand over his hair, leaning back in his

chair. "Believe me, it wasn't by choice." He stopped himself and looked apologetic. "No offense intended. I'm sure this is a nice place."

Brian gave a wave of dismissal.

Dean finished, "It was my editor's decision. He thinks I need a dose of 'civilization.' "

Molly laughed before she realized it was coming. "And this is more *civilized* than New York City?"

Dean lifted a shoulder. "More than the northern reaches of Afghanistan."

Molly decided to press; she wasn't going to get a better opportunity than this. "Why? When you're obviously most qualified in an area that few are? Why waste your talents? Anybody can write about *Smallville*."

He looked in her eyes, presenting himself so she could easily detect a lie. "I'm being punished. I disobeyed the rules, and got myself shot."

Brian slapped the table with his palm. "Damn, man. I guess getting run over by a doctor would be a step in the right direction, then."

The pizzas arrived. Molly regretted the onions now that she was in mixed company. She ordered a diet Coke from the waitress, who paused to make a fuss over Nicholas before she left the table. Brian filled her in on his name and age, as he toyed with the baby's tiny fingers.

Dean lifted his chin toward the baby. "Tell me more about why you chose to raise your son here, instead of in a great cultural center like Boston or New York. I would think the medical career opportunities alone would be enough to keep you out east."

Molly's appetite took a nosedive just as she was about to bite into her first slice of pizza. "Once Nicholas came, other things took precedence over my career." She didn't offer more. "So you're here for punishment. What rule did you disobey?"

"I was supposed to evacuate. I stayed. Then I got shot and they carried me out. All very upsetting for the powers that be."

"Will you go back?" she asked.

"As soon as they give me back my passport."

"Why?"

"Those people, they're shoved from village to town with whatever they can carry on their backs. They're starved; dying of illnesses easily prevented. If nobody tells their story, they'll be lost . . . ignored even worse than they are now. The higher we can keep the human profile, the more likely the fighting factions will be pressured to make peace. At the very least, it helps draw humanitarian aid. And, of course, there's the political story. It's important for people to know *why* things are happening. Like it or not, we live in a global community. Nothing that happens there is irrelevant—even here, to this little town."

Brian nodded thoughtfully.

Molly wondered how she could have, even in her overreactive state, thought this man could have been the "evil" person Sarah said fathered her child.

After taking a bite of pizza, Dean turned the tables on her again. "Will you go back to the city?"

"No," she said emphatically. *Never. I'll never take him back there where his father would have a better chance of finding him.*

"Even after Nicholas is older, and there will be more and better opportunities for him? He'll have so much more open to him in the city." He said it as if it was universal knowledge that all children benefited from life in a major city.

"Opportunity lies everywhere," she said. "He'll be prepared to go wherever he chooses when the time comes."

A pride she hadn't realized lived in her had been pricked. She went on, "Your condescending tone tells me you don't have any idea what it's like to live in a small town. Believe it or not, it's not like living in a third world country! We aren't isolated and ignorant. We aren't bumpkins.

"It's obvious you're going to need more than a few weeks to 'get a feel' for life here." She couldn't keep the pique out of her voice.

Dean held his hands in surrender. "Settle down, there, doctor. I'm just asking questions."

"For your article."

"Yes, for my article."

She took a deep breath. "There are a lot of advantages to raising a child in a small town."

"Such as?"

Their rapid-fire questions had excluded Brian. But now he spoke up, "Like a strong sense of community. Like living in an environment where everyone is accountable, because there's no hiding in the crowd. Like having your children walk the same school halls you did. Like the awareness you have of others in need who won't ask for help—and the way people find a way to provide that help without crushing a person's pride."

"Yeah," Molly nodded. "Like all that." She was secretly glad Brian had bailed her out. She did agree with all of those reasons, but would have been hard-pressed to put them into words herself. She hadn't thought of her return in those terms—until now.

"I see." Then Dean focused on Molly again. "You should have a very unique perspective of this town. Growing up here, moving to the big city, returning to raise a child. I wonder if after you're here a while, your opinion will change?" He paused as if rolling the idea over in his mind. "A *very* interesting perspective, indeed."

He nailed her with that probing gaze again. "I'd like to talk to you again, keep an ongoing dialogue. A progressive story, so to speak."

An ongoing dialogue. That was an interesting way to put it.

"I don't want to be a part of this story. I don't want my son mentioned in a magazine."

Dean said, "It can be done with a pseudonym. No one will know it's you."

Molly barked out a laugh. "In this town, I think my story will stand out."

Dean persisted. "All right. You won't be in the story per se. But I'd still like to talk to you about your perspective to gain insight."

Molly sighed. She didn't want to appear disproportionately belligerent. "I'm sure you'll find lots of interesting stories—varied perspectives—without mine." She lifted her palm and gestured across the table. "Like Brian. He played quarterback for Michigan, came back home, started a successful business, *and* he ran for congress." She leaned back in her seat, as if that should get the ball rolling—and in a direction away from her.

Brian added, without any trace of disappointment or bitterness, "And lost."

Molly was quick to keep things moving. "But that doesn't diminish the *experience*. He's been dedicated to making Glens Crossing a place a person *wants* to raise their kids in. *He's* your story. The Boy's and Girl's Club—" she paused "—I saw in the paper the other day that you've led the board to breaking ground on a new facility."

Dean nodded his interest, but still focused on Molly. "I want *everyone's* story. That's why I'm staying for a while. Brian's perspective." Dean pointed toward the kitchen. "Papa's perspective . . . I'm assuming there is a Papa." He didn't wait for confirmation. "The high school principal's perspective. The garbage collector's perspective. Everyone has a unique view of their slice of the world. Molly, yours is particularly interesting because of the contrast you offer and the choice you've made."

Molly nodded; there didn't seem to be any sense in arguing further at this point. She said to Brian, "We should be sure he interviews Ed Grissom." She grinned and explained to Dean, "He's a real character." Returning her gaze to Brian, she asked, "Is he still calling the Air Force and the FBI about aliens?"

Brian smiled sadly and said, "Ed died four months ago."

"Oh." Molly felt tactless in the extreme. "I didn't know."

"Yep. Massive stroke. Left Hattie totally unprepared and out there on that farm all alone. She can't make a living just selling eggs. I've been trying to get her to sell the farm and move into town. Poor woman never drew a breath without Ed telling her to. I'm not sure she even knows how to write a check. A couple of women from her church are checking on her, helping make sure the electricity's paid and such."

Molly had to strain to remember Hattie Grissom. She finally recalled a small, mousy woman, who wore ill-fitting old lady clothes and kept her eyes fixed on the ground. And Molly could never remember seeing her without her husband. She moved along like a thin shadow behind him. With his wild accusations and alien conspiracy theories, he was the one everyone noticed. It was as if his presence had eclipsed his wife completely.

"I'm sure she's absolutely lost," Molly said. "They didn't have children, did they?"

"None that lived."

For a few moments they ate quietly. Then, before the silence grew uncomfortable and Dean decided to make her the topic of conversation again, Molly said, "So Dean, you've been living in the Middle East for five years?"

He nodded and wiped his mouth with a napkin.

She asked, "Where, exactly?"

"Wherever there's trouble. Which, when you talk about the Middle East means pretty much all over. I use Saudi Arabia as my home base most of the time. But I don't actually have a permanent address. I follow the unrest, live in hotels, tents . . . whatever's available."

"A nomad," Brian offered. Then he laughed. *"That's* why Glens Crossing is so much more 'civilized.'"

"Exactly," Dean agreed.

"So, you don't have a wife and children, then?" As soon as Molly said it, she realized it sounded like she was fishing for a date. "I mean . . ."

Dean lifted a hand to signal she was off the hook. "I know what you mean; I'm the professional question asker, remember? And no. No wife. No kids. No girlfriend. Just me and my passport."

"How long before your boss decides you've been punished enough and you get to go back and do some *real* reporting?" Brian asked.

Dean leaned back in his chair and laid his napkin on the table. "As it's turning out, I'm not all that anxious to leave. This town is proving to hold some very interesting avenues."

Molly knew he wasn't referring to the streets—and didn't really want to be one of those avenues. She couldn't afford the complication. She took one last drink of her Coke, then put her money on the table for her pizza. "I need to be getting home. We walked and I hate to have Nicholas out in the air after it gets too cold." The baby had fallen asleep in the seat. She put on his hat and picked up the blanket. "Thanks to you gentlemen for sharing the table."

Dean stood and helped her with her coat. His hands lingered on her shoulders for a moment while she picked up Nicholas's blanket. She hadn't had a date in a long while, but her senses weren't deadened entirely. She knew he'd misinterpreted her questioning about a wife.

Oh well, that aside, the conversation had provided what she wanted. Dean Coletta was definitely not Nicholas's father; he'd been living in the Middle East for years. Nor did she think he had anything to do with his father; Dean had barely looked at the baby all through dinner.

But he had shown interest in *her.* Perhaps it was just the story. Still, when he looked at her, it felt like more. And a tiny place deep inside wanted it to be more. It had been a long, long time since anyone had looked at her like that. And parts of her were responding without her permission.

My God. She had to keep in mind, in the eyes of everyone around her, she'd just had another man's baby. How would it look if she responded to that interest?

She needed to get out of here, away from this crowded space, into the fresh air.

She faltered slightly.

Dean put a steadying hand on her arm. "Maybe I should walk you home."

Molly said, "I'm fine. It's just so warm in here. You two go on and share your manly stories. I don't have far to go."

Concern remained on Dean's face. "You're sure? Brian and I can talk later."

She grinned. "Absolutely. Remember I've lived alone in Boston for ten years. I can take care of myself on the mean streets of Glens Crossing."

The men laughed.

She waved and walked out of the restaurant, wishing she could shake the feeling of vulnerability that Dean's touch had just created; a vulnerability that had nothing at all to do with Nicholas.

Chapter 8

Dean sat on the sofa in the dark living room of the rented cottage on Forrester Lake. In his hand he held a five-year-old photograph of his sister. But it was only out of habit; he wasn't looking at it. He didn't need to. Its image had been burned into his heart. Instead, his gaze was fixed beyond the big window, on the moon's long, narrow reflection on the lake.

The iridescent silver of moonlight on water drew to mind Molly Boudreau's eyes—the color of morning mist, of childhood dreams, of innocence. She appeared to be just the kind of person Julie would become friends with—kind smile, bright sense of humor, independent, intelligent.

Before he met Molly Boudreau, he'd imagined her to be manipulative and calculating. He had been sure she was the link that would lead to Julie's killer. However, everything about Dr. Boudreau had taken him by surprise—knocked his perceptions askew, thrown roadblocks in the path of his well-laid plans.

Wouldn't that just play along with the manipulative mindset? She's showing me exactly what she wants me to see.

She was good. If he hadn't come here armed with the notion that she was linked to his sister's demise in some objectionable way, he would have been completely taken in. As it was, he was having to fight his own attraction to her.

He reminded himself he was attracted to an illusion. This was all part of the charisma she used to draw in the unsuspecting. He feared Julie had been the victim of a very calculated friendship.

Dean had developed a theory before he left Boston. It started when he tracked down Carmen, the girl who'd worked at the now-closed clinic where Julie had delivered her baby. Carmen hadn't had much to add to the vague and unfruitful story the police had already pieced together, except that Julie had developed a friendship with Dr. Boudreau.

When Dean tried to find Dr. Boudreau, he'd discovered the doctor had left town abruptly the same day Julie's body had been found. Far too much of a coincidence. When he'd brought that fact up to the police, they said they'd already spoken with the doctor and were satisfied she had nothing to do with the murder.

Then Dean tried to press the police about the whereabouts of the baby that the autopsy confirmed Julie had recently delivered. They still saw no connection to the doctor. They had concluded the child was either dead or untraceable. Until they solved the murder, they had no place to begin to solve the mystery of the missing baby. They knew the baby had been in the hospital emergency room with Julie. But after that, there was no trace. Repeatedly, they assured him they were doing all that was humanly possible.

All the while, weeks were slipping by, making the prospect of solving this case less and less likely. So Dean had dug deeper himself, questioned and followed every scrap of information until it died out without yielding a single thread that would tie this whole mystery together.

Dr. Boudreau appeared to be his last hope for discovering what had happened to his sister.

He'd taken Smitty's advice and accepted a leave from his job. As for the rest of his boss's suggestion, that he take a long and recuperative vacation, that was bullshit. How was he supposed to lie on a beach while Julie's killer walked around undiscovered and unpunished? Instead, he'd packed his bags and headed for Glens Crossing.

He went about it as carefully as if he were investigating a terrorist cell. If the good doctor was hiding something from the police, he doubted she'd spill her guts to the victim's brother. That, compounded with the level of cooperation he could expect in a small town like this, led him to fabricate the cover story. Contrary to Molly's accusation, he knew very well how small towns worked. They were the same all over the world. If a stranger came in asking questions about one of their own, the people of this town would shut him out. It would have nothing to do with guilt or innocence. It was loyalty, pure and simple.

This was going to take time. But he had plenty of that.

His quest was twofold. First and foremost was to discover who had killed his sister and why. Secondly, he needed to find out if there was a child, a niece or nephew, somewhere out there who needed him. This second aspect sparked a stormy mix of emotions. He knew his responsibilities to such a child. Responsibilities that would forever change his life—in ways an unencumbered, free-footed man didn't want to contemplate.

And yet, this baby was his *only* living relative—the only person on the planet who shared his blood. He'd contemplated the issue from the moment he'd been told there had been a baby. Even if he located the child, he might still offer it up for adoption. That might be the best thing he could do. He just didn't have the skills to be a good father, especially a single father—how screwed up would he make the kid? He owed it to his sister to find this baby and do what was right for it—whatever that turned out to be.

He continually pushed the thought away that his quest would reveal that the baby was as dead as Julie. Even with all he'd seen in this world, he had to believe no one would be cruel enough to kill an infant for no reason.

That line of thinking had led him right back to his current theory about Dr. Boudreau. He suspected there had been some sort of black market baby organization, and Dr. Boudreau was one of the doctors recruited to find unsuspecting expectant mothers—women who were alone and vulnerable. He'd done research on such a criminal ring years ago. This scenario played right into their mode of operation.

Dean dropped the photo on the sofa and pressed his palms to his temples. The cottage suddenly felt much too confining for all of his emotions. He got up and began to pace in the dark. His path was limited to a circle around the coffee table and a loop into the tiny kitchen. Two times around only increased his sense of claustrophobia. He grabbed his jacket and walked out the door, across the porch, past the boathouse and onto the long dock that projected from the shore.

His exhalations came in silver puffs, reminding him that winter was inching ever closer. The dock creaked and moaned under his footsteps. It was too cold for insects and frogs. Dean heard the occasional owl in the distance. Other than that, if he held still, there was only the soft lapping of the water against the pilings. He closed his eyes and concentrated on it. It was the music of the gentle sweep of time blended with the quiet voice of nature. The sound slid beneath his skin in a warm flow that immediately lessened his tension.

Until that moment, he hadn't realized how much he'd missed the sound of water. For years, his life had been filled with gritty sand and barren rocky mountains—and worrying about people he didn't know and often didn't understand. Perhaps he should have been paying more attention to those close to his heart. How could his own sister have had a baby and not have breathed a word to him?

He still couldn't understand it. If she'd been in trouble, if she had needed him, she had known to contact Smitty. That was Dean's rule. His editor would have located him somehow.

But, he knew too well, Colettas didn't call for help. They tackled their own problems and solved them alone. Colettas were never interdependent.

Her friends in New York had had no hint of warning before she'd disappeared. And every one of them had insisted that Julie hadn't been dating anyone in particular in the months before she'd vanished. That statement was usually followed by, *but you know how she was about private stuff.*

Of course he knew. He was cut from the same cloth. Again, the Coletta credo.

A dull pain centered in his chest when he thought of his sister facing trouble alone. He knew she was tough on the inside; he'd seen her mettle plenty of times. But because of her waiflike appearance, he'd always thought of her as fragile, ethereal. She always seemed to have no more physical substance than sheer silk.

Had she been afraid? Had she known death was waiting for her?

A tear rolled down his cheek. He swiped it away with the back of his hand. Colettas didn't cry, either.

If only he could have talked to her. He would have come home. He assured himself that he would have. How many times had he urged Nigel Clifford to leave because family came first?

My God, he realized, Julie had died within hours of Clifford's death. At the same time Dean had been fighting for his own life.

Ever since he'd seen Julie in the morgue, fury had fueled every one of his days.

But now, as he stood on this peaceful lake in the crisp night air, a tiny bit of that rage ebbed away. New questions began to emerge.

Had Molly Boudreau been a comfort to his sister? Perhaps the link, the trust, between her and Julie was as simple as it appeared: they'd been two pregnant women without partners bonding through the experience.

But, deep in his heart, he doubted. Julie's trust had been ill founded. When Molly had fled so oddly after the

accident this afternoon, he'd been certain the hunch that
led him here had been right: She did know something
about Julie's death. The way she'd paled when she heard
his name, what other reason could there have been? Still,
in their prolonged conversation this evening, he hadn't
been able to find anything sinister in her demeanor or her
character. A far cry from a co-conspirator in a black market baby scenario he'd thought possible.

Or maybe it was just hard for him to distrust a woman
who was a new mother. Especially one with gray eyes that
broadcast guilelessness and innocence.

Why did he keep coming back to the same circle with
this woman? He knew to trust his instincts—but for some
reason, he continually doubted himself.

He rubbed the back of his neck, trying to relieve the
cramped muscles there. Looking up at the stars in the
night sky, he longed for the uncomplicated life of survival
in a war zone. There was nothing there to cloud your emotions, every fiber of your being was concentrated on staying alive.

He blew out a long vaporous breath.

Maybe he was barking up the wrong tree. But, he con-
ceded, it was the only tree he had.

It might be much simpler to just go and tell the woman
the truth, see what light she could shed on his sister's last
days.

Easier, yes—not wiser. His instincts held him back.
And this instinct was one he was going to heed. Once the
truth was out there, there'd be no reeling it back in.

Molly's spirits began to lift immediately when she
stepped outside Papa's Pizza. With a breath of cool air she

reshuffled her perspective on this entire evening. Now she saw, as sharp and clear as the pinpoint stars in the sky, that her fears of earlier today had been totally unfounded. Dean Coletta was who he said he was; Brian had confirmed that. And he'd been living outside of the United States for years, making any link to Nicholas's father even less likely.

As she walked home, she began to restore the feeling of security she'd awakened with this morning. If the baby's father was going to come after her, he'd have been here by now. He hadn't—and she knew she had not made herself difficult to find. The man either didn't know about the baby, or he didn't care.

By the time she and Nicholas reached home, she once again felt solid in her footing. Standing on the sidewalk at the base of her front porch steps, she looked at the house next door where Mickey lived. Molly had been watching the girl come and go for three weeks. There had been no loud parties, no hot-rodding boyfriends. Mickey kept reasonable hours and Molly had seen her doing dishes through the window over the kitchen sink on most evenings. All in all, Mickey seemed to be a quiet and responsible girl.

In the most impulsive decision Molly had made since arriving in Glens Crossing, she picked Nicholas up, carried him to the Fultons' front door and rang the bell. She realized at the last second that she might not have any more luck finding Mickey at home on a football night than she did in getting a pizza delivered.

To her pleasant surprise, Mickey herself answered the door. "Hi, Dr. Boudreau."

"Hi, Mickey. I'd like to take you up on the babysitting

offer. I know it's short notice, but I wonder if after I put Nicholas down, you could come over for an hour or two. I really need to make a serious trip to Kingston's Market. It'd be so much easier by myself."

Mickey hesitated and glanced over her shoulder.

Molly heard someone approaching from inside the house.

Mickey said, "Sure. I'd love to."

Mickey's mother appeared at her daughter's shoulder. Karen Kimball Fulton was every bit as pretty as she'd been in high school; as impeccably groomed as a magazine photograph, a strong contrast to the carefree wholesomeness of her daughter.

Molly said, "Hi, Karen. I'm Molly Boudreau, Lily's sister." She shifted Nicholas so she could offer to shake hands.

Karen smiled in a distant way and shook Molly's hand as if it were distasteful to touch her. "I remember you."

Molly smiled, slightly uneasy under the woman's glare. Molly hadn't really given a thought as to how Karen would react to anyone in the Boudreau family. She should have. A couple of summers ago, Riley had been responsible for exposing Karen's ex-husband's drug dealing. Tad Fulton was now sitting in the Pendleton men's correctional facility.

Mickey didn't seem to hold it against Molly. Apparently her mother felt differently.

Molly explained, "I was just asking Mickey to babysit later. I was afraid she'd be at the football game."

Karen gave a bitter-sounding laugh. "Oh, no. Not Michaeline. Football isn't cerebral enough for her." She gave Mickey a condescending pat on the shoulder. "She's our little oddball."

Molly recoiled slightly, blinking at the backhanded insult.

But Mickey didn't seem fazed. She simply moved slightly and Karen's hand slid from the girl's shoulder. Then she asked, as if her mother had said nothing at all, "What time do you need me?"

"About eight-thirty."

Mickey smiled. "I'll be over then."

Karen remained standing in the background when Mickey closed the door.

As Molly went down the steps, she heard Karen's raised voice, but couldn't make out what she was saying.

Crap. She should have been thinking beyond her own circumstance and tested the waters with Karen before she actually asked Mickey to sit. She entered her own house feeling terrible for making trouble for the girl.

At eight-thirty precisely, Molly's doorbell rang. Mickey stood there smiling with a novel in her hand. Molly went over the list she'd spent the past half hour composing about where everything could be found, what to do if Nicholas awakened, and a list of emergency numbers much longer than it needed to be.

Mickey took the list with a knowing smile. "I'm your first babysitter."

Molly wiped her hands on her thighs. "Shows that much?"

"I've had worse," she said with a playful tilt of her chin. But she dutifully looked over the list. "We'll be fine. I've taken first aid and the babysitting class offered by the

Red Cross. I've been sitting since I was thirteen. I'm the only one Mrs. Calverson lets babysit her twins."

Molly felt ridiculous. "I know you'll do fine—it's me I worry about." Then she glanced toward her bedroom where the crib was. "He really should sleep until I get back."

Mickey nodded.

Molly picked up her purse. "I'm locking the door when I leave. Please don't open it for anyone while I'm gone."

This was the first thing that Molly had said that drew a surprised expression from the girl. Still, she said, "All right."

Molly tried to explain. "I've been living in the city— you have to be so much more cautious. . . ."

Mickey said, "I won't open the door. Promise."

Molly couldn't help but check the street for unfamiliar cars and figures lurking in the shadows as she left home. She saw neither.

Once in the market, she was swept back in time by its familiar aisles and burnt–orange-and-white checked tile floor. She had come here as a child with her father, and then with Lily once she'd gotten her driver's license. Molly had always loved grocery day. Just entering the building gave her a taste of that happiness. Back then, her dad had patiently taught her how to select bananas that wouldn't go brown too soon, cantaloupes that were ripened just right, apples that were tart and crunchy, and celery that wasn't bitter. Molly's dad knew more about produce than most mothers.

This was the "new" grocery store; in Glens Crossing that meant built in 1970 on the outskirts of town where it had plenty of parking. Everything was arranged as it had been for years; Molly completed her shopping as efficiently as if she'd been frequenting the store on a weekly basis. When she glanced at her watch, she was relieved that she'd only been gone for forty minutes. She felt like she was really getting a handle on her life, going forward.

The parking lot was nearly deserted at this hour. Kingston's was right next to the park, which wasn't lighted at night. It seemed this lot was a little island of weak yellow light in the press of dark woods. The land around Glens Crossing was very hilly, with deep ravines and heavy woodlands. The Hoosier National Forest was within a bicycle ride. When Molly had been growing up, she'd felt isolated here. Now she appreciated that feeling of isolation from the rest of the world.

As she loaded her groceries into the trunk, the faint strains of music reached her ears. It sounded like a soft string instrument playing alone. She put the last bag in the car, then paused, listening. She had to concentrate to put together the melody because it was so faint and broken. The evocative dreamlike quality of it made chills run down her spine.

A hand fell on her shoulder without her hearing anyone approach.

Yelping, she jumped away from the touch, swinging her purse at the assailant's head.

Dean Coletta ducked and threw his arms up for protection.

Molly's heavy bag thudded against his elbow.

"Don't you know better than to sneak up on a woman alone in a dark parking lot?" she shouted, her body humming with adrenaline.

He slowly lowered his arms, peeking to see if she was

going to take another swing at him. "I wasn't sneaking. I just pulled in the space behind you; I assumed you saw me since we're the only two cars in the lot—*and* I slammed my car door." Then his gaze sharpened. "As a woman alone in a dark parking lot, maybe you should be more aware of your surroundings." He paused. "Or maybe you *did* know it was me."

"Hey! Don't try and turn this around on me, mister."

"Well, I am beginning to think you've got it in for me. This is twice in one day you've tried to knock me on my ass."

A twinge of guilt nipped at Molly. She ignored it. "I *did* knock you on your ass this morning. And I obviously need to hone my self-defense skills, because I should have done it again right now." She raised a brow. "Seems you'd learn to cut a wide berth around a woman like me."

He tilted his head. "What kind of woman would that be?"

"Dangerous." She'd meant it as a joke, but from the look on his face, he certainly hadn't taken it that way.

He studied her for a moment. Then he asked, "What were you doing just standing here? I thought there was something wrong."

"Listening. Violin music. If you'd be quiet for a second, you'd hear it, too."

Pressing his lips together to emphasize his silence, he listened. After a second, he opened his mouth. "I don't—"

Just then, the strains began again and Molly raised a finger in the air.

He gave a little shivery-shake. "Kinda creepy."

"You see that radio tower? Those red lights on top of that hill." She turned and pointed.

"Uh-huh." He was right behind her right shoulder now, looking up toward the hilltop.

Molly felt a little shiver herself that had nothing to do with the fall air—or the odd music. "That's Fiddler's Hill. It's supposed to be haunted." She couldn't help the hushed, reverent tone that she remembered always accompanied talks of the Hill. "It used to scare the pants off of us as kids. You only went up there after dark on a dare."

"And the music?" His voice was soft, as if not to disturb the faraway musician.

"Played by a ghost. No other explanation's been found."

Now hearing the faint tune herself, even though she'd never given much credence to the legend, she couldn't come up with any better explanation. There *was* an undeniable otherworldly quality to it. She turned to Dean again. For some reason it seemed right to share this romantic tale with him as they stood with darkness surrounding them. "Legend says that in the early eighteen hundreds a young man brought his bride here from Virginia. This was the frontier then—very wild with Indians and bears and few settlers. He had a piece of property on Fiddler's Hill, planned on starting a mill. During the first winter, the bride fell ill and died. Her husband was so grief stricken that he lost his mind. He spent the rest of his life wandering these hills, playing his fiddle so his love's soul could find him."

The music seemed to grow the slightest bit stronger.

Molly felt a full-fledged chill and her gaze locked on Dean's.

He put a hand on her arm. It felt very protective and she nearly stepped closer. What would it be like to surrender to such protection, such a feeling of security? She couldn't deny the appeal of letting someone else take on the safeguarding of her and Nicholas from fallout from the truth—even for just a little while.

That was nonsense. She barely knew the man. The weird music and romantic legend must be getting to her. She was very tired, which she knew made her vulnerable to such things.

Dean's gaze cut quickly to the hill and back again. He whispered, "Have you heard it before?"

She shook her head and whispered back, "Never."

Dean's voice remained quiet when he said, "Maybe it's just a radio."

"Maybe." But it didn't sound like a radio, or a CD player. It seemed much more unearthly than that. And it didn't sound as if it was coming from the same direction all of the time.

"The breeze is carrying it." Dean looked into her eyes when he said, in a quiet, serious tone, "I don't believe in ghosts."

"Neither do I." Even so, when Dean's hand fell back to his side, Molly felt a little more vulnerable.

Although he wasn't touching her, his gaze penetrated even deeper. "Or love that strong. People can't stay committed for a mortal lifetime. A couple hundred years seems impossible."

Molly thought for a second. Although the legend was romantic—it was hopelessly so. She'd watched real-life couples' love die in violent explosions or in smoldering embers. Suddenly she wondered which her parents' had been. Had her mother's desertion taken her father totally unaware? Or had their relationship been slowly washed away, eroding bit by bit under the waves of everyday life?

"Maybe it was different back then," she offered weakly.

He responded with a huffing noise.

Molly said, "I assume your parents stayed together—the way you spoke of them earlier."

"They did—stayed married, at least."

"Oh." Molly was caught between curiosity and manners. In the end her curiosity won out. "Not happily?"

Dean lifted a shoulder. "I suppose it was their choice to stay together; so maybe they were happy in their own way. I think Mom just ignored the parts of life that would force her to make a different *choice*."

"Your father was unfaithful?" Molly was shocked at her own brashness. But standing here with the romantic legend hanging in the air between them, she was compelled to discover more about him.

Dean cocked his head. "The music's stopped."

"So it has." Molly closed the trunk of her car, her feelings torn between disappointment and embarrassment. "I'd better get going. Nicholas is with a sitter."

"Yeah," he said, but didn't move away. "I need to get some things before the store closes."

She stepped around him, but stopped halfway to the driver's door and turned back around. After a second's hesitation, she said, "I'm sorry—I didn't mean to be rude."

He grinned a boyish grin that took her totally by surprise. "That's all right. You're not the first woman to smack me with a purse."

"That's not—"

His laughter cut her off.

Okay, then. The man doesn't like to talk about himself.
Molly waved and got in her car, feeling a little sorry
that this conversation was over.

Mickey was reading at the kitchen table when Molly let
herself in. This was the first time Molly had felt the lack
of living room furniture.

"Is he still asleep?" Molly asked.

"Didn't hear a thing from him. I peeked in again a
minute ago." Mickey put a bookmark in her novel and laid
it down.

"I've got a couple more bags in the car." Molly set the
bag in her arms on the kitchen counter and turned to go
back out.

"I'll get them," Mickey said, getting up.

"They're both pretty heavy. We can each carry one."

They went outside together and emptied the trunk.
Once back inside, Molly said, "What are you reading?"

Mickey slid her bag onto the counter beside the others.
"*Rebecca.*"

Molly raised a brow in surprise. "That's an old one. For
English class?"

"No, for me. I just like to read."

"Classics are your favorite?"

"I love everything: mysteries, historicals, romances,
suspense, biographies—even the ones we're required to
read in school. If you read authors from varying eras, you
get more than the story, it's like a window into their time.
You see the language, the social viewpoints, the varying

levels of what's acceptable, all of it. How else can you do that?"

Molly paused in unloading a bag. "I guess I never thought of it that way." She shook her head slightly. "I admit, I haven't read much beyond what was required in school. Even now, I don't seem to have the time for more than medical literature."

Mickey sat down at the table and absently thumbed the pages of her novel. "I'd die without books."

That single statement gave Molly a pretty clear view of Mickey's lonely life: a mother who belittled her, Friday nights spent at home alone. Molly had seen several younger boys with a boy who she presumed to be Mickey's brother, but she didn't recall seeing Mickey come or go with friends. When Molly had mentioned to Riley that Mickey was her new neighbor, he'd acted as if he barely knew her. They had to be in the same grade and the school wasn't that big.

Our little oddball.

Well, there was no reason for the girl to feel like an oddball. Maybe she was just more mature than her classmates. Her interests certainly were more intellectual than most.

"Have you made plans for college?" Molly asked. Even though it was two years away, she had the impression that Mickey planned ahead.

Mickey brightened. "I'd *love* to go to the east coast— like you did. But that'll depend on scholarships."

"The east coast has a lot of great colleges. What do you want to study?" Molly stopped putting things away and leaned against the counter.

"I'm thinking microbiology or chemistry."

"Really? With your love of books, I figured you for a literature major."

"I'll always be able to read for myself. I'm not sure what you do with a literature major these days."

"Good point. Unless you want to teach. I bet you'd make a great teacher."

Mickey shook her head. "I'm not very good with groups of people—especially if I have to stand up and talk in front of a whole classroom."

Molly gave a grimace and a visible shudder. "I can't say I like speaking to a crowd myself. In fact, I got nauseous before every oral presentation in college."

Mickey gave her a look that said she didn't believe it.

"I spent the fifteen minutes before class in the restroom, then I usually couldn't speak clearly because my mouth was so dry," Molly assured her. "I'm surprised I passed some of those classes."

Mickey was quiet for a moment, then she stood and picked up her book. "Well . . . I guess I'd better go."

"Oh." Molly reached for her purse. "I'm sorry to keep you like this." She took out a ten and handed it to Mickey. "It's just nice to have company."

"I really like talking to you—you seem to . . . understand." Mickey looked at the money, and then tried to hand it back. "This is too much. I was only here an hour and he slept the entire time."

"Keep it. The extra is for babysitting me. I know I sounded . . . overprotective when I left. You were a good sport about it."

Mickey grinned. "No worse than any other new mother." She put the bill in the pages of her book. "Thanks."

Just as Mickey got to the door, Molly said, "I want to apologize."

Mickey turned around, looking confused. "For what?"

"I didn't mean to put you in a difficult position with your mom. I really didn't think before I came over . . . I realize there may be some . . . hard feelings toward my family."

"Don't worry about it. Mother has hard feelings toward a lot of people—including me." There was a moment of hesitance where Mickey looked like she wanted to say more, but she just said, "Good night," and went out the door.

For a few minutes, Molly stood thinking about Mickey. Any parent should thank their lucky stars to have a daughter like that: focused, mature, respectful. Karen Fulton needed to get her priorities straight.

As Molly finished putting away her groceries, she thought about what an unusual day this had been. In fact, so many things had happened that she could hardly believe it *was* just one day. She'd gotten a job. Run over a man. Been "telephone rejected" by her father. Argued with her sister—again. Braved her first real public appearance in town. Eliminated Dean Coletta as a potential threat—and still accosted him in a parking lot. Heard the mysterious music of Fiddler's Hill for the first time in her life. And had intriguing conversations with both Dean and Mickey—conversations that served to raise more questions, making her want to get to know each of them better.

God, no wonder she was exhausted.

Chapter 9

The next morning, Molly started looking for a sitter for her work hours. The task was complicated because she needed both weekdays and weekends. In her new job at Henderson County ER, she was to rotate four days on and five days off in twelve-hour shifts.

The odd hours, plus the fact that she'd basically been estranged from everyone in this town except her family for the past ten years, made the quest difficult. She didn't know anyone well enough to assess whether or not they would meet her high standards. She didn't think she was being extreme in her requirements—Nicholas was a newborn, after all. She didn't want him in an environment with one caregiver and six or seven small children. In addition, there were extenuating circumstances, making her need someone who would be watchful, cautious by nature. Especially since Molly couldn't explain *why* vigilance was needed.

Lily was the most obvious person to point her in the right direction, but Molly was determined to take this step on her own, partially because she'd have to begin her next conversation with her sister with an apology and she wasn't in the mood to cross that bridge at the moment. Maybe after she found a potential candidate, she'd run it past her sister. Then she would feel like she was in the driver's seat, at least.

On Saturday afternoon she went to check out and interview the three places that had placed ads in the paper, two individual homes and one "professional" day care center. None of which she'd consider hiring. The day care center was closed on Saturday and Sunday and the houses were . . . well, substandard for a variety of reasons. One woman was taking care of three infants and two toddlers while her husband slept in the back bedroom because he worked nights. The other house was so dirty that Molly had actually considered calling the health department after she left.

As she put Nicholas in his car seat after the last interview, she felt defeated and frustrated. She had no idea finding a caretaker would be so difficult. As a pediatrician she'd often listed criteria new parents should use to choose childcare, but she hadn't had a clue how difficult those criteria were to fill. She decided to take a break for a piece of pie at the Dew Drop. Maybe Mildred would have some suggestions; she'd lived here all her life and knew almost everybody.

Since the courthouse was closed on Saturday, there was plenty of parking around the square at two-thirty in the afternoon. Molly parked right in front of the café. Once inside, she and Nicholas took a booth near the back, where she could watch people more easily without having people watch her.

Mildred came over to take her order. "How's that little darlin'?" She leaned over the baby and cooed a couple of times.

She'd obviously gotten over her shock that Molly's child didn't come with a husband.

"He's great," Molly said. "We've been looking for a babysitter. I'm going to work at the hospital in a couple of weeks. This process is very frustrating."

Mildred nodded slowly in commiseration. "I understand that can be a real problem. What with every other week there's a day care center or a church that has horrible things come out in the news. Child molesters—and in small towns like ours! I just don't know what's gotten into people these days."

Molly inwardly cringed. Then she said, "That's why I came here, for your advice—well, that and a slice of your famous cherry pie." Molly pointed to the pie case and smiled. "Since you know everyone, I thought maybe you could make some suggestions."

Mildred shoved her hands on her hips. "Oh, sweetie, I'm so far out of the baby business, I couldn't begin to really know who to say. My niece, Denise, her kids are in junior high now, but she might know somebody. I'll ask her tomorrow at church."

"Thanks, I'd appreciate that." So much for bright and promising leads from Mildred.

"You want coffee with your pie?"

"Decaf, please." Molly rested her elbow on the table, then set her chin in her hand. She huffed out a little puff of frustration. Where was she going to look next?

Mildred served her pie. "I gave you an extra large slice; you look like you could use the pick-me-up."

Molly's eyes widened. She must really look dejected; Mildred had given her what had to be a quarter of a pie. "Wow."

Mildred patted Molly's shoulder before she walked away. "You take your time and enjoy that now. It'll all work out, you'll see."

Smiling her thanks, Molly picked up her fork. She had her head down, focused solely on the pie when she heard a man speak.

"You're going at that pie like you're afraid Mildred's going to come back and repossess it."

Molly raised her eyes. Brian Mitchell was standing next to her table.

She ducked her head and swallowed the huge bite she'd just shoved in her mouth. Then she said, sheepishly, "Comfort food." Then she held onto the rim of her plate. "How do I know *you're* not here to take it away? You've got a lustful look in your eye, looking at my pie there."

Brian laughed. "Can't deny my guilt. But I know better than to take food from an exhausted-looking woman. I'll order my own." He raised a hand to Mildred, who was behind the counter. "Pie and coffee, please." Then he asked Molly, "Mind if I join you two?"

Gesturing toward the seat opposite hers, she said, "Of course not. I was just about to offer—once I was sure you're not after my pie."

Brian slid in the booth. Mildred was right there with his pie.

"Hey, her piece is bigger than mine!" he said, playfully.

Mildred put one hand on her hip and pointed to

Nicholas. "I tell you what, you give birth to one of those and I'll give you a whole pie."

Screwing up his mouth, Brian appeared to consider. "In that case, my pie is just right."

"I thought so." Mildred went back to the counter.

Brian said to Molly, "So, you two out shopping this afternoon?" He then reached across the booth and touched Nicholas softly on the cheek.

She sighed and said, "Shopping for day care."

"I heard you got a job in the ER."

"Wow. News travels even faster in this town than I remember."

Brian winked. "Cell phones." He dug into his pie.

Molly tried to eat hers at a more civilized pace.

Between mouthfuls, Brian said, "Have you tried the Methodist or the Lutheran churches? I think they both have some sort of day care, or Mommy's Day Out, or something."

Shaking her head, Molly said. "No. I'll check. My problem's going to be that I need someone for Saturdays and Sundays on some weeks. ER has a weird rotation."

"Hmm."

They ate for a minute in silence.

Suddenly, Brian said, "I've got it!"

"Got what?"

"The solution."

"What is it?"

He leaned over the table slightly. He was clearly excited about his answer. "Remember I told you that Ed Grissom died?"

Molly nodded, not sure she liked where this was going.

"Hattie is really lost. She'd be a great sitter. And, as the woman has no life, there shouldn't be any conflicts. It would be good for both of you."

Molly tilted her head and squinted slightly. "Isn't she . . . a little nuts?"

Brian shook his head. "Not at all—Ed might have been, though. Hattie's just . . . withdrawn. This could be just the thing to bring her out, let her enjoy life. Besides, she's good with babies. She's worked in the infant nursery at her church forever."

Molly clucked her tongue. "I don't know."

"What have you got to lose by talking to her?"

"I don't think I want Nicholas out there on the farm. If I needed to get to him it would take twenty minutes."

"Have Hattie stay at your house. That'll get her out of that closed up box she lives in and you won't have to cart Nicholas and all of his stuff out every morning."

Molly didn't know which took her more by surprise, that he was actually serious about Hattie, or that he was aware of all the junk a person had to haul around for a baby. Then she said, "I can't just show up on her doorstep and ask her. She doesn't even know me. And how will she take it if I decide she's not the right one? She's already 'withdrawn.'" Even as she said it, she realized how much of a good thing that could be in this particular case. Hattie was cautious, shy, not about to open the door to a stranger.

What am I thinking?

Nicholas woke up and started to fuss.

Molly lifted him out of his pumpkin seat. "Shhhh. You're all right."

Brian held out his hands. "Let me take him while you finish your pie."

She glanced at her half-eaten pie. His plate was empty except for a scattering of crust crumbs. "You're asking for it. If he gets wound up, just watch that glass pie case shatter."

Brian took the baby and Nicholas quieted immediately.

"Well, I'll be calling you at two A.M.," Molly said jokingly.

Brian smiled at the little boy in his arms. "Any time. I think he likes me."

"He's probably pooping."

Brian laughed as he bounced the baby. Then he said, "Seriously, how about I bring Hattie by your place on Monday? That's the day someone brings her into town to shop. You can meet her without her knowing that you're sizing her up. If you don't want to pursue it, no harm done."

"If she has to be brought in to do her shopping, how is she going to get to my house to babysit?"

Brian waved the concern away. "One step at a time. First meet her. Something can be worked out."

Molly didn't like the idea of a creepy old lady watching Nicholas, but she was getting desperate. And Brian did seem to know the woman pretty well. "All right, bring her by."

After they both paid for their pie, she asked him if he would mind watching Nicholas while she went to the ladies' room. Brian had been holding the baby for several minutes already.

"Of course I don't mind," he said. "I'll tell him some dirty jokes while you're away."

Molly rolled her eyes and headed for the restroom.

When she came back out, Brian was gone. In his place at their booth sat a frightened-looking Dean Coletta holding Nicholas under both arms as if he was looking to hand him off to the next person who walked by the table.

The baby started to wail.

True terror showed on Dean's face.

Molly remained standing in the hallway to the restrooms suppressing a chuckle as she watched Dean's frantic eyes searching for Mildred.

Dean set Nicholas on the table edge and jostled him. "It's okay. Don't cry. Mommy'll be right back."

Even though she was enjoying the scene, Molly took pity. She stepped into the dining room.

"What's all this?" she said. "Where's Brian?"

Dean thrust the baby at her. "His beeper went off right as I walked in. He had to go on a volunteer fire run."

Molly took Nicholas and put him on her shoulder. His cries died out to whimpers. "Now that's a question I hadn't thought to ask a babysitter."

Dean immediately said, "Oh, he wouldn't have just left the baby."

Molly shook her hand and chuckled. "That's not exactly what I meant." She sat in the booth and put Nicholas in his seat. "Thank you for watching him."

Dean shrugged, looking nearly as uncomfortable as he had while still holding the baby. Then he picked up a menu. He didn't open it, just sat tapping it on the table.

She started to get Nicholas ready to leave.

"Can you stay to have a cup of coffee with me?" he asked out of the blue.

She was ready to say she had to get going; Nicholas was getting fussy and needed to be fed. But then she looked into Dean's eyes. They looked—hopeful. She felt guilty for the laugh she'd just had at his expense.

"Sure," she said. "I'll have Mildred heat up a bottle." She dug one out of the diaper bag and walked over to the counter. After she asked Mildred to warm it, she asked, "Do you have any more of that cherry pie?"

"Sure do." Mildred raised a brow. "You want *more*?"

Molly laughed. "I would if I could find a place to put it! I'm buying for Dean." She thumbed over her shoulder.

Mildred looked around her. "I see."

Molly looked from under her brows. "I'm just trying to make the man feel welcome in our town so he writes a nice story about us."

"Uh-huh." Mildred turned around to get the pie and Nicholas let loose a bellow before Molly could voice any more denials.

"What do I do?" Dean called across the dining room. "He's crying."

Nothing like stating the obvious. But, Molly thought, there was a desperate quality to the man's voice that was just a little endearing coming from such a globally seasoned character.

Molly went back and picked the baby up. She couldn't believe a man who'd spent most of his adult life dodging bullets could be so rattled by one little baby. "Just keep in mind," she said teasingly, "you're bigger than he is. Plus, you can run away and he can't come after you."

Dean looked embarrassed. "I've just never been around babies."

"I'm sorry. I shouldn't make fun. It's just here you are with the worldly reputation, having survived war zones and irate editors, and eight pounds of baby has you scared to death."

Now he looked indignant; her tactic to get him back in a place of comfort seemed to be working.

He said, "I wasn't *scared*. I didn't want to do the wrong thing. I've heard how picky mothers of firstborns are."

"Right you are."

Mildred brought a tray with the baby's bottle, a cup of coffee, and a slice of pie. She handed the bottle to Molly, then set the coffee and cherry pie in front of Dean.

"Sorry, ma'am, but I didn't order pie."

Mildred tilted her head toward Molly and said, as suggestively as any bartender in a swinging singles spot, "A gift from the lady." Then she gave a salacious wink and walked away.

Molly busied herself with situating the baby for his bottle. She didn't make eye contact when she said, "Just eat it, you'll thank me."

Once Dean took a bite, Molly couldn't tell whose face showed more bliss, his or Nicholas's.

"Oh my God. I didn't know pie could be this good."

Molly chuckled. "See what you've missed in all of your world travels by limiting yourself to strife-filled countries?"

He grinned and Molly took it like a shot in the heart. The man was one mass of charisma.

Then he said, "This could turn out to be the best story

I've ever written, considering my good fortune in these first days."

Molly didn't respond with more than a slight smile. He was flirting again, and she couldn't deny she liked it—even though he probably flirted as unconsciously as he breathed.

Dean took a break in his pie shoveling, and leaned against the back of the booth. "Tell me a little about your life in Boston."

Molly put Nicholas on her shoulder to burp him. As she patted his back, she said, "Are you asking as a journalist?"

Dean rolled his lips inward for a second, as if this had been a difficult question. "I'm not sure yet."

More flirting.

Nicholas gave a burp befitting a linebacker and Dean tipped his head in commendation. "My."

Molly said, "Yes, a talent any mother would be proud of. I can't wait until he's sixteen and realizes his full potential." She gave Nicholas his bottle again.

"Back to Boston," Dean prompted with a smile.

"Yes, Boston. I went to Boston University for both undergrad and med school. After graduation I worked in the ER at Boston General. That's pretty much it. You know med school—doesn't leave much time for anything else."

Dean raised a brow and nodded toward the baby. "Apparently you found time for a little something else."

For the briefest second Molly fought panic. Then she took a breath and said flippantly, "That can be done on a fifteen-minute coffee break."

He looked at her seriously for a second. "Is that how it was?"

"I really don't know what business that is of yours—or your magazine's."

He raised his palms. "Sorry." After a second, he looked in her eyes and said, "I wasn't asking for the magazine, FYI."

Molly decided to let that topic die right there.

Dean cursed himself for pushing too hard. He had better finesse than that. So he took a step backward in the conversation. "What made you decide to work in emergency? Was that your specialty?"

With a weak smile at the baby in her arms, Molly said, "No. My specialty is pediatrics. I just wasn't ready to set up a practice yet. Maybe it was because deep down I really didn't know where I wanted to settle for the long haul." For a moment, she seemed deep in thought. Then she gave her head a slight shake and said, "Plus, the hours at the ER allowed me to volunteer at a free clinic."

"Really! A free clinic?" He slid the pie plate away and leaned his elbows on the table. "What brought you to that? Did you like it?"

Molly thought for a minute before answering. "The children," she said with certainty. "It was the children. I thought my pediatric expertise could be of value there. Working in the ER I saw so many sick kids that shouldn't have been, and who'd often waited far too long to seek help. Aside from the injuries, most of the illnesses the kids came to the ER with could have been prevented with even a minimum of care. I guess you could say it was

frustration—I wanted to get at these problems before
they were full-blown disasters.

"As far as liking it . . . it was my life. If I'd been able
to afford it, I would have given more time there." Sadness
shone in her eyes when she added, "But the clinic was
closed down—lack of funding." She hugged the baby
tighter and kissed his forehead. "Then Nicholas came
along, and everything changed." She lowered her lashes,
hiding her eyes from him, and visibly shivered.

"Are you all right?" Dean asked, reaching across the
table and putting a hand on her arm.

It took her a second to respond. "What?"

"You look like you had a chill, are you okay?"

"I'm fine."

"It is a shame—the clinic, I mean." Dean drew back
and sipped his coffee. Then he said, as if musing to himself, "Seems like a lot of bad news out of Boston recently."

"I beg your pardon?"

He was as careful not to allow her to look into his
eyes. Lifting a hand, as if to flip the thought away, he
said, "Nothing . . . ." He sighed. "Well, not *nothing*—that
sounded disrespectful." He then concentrated on slowly
turning his cup on the table.

At first he thought she wasn't going to take the bait; he
let the melancholy silence do the prompting for him.

Finally she asked, "Is it something you want to talk
about?"

Advance carefully. He'd pushed too hard a few minutes ago; he didn't want to screw this up again. In order
to appear reluctant, he scrubbed his hand over his face
and blew out a breath.

Looking at her he said, "Someone I knew was killed in Boston not long ago."

Molly's eyes immediately dodged his and focused on the baby. "Oh . . . that's terrible." She said it softly, with a slight tremor in her voice.

He sat there for a long moment, fiddling with his fork, allowing the maximum reaction from her. When it became apparent she wasn't going to say more, he said, "Yeah. Terrible."

She quickly burped Nicholas again, then set him in his baby seat. "I'd really better get going. I'm in the process of looking for a sitter."

"I appreciate you keeping me company."

"My pleasure." She slipped on her coat and picked up the baby. "Good luck on your article."

He picked up his coffee again. "Thanks. You too, on finding a sitter."

"And," she hesitated, "I'm sorry about your friend." Then she hurried away.

Molly left the lingering scent of her perfume and baby formula. It was an exceptionally feminine mixture. But Dean made himself ignore it. Molly had not asked one question about his "friend" who was killed in Boston. Not how the person died, or if they'd been close. What kind of person can ignore basic human curiosity like that?

He knew what kind—one who had something to hide.

Chapter 10

As Molly was bouncing off the doorjamb, trying to get herself, Nicholas and all of his stuff hauled inside in one trip, the telephone rang. She dropped the diaper bag on the floor, set down the pumpkin seat, leapt across the kitchen and grabbed the receiver on the fifth ring.

"Hello?"

"Are you all right?" Lily asked. "You sound funny."

Molly sucked in a deep breath. "I was just walking in the door." She couldn't squash the little dance of satisfaction her pride was doing because Lily had called first. It surprised Molly how quickly a person slipped into childish habits once back in the family fold. What shouldn't have surprised her was the fact that Lily made the call; she never did like to leave things at odds.

"We're going to the spaghetti supper at the high school tonight," Lily said. "You and Nicholas want to come?" She didn't pause long enough for an answer. "It's a fundraiser for the basketball team."

"Oh, I don't know. I've been out all day. I'm really bushed." And she didn't want to sit through a meal in a crowded room wondering who was looking at her and forcing strained conversation. Lily was offering the olive branch, but Molly knew her sister wouldn't rest until she understood Molly's motives for her actions concerning Nicholas. Of course, that could never be. So it was going to be a long game of cat and mouse.

"You have to eat. This'll save you making a mess in the kitchen."

Molly had no intention of messing up her kitchen. Dinner was going to be a bowl of Frosted Mini-Wheats.

Lily went on, "Besides, I want to see you." Her voice dropped a little lower. "I don't like us being upset with one another."

"I don't either."

"Then you'll come?"

Molly felt a little guilty that Nicholas had been in his seat nearly all day. She looked at him now, dozing where she'd left him by the door. It certainly didn't appear to make any difference to him. "On one condition: no talk about Nicholas's father."

Lily was quiet for a second. Molly could almost see her sister weighing the answer. Lily never broke her word, therefore she was always careful about giving it. "All right. Tonight is just for fun. You could probably use a little."

Fun? Molly hardly remembered the definition of the word. She said, "What time?"

"Six. We'll come by and pick you up."

"I'll just meet you there. It'll be easier than moving the car seat."

"Okay. Don't buy a ticket. I already have one for you," Lily said cheerfully. "See you."

"Bye." Molly held the receiver in front of her and looked at it for a second before she hung it up. *That sure I'd buckle under, huh?*

"Really, Michaeline, I just don't understand you!"

Mickey rolled over on her bed and looked toward her mother, standing in the doorway. "What?" What could she have possibly done to get her mother's panties in a bunch? She'd emptied the dishwasher, done her own laundry, cleaned the cat's litter box; she'd even been nice to her ratty-assed brother. For the past two hours, she'd been in her room reading.

"I told you yesterday," Mother put her hand on her hip, "the basketball team is having a big spaghetti dinner as a fundraiser tonight."

"I know. I'm not going."

"It's the very *least* you can do to support your brother! With your father unavailable, Andrew needs all of the family support we can give him."

Mom always referred to Dad as being "unavailable." Good God, everybody in town knew Dad was in jail. And Mom hadn't been too concerned about showing *Dad* any kind of support. Both Mickey and Drew had been strictly forbidden to have any communication with him. Obviously *family* support had very little to do with being family.

"The place will be packed, no one will even know if I'm there," Mickey said. *Least of all Drew, who treats me like a leper at school. So afraid my uncool will rub off on him.* Why on earth did her mom always badger her into these things? Wouldn't they all be better off if she just stayed home?

"I'll know." Karen crossed her arms over her chest, a sure sign that Mickey wasn't going to win this one. "Besides, before you know it, high school will be over—and what will you have to show for it?"

"A diploma."

Karen gave an exasperated grumble. "You know that's not what I meant. Really, I thought when you took up with that Holt boy, things were going to turn around. He's the most popular boy in school."

Mickey started to ask her mom how she knew who was popular and who wasn't in the junior class at Glens Crossing High, but decided not to bother. If the fact that Riley Holt was rich could outweigh the fact that he'd been the one to insure that her dad was "unavailable," Mickey doubted anything else would matter.

Karen went on, "But you managed to run him off, just like you have everybody else. My high school friends and I *still* do things together. I hate it that you're missing out."

Mickey huffed and flopped back on her bed. It just burned her when her mom started throwing Riley Holt in her face. She'd thought they were friends, too. How wrong she'd been.

Mickey thought back. She could just about pinpoint the day that Riley Holt began to treat her like a *persona non grata*. Their friendship had been formed Riley's first summer here in Glens Crossing—before he knew anyone else, before he understood where Mickey ranked in the social pecking order. Back then, it really hadn't seemed to matter. Riley had been in trouble a lot back then; his parents had just gotten divorced and his dad was in rehab.

But he had been a good friend to her. He'd even put himself at risk to have her dad arrested for dealing. Riley never actually admitted it to her, but she knew he'd done it because of the bruises her dad had left on her.

They'd managed to stay friends through their freshman year in high school, even though he was quickly becoming involved in a world from which Mickey had been excluded. Then, the beginning of sophomore year, Codi Craig decided she wanted Riley to be her boyfriend. Mickey could see why; Codi had already gone through every cool guy in school. She was running out of targets.

At first it seemed like Mickey and Riley's friendship would survive. But soon it became apparent that Codi wasn't going to let that happen. Even so, Codi was too smart to demand Riley drop Mickey. She didn't have that kind of hold on him—yet. It had been slow work, but she finally achieved her goal; Mickey and Riley's friendship eroded away one tiny grain at a time.

The whole thing just confirmed that Mickey had been right in her original theory: until she got out of this town, life was going to suck.

Her mother came into Mickey's bedroom and sat on the edge of the bed. Mickey could almost recite verbatim what she was about to say.

Mother didn't disappoint. "I'm just thinking about your happiness." She petted Mickey's head. "I don't want you to be sorry you missed this wonderful time in your life."

"I'm not missing it—I'm living *my* life, just the way I want to."

Karen got up, the sympathy gone from her voice when she said, "Well, I can't make friends for you, but I can in-

sist you be there for your brother. Get up and get ready."
Then she walked out of the room without looking back.

If her mom was so worried about her happiness, why
did she keep making her do things that made her feel like
an outcast? She was perfectly happy to stay home. None
of her school friends would be at the dinner. They were
even more nerdy than her. So, she'd sit by herself, while
her mother ran around like a bee in a flower garden, chat-
ting with all of her *friends*. Karen Kimball and Codi
Craig—same person, different generations. Even the al-
literation in their names matched. How much happier
would Mother be if Codi was her daughter?

Mickey got up and went to the bathroom to brush her
teeth and comb her hair, counting the long string of
months until she could leave for college.

When Molly entered the high school, she was struck
by how little had changed in her near eleven-year absence. It even smelled the same: a mix of worn textbooks,
gym socks, rubber erasers, and floor wax. She moved
through the halls toward the cafeteria. The glass trophy
case by the gymnasium appeared slightly more crowded
than she remembered. However, the state runner-up trophy the football team had earned her brother Luke's senior year remained the center focal point. Its presence gave
her a sense of continuity, stability. She glanced down a
hall at her old locker, which had had generations of tape
and stickers peeled off and had been painted so often, she
could see the thick roughness of the finish from here.

"Better take a look, Nicholas, one day you're going to
be walking these hallowed halls."

Just saying that crystallized her future before her.

Never in a million years had she dreamed she'd be moving back to this town. But then, she'd had no way of knowing Sarah was going to come into her life—and upend it so unexpectedly and so tragically.

In pondering her future, standing in the halls that housed her teenage years, she wondered briefly if she would end up the stodgy old town doctor, unmarried, living solely for her work and the occasional visit from her only child.

Now that was quite the pessimistic leap. Shaking such dismal thoughts from her head, she moved on.

She passed an older couple who looked familiar— Molly thought the husband used to work at Duckwall Hardware. Their eyes lingered on the pumpkin seat and avoided her own. Molly was pretty sure she heard the woman say, "Such a shame," after they passed.

Molly thought about turning around and walking back out to her car. She didn't have to put herself on display tonight; she had plenty of food in the house. Granted, her dinner at Papa's hadn't been disturbed by pointing fingers and hissing gossip—but this was in the *high school*. It was easy to slip into the cliquish, judgmental mindset by just walking in the door.

It turned out to be too late to turn around. Lily, Clay, and Riley were waiting for her outside the cafeteria. Lily waved. Molly had to admit, it was a nice sight, Lily and her little family—one that counteracted her near slide back into adolescence that the building had induced. Seeing them gave her hope that happy endings sometimes do happen. Although, she thought, Peter, Lily's ex-husband, probably wouldn't agree. Did it always have to be that way—for one person to achieve happiness, another had to suffer?

It was certainly turning out that way in her case. Here she was, a woman most likely destined to be barren, but through a cruel twist of circumstance had been given the chance to be a mother. The cost of that chance was almost too much to contemplate. Each and every day she said a prayer for Sarah Morgan—and she hoped that Sarah knew her child was not only safe, but loved.

Her maudlin thoughts threatened to provoke tears. Tears she wouldn't be able to explain to her sister. So she forced a smile and tried to think of only the happiness this child brought with each dawning day.

Lily came forward and gave Molly a quick hug. "I'm so glad to see you."

Molly hugged her with her free arm. "Me too."

Clay stood a couple of feet away, looking as if he didn't know if he should come forward or not. There was a guarded look in his eye that Molly didn't recall seeing before—no doubt because she'd upset Lily again. He was fiercely protective of Lily.

"Hello, Clay." She took the bull by the horns and stepped over to him and gave him a sisterly hug. As she did, she noticed Riley shifting slightly farther away. "Relax, buddy, I wouldn't do that to you."

Riley shifted from foot to foot, looking at the floor. "I wasn't worried."

"Liar." Molly laughed. "But don't think you're safe forever. I'll collect my hug in private."

Clay said, "Riley, why don't you take the baby seat for Aunt Molly?"

Riley's horrified gaze darted between the cafeteria and the baby.

Molly almost saved him by saying she'd rather carry Nicholas. But the truth was that after lugging the seat, baby, and diaper bag around all day, her back was killing her. She held out the seat. "Thanks so much." Then she added under her breath, "Trust me, babies are chick magnets. You'll see."

Riley didn't look convinced as he fell into step with them and entered the cafeteria. They found a table that had seats available and put their coats on the chairs. Riley set the pumpkin seat on the table and before he could shove his hands in his jean pockets, two smiling teenage girls showed up.

One gasped, then said, "Ohhhhh, he's sooo little."

While the other reached for the baby's fingers. "He's adorable." Then she looked at Riley with a question in her eyes. "It is a boy, right? I was just guessing from the blue blanket."

"Uh, yeah." Then Riley seemed to get his feet back under him. "His name is Nicholas. He's my cousin."

While the girls fussed over the baby, Riley turned to Molly and mouthed, "Seniors." Then he grinned and wiggled his eyebrows.

She responded with a knowing tilt of the head.

Glancing around the room, she realized the senior girls weren't the only ones who appeared interested in their arrival. She actually caught one pair of ladies pointing as they ducked their heads together in gossip. Well, the sooner everyone got discussing Molly's unwed status out of their systems, the sooner she'd begin to blend into this town.

A horrible thought struck her. What if she never blended in? Would Nicholas grow up with whispers and shunning? *Of course not. Stop sounding like Lily.* This was the twenty-first century—even in Glens Crossing.

The senior girls moved on and Riley turned to Molly, beaming. "Wow, you were right."

"Only thing that works better is a puppy." Then she said to Lily, "You guys go on and get your food, then I'll go."

Riley piped up. "I'll stay with him. You go on with Mom."

Molly felt a stab of fear. Her first reaction was that there was no way she was leaving Nicholas in this very public place. Then she glanced down the long table and saw Sheriff Clyde with his large family. She was only going to be forty feet away herself. How much safer could it be?

Lily's hand rested on Molly's arm. "He'll be fine."

Molly forced her feet to move toward the food line. Clay stopped halfway there to chat with someone, but Molly kept going. If Lily wanted to wait for Clay, fine. But Molly was getting her food and heading back to the table without a lot of unnecessary chitchat. Besides, being in this crowd reignited that defensiveness that had sprouted earlier in the hallway. She had in mind keeping a low profile.

"Going to a fire?" Lily asked laughingly from behind.

"I just want Riley to be able to get his food, he's probably starved," she said without slowing her pace. She didn't look in her sister's eyes again until they were back at the table.

As Lily sat down across from her, she said, "See,

everyone survived." Then to Riley she said, "If you hurry, you can catch Clay and get in line with him."

"*See*—" Molly cast Lily a pointed look and mimicked her mocking tone "—if we'd stopped with Clay, we'd still be standing there."

Lily had the graciousness to laugh. "Right you are."

Riley got up. Both women watched him walk toward Clay.

Molly said, "I don't see much of Peter in him. Genetics are funny." She knew there'd come a day when people said the same about Nicholas.

Lily didn't say anything. When Molly looked back at her, Lily's gaze was fixed on Riley and Clay walking together. Something unreadable was on her face; she seemed a thousand miles away.

Molly gave her a dose of her own medicine. "Hey, you make fun of me! You look like they're leaving for Siberia or something."

Lifting a shoulder, Lily said, "It's just that Riley seems so—adult. I know it comes and goes on the wind, but the adult days are beginning to outweigh the irrational ones. Two years and he'll be in college."

"He and Clay seem to be getting along pretty well."

Lily bit her lip. "Today. It falls in the same category as Riley's mature behavior, changes minute by minute." She sighed almost imperceptibly. "I thought things would be running smoothly by now."

"Hey, with teenagers, I don't think it's ever smooth."

Smiling, Lily nodded. Then she said, "I'm sorry if I upset you yesterday. But I really can't take on Nicholas right now."

"I'm the one who should apologize. It was unfair of

me. It's just . . . nothing is working out the way I'd imagined."

Lily looked deep into Molly's eyes. "Hey, nothing ever works out the way you plan once you have a child. Get used to it."

There was an undercurrent to Lily's words that made Molly wonder if things perhaps weren't as idyllic in Lily's household as they appeared. Before she could question further, Lily picked Nicholas up out of the pumpkin scat. "I think he's grown since yesterday."

Molly laughed. "I doubt that very much. But he is pushing ten pounds."

Lily gave Nicholas a couple of manly grunts. "Gonna be a football player?"

Molly covered her eyes. "God forbid! All I can see are broken collar bones, concussions, and blown-out knees." She let her sister off the hook and didn't try to get them back on the topic of *her* family. Lily never liked to talk about her problems—which oftentimes led one to believe there *were* no problems. The fact that Lily had hinted at things being imperfect was quite a big step for her.

Molly said, "Finding a sitter is turning out to be impossible. Do you have any suggestions? I'd feel better if I could give a sitter a bit of a test run before leaving the baby for a twelve-hour shift." The very thought of it drove away Molly's appetite.

"Have you interviewed anyone yet?"

"No one I'd consider." Then she said, "You wouldn't believe who Brian Mitchell has me interviewing on Monday."

"Brian?" Lily asked with a suggestive lilt and raised brows.

"God, it's great to be back in a small town." *Gossip, no privacy . . . heaven on earth.* Then she explained, "I ran into him last night at Papa's."

"He's single again, you know."

"Jesus, Lily! I'm trying to have a serious conversation here."

"I'm just saying. . . ."

Molly looked at the baby in Lily's arms from under her brows. "And need I mention I have a new baby?"

"Brian likes babies."

Molly sighed in exasperation. "Can we get back on the subject? He actually suggested Hattie Grissom! Can you imagine?"

"Why not?"

"You can't be serious! She's ancient. She's never had children. She's probably nuts. Need any more negatives than that?"

Lily put Nicholas up on her shoulder and patted his bottom. "It might work. She's not *that* old. In fact, she looks quite a bit younger now that her husband isn't mentally beating her into the ground every day. It's not like she didn't *want* children. She had several babies who didn't live. And she's worked in the infant care nursery at church forever. I have to admit, she's not long on conversation with adults, but I've seen her with those babies. In fact, I can't believe I didn't think of it myself."

"Babies that didn't live? There's another negative."

"She couldn't carry a pregnancy to term. I only know because since Ed's death, Hattie's been the center of several discussions—everyone wants to help her. This could be just the thing for both of you. Try to keep an open mind when you meet her."

"I'll try."

"Hello, Dr. Boudreau."

Molly turned around to see Mickey Fulton standing behind her with a plate of spaghetti and a can of Coke. "Mickey!" She didn't see anyone with the girl. "Would you like to sit with us?" Molly pointed to the empty chair across from Riley's coat.

Mickey looked over her shoulder. Then she said, "If you don't mind. My mom's talking to Mr. Mitchell. I don't think I'll be seeing her for a while."

Lily said, "Well, have a seat."

Mickey sat down and looked at the baby. "Hey, Nicholas, you sweet boy, you."

"Mickey babysat with Nicholas last night while I went shopping."

"That's right, you're neighbors," Lily said. "We haven't seen much of you out at the farm lately, Mickey. You should come by, I've got some great new pot designs." She turned to Molly, "Sometimes, Mickey does some of the hand-painting and glazing for me."

Mickey nodded, but seemed totally engrossed in her spaghetti—at least with moving it around on her plate.

Riley and Clay returned. Molly noticed Riley hesitate before taking his seat across from Mickey.

Lily said, "Aren't you going to say hello?"

Riley's fork twirled in his spaghetti, his concentration centered there. "Hi."

Mickey didn't look up when she offered her quiet "Hi" in return.

There was definitely something afoot between these

two. Molly didn't have a great deal of information on Riley's social life, but she did know that Mickey had been his first friend when he moved to Glens Crossing. From what Lily had said, she suspected a romantic relationship at one time. Now they were two icebergs passing in the night.

The uneasiness between the teenagers hung in the air like a noxious cloud.

Just as Molly thought that, Lily said, "Uh-oh. Somebody needs a diaper."

So maybe the teenagers weren't the source of the noxious cloud.

Molly put out her hands for Lily to hand her the baby.

Mickey stood up. "I'll go change him. I can use the teachers' lounge."

"Oh, Mickey, you don't want this one," Molly argued.

Lily said, "Never turn down someone's offer to change a diaper. By the time he's potty trained, you'll be willing to pay strangers to do it."

Molly passed the baby on to Mickey. "You're sure?"

"Hey, a little poop never killed anyone." She picked up the diaper bag and went toward the door at the side of the cafeteria.

Molly said, "Yeah, that's what she thinks."

Lily and Clay chuckled.

Riley acted as if the entire conversation hadn't transpired.

When Mickey returned, she handed Nicholas to Molly and picked up her barely touched dinner. "Thanks for letting me sit with you."

The three adults urged her to stay and, when she

wasn't swayed, said a pleasant good-bye. Riley was silent. In fact he didn't even look up from his food.

As Dean entered the cafeteria from the street doors, he saw Brian Mitchell just inside. He was speaking to an attractive woman in her early thirties who appeared far more taken with the conversation than Brian did.

Dean stayed out of Brian's line of sight as he scanned the crowd. He didn't particularly want to be dragged into a conversation at the moment. He had his own agenda this evening.

He'd seen the notice of the spaghetti supper in the local paper. Of course, any reporter looking to cover small town minutiae wouldn't miss such an event. Thus, his presence served two purposes, both valuable; the second being of more interest, however. By being here, he validated his cover story; his secondary objective was to run into Molly Boudreau again. He really needed to get a better handle on her. Everything he read in her personality and character was contradictory to his preconception of her. But then, just when he began to decide she wasn't any more than she appeared on the surface, she'd do something totally off-base like her *non*-reaction to his mentioning the unexpected death of a friend. A part of him prayed that she was just a single mother looking for a place to raise her child—even if it did leave him at a dead end in the search for his sister's killer. He was really beginning to like Molly.

The cafeteria was crammed with people sitting, standing, and milling around, making it difficult to pick out any single target. Jittery kids scurried up and down the aisles as they waited for parents to finish eating and visiting. A couple of ladies were walking around with baskets, passing out breadsticks. Just as he was about to give up, he saw a tall blond girl. It was the pale color of her hair that captured his attention. It was the same near-white shade as Julie's. The sight gave his heart an unexpected jolt.

Julie had always been easy to pick out in a crowd because the rare color of her hair was matched with fair skin, and light brows and lashes—a natural blond always stands out.

When he calmed his heart, he saw the girl was standing right next to Molly—another woman who stood out in a group with her near-black hair, dark, gracefully-arched brows and silver eyes. The fact that she appeared to be totally unaware of her striking looks stirred grudging admiration in him. It was a rare trait in beautiful women.

His gaze cut briefly to the woman speaking to Brian, who clearly capitalized on her appearance with every gesture and every nuance of her conversation. Dean had always had a deep aversion for such women. He supposed it was because, in his work, he'd learned to value those who are true of heart above all else.

He was pulled out of his thoughts when everyone at Molly's table appeared to be moving. Dean needed to thread his way across the big room before they left. He could hardly chase the woman out the door.

He hadn't taken two steps when he heard Brian call his name.

Dean turned around, but tried to preserve his momentum. "I'll be right back."

"Hold on for just a second, I want you to meet someone." Brian's lips said the words, his eyes screamed, *Save me!*

Dean cast another glance toward Molly's table. They seemed to be settling back in after handing around the baby. He put on a smile and forced his nervous feet to stand still.

Brian said, "Karen Fulton—"

She interrupted him. "I go by Kimball now." Then she added, "Since my divorce."

Brian tilted his head in apology. "Karen Kimball, meet Dean Coletta. He's the one I was telling you about, doing the story on American towns."

Karen extended her hand. "Nice to meet you, Dean."

"Ms. Kimball." He shook her hand. Probably too soon for politeness, his eyes left her face and looked over her shoulder to make sure Molly was still there.

She glanced behind her. Then back at Dean. "Looking for someone?"

Dean slipped on what he hoped was a charming smile. "No. I noticed Dr. Boudreau over there . . . she and I have a conversation to finish."

"Oh," Karen sounded disappointed. "I thought you'd be more interested in interviewing people who actually *live* here."

He bowed slightly. "Everyone has a unique perspective. I'm looking to hear all of them."

"Well, I suppose her 'perspective' might be interesting, being raised on the 'wrong side of the tracks,' so to speak." She lowered her voice to a conspiratorial tone. "She lived over the tavern—her mother was trash . . . ran off with some man when Molly was just a baby. It's really no wonder she's an unmarried mother herself now."

Where did this woman get on her high horse? Dean didn't know why he was tempted to defend the doctor, but it burned him to hear her cast such a derogatory slur on Molly. He was ready to put Karen Kimball in her place. He'd been in town long enough to hear that her ex was sitting in jail for drug dealing.

Luckily, Brian prevented his attack by saying, "You've met Benny . . . at the Crossing House."

Dean pretended this was news to him. "Oh, that's her father." Then he emphasized, "A real nice gentleman." He looked sharply at Karen, "Before long, I'll get all of the interconnections around here."

A dark look crossed Karen's face. Quickly she recovered her smile. "Well, you know, we can't always be judged by what our family does. . . ."

Dean maintained the intensity of his glare. "I've never held that misconception. A person should be judged by their actions and their actions alone." He'd had to remind himself of that repeatedly since meeting the young doctor. Her quiet demeanor, her caring attitude, could easily be manufactured to disguise her *actions*. And she was good at it; his own urge to defend her was evidence of that. Once again, he felt like he was chasing his own tail.

He said to Karen, "If you'll excuse me. I need to catch the doctor before she leaves." He started to walk away.

Brian said, "Remind her that I'll be by Monday morning around eleven."

Dean's gaze snapped back to Brian, and he saw that Karen's surprised eyes moved to him also. Brian and Molly had a date? After a pause that broadcasted he didn't care for the idea, Dean said, "Will do."

When he stepped up behind Molly and said hello, she

turned, looking truly pleased to see him. He caught himself feeling just as pleased that she was smiling at him.

"Hi. I guess I shouldn't be surprised to see you—this kind of thing," she gestured to the crowd around them, "is pretty much what it's all about around here."

He shoved his hands in his pockets and nodded. "I suppose *everyone* is here?"

Molly laughed. "The town isn't *that* small. But they do have quite a basketball following, so it's a good crowd."

Dean didn't miss the fact that she spoke as an outsider—"the" town as opposed to "our" town . . . "they" have a following.

Molly introduced him to Lily and Clay, then offered him the seat the blond girl had just vacated. "Have you eaten?"

Dean pulled out the chair and sat. He patted his stomach. "After that huge piece of cherry pie this afternoon, no pasta for me." Then he said to Lily, "I bet you've really been looking forward to having your sister move back."

"Well, to tell you the truth, it was a surprise."

"Oh?"

Molly spoke before Lily could say more. "I didn't tell anyone in advance—get their hopes up. I didn't make my mind up firmly until after Nicholas was born. What they say is true—you don't really understand how you're going to feel about being a parent until that baby is laid in your arms. It's . . . overwhelming. Once he was here, I knew I wanted him to be raised around family—in a place like this." The words tumbled out in an unconvincing rush.

Her tone was off, it sounded . . . practiced. Something

had triggered this move for Molly—something that she obviously didn't want anyone to know. Dean wondered briefly if it had to do with her baby's father. But the idea of Molly and another man was suddenly unsettling to him.

Ridiculous. Focus on your objective, man. It bothered him that the more time he spent with Molly, the fuzzier that objective became.

Chapter 11

Molly was impressed with the easy way Dean slid into conversation with her family. Even though he asked so many questions about her it nearly set off a blush, she couldn't help but feel flattered by his interest. It was as if he really wanted to know her in depth, not just gather facts for a magazine article. As they chatted, he frequently cast smiling glances her way. Glances that made something shift inside her, a tiny molecular earthquake. She began to have such a good time she forgot to look to see if gossipers were still casting surreptitious glances her way.

Dean and Clay seemed to hit it off—which for some reason pleased her. And when Dean discovered that Lily and Clay and Riley were on the clean-up committee, he offered to help Molly carry the baby seat and diaper bag to her car. Suddenly, her insides felt just like they had when Andy Jacobi had asked her if he could walk her home from the eighth grade dance.

She tried to calm her reaction; she was much too old for such fanciful and impetuous feelings.

"I should be an independent woman and decline," she said, pleased that her voice sounded like a grownup and not a hormonally charged teenager. "But my back is killing me. So, here." She hung the diaper bag on his shoulder. He picked up the seat with his left hand. They said good-bye to Lily's family and left the cafeteria.

"So, you went to high school here?" Dean asked as they walked slowly through the halls.

"I did. My brother and sister did. Probably ninety percent of the adults in that cafeteria did. My dad was in the first graduating class from this 'new' building."

"Deep roots."

"Yeah, I guess so."

He said in a distracted tone, "These people probably know you better than anyone in Boston."

She slowed. "I suppose that's right." She'd never thought of it that way; it did seem odd. She'd lived in Boston for ten years, yet she could tell him more about the people in that cafeteria who were no more than passing acquaintances than about anyone she knew in Boston.

The wall outside the principal's office was lined with plaques. Dean stopped. "You on any of these?"

"A single-focused overachiever like me? You have to ask?" She couldn't help but grin.

"Hmm. Let me see. . . ." He stepped closer, so he could read the names. "Probably not on 'Boys Track and Field.' "

"No, but you'll find my brother there for state champion in pole vault."

"So, you're not the only overachiever in the family."

"Luke was athletically gifted—not academically dedicated."

"Ooooh. Do I sense a little sibling rivalry?" He narrowed his eyes as he looked at her. "And with your *brother*."

She laughed, shaking her head. "I'm just stating the facts. Luke is a great guy, very bright, just didn't like to study. Believe me, I'm not in the least jealous of his life."

"What does he do?"

"Until recently, he was an army Ranger."

"What made him give it up?"

"An accident. Messed up his knee and took him out of the field. Then he fell in *lo-ove*—" Molly batted her eyelashes and gave the word as much prepubescent drawl she could muster. "Now he lives in Mississippi with a wife, a brother-in-law and the biggest bloodhound you've ever seen."

"You sound like you don't believe in *lo-ove*."

"My current circumstance makes my belief in love a moot point."

He glanced at the baby he was carrying; he obviously understood her comment. "No love . . . before?"

She gave an exaggerated huff. "I thought we covered that territory already. My stand remains the same: None of your business."

He looked apologetic. "Sorry. Male curiosity."

"You want to know if I fall into bed with just anyone? Scouting out your chances?" she said with a flippancy she didn't feel.

He appeared aghast. "Damn, woman, I said I was sorry. I'm just trying to make conversation." Then he added, "And we were talking about *love*, not sex."

She raised her hands in the air. "I guess I'm overly sensitive tonight—people around here aren't used to my . . . situation, yet."

Realization shone in his eyes. "Not quite like Boston."

"That was the whole reason I moved. I just forgot some things about small towns."

He smiled. "You're one of theirs. They'll forgive you." Then he directed his attention back to the plaques. "Let's see here . . . I'll bet this is the one with your name: 'Valedictorian.'" He read down the list. "Bingo!"

"Enough of that." Molly nudged him forward with a mingling of pride and embarrassment in her chest.

When they stepped outside into the dark evening, it was raining. Molly threw a protective blanket over Nicholas. "My car's just over there." She pointed to the first row in the lot.

They trotted side by side to the Jetta, standing water in the parking lot splashing knee-high with every step. She opened the back door for him to put Nicholas in.

He ducked inside, then she heard his muffled voice say, "How in the heck does this thing work?"

She ran around to the other side and opened the back door. Kneeling on the seat, she fastened the baby securely in place. "There. Looks more complicated than it is." She leaned over, pulled away the damp blanket and gave Nicholas a noisy smooch on his cheek. "Sweet boy. Didn't get wet at all, did you?"

Then she asked, "Where's your car parked? I can drive you to it."

He looked a little sheepish in the light from the dome of the car. "It's on the square."

She gave a disbelieving tilt of her head. "The square?"

"I wanted to get a feel for the neighborhoods, so I parked there and walked. I didn't know it was going to rain."

"You'd better get in then. You'll be drowned by the time you get to the square."

"I should be a macho man and decline," he said, throwing her words back at her with a grin, "but I hate wet socks. So. . . ." He got out of the back and climbed in the front passenger seat.

As soon as the car doors were closed, the windows began to fog over. Molly started the car and turned the heat up and the defroster on. "This kind of weather makes me want hot apple cider."

Dean nodded with a boyish grin on his face. "My mom made the best hot cider. It was Grandma's recipe, she had an orchard upstate." Then he added with a hint of mystery in his voice, "It uses a very important secret ingredient."

"Ooh, what is it?"

He looked shocked that she would ask. "It's *secret.*"

She chuckled, "You don't even know yourself."

"Oh, but I do." After a second, he said, in a voice filled with reminiscence, "I haven't had hot cider for years." He made a little smacking sound with his lips. "Tell you what, if you go by the grocery store, I'll buy the stuff and make it for us."

Before she even thought about it, she said, "And I'll make oatmeal cookies." She nearly moaned, "Hot cider and oatmeal cookies."

"Deal. But you can't go into the store with me, that'd give away the secret ingredient. If you need anything for the cookies, I'll get it."

It sounded like so much fun that Molly refused to let her usual pragmatism interfere. "Deal."

The windshield was finally clear. She turned on the wipers, put the car in drive and headed out of the lot. It was one of those gloomy fall nights that gobbled up head-light beams and made roads unpredictably slick. The rain was knocking the few remaining leaves off the trees. They fell limply through the light of the streetlamps into dark puddles, making it seem that much colder outside. She shivered and could almost taste the cider already.

Molly said, "We'll swing by the grocery first, that way I can let you off at the door. Then we'll get your car." She cast a glance at him; he had a strong jaw, and lean cheeks that looked even leaner in the odd light coming through the rain-streaked glass. He was an easy man to look at.

She said, "I should warn you, I don't have any furni-ture. I have a big empty fireplace and no logs. It'll just be you, me and the kitchen table."

"What more do we need?" Then he asked, "You *do* have a stove?"

She laughed. "Yes, it's not quite that bleak at our house."

"Okay, then."

The rain increased as they drove toward Kingston's Market. Molly stopped to let Dean off at the store en-trance. When he opened his car door, she thought she heard the same single violin she'd heard the other night.

From the look on Dean's face, he heard it too.

"How can that music carry through the rain?" he asked.

"Must have to do with the hills." She had no idea if

that was true, but there didn't seem to be any other explanation for that faint music overriding the pelting rain.

He held her gaze for a moment. His face was taut with seriousness. "Maybe it's because it's not really of this earth," he said eerily.

"Oh, shut up and get out of the car."

He was laughing as he did.

He could laugh all he wanted; that music was creeping her out. In her entire childhood, as much as she'd *wanted* to hear the legendary music, she never had. Now, two days in a row, she'd heard it floating around. Weird.

Dean emerged a few minutes later with a brown paper bag and a plastic gallon jug of cider. When he opened the car door, Molly listened intently, but didn't hear any hint of the mystery melody.

He kept the bag on his lap and set the jug between his feet on the floor of the car. "Prepare those taste buds for a treat."

"You're sounding pretty cocky there, Chef Coletta."

"Well, I don't like to brag. . . ."

"So I see." She drove out of the lot and headed back toward the center of town.

The wind picked up, driving the rain in sheets. The windshield wipers were having a hard time keeping up with the downpour. Molly kept cautiously below the speed limit.

About halfway to town, an SUV raced up behind her, then swung out, passing her on the left.

She clucked her tongue. "If I had a dollar for every stitch I put in an SUV owner who thought four-wheel-drive made them invincible, I'd have my student loans paid off."

She'd no sooner gotten the words out when the brake-lights flared and the SUV swerved, skidding off into a shallow ditch on the right.

"Watch it!" Dean needlessly shouted.

She hit the brakes and saw what made the truck swerve in the first place. Her car came to a stop only a handful of yards before the bicycle that lay in the road. An orange triangular flag stuck straight up on its flexible plastic shaft. The front wheel was still spinning, its yellow reflector a racing circle in the headlights.

She turned on the hazard flashers and jumped out of the car, leaving the driver's door open. "I have flares in the trunk," she shouted before she sprinted toward the bicycle.

Dean was amazed that her reactions were quicker than his. He was still buckled in his seatbelt and she was out and running. He glanced at the car seat in the back. He didn't like the idea of leaving this car in the driving lane with the baby in it.

He looked out the windshield. Molly was on her knees on the left side of the road.

He quickly got out and ran around to the driver's seat. He moved the Jetta to the shoulder, then got the flares out of the trunk and put them several yards behind them on the road.

A man got out of the SUV and ran toward Dean.

"I didn't see him! I swear! This rain. . . ."

Dean shouted, "Did you call for help?"

"What?" The man appeared dazed, but unhurt.

"A cell phone! Call nine-one-one!"

"Yes. My wife's in the car—she's calling."

Dean looked back at the Jetta with Nicholas sleeping

inside, then to Molly ten yards away, moving with frantic desperation beside the bicycler. The bicycler wasn't moving at all.

Dean swiped the rain out of his eyes. "Take one of those flares and make sure you flag any car coming this way. We don't want anyone else run over."

"Right," the man said, then he hurried to the first flare that Dean had set in the road.

Dean sprinted to Molly with another flare in his hand. He dropped it on the edge of the road beside her.

"I need some light!" she shouted. "Plastic case in the trunk."

He ran back and was relieved the baby wasn't crying when he opened the car door and checked. He popped the trunk and grabbed the kit. When he reached Molly again, he dropped to one knee and opened the case. Once he found the flashlight, he shone it on the victim's face. He was surprised when it was a grizzly old man and not a kid. Rain matted his long wiry gray hair where it stuck out from under a knit watch cap. His eyes were closed. His jaw jutted at a grotesque angle. And there was a *lot* of blood.

Molly was doing something in his mouth. She didn't stop when she said, "His leg. Check his leg. I think he has a fracture that broke the skin. I need to know how much he's bleeding. But don't touch it without gloves!"

Dean shifted, ran the light beam down each of the man's legs. On the right thigh a jagged, bloody bone protruded through the torn pant leg. The grisly sight stole his breath momentarily. He tried to detach himself, to think of it clinically, assess the damage. He moved quickly, his war zone instincts finally up to full speed.

"It's a femur fracture. Through the skin. Can't tell about the blood, too much rain," he said.

"Jaw's broken, I need to keep his airway open," Molly said. "Put on some gloves. Take the heel of your hand and apply pressure at the top of his broken leg—groin area. Then try to feel with your other hand if warmth is still flooding under his leg."

Dean did as she said, all the while unable to vanquish the picture of his own blood puddling on that hotel floor.

"I don't know if I'm helping." He could be missing the artery by a mile for all he knew. When he tried to probe under the man's leg to feel for a warm flow of blood, the rain and the pavement were so cold, nothing felt warm.

"Just keep the pressure there. Has anyone called for help?"

"Yes."

Then he heard her curse. "Lost his pulse." She shouted, "You know CPR?"

"Yeah."

"I need you to do chest compressions. It's going to take both my hands to keep the airway open."

"What about the leg?"

"Leave it! In the kit, a plastic pouch, hand me the Rescue-Breather—flat plastic sheet with a valve in it."

Dean handed it over, then took his position on the other side of the man ready to give compressions.

She put on the mouth barrier and gave the man two breaths. Dean felt the chest rise under his waiting palms. Then she counted his compressions.

With both of his hands occupied, the rain ran unchecked into his eyes. He really couldn't see, but he was working by feel anyway.

They'd gone through the breath/compression rotation fourteen times when Dean finally heard a siren.

"Stop." Molly checked for a pulse. Just as she had the last two times, she shook her head and they resumed CPR.

When the paramedics arrived, Dean quickly moved out of the way. He was surprised when Molly did too. She removed the resuscitation barrier, identified herself as a doctor and shouted some medical jargon at them as she stepped back. Then she looked at the blood on her hands—her *ungloved* hands.

At that moment, the magnitude of what she'd just done struck Dean. It hit him in the pit of his rolling stomach. In this age of biohazards and latex gloves, Molly had opened a man's airway with no protection. The guy looked like a bum—who knew what diseases he was carrying? Molly could see it just as easily as Dean had. Still, she hadn't hesitated when she saw what needed to be done. Her selflessness awed him. But it also made him afraid for her.

He watched the properly protected paramedics go to work. He stepped closer to Molly. "Aren't you more qualified than them?"

She shook her head. "Not for trauma at a scene like this. I usually have more help . . . more equipment." She stared with her arms crossed over her stomach as the trauma team worked.

After a moment, she reached into the paramedic's kit and pulled out a bottle. Dean watched as she squirted a solution over her hands and rubbed them vigorously together. Then she looked at him.

He held up his still gloved hands. Then he removed the

gloves, tossing them next to the medics for proper disposal.

Two county sheriff's cars arrived with lights and sirens. Molly didn't take her eyes away from the rescuers working on the man.

Dean went over to talk to the police and check on the baby, who by some miracle was still sleeping.

When he returned he asked, "Why aren't they loading him up and getting him to a hospital?"

"They have to get him stabilized enough to move him."

Suddenly, the feet of the man on the ground started thumping against the ground, even the one at the end of the horribly broken leg.

Molly leaned forward, ready to shout something, when one of the paramedics injected something into the man. She backed up. Whatever it was seemed to stop the seizure.

Dean put an arm around her shoulder.

She turned toward him. "He's not going to make it." There was true regret in her eyes.

As Dean looked at her face, he saw a dark streak of blood mixed with the rain. He unbuttoned his soaked shirt and took the tail to wipe her cheeks. She stood there like a child in the rain and let him do it. Last he gently dabbed her lips.

"That's it!"

Molly jumped at the paramedic's words.

The rescuer sat back on his haunches. He looked at Molly. "He's gone."

She stood stiffly for a moment, her head bobbing slightly in affirmation. Then she closed her eyes. For a second Dean thought she was going to topple over, he put his hands on her shoulders. She let out a long quivering breath, then opened her eyes and said, "Dammit."

Then she leaned into him for a moment. His arms went around her as the rain continued to drench them. He pressed his lips against her wet hair and she trembled slightly.

Suddenly, her head snapped up. "Nicholas!" She broke free and sprinted to the car.

Dean was right behind her. "I've been checking on him."

Molly yanked open the back door and climbed next to the baby. Now she was shaking violently. "I can't believe I did that—I just *left* him."

"You left him with *me*," Dean said.

She didn't seem to hear. The self-incriminating look on her wet face appeared even more heartbreaking in the garish parade of blue and red lights that pulsed across it. Her hand hovered over the baby's sleeping head, a touchless caress. She was careful not to let water from her saturated coat sleeve drip on him.

Dean stood in the rain beside the open door for a minute, watching her.

Then she looked at Dean. "Will you drive?"

He closed the door, then made sure the police had all of the contact information they needed. One of the deputies told Dean they couldn't leave the scene yet.

"That woman just put herself at risk trying to save that man." Dean pointed to the Jetta. "She's drenched and freezing and has a baby in the car. I'm taking her home. You know where to find her if you need anything else."

He didn't wait for a rebuttal.

*   *   *

Mickey looked at her watch. It was going on thirty minutes since her mother had *promised* for the fourth time that she'd be right there. The crowd was thinning. The volunteers were beginning the clean up. Mom was back to talking to Mr. Mitchell again. Drew had long since left with his crew for a night of sneaking beer in the Boswells' basement.

There was no sense in prodding her mother again, that would just lead to a lecture once they got home about how Mickey had *no* social skills, and how utterly *embarrassed* her mother had been over Mickey's rudeness. If it weren't raining cats and dogs outside, she'd just walk home. It would be great to have a car of her own. She was saving her babysitting money, but she knew it'd probably never go for a car. College tuition was going to be much more important; the car would only offer short escapes, college would be the real thing.

As long as she was going to be stuck here while her mother exercised *her* social skills, Mickey decided she might as well make herself useful. She started helping stack unused chairs so the floor could be mopped. Riley was doing the same thing, but on the other side of the cafeteria. With the room between them, Mickey felt she should be fairly safe from catching another dose of the cold shoulder. But it was hard not to look at him. She missed their friendship—it had actually been better before she met him, then she hadn't known what she was missing.

Why did guys have to be such jerks?

Riley, of course, hadn't cast a single glance her way, even when she started stacking chairs. He did, however, make plenty of eye contact with Codi Craig, who had perched herself, legs crossed, on the table where the cash had been taken. She swung her foot and leaned back on one arm, giving everyone a better view of her navel ring—which was forbidden to see the light of day during school hours. Apparently the principal, Mrs. Beaver, didn't have the authority to enforce the dress code at a public dinner.

Two girls stopped to talk to Codi. Mickey was close, but not close enough to hear their conversation clearly.

Then Codi spoke louder. "No, thanks, I'm waiting for Riley. We're going to hang out by the dam."

Even someone as uncool as Mickey knew that's where everybody parked and made out. Mickey pretended she didn't hear.

The other girls said something that Mickey really couldn't hear, followed by girlish giggles. Nothing got under Mickey's skin as much as stupid giggling.

Then Codi said loudly, "Could be . . . if he doesn't make me wait much longer."

More giggling.

Mickey's ears started to burn; she was glad she wore her hair down tonight. She moved farther away.

Out of the corner of her eye, she saw Codi get up and walk over toward Riley.

Mickey knelt down to wipe up a puddle of spilled lemonade from the floor. From there she could watch without being seen. Codi leaned close to Riley and whispered something in his ear.

He stopped in mid-motion, surprise on his face. Then he broke out in a grin—and *his* ears turned red.

The girls next to the cash table twittered like a couple of ninnies.

Codi took a single step back and looked at Riley for a minute, then turned around and walked back to her friends.

Riley started moving faster.

Codi returned to her perch. She caught sight of Mickey and gave her a catty smile before Mickey could turn away. It was all Mickey could do to keep herself from bitch-slapping her.

She walked to the trash can, threw away the paper towels she'd been using to wipe up the spill and kept on walking right out the cafeteria door. Who gave a shit if it was raining?

Molly was silent all the way home. She didn't say anything when Dean drove straight to her house. At this point he didn't really care if she questioned how he knew where she lived. For two days, he'd been fighting the obvious, trying to find deceit where there was none, cunning where there was nothing but an honest woman in a difficult situation. He'd recognized the type of person she was at their first meeting and hadn't trusted his own instincts. But that all ended tonight. There was no way a woman who acted as selflessly as Molly did could have had anything to do with his sister's murder.

He'd already engaged his investigator to dig into Molly's finances, see if there had been any big loan pay-offs or unexplained deposits into her bank accounts. It was too late to stop it, so he'd just see what turned up. Still, he knew, Molly was not criminally involved.

Now he had to decide. Would he finish this charade and creep quietly out of town? Or would he admit his duplicity to Molly, hope she wouldn't kick his ass; that she'd take pity on him and share a glimpse into his sister's last days? He just didn't know.

With the stopping of the car, Nicholas began to make little noises that reminded Dean of a kitten.

Dean got out and opened the back door as Molly unfastened the baby seat. As she stood, a litter of soiled baby wipes fell from her lap to the ground.

He bent to pick them up.

"I didn't want to risk getting blood on the baby's things." Then she started to lean back toward the car to get Nicholas.

Dean put a hand on her shoulder and stopped her. "Go on and unlock the door. I'll get him."

She looked up at him. "He's gonna cry."

"I can take it."

She gave him a doubtful look, but stepped away from the car. Just as Dean stuck his head inside to lift out the seat, Nicholas found his voice.

By the time they reached the front door, he was in full fury. Molly turned the light on in the kitchen. As Dean walked through the living room, he realized she hadn't been exaggerating about the place being bare. There wasn't a stick of furniture or a TV in it. He followed Molly into the kitchen and set the baby seat on the table.

Molly looked at the front of her clothes.

Dean read her concern and checked his own. The only blood on him was on the tail of the shirt he'd used to wipe Molly's face. He said, "You go on and clean up. I'll take care of the baby. What does he need? Diaper? Bottle?"

"Both, diaper first. Thanks, I really don't want to touch him like this." She started out of the room. "I hate to impose—"

"Just go. You're starting to shiver again."

She nodded with a grateful look in her eye and left the room.

Dean stripped off the wet and soiled shirt. He checked his T-shirt for signs of contamination before he washed his hands and picked up the crying baby.

Molly stuck her head back into the kitchen. "The bottles are in the fridge." She paused as she ducked back out. "*Can* you do a diaper?"

He made a *pfft* of dismissal. "I've seen commercials. How hard can it be?" He cradled the squalling baby in one arm and picked up the diaper bag with his free hand. The child felt unbelievably small against his ribs.

Molly said, "You can lay him on my bed to change him."

He followed her into her bedroom. At least this room looked like someone lived here. The bed had a sunny yellow comforter, there were a couple of books on the nightstand, and the crib had a colorful mobile hanging over it.

He laid the baby on the bed and dug around in the bag for a diaper and wipes. He looked at Molly, hovering nearby. "Really, I can do this. Get in the shower; your teeth are chattering."

She looked apologetic. "I didn't mean to imply . . . I just . . . oh, never mind. You're doing great." She left the room.

"Thanks." *Great*. He hadn't done anything but put the kid down and locate a dry diaper. Pretty hard to screw that up.

He unsnapped the sleeper and wrangled the baby's feet free, then pulled the tape tabs of the old diaper and took it off. Nicholas was red all over from crying. He stiffened his little legs. Dean couldn't believe something so small could be so strong. Those legs were like two boards glued together, making it impossible to shove the bulky diaper between them.

Dean looked over his shoulder to make sure Molly hadn't snuck back in to watch the show. They were alone. Dean got an idea; he rubbed the baby's tummy trying to get him to relax. "Come on, little guy. Give me a break here."

Nicholas cried louder and peed all over the front of Dean's T-shirt.

"Whoa!" Dean flipped the dry diaper over the baby too late to save much of the mess. He screwed his mouth to the side. "That wasn't fair. A sneak attack—totally ungentleman-like. Is that the kind of man you want to grow up to be?"

Nicholas quieted and kicked his legs.

"Ah! That's the way." Dean shoved a new diaper under Nicholas's bottom. After getting the tape stuck on the baby twice, Dean managed to get the diaper affixed in a close proximity to where he thought it should be. When he picked the baby up, he saw the wet spot on the comforter. He dabbed it with a couple of Kleenex and hoped it would dry before Molly noticed. Then he went to the kitchen to get a bottle.

Nicholas was sucking his fist, apparently not overly judgmental about the diaper job.

When Dean pulled the bottle out of the refrigerator, he realized Molly hadn't said anything about heating it. Weren't baby bottles supposed to be warm—something about putting the milk on the inside of your wrist to make sure it wasn't too hot? He looked around the kitchen.

There didn't seem to be anything that shouted "bottle warmer" to him.

Nicholas was becoming unhappy with the fist. Before he started yowling again, Dean went to the bathroom door and knocked.

"Sorry!" he shouted. "How do I warm the bottle?"

"What?"

"The bottle," he yelled louder. "How do I warm it?"

The baby broke into a howl.

The door opened just a crack. Molly's hair was lathered and she had a towel wrapped around her that didn't cover very much.

Dean cleared his throat. "Um. I don't know how to warm the bottle."

"Hot tap water in a pan. Just let it sit for a couple of minutes and give it a shake."

"Right." He turned around before she caught him staring at things he shouldn't.

By the time Molly entered the kitchen several minutes later, dressed in a light blue sweatsuit and bare feet, Dean was sitting at the table proudly feeding a very happy baby.

Molly raised her brows and gave a nod. "Well done, Mr. Coletta."

He was pleased with the praise. "I wrapped him in this blanket, trying to keep him from getting too wet from my shirt."

She smiled and tilted her head slightly to one side. She looked like a kid standing there, barefoot with wet hair and no make-up. Suddenly he wanted to hold *her*.

She sat down heavily in a chair across from him, looking very tired. As she pushed her hair away from her face, she said, "You must be freezing."

Lifting a shoulder he said, "Nothing a little hot cider won't fix."

Her eyes widened slightly. "I'd forgotten about the cider . . . and your car! I'm sorry, I've been holding you hostage here."

"I'm not planning on going anywhere for a while. Not until I've demonstrated my cider-making prowess." And he realized in that moment, he'd much rather spend the evening here in this barren house with Molly than in his own warm and comfortable cottage alone.

"Burp," Molly said.

"Pardon me?"

"It's time for a burp."

He tried to pull the nipple from the baby's mouth, but Nicholas sucked harder. "He won't let me."

Chuckling, she said, "He's not the boss."

"But he'll be mad."

"If you don't, he'll have a bellyache and *I'll* be mad. Who are you more afraid of?"

He looked at her seriously for a long moment. Then he looked at the baby. Then back at her. Finally he said, "Him."

She laughed. "Wrong answer." She put out her hands and stepped forward. "Do you want me to take him?"

"Nope. I like to finish a task once I start it." He scrunched up his face. "Here goes." He took the bottle away and Nicholas began to fuss.

"Up on the shoulder," Molly coached.

Dean shifted the baby and before he even got him to his shoulder, Nicholas let out a robust burp.

"Damn, I'm good," Dean said with a satisfied look on his face.

Molly said, "Yes, it's all in the technique, Dr. Spock. I'm going to dry my hair." She left the room.

As Dean finished feeding Nicholas, thoughts of another baby crept into his mind. Where was Julie's child? Was it being well cared for? Worry pinched a place deep in his heart. Now that he realized he was looking in the wrong place for his sister's killer, he needed to find a new direction as quickly as possible. Somewhere, there was a child as tiny and helpless as the one he held in his arms that needed him.

A squeaking noise signaled the end of the formula.

Dean put the baby on his shoulder. "Time for another burp."

Molly came back in the room. "Weren't you two doing that when I left?"

Dean patted the baby's back. "We ran out of milk. What if he's still hungry?"

"Trust me, if you fed him any more, it'd be running down your shoulder right now."

Nicholas rewarded Dean with another burp, followed by a warm wet feeling on his shoulder. "I think it did anyway."

Molly took the baby. "Think of it as a christening. Now you're duly qualified to feed a baby."

Dean suddenly felt like a traitor for taking pleasure in feeding this baby when his own niece or nephew might be hungry. That thought surprised him, but not for the reason he would have expected: he had been *enjoying* himself.

She looked at his T-shirt. "If you want, you can put

that in the dryer. It's in the basement. I'm going to give this guy a bath." She threw him a challenging look. "Wanna help?"

"No, thanks. I think I've added enough new skills to my repertoire for one evening. I'll make the cider. That way I'll be sure you're not peeking and discovering the secret ingredient."

She paused on her way out the kitchen door and asked, "Will you feel too cheated if I renege on the cookies?"

"Not if you promise to make them another time," he said. Suddenly he felt oddly sad; there most likely wouldn't be another time.

Chapter 12

Codi kept her eyes on Riley while he stacked chairs. Before he finished she was shifting with impatience. He knew she was getting pissed, but what was he supposed to do? He couldn't take off before the clean-up was finished, not with his mom right here.

He worked as fast as he could, his urgency fueled by Codi's whispered promise. He finished his job, then helped Clay haul trash out to the Dumpster to move things along more quickly. Finally, his mom gave him the nod of approval to leave.

He grabbed his jacket and Codi met him at the cafeteria door. They held hands as they raced to his car through the rain. There really weren't too many left in the parking lot, so when they got inside and Codi leaned across and kissed him, he wasn't too worried. But then she slid closer and added some tongue. He felt her breasts press against him and he about shot out of his pants.

When she put her hand between his legs, he started to get nervous. His mom and Clay hadn't come out yet. The last thing he wanted to think about tonight was a lecture from his mom about how girls should be "respected." This whole thing was Codi's idea, after all. He hadn't asked for it . . . directly.

Codi had him all but coming by the time she slid back to her seat.

She smiled, dipping her head shyly. "Let's swing by Papa's to see if Jen and Jeff are there."

"Why?" What they were going to do didn't require company.

"Because I need to tell her something." Codi sounded like she was bordering on getting her panties in a bunch.

"Use your cell." He wasn't sure he could wait until they got out to the dam, let alone drive all over hell's half-acre looking for Jen.

"Riley!"

"Okay." He didn't want to piss her off and have her change her mind. He started the car and pulled out of the parking lot.

He didn't buy her story for a second. There wasn't anything that urgent that she had to tell Jen. She was punishing him for making her wait by making him wait. Not that getting what she promised wasn't worth driving around and wasting a little gas.

He'd just turned onto Grant Street when Codi said, "Oh, look! There's Mickey." She pointed to a lone figure hurrying along the sidewalk, huddled against the rain.

"It is not."

"Slow down!"

Thinking he was in danger of splashing a puddle all over the person, he braked.

Codi rolled down her window. "Mickey! Hey, Mickey!"

When the girl on the walk turned, Riley saw it was Mickey. He felt like sliding down in his seat, hiding. Not that it would do any good—he had the only Mustang in school.

Riley hissed, "Shut up!"

Codi ignored him and called, "You want a ride home? C'mon, get in!"

Mickey raised a hand.

Was she giving them the finger? Riley's mouth fell open.

"Bi-a-tch!" Codi yelled. She rolled up her window. "Go on. You just can't be nice to some people. She is such a freakin' *loser*."

When the Mustang accelerated past, Mickey's brief sense of victory leached away in the rain. Shame replaced it. What was wrong with her? She wasn't acting any better than those stupid girls at school. It really wasn't like her to flip people off. Even if they deserved it as much as Codi Craig did.

Still, she felt embarrassed doing it in front of Riley. *He* knew she was a better person than that.

As she stepped off the curb at Sycamore Street, she stomped as hard as she could into a puddle. Cold, muddy water shot up her pant leg and flooded her already soggy shoe.

She trudged on, her left shoe squishing loudly with every step.

She was so pissed at herself. Why did she give a rat's ass what Riley Holt thought of her? He sure wasn't giving *her* any thought. She didn't, she told herself. She didn't care what he thought, who he hung out with, or who was going to give him a blow job out at the dam.

Suddenly, she was short of breath and a little dizzy. Maybe she'd given herself a stroke or something. She nearly sat down right where she was, on the brick retention wall at the edge of the sidewalk in front of Mrs. Jacobi's house. It didn't matter if she went home, or stayed out in the rain all night. Nobody cared.

A huge lump stuck in her throat. She walked on, raising her face to the rain so she could deny her tears.

By the time Molly had Nicholas bathed, sung to, and put down in his crib, the entire house smelled like mulled cider. When she stepped into the living room, another surprise awaited her. There was a crackling fire in the fireplace.

Dean sat on the floor in front of the hearth, the flickering flames lighting the angles of his handsome face. It caught the gold in his hair, which had curled from his dousing in the rain. It was strange, how comfortable she felt with him—especially considering their initial meeting. Maybe it was because he was so comfortable with himself. She studied him for a long moment, until he looked up and caught her at it.

She put her hands on her hips and said, "Please tell me you're not burning my kitchen table."

With a shake of his head, he alleviated her fear. "You've had enough trauma for one night. Burning your only stick of furniture would be too cruel." He lifted his chin in the direction of the Fultons' house. "I *borrowed* some firewood from your neighbor."

Molly thought of Karen's cruel words to her daughter and of the lonely girl who had joined them for dinner. "Good. I hope she misses it."

The wind blew rain against the window, the sound giving Molly a little chill.

Dean beckoned her. "Come and sit down and warm up by the fire. You look exhausted."

She was exhausted. Since her shower, she felt completely drained. She sat next to him and he handed her a mug.

"Your cider, as promised," he said with a smile that warmed her as much as any fire.

She took it, trying not to notice her fingers brushing his as she did. Breathing in the steam rising from the mug, she moaned. "Heavenly." Then she looked at him and said, "Let me see if I can guess the secret ingredient."

Dean leaned back on his elbows, the damp shirt clinging to his chest. "Sure. Go ahead. But if you do, you'll have to marry me and become an official Coletta. Can't let the secret out of the family."

"There you go, flirting again." She tried not to look at the definition of his chest muscles.

"I don't flirt."

She raised a brow and gave him a disbelieving look.

He sat up. "I don't."

"Whatever." She closed her eyes and drew in the vapor again. "Cider . . . orange . . . cinnamon . . . ." Opening her eyes, she started to look into the cup.

Quickly, he put his hand over the top. His fingers were practically against her lips. "No fair. Nose and taste buds only."

She gave him a suspicious look. "I think you're making the rules up as we go."

He lifted a shoulder, leaving his hand lingering on the cup and near her mouth. She had the totally improper impulse to kiss his fingers. She resisted—barely. He did have incredibly nice hands.

"They're my rules," he said cockily. "I can make them whenever I please."

"*Humph.*" She looked down her nose at his fingers. "Well, I can't use either with your hand over the cup."

He held her gaze for a moment before he moved it away.

Closing her eyes again, she took a tiny sip and let it rest on her tongue. Then she drew air in through her nose and her mouth at the same time. She swallowed. "Cloves."

"So far you've guessed all of the *standard* ingredients."

"Hey, I'm working my way along here. Have I been wrong yet?" she asked smartly.

"You're not looking in that cup, are you?"

"I'm no cheater. Once I know the rules, I play by them. Besides it's so dark in here, I couldn't see anything floating around in there if I tried."

He scooted nearer and looked into her cup. He was so close, Molly could feel the warmth from his skin, the moisture evaporating from his damp clothes in the heat of the fire. She stared at the top of his head for a long moment, tempted to reach out and curl her fingers into his hair. It was a fascinating mixture of colors, deep brown underneath, sun-lightened to a hundred shades between brown and blond. And it curled slightly and fell so temptingly over his forehead since they'd been out in the rain.

Then he raised his gaze to meet hers and she flinched guiltily.

"Just checking to make sure you really can't see anything in there," he said softly.

"I think you have trust issues, Mr. Coletta." The words came out much more slowly than she'd planned. Now it sounded like she was flirting . . . and maybe she was.

He raised a hand and rested it on the side of her face.

Her heart responded with a double beat. The skin beneath his fingers tingled as if a spontaneous current passed between them. She felt like an eighth grader again.

He held her gaze and said, "I saw you do an incredible thing on that road tonight. I'm convinced I can trust you."

With slowness that heightened Molly's anticipation, he kissed her. It was sweet and tender and filled with respect.

When he pulled away, Molly said, "But he died." She'd known the outcome was doubtful when she'd begun to attend the man, but it still felt like failure to lose him. She hated failure more than anything—and to receive praise for it was unthinkable.

"That wasn't your fault. It was the fault of the guy who ran him over—I *don't* trust him."

She smiled and looked into the fire, her heart suddenly aching with the stark reminder of her inadequacies.

"What's wrong?" Dean asked softly.

She shook her head and kept her gaze fixed on the fire.

Then he touched her, sliding his hand under her hair on her neck. "Tell me."

Tears blurred the flickering flames. "I did a horrible thing—I got out of that car and ran to help a stranger without a *thought* to my son in the back seat."

"You acted on instinct."

"That's what frightens me. My first instinct should have been for his safety. I acted as a doctor—not a mother."

"You knew I was with him."

She turned her glistening gaze on him. "Did I? Did I *think* at all? What if I'd been alone?"

He leaned closer, so close his breath was warm on her cheek when he said, "You did the right thing in the circumstance—which was a man dying on the road and me inside the car with your baby. If that man had lived . . . would you be feeling this way?"

How could he see so clearly into her heart? "I don't know."

His hand moved her hair behind her shoulder, then his thumb traced the line of her jaw. The hunger he sparked in her threatened to come forth without her permission. His gentle touch felt undeniably good—dangerously so. She wanted to sink into these feelings, to let them obliterate her doubts and fears.

No. She needed to keep her wits—and his nearness threatened to snatch them away. Still, she drew strength from his presence and couldn't force herself to put more distance between them. The most she could make herself do was return her gaze to the fire and take a distracting sip of cider. Then she tried to concentrate on the mesmerizing movement of the flames.

She could feel his gaze still on her. But she was afraid to look at him again. Afraid she would fall completely into his strength and absorb it as her own. And she could ill afford to depend on anyone, let alone a man who was leaving town in a few days. Even if he did make the most incredible mulled cider she'd ever tasted.

Then it struck her. "Raspberries!" In her excitement, she sat up straighter and faced him. "Your secret ingredient is raspberries."

Oh, but he was close—close enough to kiss again. She slid backward, putting more space between them.

"Ah." He raised his index finger. "But what *kind* of raspberries? Red? Black?" he asked seriously.

She narrowed her eyes and tilted her head, trying to regain a playful attitude and dissipate some of the desire that lingered in the air. "As I'm not ready to become Mrs. Coletta, I think I'll leave that question unanswered."

"I'm not sure you haven't given up your freedom already. No one's ever guessed raspberries before."

"Even with the berries floating around in there?" she asked disbelievingly. "Why, you probably have five wives already."

He remained looking serious despite her teasing and shook his head. "I always strain them out. No telltale signs to give it away. And *you've* guessed the family secret." He inched closer, making a mockery of her effort to reduce the sexual tension. "So you see . . . you're entirely at my mercy."

That's just the way she felt at the moment, as he held her motionless with a penetrating stare, his eyes a dark blue in the firelight. He was sucking away her self-control; she could feel it draining so rapidly there was probably a raging vortex somewhere around her ankles.

Suddenly she understood, for the first time in her life, how a woman could fall victim to a man's will.

He took the mug from her and set it on the hearth. As he slid his hand behind her neck to pull her closer for another kiss, Molly thought vaguely that she shouldn't be doing this. As his lips touched hers she must have mumbled something to that effect.

Pausing, but remaining a breath away, he said, "Why?"

"Never mind." And she gave into her urge to touch his hair, running her fingers through it as she kissed him. She had never wanted to touch a man as badly as she wanted to have her hands on Dean Coletta. *Which proved his gaze must have hypnotic powers. Probably something he learned in the Middle East.*

He stopped kissing her, but held her face close to his. "Will you stop thinking?"

Her brows furrowed. "How do you know I'm—"

He nipped her lower lip. "I *know*. Just let yourself go for a single moment. No thought, just feelings." When he kissed her again, she rode the sensation alone and was astounded at her internal response. Not only was her reaction changed, but his kiss was entirely different too; sweetness succumbed to hunger, desire overrode tenderness, and passion replaced respect.

She wanted more than his mouth. Secret places in her body ached to be touched.

She was breathless when he stopped.

"Wow," she whispered.

"Yeah. I knew it was in there somewhere." He blew out a breath. "We're a dangerous mix, you and me."

Before she could ask him exactly what he meant by

that, he held her close and lay back on the floor. She curled on her side next to him, resting her head on the crook of his shoulder. He held her tightly and kissed the top of her head. She was very thankful he didn't attempt to take them further. In her current state, she wasn't making very good decisions.

She watched the fire and tried to figure out what it was about this man that reached so deeply inside her.

He said softly as he stroked her hair, "You're thinking again."

"Thank goodness."

"I promise not to take advantage of you while your brain is disengaged." He rolled her onto her back and looked into her eyes. "So you can enjoy this."

When his mouth covered hers this time, her brain took immediate leave. She wrapped her arms around him when he trailed kisses down her neck. He nudged away the neckline of her sweatshirt, running his tongue along her collarbone. Just when her body took the driver's seat, cutting off all communication with conscious thought, he returned to her lips for a lingering kiss.

Whispering in her ear, he said, "If I'm going to be a man of my word, we'd better knock it off." Rolling onto his back, he took her with him.

Her mind thanked him while her body screamed in protest. She rested her hand on his chest and her chin on her hand. Looking at the scar on his neck, she said, "Does that give you much discomfort?"

"Not really. It was a fairly clean shot, so they tell me."

She ran her finger lightly along the scar.

He added, "Not that it wasn't dangerous—I *did* almost bleed to death."

"Oh, I'm very glad you didn't."

He laughed. She liked the way it sounded this close to his chest—very masculine.

Then he said, "Me too," as he stroked her hair.

Turning her head to face the fire, she laid her cheek on his chest. The steady thump of his heart echoed in her ear. It made her a little miffed that his was beating so regularly while her own was doing advanced aerobics.

After a second she noticed an odor. Then she buried her nose in his shirt. "You smell like pee."

"Don't suppose anyone ever accused you of being a romantic?"

"Never." She relaxed against his chest once again. "Romance is for dreamers. I live firmly in the real world." Although this little break from reality certainly tempted her to change her ways.

Molly was drifting very near sleep when the telephone rang. She gave a start, drawing in a quick breath as her head came up off of Dean's chest.

"My gosh, what time is it?" she asked as she rubbed her eyes and got up to answer the phone. She'd never fallen asleep in the company of a man—never felt at ease enough to. And here she barely knew Dean.

He looked at his watch. "Eleven." He sounded as groggy as she felt.

Picking up the phone in the kitchen, Molly wasn't overly surprised to hear Lily's voice.

"Sooo—" there was a suggestive lilt to her voice "—did you get home okay? I didn't want to call too soon . . . in case you had company."

Molly decided to put an end to this right now. "As a

matter of fact, I had quite an eventful drive home. There was an accident—"

"Oh my God, are you all right?"

"I didn't say *I* had an accident. A guy on a bicycle was hit by an SUV . . . I tried to help, but he died."

"Jesus, how awful. Do you know who it was?"

"No. An old guy, looked pretty bedraggled."

"Old guy on a bike . . . Buddy Biggs? Remember the Bible-banger who always hung out at the gate after football games trying to save everyone's soul? Was it him? I can't imagine who else would be out on a bicycle on a night like this."

The memory clicked in Molly's brain. Buddy Biggs had ridden around town on his bicycle shouting for people to repent for as long as Molly could remember. When she was a kid, he used to circle the perimeter fence around the park swimming pool on that bicycle, reciting Bible verses at the top of his lungs. She never looked directly at him, for fear of inviting a lecture, so she couldn't say for certain what he looked like, even when she'd lived here. She had always just had a general impression of grubby craziness. He'd seemed ancient then; she'd just assumed he was long gone by now.

"It might have been."

"Dad will be upset."

"Really?" What connection could her father—a bar owner—have with a mentally unbalanced religious fanatic? Dad didn't even go to church.

"Oh yeah. Dad pretty much takes care of the old guy. Leaves a boxed dinner outside the back door of the Crossing House every day at five o'clock. I'm not sure how it all got started—it happened while I was in

Chicago. It's really weird, neither one of them will admit it's going on. Faye doesn't even understand it."

"That's Dad, always looking out for someone else— as long as it's not a family member who 'disappointed' him."

Lily sighed. "You really should call him. You can use this as an excuse."

"I don't need an excuse. Besides, nothing's changed with *me*." She lowered her voice. "I still have a baby and no husband. Can't see what my calling him will do. He can call me."

"I suppose one of these days one of you stubborn mules will budge," Lily said with an uncharacteristic biting tone.

Molly didn't respond.

Lily, in a confrontation-avoiding fashion much more like herself, abandoned that avenue and returned to her original path of discussion. "So, Dean Coletta seems nice."

"Yes." Too nice. In just a couple of days, she'd really grown to like him. In a few more, he'd be gone to New York, or Istanbul, or wherever his job would take him next.

"I think he's interested in you."

"I'm a good small-town coming-home story," Molly said dismissively, trying to keep her voice low enough that Dean didn't hear without tipping her sister off to the fact that he was sitting in her living room.

Although, inside Molly decided she wouldn't mind at all if Dean was truly "interested." But it was all too new to know. Maybe he kissed every woman he spent an evening alone with. Maybe the kisses they shared were ordinary to him, not the sky-rocketing pyrotechnics they were for her.

She finished with, "Besides, *you* thought Brian Mitchell was interested in me."

"Oh, Brian's interested all right. He was very upset that you left the dinner before he had a chance to talk to you."

Molly gave an exasperated sigh. "Honestly, Lily." Maybe her sister was just anxious to get her married off, making the baby less of an issue for gossip.

"You can't fight love," Lily said.

"Yes I can." For some peculiar reason, she thought of the odd music she'd heard while at Kingston's. "Have you ever heard music on Fiddler's Hill?"

Lily laughed softly. "Actually, I think I did once . . . a long time ago."

"Who were you with?" The question came out without thought.

"Clay. We were kids, and I was with Clay. But I'm sure it was just an overactive teenage imagination."

"Probably."

"Why do you ask?"

"I just remembered the old legend and was curious."

"Did you hear it? I think you did. Who were you with?" Lily was picking up steam.

"Uh-oh, gotta go, I hear Nicholas," she lied. "Talk to you later."

Curious. It had to be a fluke—or her imagination.

But Dean had heard it, too.

She brushed away the thought as she returned to the living room and found him standing in front of the fireplace, looking at the only thing sitting on the mantle: her Tinkerbell clock.

Dean leaned his face close to the little glass-domed clock and watched Tinkerbell fly back and forth on her fairy wings. The presence of this childish decoration was a surprising contrast to the pragmatic woman who lived here. He might have guessed she'd bought it for the baby, but it looked old.

He kept an ear on the telephone conversation in the kitchen. He couldn't help it really, the empty house conducted sound like a megaphone. Molly was telling someone about the accident. Then something about her dad. When he heard Molly mention Brian's name, he strained to hear more clearly, but she seemed to be making an effort to muffle her voice. Jealousy nipped at his heart. He tried to logic his way around it, but it remained there like a splinter.

He stared at Tinkerbell, trying to let her soothing motion erase a feeling of possessiveness he had no right to have.

Molly surprised him by speaking; he hadn't noticed her return to the room. "My father gave me that when I was five."

He looked at her, framed by the backlight from the kitchen with her dark hair mussed from their activities on the floor. The sight made him want to finish what they'd started, to make Brian Mitchell disappear from her mind altogether. But he'd made a promise, so he didn't give in, throw her to the floor and ravish her. Instead he ignored his own desire and tried to carry on a conversation like a civilized person. "I met your father."

Straightening, she said, "You did? At the Crossing House?"

"Yeah. Nice man." Dean leaned his shoulder against the mantle and crossed his arms over his chest.

"Yes, he is." There was a grudging tone to her voice.

"You sound . . . unhappy about it."

She crossed the room and stood in front of him, looking at the clock. "He and I are having a hard time at the moment." She took a slim finger and traced the arch of the glass dome.

Dean paused, wondering if she truly wanted to talk about it. He didn't want to ruin what they'd started to build here this evening. He wanted it badly enough, that he'd decided to keep his own admissions to himself for tonight. Molly had had enough to deal with today; she didn't need to know about his lies just yet.

Finally he asked, "Because of the baby?"

"I don't understand it!"

Apparently, she did want to talk about it.

She ran a hand through her hair, looking sweetly distracted. "He's always been so reasonable. We could always talk through things. And he's the first to help most anyone in a bind. But me . . . his own daughter. . . ."

"I imagine it's complicated for him. He has more invested in you than he does in friends and acquaintances. Parents always have ideals in mind for their children. And so far you've delivered. This is probably the first time you've disappointed him in your adult life."

She nodded, biting her lower lip.

Dean went on. "I'm sure he made sacrifices so you could have your education, your career. He doesn't want those sacrifices to be dishonored—which is how he probably saw it at first. Then there's the whole father-daughter relationship—"

"Right now we have *no* relationship."

"Is that the way you want it to be?"

She looked shocked. "Of course not. I came home so Nicholas could grow up with a supportive family."

"Then it's going to be up to you to pull that family back together. Don't wait until it's too late."

"That sounded grim. It's not like he's on his deathbed."

"You never know. Here one day, gone the next. Just look at that guy on the bicycle."

Molly gave a visible shiver and cast her gaze to the fire. In a small voice she said, "How did you get so insightful about parental relationships? You don't even have kids."

"No. I had two parents who were professors of psychology." He pulled her against his chest and held her. It felt so right. How could he have ever thought this woman had led his sister to her death?

And now he was the duplicitous one. What was he going to do about that?

Riley drove past Mickey's house. First he cruised slowly down the street. Then he turned his headlights off and drove along the alley behind her house. Mickey's bedroom was on the second story in the back. Her light was on. He imagined her sitting up there alone, wrapped in an old quilt (Mickey loved old stuff) trying to get warm after walking in the rain, maybe reading one of her thick books—and it made his stomach hurt. Sharp stabbing pains that he hadn't felt in a long time.

He could hardly remember how they used to be together. Mickey was unlike any girl he'd ever met. Honest, opinionated (in a good way, not spoiled), smart. What had seemed so straightforward that first summer had become twisted and knotted into a mess. Everything about Mickey had made him feel confused. He wanted to be with her, but at the same time, the feelings that burned inside him made him afraid.

Now he was older and knew more about those kinds of feelings—but they still made him afraid. It was easier with a girl like Codi, who just wanted to have fun, and who, he knew, would move on to the next guy at some point. Being with Mickey was different. Stuff mattered with her. What if he let himself feel those things for her and she left him? And with all the stuff about her dad, someday she would. One day, when all of the bruises healed and she forgot the fear, she'd stand up and blame Riley for sending him to jail.

When they'd started school after Riley had tricked Mr. Fulton into making a drug deal under surveillance of the sheriff, everything changed. What Riley had thought would bring him and Mickey closer together, ended up tearing them apart. News had spread by September, and Riley started at his new school as something of a hero. The story of the drug bust had been exaggerated by then to the point that even Riley was impressed with what supposedly transpired.

But it had been the opposite for Mickey. She was already different from most kids. She withdrew even further.

Everyone had thought him brave. But he never would have done it if it hadn't been for Mickey. The bruises he'd seen on her collarbone had ignited a fury in him that he'd never experienced. The only thing he could think about was how to keep her dad from doing it again. Even after all that, somehow it seemed wrong to accept praise for ruining her dad and staying close to her at the same time.

And as she slipped away, Riley let her go. Because it was easier to fall into his familiar role of popular guy, class leader, to bury himself in things he knew, than to face his confusing feelings about a girl who changed his entire view of life—at least for one summer. It took a long, painful time for Mickey to completely give up on their friendship. But eventually, he wore her down with his feigned indifference.

For a while his stomach had given him so much trouble, his mother had taken him to the doctor. He'd prescribed something to reduce the acid in Riley's stomach. In time, the pain lessened. Sometimes Riley thought it had more to do with avoiding Mickey than with the medicine, though.

And now the stomach pain was back, worse than ever.

Sitting across from Mickey at the spaghetti supper had been awkward, but it had started him thinking. And most of those thoughts had to do with how much he missed her.

He'd been so furious with Codi for making fun of Mickey that he'd driven her straight home instead of out to the dam like they'd planned. He said he wasn't feeling well—which was true enough. He felt sick.

Codi was pissed. She told him that he'd missed his "chance" with her. Then she slammed the car door so hard, he was afraid she'd crack the glass. Which bothered him more than her being mad. Guess that told him just how much he really cared about Codi.

He drove for a long time. Over and over in his mind, he kept seeing that huddled figure turn, Mickey's pale face in the night, then her defiant gesture that made him want to kick Codi's spoiled ass out to the curb and put Mickey in the warm, safe car instead.

Now he sat in the dark alley, beside the trash cans and the utility poles watching her window like a pervert. What in the hell was wrong with him?

He took his foot off the brake and drove to the end of the alley. Once there, he turned on his headlights and took off so fast that the Mustang's tires spun on the wet pavement.

"Are you sure? Nicholas will be up in a few minutes anyway for a feeding." Molly stood with Dean at her front door.

"It's hardly raining. There's no need for you to drag the baby out." He took a deep breath and released it. "I feel like I could use a walk anyway." *Nothing like a walk in the rain to wash away your sins.*

It was nearly two A.M. He should have been gone hours ago. But he'd been enjoying his time with Molly enough that he deprived her of the few hours of sleep she'd get before the baby needed to be fed again. And for that he was sorry—but not as sorry as he was about what he'd have to tell her the next time they met; that he'd lied about his reason for being here.

He lingered in the doorway, absorbing the expression on her face. That caring look in her eyes would vanish the next time. It would be replaced with wounded betrayal.

But there wasn't a thing he could do about it now. It was too late.

He kissed her on the mouth, committing her taste to memory, then said good night.

She lingered in the open doorway for a long time. He was halfway down the block when he heard the door close in the quiet darkness. The rain had reduced itself to nothing more than thick misty fog that amplified the sounds of his footfalls against the still night.

An alert dog barked inside one house he passed. But no lights followed. Dean supposed it was rare that a person walked the streets at this time of night in Glens Crossing. In fact, he hadn't even seen a car pass—and it was Saturday night.

As he walked, he wondered what it would be like to live in a place like this. Where the night was left to the owls and the tomcats, where high school football was the focus of the Saturday newspaper, where people ate sticky spaghetti and doughy cookies to support their basketball team. Would he die of boredom in a place like this, as he'd always sworn he would? Or would he get caught up in the simple rhythm of life here and open that Saturday paper to see if he knew the kid who caught the winning touchdown pass?

He shoved his hands in his pockets and hunched against the chill. His jeans were damp and chafing; he'd be glad to climb into the claw-footed tub and pull the shower curtain around it. The ceilings were so low in the upstairs of Brian's cottage, he felt like a giant when he stood in the tub, his head almost scraping the ceiling.

Tonight he would welcome that feeling of largeness because he was feeling very small inside. He'd done nothing in coming here but lie to a decent woman. He was just as far away from discovering his sister's killer as he'd been a week ago.

The only chance he had at making something good come of this would be if he could convince Molly to share any detail of his sister's life that she could recall. If he was lucky, he'd find the key in those memories.

Lily sat with her lips pressed tightly together for fear of saying something she'd be sorry for. Clay sat across their kitchen table, his expression as dark and dangerous as she'd ever seen it. She'd thought this was settled right after Molly arrived. Why did he have to be so set on this *now*?

She glanced at the clock. It was nearly midnight. Riley had gone out with Codi after the spaghetti supper and would be home any minute. Lily needed to get this conversation finished.

After taking a calming breath, she said, "I don't see what waiting another couple of months is going to hurt."

Clay's eyes snapped with anger. "A couple of months, and then what? Something else will happen. I've tried to abide by your wishes in this, but we decided *together*. We've already prepared Peter. It's time Riley knows who his real father is. My God, Lily, in a couple of years, he's going to be off on his own. The longer we wait, the more he's going to feel we lied to him."

Her stony gaze met his. "We did. Nothing will change that."

This discussion had always been very painful for the two of them. It was coming around more and more frequently. And it never became less complicated. That seemed to be their lot, a relationship filled with complications.

It had been that way from the beginning, back when they'd been teenagers. Clay and Peter, her ex-husband, had been summer people from Chicago and friends of her brother Luke. Lily had tagged along, pining secretly over Clay for years. Then, the summer she'd been eighteen, everything changed. Clay saw her for the woman she'd become. But they kept their relationship secret throughout the early weeks, knowing it would upset the balance of their friendship with Peter. Not to mention the fact that Clay's wealthy and powerful father would disown him if he became involved with a girl he'd made very clear he thought was trash.

Clay had left her that summer in anger. He had wanted to tell his father, consequences be damned. She'd wanted him to wait another year, until he'd finished college, fearing he'd regret a rash decision. So they argued right before he left for Northwestern in the fall. And then Clay disappeared—completely.

When Lily had called after cooling off for a couple of weeks, Peter, who was also Clay's roommate, said Clay had fought with his father and was now gone.

Lily waited to hear from Clay. Then she discovered she was pregnant and could wait no more.

She confided in their friend, Peter. He admitted his own feelings for her and convinced her to marry him and the three of them, Lily, Peter and the baby, could become a family. And she did love Peter—as a friend. However, what Peter never told her was that he *knew* where Clay was.

So they married. And Lily tried to make it work. But

Peter's secrets soon started eating him alive. Before long he took refuge in alcohol. Living with Peter became much more destructive for her son than living through a divorce, so she made a painful choice and ended the marriage.

But Riley continued to spiral out of control, his exploits becoming more dangerous and more destructive. In desperation, when Riley was thirteen, Lily moved them back here to Glens Crossing, seeking distance from Riley's meddling wealthy grandparents and the stability of a small town life.

She didn't discover the truth of what had happened until she returned, and found that Clay had moved to Glens Crossing the previous year. He *had* told his father about her—and his reaction was far worse than even Clay had anticipated. His father had disowned him completely, recalling money, car, and all clout of the family name.

Clay left his father's house on foot and ended up in a bar on Rush Street. There, while intervening when a man was beating a woman, he was arrested. The other man suffered a knife wound in the process. Unluckily for Clay, the woman sided with the knife-wielding boyfriend and Clay, unable to make bail, sat in jail awaiting trial for nearly a year. His father made good on his promise that Clay was dead to him, refusing help of any kind. Clay thought perhaps his father had even used his influence to make things drag on longer than they would have otherwise. No one crossed Douglas Winters without retribution.

When Clay was finally released, Lily and Peter were already married and Riley had been born. Clay assumed the baby was Peter's. Clay left Chicago, without having spoken to Lily or Peter, the stinging whip of betrayal snapping at his heels.

When Lily and Clay had worked through their painful past and decided to share a future, he'd only asked to be a part of Riley's life. He'd promised to leave the decision of whether or not to tell the boy up to her. But as time passed, Lily knew it was unfair to both Riley and Clay not to have the truth in plain sight. But there never seemed to be a good time to break the news. And the longer she waited, the worse it got.

They had settled on telling him the week that Molly arrived with Nicholas and turned the entire family upside down. Clay had been patient, but his patience was running thin. He'd readied himself; now he wanted it done. Lily still feared the aftermath, she lay awake night after night worrying about it. They'd all been doing pretty well living together. After this, who knew what would happen.

Clay got up and walked around the kitchen table, kneeling beside her chair. He took her hand. When she looked in his face, the anger was gone. What she saw there was much more powerful . . . he, this proud man, was begging her. "Seeing Molly's baby tonight—and the way Riley was with him. It broke something free inside me. I've missed most of his life already. I *need* him to know."

She pulled his head against her chest and kissed it. "I know."

But telling Riley meant telling her father, her brother and sister, Peter's parents. She just didn't want to face it—and she knew she never would. It had to be done. Clay was right; the sooner the better.

"All right," she said with her lips pressed against Clay's hair.

He pulled away and looked into her eyes. The gratitude she saw there made her feel selfish and miserly, refusing him this for so long.

Then he said, "Tonight. When he gets home."

Her heart took flight like a startled bird. It beat frantically against her rib cage, until she feared it would stop beating. *Tonight?* Why couldn't they wait until tomorrow? Even as she thought it, she knew tomorrow would become the next day, then next week, and they'd be back where they started.

Her mouth was dry and her stomach rolled when she said, "Tonight."

She didn't have a moment to recompose herself because she saw Riley's headlights as he pulled into the drive.

Her startled gaze shot to Clay.

He took her hand and squeezed. "It's going to be all right. You'll see." Then he stood behind her chair and put his hands on her shoulders.

Thank God she was sitting; otherwise she would have fallen down.

Riley's car door slammed, then his feet thudded up the back steps.

The instant he threw open the kitchen door, she knew something was wrong. His face held the old anger and tension she thought he'd long since released. But would Clay see it?

Riley started to pass through the kitchen with only a quick, "Good night." But Clay stopped him.

"Riley, sit down for a minute."

Lily wanted to leap out of her seat and stop this, but she knew Clay would just see it as another stalling tactic.

Riley didn't move toward a chair, but hovered in the doorway. "I'm really tired."

Clay's fingers tightened on Lily's shoulders.

Please don't do this now.

After a moment's hesitation, Clay said, "Go on to bed."

Lily nearly fainted from relief.

Clay took his seat at the table again. His face held so much disappointment, Lily wanted to cry.

After Riley's bedroom door closed, Clay said, "Dammit." Then he blew out a long breath. "Obviously, something's wrong."

Lily got up and sat on her husband's lap. She kissed him on the forehead. "You're a good father. Not every man can read a child's mood so quickly." She pushed his hair away from his forehead. "Thank you." She kept her words simple, trying to hide the relief she felt.

Still, Lily knew it was all just borrowed time.

Chapter 13

Molly awakened on Sunday morning to the sound of the soft squirming sounds Nicholas made before he completely woke up. She lay in her bed, looking at the pre-dawn shadows shifting on her walls and listened with her heart near bursting. How could one tiny being fill up one's soul? He was a miracle with every breath he took, in every moment of his being.

She got out of bed and tiptoed over to the crib to watch him come awake in the pale gray light. She nearly held her breath, wanting to capture this instant forever in her heart. His innocence, the gentle sound of his breathing, the way his small fingers clutched as tightly in sleep as if they were holding a treasure of immeasurable worth.

The meaning of that thought suddenly seized her heart. *A treasure of immeasurable worth.* That was exactly what this baby was to her. The daunting responsibility of those first days had faded away and been replaced with a fierce love that she could never have imagined.

Her hand moved gently to cup his head, a perfect fit into the curve of her fingers. This child may not have come from her body, but he was as much a part of her soul as if he had grown in her womb.

His lower lip began to twitch, his breathing grew louder and before he even opened his eyes, his cry broke free.

"Oh, there, there, little one," she whispered as she picked him up and held him to her heart. "Mama's here." She kissed the silky dark baby hair on the top of his head and breathed in that very special scent only to be found on babies. Her hand cupped the back of his head as it bobbled in his effort to hold it upright. Already the sides of his dark hair had worn away, replaced by a much lighter color that said he was going to be a blond. Sarah would have liked that.

"I'll always be here."

She began her day, as she had each one since she moved into this house, as a mother. Her happiness was soon overshadowed by a growing sense of guilt. She was only a mother because Sarah was dead. Nicholas would never know anything about his biological parents. That meant she had a lot to make up for; she couldn't let him down.

That also raised another question; would she tell him the truth? She had arranged for the birth certificate paperwork to be processed in Boston through the defunct clinic with the birth mother as Jane Doe, Nicholas as live birth, Baby Doe, leaving the possibility wide open for the future. It was a question she was ill prepared to answer today. So she tried to forget it for now.

For the rest of the morning, she puttered around; reading the paper, lying on the bed with the baby cradled next to her while she sang all of the old nursery songs she could remember, walking aimlessly around her empty house.

A peculiar restlessness began as an undercurrent to her loving contentment of early morning. It seeped in so quietly she didn't notice the moment of its arrival. It grew until it tainted all else, yet it remained elusive in definition, vague and unnameable.

She stared out the window at the starkly bare tree branches, the browning grass and the dismal mist that wrapped everything in a blanket of chilly dampness. When she caught herself glancing at the silent telephone for the fourth time, she recognized the source of that restlessness. She was sitting around like a teenager waiting for Dean to call. The way he'd looked deep in her eyes last night, respectful kisses that quickly gave way to passion, had all gotten under her skin much more deeply than she'd realized. He'd awakened her to something she was probably going to be missing for the rest of her life. Her sexuality sat like an exposed nerve at just the thought of him.

Well, that was a relationship that was going nowhere fast. So she might just as well push it out of her mind completely. Besides, she had enough to deal with at the moment without getting all emotional over a man.

After realizing she was harboring secret hopes about Dean Coletta, her feelings were as raw as the miserable autumn weather—much too raw to remain alone in this house with only her thoughts and one tiny baby. She got Nicholas and herself ready and headed out the door with no real plan.

She began with a drive around the lake, past the old summer houses owned by out-of-towners, which were mostly closed up for the season; past the marina with its empty slips and storage yard filled with boats awaiting another summer; past Arctic Express—

Oooh, Arctic Express.

Immediately she braked and made a U-turn. She pulled into one of the spaces served by an old-fashioned car hop. For a Sunday afternoon, the place was unusually deserted. Molly supposed not many people wanted ice cream on a wet and dreary day like today.

She unfastened her seat belt and twisted to look at Nicholas. As always when in the car, he was fast asleep.

The server came out of the building with a scowl on her face that said she wasn't happy about being dragged out in the cold. The girl leaned near Molly's open window, with her hands stuffed under her arms, bouncing slightly to keep warm.

"I'll have a hot fudge parfait, extra whipped cream."

"That all?"

"Yes."

The girl trotted back inside and Molly cranked up the heat in her car. She also turned on the CD player loud enough to drown out the fifties and sixties oldies the drive-in had blaring on their outdoor speakers.

When the server returned with her parfait, Molly gave her an overly generous tip. Lily used to work here and the thought of her sister running back and forth in the cold for minimum wage drew on her sympathies.

She dug into the ice cream, not in the least concerned about the fit of her jeans. The stress of the abrupt changes in her life was eating away pounds better than a new gym membership and a low-carb diet combined.

As she listened to a sentimental ballad sung soulfully by Faith Hill, she thought of growing up in this town, of Christmases past, of the family warmth she'd hoped to pass on to Nicholas. Pretty soon, Dean's words started kicking around in her head.

Then it's going to be up to you to pull that family back together.

As much as it galled her, she knew that was exactly what she needed to do. She had to straighten this out before it grew too big to overcome. Her Dad was the second most stubborn person on earth—only surpassed by herself. She was woman enough to admit her own flaw. Was she woman enough to take the first step in mending her damaged relationship with her father?

She thought of the baby sleeping in the back seat and set the half-eaten parfait in the cup holder, then put the car in gear. Within ten minutes, she was sitting outside the Crossing House.

Being the middle of Sunday afternoon, there were few cars in the lot. Faye had been trying to get her father to take Sundays and Mondays off for a year now. But, having the obstinate Boudreau blood running in his veins, her father had fought it tooth and nail. Last Molly heard, Dad was taking every other Monday afternoon off, but not during NFL Monday Night Football season. Which in effect, meant he wasn't taking any time off at all.

Molly could understand his compulsion. She suffered from the same type of fixated drive. If she was in, she was in up to her eyeballs or not at all. That's what had drawn her to the free clinic, she supposed—that pressing need that justified her obsessive commitment. This bar was her father's life, his link to the town, a child in its own right—one he'd raised from infancy like his other children, but this one didn't disappoint and frustrate him by making decisions he couldn't understand.

She could see it much more clearly today. And just a few words from Dean had cut through the bullshit for her.

Maybe I should send Dean to talk to Dad first, too.

She took Nicholas out of the car and went inside. She felt good about it . . . strong.

Up until a couple of years ago, when her father had re-modeled and added a dining room separate from the bar, she wouldn't have been allowed to bring the baby inside. As a child, she had never been permitted on the first floor. The law said no one under twenty-one. And in Benny Boudreau's eyes, that included his own children. He apparently didn't see the irony that they slept right above the beer cooler.

Of course Molly, being the bullheaded child she was, managed to sneak in on plenty of Saturday nights while her dad was swamped at the bar. Her advantage was that she was so much shorter than all of the adults. She was hard to see from his position behind the bar. It became a challenge she issued to herself: make it through the kitchen without Henry the cook catching her, slip into the room with the pool table in back, rub a little blue chalk on the end of her finger as a symbol of her achievement, snake her way all the way to the front of the bar unde-tected, go out the front door and then around to the out-side stairs that led back up to their apartment.

Dad caught her when she was twelve. She blamed it on her growth spurt that put her over five-four. It was the very last time she attempted it. She was stubborn, not stupid. Losing her father's trust was the worst thing she could have imagined. She suffered for weeks, and he really didn't do much more than say only once, "I'm disappointed."

She never heard those words from him again—until six weeks ago. And they cut her as deeply as they had when she was twelve.

Squaring her shoulders and lifting her chin, she opened the door and stepped inside. The dining room was empty. Five or six men gathered at the bar, watching football on the TV suspended from the ceiling. Her dad was standing behind the bar with his back to the door, watching the game.

Nicholas was awake, which meant she only had a short while before he needed attention. As she gathered her composure, Faye appeared at her side.

"I'm so glad you're here, darlin'. He's been cross as a bear with an arrow in his butt."

Faye's frankness helped take the edge off her mood. Molly knew Faye and Lily were sometimes at odds, but she liked the woman. You never wondered where Faye was coming from, with her it was always up front and in your face.

Faye cooed at Nicholas. Then she said, "Can I take him for a minute? Henry's been wanting a look at him for a month now."

Molly smiled her thanks and handed the baby seat over. "You might want this too." She took the diaper bag off her shoulder. "It's about time to feed him."

Faye looked surprised. "You're not nursing?"

"No. Complications." Actually, Molly had expected

this question much earlier; most pediatricians espoused the benefits of breastfeeding. She'd been prepared with a sad look and a ready answer for weeks.

Faye looked appropriately sympathetic. She patted Molly's shoulder. "Plenty of babies are on formula. They grow just fine." Then she smiled. "I'll send Henry out to babysit the bar. You don't want to talk to your daddy with all those men around." She nodded at a booth near the back. "Why don't you just wait there a minute."

Molly was thankful for Faye's consideration. Sitting in a quiet booth waiting for her dad made her feel a little less awkward than having to walk into a crowd and wait for his reaction in front of everyone.

In two minutes (her gaze had remained steady on the second hand of her watch) her dad came into the dining room. He stopped short when he saw her. Then he came and slid in the booth across from her.

His face was creased with worry when he asked, "Is something wrong? You look thin. Where's the baby? Is he all right?"

Oh, he knew her too well. It had to be something of a monumental nature to get her to be the one to surrender first. "The only thing that's wrong with the baby is that his grandfather won't acknowledge him."

He leaned back in the booth, his palms down on the table. "I didn't disown him."

"Only me?"

As he scrubbed his hands over his face, Molly noticed the dark circles under his eyes. He looked more tired than she remembered.

He said, "I never said I 'disowned' you. I said I was

disappointed. And can you blame me? My God, the things you've thrown away."

"Dad, I can practice medicine anywhere. In fact, I was thinking about leaving Boston before.... But I have something I never thought I would. You know after the surgery they said I might not have children."

"Did you have to run right out and put it to the test? Is that what this is all about?"

A terrible thought grabbed her. If she were to be found out, if the police discovered she had Sarah's baby, her own potential infertility would be damning evidence. Maybe they'd even think *she* killed Sarah for her baby. For a second, she couldn't breathe. Why hadn't this occurred to her before now?

When she finally pulled in a breath, she told herself, if she was caught, it wouldn't matter. In the eyes of the law she'd kidnapped the child. Nothing else would be an issue. She would go to jail. And if she *ever* told her family, they could be charged as accessories, or for harboring a fugitive, or something equally awful.

She felt her dad's hand on hers. "Are you all right?"

Unable to spare the oxygen for words just yet, she nodded.

"I'll get you something to drink."

He was up and gone before she could stop him. She didn't need anything to drink, she needed a miracle to sustain this deception.

Setting a glass of ice water in front of her, he sat down on the same side of the booth and put an arm around her. "You look like you're going to faint."

She took a sip of water. "I'm all right. I guess I'm just overly emotional right now." Not exactly a lie.

"Your mother was the same way—for months after you kids were born."

She forced herself to look into his brown eyes. She tried to arrange her words so they weren't blatant lies. "Dad, I came home so Nicholas would have a family. I don't want to raise him alone."

He stiffened. "Then you should have brought a father, too."

Molly saw this for what it was; his last defense. Eventually, they would find their way back to one another. She hoped it wouldn't take years. But if it did, she wasn't giving up.

Faye brought the baby out at that moment, her timing giving away the fact that she was probably peeking out from the kitchen the entire time. She had a huge smile on her face as she tried to hand Nicholas to Benny.

"Whoa!" He held her off. "I'm too rough to hold something that tiny." To emphasize his point, he held his large, calloused hand next to the baby's tiny face. "Look at that. I'd crush him."

Faye looked as disappointed as Molly felt when she sat in the booth across from them. "Just look at what a big man he is," she cooed.

Nicholas performed nicely with a gummy smile.

Benny looked more closely. "He is a handsome devil."

"Of course," Faye said. "He takes after his grand-daddy."

Benny made a sound of dismissal, but Molly saw him study the baby just a little more intently.

Don't look too close there.

Henry brought over an appetizer platter and three drinks. Faye asked questions about the baby, his delivery and a thousand other things that Molly really wanted to avoid. But she pulled it off admirably well, she thought.

Then her dad took the conversation on a new tangent. One that rankled, but things being what they were, Molly could hardly cut him off.

"I hear you had dinner with Brian Mitchell Friday night."

"I ran into him at Papa's," she said flatly. "We shared a table; it was very busy."

"A good man—had his share of troubles. Still, I say it's the best thing that happened when that snooty wife of his up and left town. He deserves some happiness."

"I'm sure he does." Dad was anything but subtle.

"You could do worse than a man like Brian."

"Like not have a man at all?" She knew she should have kept her mouth shut; couldn't she just quit while she was ahead?

Benny's brow grew stern. "You know where I stand. That won't change."

"I know." In the effort toward peace, she decided to throw the man a bone. "Brian is nice."

One of the creases left her dad's brow. "Keep that in mind."

He got up and went back to the bar.

Molly tried not to feel defeated, or like a cheater in her last admission. If thinking there was a man in the near future for her made her dad feel better, then fine. Clearly, Benny Boudreau wasn't going to be happy until he saw Molly married. And he was right; she could do worse than Brian.

*   *   *

After Molly put Nicholas to bed, she poured a red plastic Solo cup of cheap wine. Having always lived on a tight budget, cheap wine was the only kind she'd ever had, so the glassware fit perfectly. But as she did it, she realized she was going to have to arrange to have her apartment emptied and the stuff shipped here. There was no way she was taking Nicholas back to Boston, even for a few days, so she would have to hire a mover.

After a moment, she had second thoughts. It would probably cost more to pack and ship the stuff than it was worth. The only things of value she'd left behind were her books. Maybe she'd call her landlord tomorrow and ask if he would pack up the medical books and ship them to her, and then donate the rest of her belongings to charity. It seemed much more practical. Then she should move her bank accounts—not that there was much there either. Good thing she'd found work quickly.

She turned off the kitchen light and took her wine to sit on the floor in front of the cold ash-filled fireplace. Without the fire, the room felt every bit as stark as it was, even when masked by darkness. Last night, with Dean by her side and the yellow flames lighting the room, it had almost seemed like home.

She pushed thoughts of Dean away and embraced her day's success. She and her dad were at least back on speaking terms again, even though it was partly due to false pretense on her part. She couldn't see herself married to Brian. Although, the man would make a good father. Maybe she should consider something like that for Nicholas's sake.

She shook her head, putting those thoughts aside.

Today was a beginning with her father; she made herself happy with that.

Molly came awake, lying on the floor in front of the fireplace, tipping her empty Solo cup over with her elbow.

There had been a sound. She listened intently.

The baby was quiet.

Then she heard it again, a quiet tapping on the front door glass. Her heart sped up. She had no idea how late it was. Was it someone just testing to see how soundly she was asleep before they broke in?

She quickly negated that thought. Who would use the front door when the back was so well-concealed from the street and neighbors?

Thank goodness she'd tacked a towel up over the glass.

She got up, shaking off the lingering grogginess, and went to the door. Flipping on the porch light, she pulled the towel slightly aside to peek out.

Dean stood there with a concerned look on his face.

Unlocking the door, she couldn't deny the gladness in her heart at the sight of him.

As soon as she opened it, he said, "I was getting worried. Your car's out back, but it's so dark around here . . . I was afraid something was wrong. . . ."

His concern touched her, as did his apparent uneasiness over it. "I'd fallen asleep. What time is it?"

He looked at his watch in the porch light. "Nine-twenty."

She hadn't been asleep long at all.

"May I come in?" he asked.

Molly shook off the last of the nap-induced cobwebs. "Of course." She opened the door wider.

He looked rather apologetic when he said, "I was actually interviewing your next door neighbor. I don't normally just barge in—"

Molly waved away his comment. "I can see you need lots more research before you're ready to write your article. In small towns, no appointment is necessary. It's considered rude not to stop by when you're in the neighborhood." She gestured toward the kitchen. "You want some coffee? I can also offer a fine red wine, vintage 2003, the best that seven dollars can buy." It gave her a slight rush of pleasure that he came to see *her* after talking to prom queen Karen Kimball.

He grinned, all of his discomfort seeming to melt away. "I do like a quality wine. I usually draw the line at six bucks, though." With no light in the living room, most of his face was in shadow from the porch light. It highlighted his lips, the line of his jaw—and made Molly want to pick up where they'd left off last night.

She turned around and started toward the kitchen before she did something about it. As she walked past the fireplace, she kicked the empty Solo cup. "See," she stooped to pick it up, "your stopping by saved me from drinking alone. I'd hate to get a reputation."

Behind her, he chuckled. There was a knowing edge to it that bothered her.

Once in the kitchen she turned on the light and faced him with her arms crossed over her chest. "That sounded like you know something I don't."

His smile was slightly lopsided when he said, "Just that you have a jealous neighbor."

"Karen? Jealous of me?" She splayed a hand over her heart. "I'm sure you're mistaken. Boudreaus have always been a few notches below her radar. We didn't gain much when my nephew set a trap for her drug-dealing ex, resulting in jail time."

He looked puzzled. "She spoke very highly of your nephew."

Molly cocked her head slightly. "Really?"

"She seemed quite upset that he and her daughter aren't seeing each other anymore."

"Did she call it that—'seeing each other'?"

He nodded. "Made it sound like a real case of puppy love."

"Huh." Then she asked, "Did you meet Mickey?"

"No. Is she a younger version of her mother?"

Molly had to laugh at that. "Hardly. Mickey is kind and responsible and sensitive and smart."

The crooked smile was back. "And you don't think Karen is any of those things?"

Molly couldn't help but raise her brow. "I don't know that I should comment on that. You doing an interview and all." She drew a breath. "It's just . . . Mickey is very special, and her mother doesn't see it."

He nodded slowly. "But you do."

"Jesus, a blind man could see it! If Karen would take her head out of her stuck-up ass long enough, she'd see it too. But she rides the poor kid into the ground because she's not popular and concerned with what's cool." She chewed the inside of her lip for a second. "I'm sure the only thing Karen *really* likes about my nephew is that he's a Holt. Riley's grandparents were Chicago summer people, they're very well off. *That's* what matters to Karen."

He stepped a little closer. "Just for the record, the interview was scheduled by the interviewee." He touched her cheek. "I'd much rather have been here."

Suddenly, Molly couldn't remember what they were talking about.

Leaning close, he kissed her lightly, yet with a lingering sweetness that reached right down to touch her soul. When he stopped, she realized her knees were trembling.

"Wi—" her voice broke off in a squeak. "Wine?"

He nuzzled her ear. "I think I prefer the way you taste." Backing her up against the cabinets, he lifted her onto the countertop and stood between her knees. When his lips returned to hers, he parted them slightly with his tongue.

Her entire body was abuzz with his nearness. He roused sexual awareness in her with just a glance; touching commanded total absorption of each and every one of her senses. There was nothing but the smell of him, the warmth of his body, the quiver he set off in her skin where his fingers grasped her waist, the taste of his lips, the fervent rhythm of his breathing.

She wanted to be closer. To toss aside clothes and inhibitions. To know him fully and unequivocally—feelings heretofore alien to her.

Molly kissed the scar on his neck, then wrapped her arms around him, holding him close, burying her face on his shoulder. She liked the tension in the muscles of his shoulders that said he was holding himself back, the tickle of his breath against her ear, the strong feel of his hands as he pressed her closer.

He whispered, "You're an incredible woman."

How could he, a man of war zones and international politics, think she was incredible? She would have argued, but he began tasting her neck and it stole her voice away.

As Dean allowed himself to slide into another kiss, he cursed himself for a coward. He truly hadn't planned to come here tonight. He wasn't quite ready to brand himself a liar in Molly's eyes. But when he'd seen the car in the drive and no lights in the house, a shaft of icy panic shot through his chest. What if she was sick? Or hurt? What if the baby was ill? The worrisome questions mounted until he walked up the front steps and knocked on the door.

When Molly had peeked out with anxious eyes, he'd wanted nothing more than to comfort her, to erase that anxiety. Once he was inside the door, the need to touch her eclipsed good intentions. When she'd responded to his kiss, he could think of nothing else. This woman robbed him of his senses with no more than her nearness. He realized she'd robbed him of his heart the moment she climbed into the car next to her baby, a soaked and bloody mess after trying to save that bicyclist. Her need to be near her child after such an event, her refusal to touch him with contaminated hands, spoke so much about the depth of love she carried.

And he selfishly wanted to bask in her goodness, not have her turn against him in the face of his deception—which would only make his lies more hateful when he admitted them.

He forced himself to stop kissing her and step away.

He realized he'd continued the charade by interviewing Karen Kimball only to be close to Molly again without actually seeing her and having to tell her the truth.

It was time to act like a man.

Her eyes were questioning as they held his. "Something's wrong."

"I have something I have to tell you—and I'm not sure where to begin."

She slid off the counter and stood in front of him. "Listen, you don't need to explain anything to me. I know you're just here for a short time. I don't expect . . . anything."

"It's not that. I—"

Suddenly Nicholas started to shriek.

Molly moved immediately, leaving the kitchen at a trot. Which told Dean just what he feared; this was no normal cry.

Instinctively he followed her into the bedroom. She flipped on the harsh overhead light and hurried to the crib. She picked him up with confident hands, not with the panic he himself felt at the moment.

Talking softly to the baby as he continued to scream, she pressed her cheek against his forehead.

"No fever."

The baby was crying and turning purple.

"Shouldn't he breathe?" Dean asked anxiously.

"He will eventually." She laid him on the bed and checked his diaper, then she pressed on his abdomen gently.

"What's wrong with him?" Dean stepped closer.

"I don't feel a hernia. His stomach is tight though. See the way he's drawing his legs up?" She picked the child back up and held him against her, stomach to stomach. "He has a bellyache—probably gas pains."

Nicholas continued to scream.

"Sounds more serious than that to me," Dean said.

She jiggled the baby slightly and kept him tightly against her. "Have you ever had gas pains—*real*, trapped gas?"

"Now you're getting kind of personal. . . ."

She half-smiled and shook her head. "They can bring a grown man to his knees; make a football player break out in a sweat. And this guy's only ten pounds."

"Can't you do something?"

"I am."

"I mean give him something, some medicine."

"Not for a one-time gas attack. If it gets to be frequent, then maybe."

The screaming was rubbing Dean's nerves raw already, and it didn't look like there was an end in sight. It was all he could do to not cover his ears with his hands. How could Molly remain so relaxed?

She held Nicholas tightly and jostled him a bit as she began to walk. The baby quieted some, his screams became less piercing.

"I'm sorry," she said. "You don't need to hang around. This is likely to take awhile."

He watched her make a circle of the room, talking softly to Nicholas.

The boy continued to cry, but Molly seemed unfazed.

"Maybe I should stay, in case you need something from the drug store. I could take a turn walking with him," he said.

Nicholas stiffened and let out re-energized howl.

Molly patted his bottom and continued to walk. When the screaming had reduced to the point she could talk over it she said, "There's nothing you can do." Then she smiled at him. "But thanks for offering. There's no sense in two of us having our hearing ruined. Go."

"Well . . . then." He took one reluctant step toward the door.

"We'll be fine." She stopped circling and led him out of the bedroom to the front door. "Good night, Dean." She stood on her toes and kissed his cheek. Nicholas didn't approve of the halt in movement and responded with an ear-shattering shriek.

He felt like a rat deserting a sinking ship. But she seemed to want him to leave. He could hardly throw himself on the floor and refuse to go. He touched her hair. "I'll call you tomorrow."

She simply nodded and began walking the floor with the baby again.

He let himself out the door and walked to his car, feeling guilty that he was so relieved that he hadn't had to tell Molly the truth. It only put off the inevitable. But he hated the thought of seeing recognition of his betrayal in her eyes.

He told himself he was just imagining a growing relationship with Molly. It was based on lies. Lies that had to come to light. Once he told her the truth, her illusion of him would be shattered. Then he'd be back on the road, trying to decipher the mystery of Julie's murder. And then . . . he supposed back overseas.

For some reason, that idea held less appeal than it ever had in his life. In fact, dread crept up the back of his neck on cold spider's legs as he thought about it.

He drove around town for thirty minutes with his insides as unsettled as a palm tree in a hurricane. Then he found himself passing Molly's house again. As he cruised slowly down the street, he looked in her living room window. He saw her pass, slowly walking the baby. He stopped completely and strained to see her face. As impossible as it was to believe, she looked serene, contented. Five minutes with the screaming baby and he'd been ready to lose his mind.

He couldn't deny that he wanted to march right back up to her door—howling baby or not. But he'd intruded on her enough for one night.

As he drove toward the lake cottage, he tried to decipher the reason for his newly discovered aversion to returning to his life. A life he'd worked hard for. A life he'd thrived on for years.

Was Julie's death at the center?

He tried to look honestly into his heart. While he was driven to solve the crime, claim justice for his sister, he had to admit he didn't think that was the root of these life-altering questions.

Was it his own brush with death, then?

Was it the fact that if there wasn't a baby out there somewhere, Dean was truly alone in this world?

Or was it a woman with pale smoky eyes and a stubborn, yet generous nature—a woman who appreciated cheap wine, who needed little in the way of material things, who gave up an established career to do what she thought was best for her child, who heedlessly risked her health to save a stranger?

Oh, God. He hoped it wasn't that. Because tomorrow she was going to be lost to him.

Chapter 14

All day Sunday, Riley's mom and Clay acted weird, like he was in trouble. But he hadn't done anything. In fact, he was home before his midnight curfew on Saturday night. A couple of times, when Riley made the mistake of coming out of his room, Clay even made noises like he wanted to "talk," which *never* meant anything good.

So, while Mom and Clay were busy in the barn, Riley left a note on the kitchen counter explaining he was going to the marina to winterize boats. That couldn't piss them off; it was his job, after all. He didn't return home until suppertime. By avoiding eye contact and complaining of a bad headache from the muratic acid fumes, he'd managed to make it to his room without a "talk."

Monday morning, Riley awakened feeling like he had ants crawling under his skin. The sound of his alarm clock grated against his nerves. He took such a wild swing at shutting it off, it clattered to the floor. But it did stop beeping.

He hadn't slept well since Saturday night. Every time he closed his eyes, she saw Mickey's pale face in the rain. Accompanying that image was a shame so deep, he would have done anything to wipe it away. Twice he'd dreamt of the day they met, in the woods out by the dam. They had only been thirteen—nearly three years ago. She'd been there reading. He'd been running from Clay:

Riley walked against the current, watching the way the water rolled around his shins. Soon the sound of rushing water intensified and he found himself at the foot of the dam's spillway.

After he tossed his shoes to the dry bank, he let himself fall backward with his arms spread. He floated there, in the knee-deep water, watching the sun wink through the fluttering leaves overhead.

"There's a water moccasin nest over there."

Riley's arms flailed as he folded at the waist and his feet sought solid ground. His gaze shot in the direction of the voice and he saw a blond-haired girl with knobby knees pointing at a spot not twenty feet from him.

He spit out the mouthful of water he'd just sucked in. "What?"

"Water moccasins. Cottonmouths. Snakes. They're poisonous."

Every nerve in Riley's body snapped to attention. His mouth went dry and his heart jumped in his chest. Standing slowly, he curled his toes in order to make less of a target for any snake that happened to be swimming by. It took all of his willpower not to run screaming out of the stream.

He managed to stay put. "How do you know?"

She tilted her head to the side. "Everybody knows that water moccasins are poisonous."

"No." Girls always had to make everything so complicated. "How do you know there's a nest? I don't see anything."

"My brother told me."

"Oh, and he's a snake expert. Did you ever think he said it just to scare you?"

"Nope." She wrinkled up her nose.

"No, he's not an expert? Or no, he didn't do it to scare you?"

She blew out a frustrated sounding breath. "Just get out of the water and I'll show you."

He started to say he'd get out of the water when he was good and ready, but the slim chance that there actually were poisonous snakes in here with him kept his lips sealed. Stepping very carefully, he climbed up onto the bank beside her.

She bent down and picked up a rock, then looked at him. "Ready?"

He nodded, the water from his hair running in his eyes.

With amazing accuracy for a girl, the rock sailed from her hand and landed in the water just short of the far bank, about twenty feet downstream. Immediately, the water began to ripple, then it looked like it was boiling.

"Jesus Christ!" Riley couldn't keep the fright out of his voice any longer. "How many are there?"

The girl shrugged. "Dunno. A bunch."

Riley watched the water slowly settle back into stillness with rapt revulsion. "Why doesn't somebody just kill 'em?"

She turned an astonished gaze in his direction. "Du-uh! They're on the state's endangered list."

"Why would anybody want to keep poisonous snakes around? Seems like extinct would be just about perfect."

"Well," she said, squaring her shoulders. "What if we got rid of everything that annoyed us? Kill all of the mosquitoes and the bats go hungry. Kill all of the bats and the mosquitoes take over. Mosquitoes take over and people get more diseases. Everything is connected, everything counts. Besides, if we thought that way there wouldn't be any teenage boys left around."

Mickey had been the most unusual girl he'd ever met. She saw things differently than anyone else, and, at least for awhile, made him see too. There were still days when he longed to talk to her, to get her opinions—Mickey was never in short supply of opinions.

But Mickey would probably never talk to him again. And he couldn't really blame her.

As he drove to school, he was even more pissed at Codi than he had been on Saturday night. If she'd just left things alone, maybe he could have gotten some sleep. What she'd done was hateful and scheming, and it made him see clearly what he'd been trying to ignore for months; Codi was *not* a nice person. Popular, yes. Hot, totally. Willing to do things he'd only imagined before, oh yeah. But what lived inside her was ugly.

What could she possibly have gained by being so mean to Mickey?

When he parked in the school lot, he saw Codi riding shotgun in Nathan Pryor's car. She flung Riley a smug look as they drove past.

He was surprised when instead of feeling betrayed, he

felt nothing but relief. Nathan could have her. Just the thought of kissing her again made a bitter taste rise in Riley's mouth.

As he got out of his car, he caught sight of Mickey walking toward the building from the other direction. Her pale hair made her stand out in the flow of kids. He hurried in the door at his end of the building and managed to be passing the door she was using just as she came in.

She walked right past him without as much as a glance in his direction.

He almost called out to her, but a bunch of his guy friends were passing by. He kept his mouth shut and fell in with them.

Finally, after third period, he saw her at her locker. It wasn't much of a coincidence as he'd been making a point of passing it every time he was in the halls.

He stopped behind her. "Hi, Mickey."

She froze for a second, then turned to face him. She didn't look happy. "Hi."

He should have been better prepared, but suddenly he didn't know what to say. He scrambled for a common thread. "Aunt Molly said you babysat for Nicholas."

"Yeah."

She wasn't going to help him out here.

"He's really little. Weren't you nervous?"

"No." She turned and put a book in her locker.

He closed his eyes for a second. "Listen, I—I'm sorry . . . about Codi—"

She spun and faced him, her brown eyes narrowed. "Why would you be sorry? Did you ask her to yell out the window at me?"

For a moment, he couldn't even breathe. "No."

"Then don't apologize." She slammed her locker and brushed past him.

He stood there, feeling as if she'd punched him in the gut.

Brian Mitchell showed up at Molly's door at exactly eleven A.M. Monday morning. Thankfully the dreary weather had slipped away in the night like an unwelcome houseguest. The sun shone brightly in a brilliant blue sky, the kind that only comes on crisp autumn days. That alone lightened Molly's mood; so much so, she'd nearly convinced herself that Brian's plan for child care would work.

But when she opened the door and saw Hattie Grissom all but swallowed up in her gray overcoat, Molly's doubts returned. The woman stood almost a foot shorter than Brian and had an old-fashioned flowered silk scarf covering her gray hair and tied under her chin. When Molly invited them in, Brian actually had to put a hand on her shoulder and nudge her forward. Molly's hope evaporated like yesterday's fog. To think this shy, frail woman could take care of an infant for twelve straight hours was ridiculous.

"May I take your coat?" she asked Hattie.

Hattie didn't look at her, but dutifully unbuttoned the coat and handed it over.

"Let's sit in the kitchen," Molly suggested, as if there was another choice available.

Once again, it took Brian's hand on Hattie's elbow to set the woman in motion.

Although this was clearly a waste of time, Hattie looked so forlorn that Molly decided to at least go through the motions. She hoped that Brian had been true to his word and had not divulged the real reason for this visit.

That hope vanished as soon as they were seated at the table with coffee in mismatched mugs from Lily's Goodwill box.

Brian said, "Hattie is very interested in the position. In fact, she has several letters of recommendation from young mothers at her church."

Wordlessly, Hattie took six envelopes out of her handbag and slid them across the table toward Molly.

Molly cut a nasty look Brian's way. He pretended not to notice, but she saw the slight smile he tried to hide.

To Hattie, she smiled and said, "Thank you. I'll be sure and read these carefully." She licked her lips. "I don't think Brian has explained the job very well. I'm going to be working odd shifts, twelve hours at a time, with four days on and then five days off. I'm sure such long hours won't be what you're interested in."

Hattie cast a furtive glance at Brian, who nodded encouragingly. Then she said, "I'm not afraid to work—worked all my life. I'm stronger than I look. Been taking care of the livestock since Ed passed."

"Oh, I didn't mean . . . it's just that taking care of an infant for twelve hours is much different than for an hour or two during church services." Good God, the woman couldn't weigh a hundred pounds. Molly looked to Brian to help out, but he just took a long sip of coffee.

"Pastor Mark says I have a gift with babies. Says I should use it." Hattie paused and looked into her coffee for a moment. "I'd take real good care of your boy."

Molly scrambled for a way out. "If you've been taking care of the livestock yourself, how could you spend twelve hours here? And then, of course there's the problem of transportation."

"Sold the stock. 'Cept for my chickens. They manage fine once the feed's out and the eggs is brought in."

"I see. But it would be impractical for me to load up the baby to drive out to the farm and bring you back here every day."

Hattie looked directly at Molly for the first time. Her blue eyes were sharp and clear. The woman might be shy, but Molly saw a bright intelligence burning there. "I can drive myself."

At that, even Brian perked up. "You can?"

Hattie waved a bony hand in the air. "'Course. Don't live on a farm your whole life and not learn to drive."

Molly said, "But I thought the ladies of the church brought you to town for your weekly shopping."

Hattie tilted her little head, reminding Molly of a bright-eyed bird. A grin slowly spread over her face. "If I didn't let them do that, they'd be lookin' to do somethin' else. Ever'body wants to do for me now that I'm a widow. It's kind of them, but I can't be having someone underfoot every day. Just 'cause Ed always drove, they think I can't. So I let them drive me to church on Sunday and shopping on Mondays. Keeps ever'body happy— them doing their Christian duty and all. Pastor Mark thinks it's a good idea."

Brian slapped the table and laughed aloud.

"I can do house chores when the baby's sleeping," Hattie said, seeming to gain confidence as she spoke. "But when the baby's awake, it's time for him. I don't do anything else but care for him—read or sing—babies need lots of stimulation."

Just then, Nicholas erupted in a scream much like he had last night. Molly started to get up, but Hattie put a hand on her arm and said, "Let me."

"Oh, I don't know, I think he's getting colic." Molly felt Brian step on her toe under the table.

Hattie pointed to the stack of envelopes on the table. "The one there from Sharon Middleton tells 'bout colic. I helped her with her little Emily and the colic." Then she left the room, following the baby's cry straight into the bedroom.

Molly got up to follow, but Brian caught her hand. "Give her a chance."

Molly waited for a full two minutes before she followed Hattie into the bedroom. The baby was still crying furiously and she couldn't stand to wait any longer. But she stopped at the bedroom door and watched in surprise.

Hattie had already changed the baby's diaper and had Nicholas cradled against her middle, as Molly had last night. She was swaying slightly and singing to him. Gone was the timid mouse; Hattie moved with quiet confidence with the child in her arms.

When she looked up and saw Molly she said, "If you'd turn the shower on hot, then close the bathroom door, I think I can help him."

Brian answered from right behind Molly. "I'll do it."

No way was Molly letting Hattie go into that bathroom alone with her baby with scalding water running. She was right on the woman's heels when she crossed the hall to the bathroom door.

Hattie looked over her shoulder and said, "'Course, you'll want to come in too, so you can see and do for yourself when I'm not here."

The bathroom was very small, so Brian stepped out when they entered. By then the steam was thick near the ceiling and the mirror was fogging over. Hattie sat on the closed toilet lid and put Nicholas, still crying in what most certainly had to be pain, across her knees on his stomach.

"It'll take a minute for the steam to get down here to him," she said as she alternated lifting each heel off the floor just a fraction of an inch. She spoke softly, even though there was no way the baby could hear over his own crying, and rubbed his back gently.

Nicholas's cries became less frantic.

"You want to do this right away," Hattie said. "Let him get too worked up, he just gulps more air and makes it worse."

That made sense to Molly.

"Babies like the sound of the water," Hattie said as Nicholas calmed even more. "Steam soothes 'em."

By the time Molly's face felt dewy with the steam, the baby had quieted.

Hattie looked at her with a grandmotherly smile. "You can go on out. No sense gettin' into a sweat. I'll sit for a bit, until he's settled for sure."

Molly thought of the three hours she'd paced the floors last night with little effect and her admiration for this woman's instincts multiplied. She asked, "Could you come and spend a few hours with us, maybe do a short stay, before I start work?"

"I 'spect that'd be a good idea." She continued to rub Nicholas's back. "Go on now. Afore you melt."

Molly stepped back into the hall.

Brian was leaning against the wall with his arms

crossed over his chest. "Either she fixed him, or you two duct taped his mouth closed in there."

"She fixed him." Then she said, "But it could be a fluke. We're going to do a test run."

Brian grinned. "Great. You won't be sorry. And don't forget to read those letters."

In a couple of minutes, Hattie emerged from the bathroom, her gray hair frizzed from the steam. Nicholas rested quietly in her arms. She looked around, then frowned. "You got a baby and no rocker?"

"I haven't had much time to get things set up. I'll get one."

Hattie walked into the kitchen and sat down with the baby in her lap. "No need. I'll bring mine."

Brian offered, "I could move it for you."

With a calm confidence that surprised Molly, Hattie looked him in the eye and said, "Don't talk foolish. It don't weigh as much as them feed sacks. I'll put it in the truck when I come."

Hattie fed Nicholas while Molly and Brian drank coffee. It was lunchtime, but Molly didn't have anything suitable in the house to offer company.

"Can I take you two to the Dew Drop for lunch?" she said, feeling more relaxed than she had in a month. This could all actually work out.

Brian looked to Hattie.

She shook her head. "I need to get on home. I got painting to finish today."

Molly said, "You're an artist?"

Hattie chuckled shyly. "Good lands, no. The gutters. Gotta get 'em finished while the weather's good."

She handed over a well-fed, happy baby. Then Brian

helped her into her coat. Molly promised to call and set up a time for their trial run and Hattie placed her age-spotted hand tenderly on Nicholas's head.

"He's a fine boy."

"Thank you. And thank you for your help."

She nodded and pressed her dry lips together as if debating whether or not to say something, then went out the door.

Molly caught Brian's sleeve before he followed her out. "Sorry I doubted. I don't know how to thank you."

He looked at her for a long moment. "Have dinner with me. That can be Hattie's trial sitting job."

Panic bubbled forth. Brian was a nice guy, a friend. If anyone saw them out together, this town would have them married before they got home from dinner. "I don't—"

"You look like I just asked you to run away with me. It's just dinner." He smiled that charming smile that he was so famous for.

"All right."

"Good, I'll call you and we can set up a date."

Date. She looked at him, but Dean's face flashed in her mind. *Stop it.* She was here for the long haul. Dean wasn't. Maybe someday that idea of a date with Brian would appeal to her. She managed a smile and closed the door behind him.

Riley cut his last class. He couldn't stand sitting still any longer. He got in the car that his Grandpa Holt had given him for his sixteenth birthday and drove away from school. He wasn't even careful about sneaking out. He walked out of the front door as if it was what he was supposed to be doing.

He really wanted to try to talk to Mickey again, even more since she cut him off this morning. Her contempt showed him just how big of a jerk he'd been. But it looked like it was too late to do anything about it; Mickey wasn't in a forgiving mood. And he really couldn't blame her.

It was way too early to go home, so he drove around the lake. When he got to the Holts' lake house where he and his mom had stayed when they first came to Glens Crossing, he stopped. It was closed up, as were most of those on Mill Run Road. These houses belonged to people who only came in the summer—mostly from Chicago. But unlike the other houses, the Holt house was closed up permanently. His dad owned it and swore he'd never set foot in this town again. But he couldn't sell it because it had been in his family forever and Grandpa Holt would have Dad's ass in a sling.

Riley pulled into the lane that wound its way through the trees until it stopped beside the big house on the lake.

The house was dark green with white trim and deep eaves that shaded the upstairs windows. The rooms had high ceilings and hardwood floors that made the house echo when you walked around in it. When he'd first arrived here, he'd hated this house—he'd hated everything about this town. But by the time he and his mom moved out, he discovered at some point he'd actually grown to like it.

He wished he had a key so he could go inside. Years ago, when his dad was a kid, you could sneak in and out of the coal chute. But that first summer his mom had that fixed. After he got out of the car, he went to the porch and tried to peek in the windows, but all of the draperies had been closed. Then he walked down the slope of the yard to the boat dock.

The sun was bright, glinting off the water in a festive way. Riley didn't feel festive. He felt dark and alone. There was a cold ache deep in the center of his chest. He didn't want sunshine. He turned around and walked back toward his car.

There was one place that not only suited his mood, but he would be guaranteed not to be bothered by anyone. He left his car in the drive and started to walk down Mill Run Road.

In fifteen minutes, he left the road on a narrow deer path that cut through the woods to Blackwater Creek. The first time he'd walked this path, he'd been angry, frustrated and confused—pretty much like he felt now, but for different reasons.

He followed the creek to the spot where the dam's spillway emptied into it; to the place where the water moccasins nested—the place he'd met Mickey. He sat down on a fallen tree trunk and watched the water flow past. It was shadowed here in the ravine at the bottom of the dam. Even with most of the leaves off the trees, the branches were thick enough to break up the sun. This place suited his mood. He hadn't been here for over a year and had forgotten how peaceful it was.

Breathing in the scent of decaying leaves and muddy creek bank, he tried to find a bit of that peace in himself. This had been their special meeting place, his and Mickey's. If anyone had found out they had been meeting here, where it was so secluded a boy and girl could do anything and not worry about being caught, they might have gotten in trouble. But it hadn't been that way between them. They'd never even kissed. If they had, it would have messed everything up. That thought stopped Riley in his mental tracks. How could it have screwed things up more than they were now?

Maybe if he had kissed her, things would have been different. Maybe if they'd started school and everybody knew she was his girlfriend, she would have been accepted into the crowd. *Or, maybe I would have been locked out like she is.* Could he have stood it, living on the outside of everything?

He sat there for a long time, wondering how life might have been different, if it would have changed anything. Finally, he came to the conclusion that Mickey wouldn't have wanted to have been accepted into the crowd, especially if she would have had to compromise her unconventional attitudes and beliefs to do it. And, he thought, if Mickey gave up her uniqueness, would she still hold as special a place in his heart?

He groaned. It was true—he'd tried to ignore it by being in the middle of everything going on at school, by making out with Codi Craig—Mickey was in his heart, deep down where she could lie hidden but never, never be removed.

A part of him wanted to move away from the creek, to go to the place tucked under an outcropping of limestone where they used to spread a blanket and talk, or read. But that was Mickey's special place. He felt funny going there without her—especially now. It would be like snooping around in her room.

He didn't feel a whole lot better when he got up off the

log and started back on the path to the road. But he did know that he wanted to have Mickey in his life again. How was he going to fix this?

Mickey held her breath as she watched Riley sitting on the log. She'd nearly blundered right into him. After signing herself out sick at lunchtime, she'd come to the spot where she could always be alone with her thoughts. For a while, Riley had shared it with her. But that was a long time ago. He didn't come down here anymore.

But there he was. His eyes had been closed, so she'd managed to take two silent steps backward and slip behind the trunk of a giant sycamore.

She risked the occasional peek to see if he was still there. Just seeing him there alone made her heart feel like someone was wringing the life out of it. His apology this morning had shaken her, and for a brief second had given her a false glimmer of hope. But she had to be strong. She had grown accustomed to life without him. She couldn't risk thinking they could go back.

Why was he here? Why today, when she needed to be as far away from him as she could be? It was as if God was trying to punish her by setting what she couldn't have within the illusion of her grasp.

Then she heard him groan. It was sound from the soul—of torment and pain—she recognized it because she herself had made it so often. She nearly stepped out then, nearly went to him with her friendship—and her heart—offered up in her open hands.

Lucky for her, before she could do it, he got up and walked away.

Chapter 15

Molly had gained valuable insight today from the simplest of women. Some things just couldn't be learned from medical books. Hattie's miracle remedy worked brilliantly a second time, when Nicholas started in again after his evening bottle.

Even though sitting in a steamy bathroom for forty minutes with a mildly fussy baby wasn't her idea of a pleasant evening, it beat the hell out of walking the floors with him screaming in discomfort. Whether colic was caused by digestive distress or, as some proposed, from an underdeveloped nervous system going into overload from too much stimuli, it didn't really matter; the shower and steam treatment was working for this baby. By ten o'clock, after a relatively quiet evening, Nicholas was snuggled in his bed.

As she returned to the kitchen, she felt really good for the first time in weeks. Her life was finally falling into some kind of order. She squirted dish detergent in a sink of hot water and dropped in the dirty bottles and nipples.

Then she heard a familiar tapping on the glass of her front door.

Her heart lightened further. She wiped her hands on a dishtowel and hurried to let Dean in.

When she opened the door, his face was in shadow from the porch light. She was really going to have to hit a few garage sales and get some furniture in this room. Letting people in during the day wasn't so bad, but admitting guests to a completely darkened room was very inhospitable.

Dean stepped in the door and she slid her arms around his waist. This was a very good day. "Hello, you."

He held her surprisingly tightly when he kissed her. But Molly sensed something wrong in the kiss. The tension she felt coming from him had nothing to do with sex or desire.

She backed up a step, sliding her hands to his chest. "What's wrong?"

He rubbed his forehead with his fingers and thumb, as if to ward off a headache. "I've been waiting outside until I saw you put the baby to bed."

A chill danced at the base of her spine. She didn't know if it came from the idea of him sitting outside watching her through the windows, or his ominous tone.

He said, "I have something to tell you. And I need your full attention."

She put another step between them, dropping her hands to her sides. "You certainly have it now."

Her eyes were adjusting to the dimness enough that she could see his glance around the room. "Maybe we should go in the kitchen."

"I need to be sitting down, is that it?" A tightness formed in her stomach.

"Something like that." There was no humor in his smile.

As she turned around and led him to the kitchen, she quickly sifted through a dozen different reasons for his seriousness. None of them were good.

"Do you want some coffee, a Coke?" she asked. She needed something herself, if only to occupy her hands.

"No thanks. My stomach can't take it." He took off his jacket and hung it on the back of a chair, then sat down.

"Well, my stomach is definitely calling for a Coke." She opened the refrigerator and took out a can. Then she sat down at the table with him. "All right. What's going on?" She didn't like the way he was avoiding looking her in the eye.

And then he did—look her in the eye. His gaze was intense, yet bleak; her heart settled to the pit of her knotted stomach.

"There's no easy way to say this, so I'm just going to put it out there."

He held her motionless with his gaze. The fact that he had such power over her frightened her. His passion had drained her will; now the intensity of his presence stole her ability to move.

"I didn't come here to write a story," he said flatly.

That chill that had been teasing her spine mushroomed, consuming her whole being. Unable to articulate with her frozen lips, she remained silent.

He continued to stare into her eyes. "I came here because of Sarah Morgan."

Molly was trying to breathe in a vacuum. Her mind raced.

He reached out to touch her arm and her paralysis vanished. She jumped out of the chair and backed against the cabinets.

"Molly," he stood. "She was my sister." He looked earnest enough, as if his heart was in his hands, but it couldn't be.

"No." She shook her head; in her fear it was no more than a twitch. "That's not possible."

"Please, sit down." He sat himself. "I have so many questions I want to ask you."

She stood rigidly in place. "I have a few for you, too."

"Fair enough." He motioned for her to take a seat.

She remained standing, glad for the distance between them. "Sarah Morgan didn't have a brother. She had no family at all. So who are you really?"

"The question you need to ask is: Who was Sarah—really?" He paused, then shifted and reached behind him.

Molly snatched a paring knife off the counter. It was a pitiful attempt at protection, but it was all she had.

He halted. "I'm just getting my wallet." But he didn't start moving again until she nodded her assent. "Her real name is Julie Coletta." He opened the wallet and held up a photograph.

Molly had to step closer in order to see it clearly, but the knife stayed in her hand. The picture was of Sarah Morgan in a black cap and gown standing by Dean with his arm around her. They both looked younger.

He said, "When she got her master's at Columbia."

Molly's voice was weak but she mustered a bit of a

challenge in it when she said, "Why would she have told me she had no family?"

Dean set the photo on the table. "I was hoping you could tell me."

Molly's life for the past six months tumbled like a colorful kaleidoscope in her mind. The green dress Sarah wore the first day she'd asked Molly out for coffee. The bloodred sunset they'd watched at the end of a day of shopping thrift stores for Sarah's baby. Nicholas's birth in the silvery sleet storm. Sarah's frightened blue eyes the day she'd shown up at Molly's apartment with the baby. The cold gray light of morning when Sarah's image was shown on the morning news. Dean's embrace by the cheerful yellow fire. It finally settled on the image of Nicholas wrapped in a pale blue blanket sleeping sweetly in the crib in her bedroom.

My God, what was she going to do?

She stopped herself before she blurted out something that she'd regret, forcing herself to take a mental step backward. He hadn't said anything about the baby yet. Had he not put together that piece?

After a moment, she said, "You've been lying to me from the day we met."

"Yes."

"Why?"

"Because . . . I thought there was a possibility that you had something to do with her murder." As Molly struggled to take in a breath, he rushed on, "I know that's not true now."

She gathered an edge to her voice when she said, "You came here . . . weaseled into my life—" her fingers went to her lips "—last night, we . . . ."

He stood and started to take a step toward her.

"Stay where you are."

"Everything I've said to you, except for my reason for being here, has been the truth. But I had to be sure before I said anything."

"And *how* are you sure now?" Her spine stiffened. It was clear that he didn't know everything. What was she going to do about that? The very thought of giving up Nicholas made her nauseous.

"I know you now."

"But when you arrived, you thought I killed your sister."

His fingers massaged his forehead again. "Not killed her yourself. I didn't know what to think. Maybe it had to do with selling the baby . . . she had a baby in your clinic, then that baby disappeared and she was murdered—you left Boston unexpectedly that same day. It was all I had."

Molly threw the knife back onto the counter. The sharp clatter sent fresh shivers down her spine. In all of the horrible scenarios she'd envisioned that would threaten her and Nicholas, she never even considered something like this.

"Did you know she was going to have a baby?" she asked, not looking at him.

"No. I've been in a war zone in the Middle East for months and months. I last spoke to her in May, but she didn't say anything about a baby. I also have no idea why she left New York and went to Boston using a fake name. I don't know *anything*." His voice sounded bleak enough that she almost felt sorry for him. Almost.

A cold thought grabbed her. The truth was *she* didn't know Dean at all. His entire presence had been a lie.

Sarah had kept her pregnancy a secret from him for a reason, maybe the same reason she'd told Molly that she had no family.

She decided she wasn't going to say any more, not tonight. She wasn't just going to hand over this baby just because Dean was Sarah's brother. Nicholas had to be protected, cared for. "I want you to leave."

"Molly, please, I need your help."

She looked in his eye. "You should have said that in the beginning."

He simply stood with his hands at his sides.

"I don't have the answers you need," Molly said. "She had the baby at the clinic, then disappeared from the ER. I don't know why she used a fake name. I don't know why she came to Boston."

"You were friends."

"Yes. But I obviously didn't know her very well if I didn't know her real name."

"Do you know who the baby's father was?"

Molly shook her head. "I really want you to leave now."

He walked to the kitchen door. Then he stopped and looked at her again. "I'm sorry you're angry. I just want to find out what happened to my sister."

"And toying with me was just a little entertainment on the way? Or was that part of your *investigation*?"

His expression couldn't have been more stunned if she'd slapped him. She forced herself to ignore the tug at her heart.

"I said it once," he said, the earnestness back in his eyes, "and I'll say it one more time. But I'm not going to beg. Those moments you and I shared are real. I think you're beautiful, intelligent, brave, and dedicated. I can understand why my sister chose you as a friend." Then he turned around and walked into the darkness of the living room.

Molly held her breath until she heard the front door close behind him.

Dean stood on the front porch fighting the urge to turn around and walk back into Molly's house. Had he actually hoped he could make his admission and have her still trust him, continue to look at him with caring eyes?

The sad fact was, even though his conscious mind knew the outcome of this visit, somewhere deep in his heart he held onto the hope that she would comfort him, share in his loss, embrace him, vowing to help him find the person who murdered Julie. What a fool he was—no woman on earth could be *that* forgiving.

He'd achieved nothing but to disrupt her life, betray her trust. He never should have allowed himself to become personally involved with her. At first, he'd justified it as a means to discovering a murderer. He now saw that's all it had been—justification. He'd been attracted to her from the moment she got out of her car after running him over. As they shared more time, it only drew him emotionally closer to her. All of the bullshit about her being so cunning, creating an innocent front was just that . . . bullshit—an excuse to get closer, to know her more deeply.

The poor woman had enough trouble: a baby with no father, a father who had cast her out, a jealous neighbor ready to stir trouble in a town already filled with gossip—good God, she didn't even have any furniture to sit on.

He stalked down the steps, got in his car and headed for the Crossing House.

When he walked in, a tight knot of Monday Night Football watchers stood at the end of the bar near the TV. The Indianapolis Colts were up by a good margin, the atmosphere was relaxed and jovial. This late on a Monday, everyone appeared to be nursing their beers, leaving Benny free to tidy the bar.

Dean took a seat at the end of the bar near the entrance, not far from Benny.

"Evening," Benny said with a nod.

Dean nodded. He had intended on ordering a beer, but what came out of his mouth was, "Vodka."

"Any preference?"

"Absolut."

Benny poured, then set the drink in front of Dean.

Dean took a swig and let the vodka burn its way to the pit of his stomach.

Benny moved on and let him drink in peace. After a while, he drifted back to Dean's end of the bar and asked, "Bad night?"

"Bad month." Then Dean drained his glass and nodded for a refill.

"How's the magazine article coming?"

Dean ignored the question, not intentionally, but the vodka had temporarily assumed command of his senses.

Benny fiddled with some glassware, then said, "Does this 'bad month' have to do with my daughter?"

Dean's gaze lifted from the glass to Benny's beefy face. The movement felt sluggish. He hadn't had any hard liquor for months. Muslim countries didn't allow it, and he couldn't afford to have his wits dulled on the rare occasion that a bottle appeared. Now the vodka went straight to his tongue. "Listen, I came here to save you some heartache."

Benny's black brows arced high. "Is that so?"

Dean finished off another shot. This one went down much more smoothly. "Yes." He tapped the empty shot glass on the bar twice and looked at the bottle near Benny's hand. "You're going to regret it."

"I think you'd better slow down a bit. Why don't we get you a little something to eat?"

Dean raised a palm in the air. "No food, thanks." He tapped the glass again.

Benny put no more than a splash in the glass. "Regret what?"

Dean leaned his face close to the glass and peered at it. "Hey, I think you're trying to cheat me."

"This one's on the house." He looked over his shoulder and said, "Faye, let's have an order of nachos down here."

Dean held the glass, turning it slowly and watching the tilt of the clear liquid. "Heartache."

"Ah, yes. You were going to save me," Benny said as he put the bottle of Absolut under the counter.

"Damn straight." Dean nodded curtly. "Your daughter came here because she needs you. She's given you a gift—family, a boy to carry on your name, someone to keep you when you're old."

Sorrow pooled in Dean's gut. His mind started to run in circles like a chained dog around a tree and made just about as much sense. No family for him. No more Colettas. Why didn't Julie tell him she was pregnant? He was alone in the deepest sense of the word. Why did he have to fall for a woman who would never want to look at him again?

Benny looked narrowly at Dean. "And what is it to you—my relationship with Molly?"

Dean scrubbed his hand over his face. Was the man too stupid to see? "She's an ex-extraordinary person—smart, beautiful. You s-s-should have seen her—the man on the bicycle. . . ." He paused, unable to form a more articulate argument. Why did he drink so much? Now he was screwing this up, too. "You should be proud."

Faye bustled up and set a plate of nachos in front of him. "Darlin', you look like you lost your best friend."

He pointed a finger at Benny. "Don't let him mess up too."

Faye cast Benny a confused look. He gave her a nod and she left them alone.

Then Benny leaned close to Dean's face, his elbows on the bar. "You're not here to write a story, are you?"

Dean didn't say anything.

"That smelled rotten from the moment I heard it," Benny said. "A man of your reputation. . . ." He engaged Dean's gaze. "You're here for Molly."

"Not in the way you're thinking."

"And how do you know what I'm thinking?"

Dean lifted a shoulder, wishing he hadn't taken that last drink of vodka.

Benny lowered his voice. "Just so you're clear on what I'm thinking, I'm going to tell you. You're not here for your magazine—the only person you've been talking to in this town is my little girl."

Dean opened his mouth to say he'd spoken to others, but Benny held up a hand.

"I think you came here because of her. Now I don't know what's going on between you two. But if you're that baby's daddy, it's time for you to step up and take responsibility. Save *yourself* some heartache."

Dean blinked in surprise. "*That's* what you think?"

Benny nodded, and stood up straight again. "And that's all I'm going to say on the matter." He turned around and walked away.

Dean sat there for a long moment, wishing his problem was that simple; that he had fathered Molly's baby. That he could fix in a heartbeat.

Riley had refused dinner, saying his stomach was upset. At eleven o'clock, Clay tapped on his bedroom door.

"Yeah?"

"Can I come in?" He wanted to get whatever was bothering the boy worked out. There was no way he and Lily could explain his paternity to him in his current frame of mind. Over the past few days, Clay felt Riley drifting farther away. And it worried him.

"Sure." It was acquiescence without enthusiasm.

He and Riley had been getting along decently. Riley had seemed happy these past few months. There had been the little uproar in their house when the Mustang arrived from Riley's grandparents on his sixteenth birthday without a breath of warning to Lily. But they sat down, the three of them, and worked out ground rules that didn't actually please Riley, but were much preferable to returning the car—which had been Lily's first reaction.

Clay wondered if, when the Holts learned the truth, they would repossess the car. Well, if they did, that would show Riley just how shallow they were. For sixteen years, they'd loved him as a grandson. Clay fervently hoped they would behave well and not cause the boy more hurt than he was already in for.

Riley was stretched out on his bed in the dark. From the light spilling from the hallway, Clay could see he was still dressed. He crossed the room and sat at the foot of the bed. "Something's bothering you. Do you want to talk about it?"

Riley rolled over on his side and faced the wall.

Clay sighed. "Okay, if you change your mind. . . ." He got up and started to leave.

He had his hand on the doorknob ready to close the door when Riley said, "Did you ever do something you were sorry for, but waited too long to undo it?"

Clay stopped. He didn't rush back in the room as he was tempted to do. From where he stood, he said, "More times than I care to admit."

Riley rolled onto his back. "How do you know when it's too late?"

Clay accepted this as an invitation back into the room. He moved slowly, as if he feared any sudden movements would close the door Riley had just opened. "If you were wrong . . . and it hurt someone else, it's never too late to do something about it."

Propping his head on one hand, Riley faced Clay. "I don't think it'll make any difference."

"For you? Or for the other person?"

After a moment, Riley said, "I don't think she'll forgive me."

"Sometimes you have to say it anyway. The forgiveness is for you; the apology is what you give to someone else." Clay chanced sitting back down on the bed. Riley didn't withdraw. Clay finally asked, "Is this about Codi?"

After flopping on his back and blowing out a long stream of air, Riley said, "Codi never forgives. That *would* be wasted breath. She's hooked up with someone else anyhow."

"Sorry."

Riley said, "I'm not. Am I terrible? She left and I don't even care."

"I'd say it meant you didn't care that much for her in the first place."

Riley started thumping his fist rhythmically against the mattress. "Yeah. But there's someone else . . . I hurt her feelings a long time ago. I want to undo it."

"There's no undoing. Once something's done, you have to deal with it or walk away." He paused. "A man deals with it and doesn't make the same mistake again."

"I don't know if I can stand it if she hates me."

"Do you think she'll hate you any less if you don't do anything?"

Riley shook his head. "But I wouldn't have to face her rejection head on."

Clay put a hand on Riley's shoulder. "Anything worth having involves risk. My advice is be a man, step up and face her. You can't be any worse off."

"That's what you think."

It was four in the morning. Molly felt as if someone had taken a garden shovel and dug out her heart. There was nothing in the center of her chest but a cold, dark, aching void. She'd been pacing the floor of her empty house for hours, listening to her own ragged breathing, trying to corral her stampeding thoughts, fighting the urge to do the unthinkable.

Why had Sarah (she just couldn't think of her friend as Julie Coletta) lied about not having family? Had she been hiding from her brother too?

Molly had made a promise—and it weighed more heavily on her in this moment than when she'd been coerced into making it. Now she loved this child as her own. She would lay down her life to protect him. If there was some reason Sarah wanted to keep Dean from her child, could Molly just hand him over?

Stop! She crushed her temples between her palms. *You're just looking for excuses to do the* wrong *thing*.

She paused before the living room window and looked out on the quiet night. A light-colored cat trotted across the deserted street beneath the weak glow of the streetlight, giving her a greater sense of isolation. It seemed the whole world slept; it was just Molly and the creatures of the darkness. Would she ever again pass a peaceful night? It seemed no matter what choice she made, it was going to haunt her for the rest of her life.

How easy it would be to just let Dean go back to where he came from. She would never have to see him again and he could think whatever he wanted about the fate of Sarah's baby. It hardly seemed in Nicholas's best interest to give him to someone who lived Dean's nomadic life. Would he even *want* Nicholas?

She quieted the little voice that said Dean had adapted with amazing swiftness to handling a baby. Especially considering the initial terror he exhibited the first time he held Nicholas. In fact, Dean looked . . . blissful . . . as he gave Nicholas a bottle.

Her promise had been to keep Nicholas safe from *his father*. No more. She should stop trying to read more into Sarah's motivation. Dean had been overseas, difficult to get in touch with—how could Sarah possibly have turned to him in this situation?

That spawned another question. Now that Dean had reached a dead end in Glens Crossing, would he continue to probe until he found the baby's father—and Sarah's killer?

She pounded a fist against her palm. "Sarah, why did you keep so many secrets? You trusted me with your son, why not the truth?" Molly's voice bounced around the empty living room off the bare windows and stark walls, sending a chill over her.

She tried to think of that last day with Sarah. Had she offered any clues that Molly had been too stunned to notice at the time?

Clearly, Sarah had been afraid. But Molly didn't for a moment think she'd planned on getting killed. On the contrary, she had planned on setting something in motion that would free her from the baby's father forever. Something that would allow her and Nicholas to start over—safe.

If she'd only told Molly *who* the father was, then perhaps she could piece together what Sarah had been doing on that last day.

Had she gone to see the father? That seemed unlikely, but she had insisted wherever she was going, the baby could not. Had she been arranging transportation? Her body had been found near enough to the train station, bus terminal, and airport to make it possible.

As Molly asked all of these questions, she realized none of them mattered in this moment. She was using them as a way to avoid asking herself the single question that meant *everything*: Was she going to tell Dean that Nicholas was his missing nephew—knowing that once she did, he would not only take her son away, but would have the power to ruin her?

Chapter 16

E ven though this was a parent-teacher conference day and there was no school, Riley got up early. He skipped breakfast, slipping through the kitchen too quickly for his mom to ask her usual thousand questions.

Getting in his car, he drove past the path that led to the foot of the dam, past the lake house, then into town to Mickey's house.

At the last minute, instead of stopping, he drove on by. It was probably too early; she probably wouldn't even be up yet.

He circled the square, looking at all of the people heading to work at the courthouse. They reminded Riley of ants hurrying toward an anthill. It made him sort of depressed. He'd had a weird mix of eagerness and dread since he'd awakened and thought about seeing Mickey. Seeing all of these people, none looking too happy, trudging into work, made the future appear as bleak as it felt at the moment. Was that what he had to look forward to?

He left the square and headed toward the edge of town.

He passed Kingston's Market. Then he turned right, passing between the big rock pillars that flanked the narrow road that curled deep into the wooded park. He drove to the playground and shut off the engine. The mists of early morning were still clinging to the ground, the sun was not high enough to do more than add a ghostly light. It made the deserted swings and teeter-totters look like something out of a horror movie where all of the children had vanished.

As he sat there, he stared at the spot where he'd led Mickey's father into a trap. It seemed so long ago when he thought of his and Mickey's friendship, but just like yesterday when he recalled how frightened he'd been. Closing his eyes, he leaned his head against the back of the driver's seat. What if he had never set that trap? Would he and Mickey still be friends? He ran his hands through his hair and felt like screaming. It was too complicated to even try to figure out.

He started the Mustang and drove back to Grant Street. When he pulled up in front of Mickey's house, she was just coming down the front steps. *This might make it easier. It'll look like I just happened to be driving by.*

He pulled to the curb and rolled down the passenger window.

"Hi!" he called.

She gave him a sideways glance. "You're up early."

He shrugged. "Can I give you a ride?"

The look she cast him nearly made his heart stop. How could he be so stupid? He'd used nearly the same words Codi had taunted her with.

Mickey started walking toward town. "No."

"Come on! I'm trying to be nice," he called after her.

She stopped in her tracks. Her back was stiff when she turned around and walked to where his car sat at the curb. "Riley Holt, I don't need you to be nice to me."

He gripped the steering wheel so hard it set off cramps in his hands. Then, in desperation, he blurted out, "I want to go back to the way things used to be."

She tilted her head, her pale hair sliding over her shoulder. "For how long? Until we go back to school tomorrow?" Without waiting for any form of response, she turned around and stomped back up the steps and into the house.

Feeling as if he had swallowed a bunch of bees, Riley peeled away from the curb. He drove too fast, but he didn't care. Why couldn't Mickey just give him a chance?

When he got back home, his mom and Clay were upstairs. He heard footsteps on the floor overhead and muffled voices coming from their bedroom. They were going to the high school conferences later this morning, so Clay hadn't gone to the marina as usual. Riley couldn't understand why Clay wanted to go to conferences in the first place.

As he entered the downstairs hall, their voices carried down the stairwell. Why couldn't they have been gone? He already felt like breaking things; he didn't want a bunch of stupid questions about why he was upset.

When he heard his mom mention his dad's name, he froze. Were they arguing about his dad? Things had been weird the last time he and Dad talked on the phone. For a heart-stopping moment, Riley feared his dad was drinking again. He held his breath, inched silently up the steps and listened.

Clay said, "Peter's made this threat before."

"I think he means it this time." His mother sounded like she'd been crying.

"What does he have to gain?"

"At this point, I think he just wants to hurt anyone he can—even Riley."

Riley continued to creep up the stairs, anger balled in his chest burning like a fire.

Clay's voice grew rough. "Dammit. I *knew* we should have told him right away. It was just a matter of time before Peter would start with these stupid power games."

"We were going to . . . but so much keeps happening."

Clay lowered his voice, sounding sad. "We've *allowed* other things to get in the way. It's time Riley knows. And I want it to be from our lips, not Peter's."

There was a pause and Riley heard his mother sniffle.

"We'll tell him today," Clay said softly. "As soon as he gets back. There's no school. He'll have time to adjust before he has to see other people. And this way we can be certain to tell him before Peter does."

Riley shoved the partially open bedroom door open and it cracked against the wall. "Tell me what?"

After Nicholas went down for his morning nap, Molly's head was splitting. Lack of sleep, wrestling with her sense of right and wrong, multiplied by the stress of fearing Dean would call—or worse, show up—before she was ready, had all taken their toll. She took a hot shower and lay down on her bed for a few minutes.

She didn't open her eyes again until she heard Nicholas cry. Bolting upright, she struggled through the confusion of being pulled from a deep sleep. She looked at the clock. Crap, it was one o'clock already. She had too much to do today to have lost that much time.

Lily had said there was no school today, which worked perfectly with Molly's needs. Before she got Nicholas out of his crib, she fired a quick call to Mickey, to ask her to babysit at three. That should give her enough time to get Nicholas fed and herself together.

Promptly at three, Mickey knocked on the back door. Molly liked that, the backdoor neighborliness that Mickey was adopting. Molly hoped that a true friendship would develop between her and the teenager—Mickey could use someone on her side. As soon as Mickey had her coat off, Molly handed Nicholas over; that was another thing she liked about Mickey, the calm confident way she handled the baby.

Molly then gave Mickey both written and verbal instructions—which the girl accepted graciously. Mickey might not actually need to hear all of this, but Molly still needed to say it. She hadn't gotten a cell phone yet; she'd feel a lot better leaving him after—

This could be the last time you ever leave him. The truth of that thought caused a hitch in her breath. But she'd made her mind up; she wouldn't allow herself second thoughts now.

Mickey was talking silly baby-talk to Nicholas. He responded with a sweet toothless smile that reached right in and wrung the life out of Molly's resolve. He'd only been smiling for a week, and it defined him as a person unto himself—just as Sarah had sworn he would be.

Molly turned quickly, swiping her tears so Mickey wouldn't see. Then she put on her jacket. It was about twenty minutes to Brian's lake cottage where Dean was staying. Give twenty minutes for him to raise holy hell; twenty minutes back; she should only be gone an hour or so.

And then . . . would he demand she hand over the baby instantly? She wished for more time, even though she knew that would do nothing to dull the pain of separation.

She kissed the baby on the head, drawing in the sweet scent of him as if it were the last time. She had her hand on the back door when the telephone rang.

"Want me to get it?" Mickey asked.

"Yes." Molly was afraid it might be Dean. What she had to say needed to be said in person. She lingered a moment to see who it was.

She could tell by the look on Mickey's face that something was wrong.

"No, Mrs. Winters, she's right here." She handed the phone to Molly. "She's really upset. Something about Riley."

Molly snatched the receiver. "What's wrong?" Even as she asked, her mind conjured the picture of Riley's red Mustang wrapped around a tree.

"Riley's gone. He overheard Clay and me talking today and . . . oh, Mol, we've never told anyone . . . we were going to tell him, but everything's messed up . . . I don't know where he could have gone. Clay's looked everywhere and checked with all of his friends. He might come to you, that's why I called." The words tumbled over one another as they rushed out of her sister's mouth.

"Take a breath and tell me one thing at a time."

Lily gave a hiccupping sob. "Oh, Mol, Peter's not Riley's father—Clay is."

Molly felt as if someone had just spun her head completely around on her shoulders, leaving her eyeballs to rattle back into place. "What?"

"It's a long story. Clay and I were together, then he disappeared, I married Peter . . . I was trying to do the right thing for the baby . . ."

Molly could certainly understand that motivation; every move she'd made for the past six weeks had been trying to do the right thing for the baby. "All right. So he overheard you talking and you had to tell him. Obviously he didn't take it well."

Another sob bubbled from Lily.

"When did he leave?"

"He was in his room. He must have gone out the upstairs window. Sometime between ten and one."

"He took his car?"

"Yes. Oh, that car is too fast for him. We never should have let him keep it. And he was such a mess . . . what if he's had a wreck?"

"You'd have heard from the sheriff if he'd wrecked." Molly knew it sometimes took hours to notify families, but she kept that to herself.

"Did he take anything with him? Maybe he went to see his da—Peter."

"He knows he's not allowed to drive to Chicago!"

"Lil, I don't think he's considering the rules right now."

Lily sniffled loudly. "I didn't notice anything gone. Clay called Peter—just in case he was headed there. Oh, God, I don't want him to run to Peter!" Hysteria was edging back into her voice.

"I'm sure he's not far." Molly glanced at Mickey; she looked as worried as Lily sounded. "I'm coming out."

"No!" Lily took a breath. "No, Clay's in and out. I want you to stay there in case Riley wants to go someplace other than home. I've called Dad, too."

Molly wanted to ask if she'd told Dad *why* Riley left, but felt now wasn't the time. "I could have Mickey stay here and wait for him."

"I'm fine. Just stay there and call me if he shows up."

"All right." She paused. "Lily, I'm sure he's fine. This was a really big shock. He just needed some time alone to think."

"Thanks." It was little more than a strangled sound. Then Lily hung up.

When Molly replaced the receiver, she turned to Mickey. "Riley's run off. There was some . . . troubling news. I guess I'm not going anywhere after all. Lily wants me to wait here in case he shows up."

Mickey said, "I'll go ahead and put the baby down for his nap." Then she walked out of the kitchen before Molly responded.

Odd as it seemed, she was glad to have Mickey here. She only felt badly that Lily was alone. But Lily's plan made logical sense; best to keep family members where Riley could find them. Poor kid. What a thing to discover at sixteen.

And when were you planning on telling Nicholas?

As things were working out, she might never have to answer that question.

Molly tried to focus on the immediate problem. She wracked her brain, trying to think of places she would have gone when she was a teenager and mad with her dad. Suddenly she realized, impossible as it seemed, she had never felt the need to run and hide, even through those turbulent adolescent years. She and Dad might have huffed and stomped at one another, they might have had fire shooting out of their nostrils, but they always locked horns and stuck with it until the issue was resolved. It was probably because they were both too stubborn to be the first to walk away. At least that had been true until she arrived in town with Nicholas. Molly *had* walked away then, she realized now, because she was trying to ignore the fear that she was doing the wrong thing.

She took off her jacket and sat down at the kitchen table, hoping for a call saying Riley had arrived back at home, safe and sound. If he didn't show up by nightfall, they had a problem.

She heard Mickey softly singing to Nicholas in the bedroom and her heart turned to dust. Once Nicholas was gone from her life—would she stay here? It didn't seem to matter; life was going to be bleak and painful wherever she was. Perhaps Dean wouldn't damn her with bitter punishment. Maybe he would even allow her to visit; perhaps she could become Nicholas's favorite "aunt." It would be better than having him ripped from her forever.

Most likely she was headed to jail, or probation with immediate revocation of her medical license.

Molly had her face buried in her hands when she heard Mickey come back into the kitchen.

The girl put a hand on Molly's shoulder. "Are you okay?"

Molly raised her face with a weak smile and patted Mickey's hand. "Yeah." Then she sighed and picked up her purse. "I'll go ahead and pay you."

Mickey sat down at the table. "No."

"I can't ask you to come over here for nothing."

Mickey gave a dismissive wave. "I love being with Nicholas. Besides I didn't do anything."

"Anyone ever tell you you're a great kid?"

"Not recently."

Molly had meant it as a light comment, but Mickey's response was anything but light.

Molly said, "Sometimes it's hard with mothers and daughters. I didn't have a mom, so I didn't actually go through it myself. But my dad and I sure went some rounds."

With a slight lift of the shoulder, Mickey said, "I know Mom loves me. She just doesn't *get* me." She concentrated on twisting the silver ring she wore on her right hand.

"Mothers want the best for their children; your mom just sees things differently than you do. Someday you'll find a way to make things work between you."

Mickey's sigh tore at Molly's already bleeding heart. "I hope so. Maybe it'll be better after I move away."

Molly tilted her head. "You're set on leaving here?"

"Oh yeah!" There was no room for doubt in that answer.

Molly said, "It's important that you do what you think is best for yourself—not what others want for you." Then she gave a dry chuckle. "But I think you've already figured that out. You're miles ahead of the game."

Mickey sat in silence for a moment, then she asked, "Do they think Riley ran away?"

"I don't think so. He didn't take anything with him. He

just needed to be alone. But I wish he'd told his mom, she's worried sick."

Mickey took the salt shaker and turned it in a slow circle. "Did they check with—Codi Craig?"

"I think Clay's covered most of his friends. Lily said he's looked everywhere."

After a moment's hesitation, Mickey looked into Molly's eyes and said, "Not everywhere."

"Do you have an idea where Riley could be?" Hope sparked in her chest.

The girl hesitated. "Maybe."

"Well, tell me and I'll call Lily." Molly started for the phone.

Mickey looked pensive.

"What?" Molly stopped and looked at her. "Why can't you tell me?"

"It'd be a breach of trust."

Molly recognized the steadfast resolve in Mickey's eyes. It reminded her of herself. She tried anyway. "Mickey, really, you need to tell me."

With a shake of her head, Mickey said, "I'll go and see if he's there. Maybe I can talk him into going home."

"What if you can't? His parents need to know where he is."

"If he's there, he's perfectly safe. I'll tell his mother that."

Molly pushed her car keys across the table toward Mickey. "Take my car."

All through the dark hours, beginning sometime after the vodka had released its disorienting hold, Dean's mind had swung from one problem to the other and back again.

Even as each thought had stampeded over the other, Molly had dominated his mind. It made him ashamed that he'd spent more of the night trying to figure out how to cultivate her forgiveness, how to win back her trust, than he had on pondering his sister's death.

He had watched a dazzling pink sunrise from the narrow pier that jutted out from the shore. Before his eyes, the lake had transformed from cold black to deep purple. Then the water caught the pink fire from the sky. At that point, he'd finally gone to bed.

Now it was mid-afternoon. He awakened with a rolling stomach and splitting head. He forced himself to start moving. After he took a shower, he looked out the window and saw his car was missing.

Suffering a brief moment of panic, he finally recalled Benny taking his keys and having someone—Dean couldn't remember if it had been a man or a woman— drive him home.

Now he had to fetch his car somehow. He certainly didn't feel like hiking several miles with this throbbing head. So he went back to the living room and sat on the couch.

He should really leave town today; go to New York and start backtracking Julie's life prior to her disappearance. There had to be clues that her friends and the overworked police had simply missed. The father of her baby was most likely a New Yorker. If he located that man, perhaps new light could be shed on the investigation.

All that was logical, and still he couldn't bring himself to pack his suitcase and make a flight reservation. Not until he saw Molly again.

He dug around the kitchen cabinets and found an old

phone book. He checked the Yellow Pages for a listing for a taxi service.

Of course he didn't find one. What did people around here do when they needed a ride somewhere?

They called a neighbor or a friend. People here helped one another out.

Well, Dean didn't have many friends around here.

He called Brian Mitchell and offered to buy him dinner at the Crossing House if he would come and get him. Brian agreed and said he'd be there around five-thirty. Dean decided he'd head over to Molly's after that and see if she'd let him in the door.

Then he put a call in to his investigator in Boston. Harry Amundson was three days overdue with his report. Which for Harry was still about four days shy of his normal tardiness. Dean had been in no particular hurry, as he'd already made his own personal assessment of Molly Boudreau. But if he was leaving town, he should see if Harry had happened to turn up anything of value. Besides, he was thinking of sending Harry up to New York City to get a head start on working up Julie's last days there.

Harry's voice mail picked up. Dean left his message with a firm request for a call back today. Then he got out a tablet of paper and began to write down every last scrap of information he'd discovered about his sister.

There wasn't a safe place to park Dr. Boudreau's car near the narrow path that led down to Blackwater Creek, so Mickey parked at Riley's old summer house. She was careful to pull across the lawn and park on the lake side of the house, tucking the car in beside a huge spruce. If one of the adults saw the car, they might just figure out where to look. She couldn't risk violating the sanctity of their secret place.

Then she walked fifteen minutes to where the path cut into the woods. The sun was going down, casting a brilliant orange glow in the western sky and letting the temperature begin a downward slide into night. It was even chillier as she made her way to the bottom of the ravine. She hadn't brought gloves so she stuck her hands in her jacket pockets. If Riley was down here, he had to be freezing.

As she followed the winding creek, butterflies began to flit around in her stomach. She'd been praying for something like this to happen, something dramatic and life-altering that would bring her and Riley back together. But now that something terrible had happened and Riley was suffering, she battled guilt over her selfishness.

What if his words this morning asking to reestablish their friendship meant as little as she initially feared? As her feet slipped on the muddy bank she told herself that really didn't matter. What mattered was making sure he was safe—and then putting his mother's mind to rest, at least as far as his whereabouts were concerned.

She hoped Riley would come back with her. If he refused, the parents were sure to put the screws to her to divulge where he was. She could never do that. This place would lose all of its healing power if people knew where to find them.

What made her so sure he was here?

Because I know him.

Even though they'd been acting like strangers for over a year, she knew him inside and out. They'd formed a bond during that first summer and Mickey doubted it would ever truly be broken. If she'd really needed him, he would have come through—she just knew it in her heart. His attempt to apologize told her the bond was still there, buried beneath high school bullshit.

There was no lingering twilight in November. It was rapidly getting dark. Why didn't she bring the flashlight? As she'd left the house, Dr. Boudreau had shouted out the door that there was an emergency kit in the trunk of the car. Mickey had been so anxious to get to Riley, her common sense had deserted her. And now that flashlight was twenty minutes behind her.

She caught her toe on a root and nearly fell on her nose. As she flailed her arms to save herself, she caught a branch and scraped it across her face just below her eye. It stung like a whip, but at least she hadn't fallen into the creek. Taking a minute to calm herself, she decided she'd better slow her pace.

Once she reached the base of the dam, the rushing water made it difficult to hear if anyone was nearby. It was very dark now and she didn't relish the idea of veering away from the creek. But the place she and Riley shared was still fifty yards away. If she called for him, he might just step behind a tree and she'd never find him in the dark.

She saw the white-barked sycamore that sat near the path that led to the stone outcropping where they used to hang out and started in that direction. It was difficult not to sound like a bear crashing through the brush as she felt her way along, but it couldn't be helped. There was another sycamore, whose bark shone eerily in the darkness, just at the edge of the clearing. Mickey stopped and listened. Then she saw a tiny orange glow right about where the limestone shelf should be.

She moved toward it, biting her tongue to keep from yelling at Riley for smoking.

Suddenly the orange dot raised a couple of feet higher. Riley had either seen or heard her and stood up.

"Riley, it's Mickey." Just then, she stepped on something that turned her ankle so hard her knee buckled and she saw stars. "Ouch! Oooohh." She went down on one knee.

"Mickey! Stay right there! Are you all right?"

She heard him moving her way.

"I twisted my ankle."

"Don't put any weight on it. And don't move."

Then he was beside her, with one arm around her waist, pulling her arm over his shoulder, helping her to stand. "Now, try it—not too much, easy."

The instant Mickey put the slightest pressure on that leg, bright white shafts of pain exploded from her ankle. It stole her breath, making her shout of pain no more than a hiss. She wiped her watering eyes with her free hand and forced in a deep breath before she passed out. "Ow! I think I broke it."

"All right." He twisted as he looked around. "The cold water in the creek would probably be good for it."

"Probably, if I don't freeze to death."

"Let's get you set down someplace. If I support you, can you get over to the rock?"

"Yes. But shouldn't we be moving in the other direction?"

"Mickey, you can't think you're going to walk out of here."

"Shit." How could she have screwed up something as simple as coming here and finding him?

"Come on." He moved them toward the rock.

By the time he lowered her to the ground beneath the outcropping, with her back against the exposed limestone, she'd broken into a sweat from the pain.

"You should take your shoe off."

"I'll never get it back on."

"You're not going anywhere. Take it off, but leave your sock on."

She untied her shoelaces and loosened them. "I can't pull it off without turning my ankle. Can you take it off for me?"

He moved with reluctance, but he grasped her calf to support her leg and removed her shoe.

She yelped.

"Sorry," he said softly.

"Not your fault." She leaned back against the cold stone again and blew out short breaths until the pain settled.

He sat in front of her. "What are you doing out here?"

"Looking for you."

"Why?" He sounded surprised.

"Everybody's looking for you. I was at your aunt's when your mom called. I thought you might be here— but I didn't want to tell anyone about this place. So I came to find you."

He spun around and leaned against the limestone beside her. He blew out a long, heavy breath. "So you know?"

"Just that something that happened at home upset you."

He sat quietly for a minute.

"You don't have to tell me. I just wanted to make sure you're all right."

After a moment, he said, "I want to tell you. You're

probably the only person now who will understand how I feel."

She wanted to say she had *always* been that person, but she let it lie.

He finally said, "I just found out that Dad's not my real father."

"Oh." She didn't dare say more.

"Clay's my father."

Mickey sat up straighter. "That's interesting."

"It's insane."

"No. It's life. It can get real messy sometimes." Her own was a perfect example.

"I can't understand why they didn't tell me before."

"I imagine it wasn't easy—plus there's your dad and grandparents to tell, too. This could get really complicated." She tried to say all this in a tone that didn't condone what his mother had done, but maybe would open his eyes to the other side of the problem.

"That's what pisses me off the most. Dad knew. He's always known."

"Hum. How about your grandparents?"

"They *say* no one else knows. Mom even said Clay didn't know until we moved here. They had some long involved story about them having a fight and Clay getting arrested, but Mom didn't know where he was. Then she married Dad."

"So, what do you propose to do; live out here in the woods?"

She felt him tense beside her. For a minute, she thought he was going to be mad, but he finally laughed. "God, I've missed you."

Mickey smiled, even though her ankle was throbbing.

Riley said, "Actually, I was about to go home when you showed up. I just needed to be away from everyone for a while."

"You might have left a note."

"Okay, so maybe I wanted them to be upset." He didn't sound very sorry.

"That's very mature of you to admit," Mickey said in her most school-counselorish voice.

"Well, now we've got a real problem. I can carry you piggyback, but not in the dark without breaking both of our necks."

"Don't you have a cell phone?" she asked.

"Yeah. I left it in the car. It wouldn't work down here anyway."

"Maybe after I rest for a few minutes, I'll be able to walk with your help."

"Again," he sounded like he was trying to maintain patience with an uncomprehending child, "not in the dark without further broken bones."

"You should go back. Everyone is going to be crazy with both of us gone. You can come back for me with help."

"I'm not leaving you down here in the dark."

Mickey liked the way he said it with such firm commitment.

But practicality forced her to say, "I don't think there are any bears to worry about. Bigfoot is two thousand miles away. Nobody knows about this place. I'll be perfectly safe." If only she felt as confident of that as she tried to sound. The thought of being stuck down here alone in the dark with a bad leg gave her the creeps, big time.

"Forget it."

"Where did you leave your car? Maybe someone will find it and come looking."

"Nope. It's parked on a closed off access road to the lake. I put the chain back up after I drove in." He put an arm around her and pulled her closer. "It's just you and me . . . like old times."

Mickey wished with all of her heart that it was true.

Dean spent an unusual dinner with Brian. He was having a difficult time keeping his mind on the conversation. He looked up at the door of the Crossing House every time someone new walked in. After he did it for the fifth time, he realized he was hoping Molly would show up.

There was another problem. Every other sentence out of Brian's mouth seemed to be about Molly—or Molly *and Nicholas*. It was getting on his nerves. He nearly asked Brian if he was interested in dating her. But he was afraid the answer might be yes.

At seven-thirty, he and Brian parted company in the parking lot. Dean drove past Molly's house, but her car wasn't in the drive. He took the long way home, driving all the way around Forrester Lake. Brian's interest in Molly had settled like a thistle thorn under his skin. Did Dean actually have any right to think the possessive thoughts he'd been having all evening? He was leaving, after all. Molly and Brian would live in this town for years. The thistle thorn became a sting weed. He didn't even want to think the thought.

Once he got back to the cottage, he found himself too restless to concentrate on a plan for tracing Julie's last months.

Just when he stepped outside to take a walk down to the dock, his cell phone rang.

"Hello?" He stopped on the front porch.

"Dean, Harry here."

"Hey, Harry. I have some more work for you. How would you feel about a few days in New York?"

"Somehow I don't think I'm going to have time to take in a Broadway show."

"You find what I need, and I'll buy you front row tickets." He explained what he wanted done, gave him a list of Julie's friends, her employer and favorite restaurant. "There's nothing left at her apartment. The super had it cleaned out after she disappeared. The stuff is in storage. I already looked through it once. The main objective is to locate a man she had a relationship with—a very quiet relationship."

"I've got all I need. I have a couple of other cases right now. I can go on Thursday."

Dean wanted to tell him to forget the other cases, but a couple of days wasn't going to make a huge difference at this point. He asked, "Do you have the financials on Dr. Boudreau?"

"Uh, yeah. Let me flip to my notes." After a pause, he said, "She did go to the hospital after your sister was transported to the ER, but the nurses said Julie was already gone by then. Someone snatched Julie's medical record at some point. As far as the financials go, nothing. No big deposits. No new car. No credit card payoffs . . . in fact she missed her last student loan payment."

"Hum. That's probably because of the baby."

"What?"

"She just had a baby—that's probably why she's behind."

"You've got your wires crossed, buddy. I've been all over her employment records—you see, I know a lady . . . well, that's really beside the point—anyway, Dr. Boudreau didn't have a baby. No time off. No medical insurance claim."

"You've made a mistake."

"No mistake. She hasn't missed a day of work since she started at Boston General. Her departure was abrupt because of her father's health. I think they would have noticed a little thing like a ninth-month pregnancy."

Her father had seemed in fine health to Dean. Molly had never once mentioned that as the reason she'd come back. It was all about the baby.

The phone fell away from his ear. His entire body caught fire as the little things fell into place.

How stupid could he have been?

Chapter 17

"You know, it does piss me off," Riley said.

At first Mickey had felt awkward, nervous, and exposed being this close to him. She didn't want to open herself and be played for a fool. But the longer they were together, the more relaxed she became. He'd been talking pretty much nonstop since they'd snuggled close for warmth. She didn't know if he was trying to take her mind off of her painful injury, or trying to unload things that had built up over the past eighteen months, but she didn't care. She loved the sound of his voice. He could talk all night long and she wouldn't tire of hearing him.

"What pisses you off?" They were lying on the ground now, next to the small campfire he'd built. She didn't want to admit that there was something good about the fact that he'd been down here smoking, so she didn't remark about the lighter. Her head rested on his shoulder. He'd taken his coat off and put it on the ground beneath them and hers went over them. The little blaze and their shared body heat kept them pretty warm. The only thing that was cold was her unshod foot, and that was probably a good thing.

"Just yesterday Clay and I had this big talk about . . . well, it was about something that I was wishing I could undo. He was all, 'step up and be a man,' and 'you have to deal with what you've done,' and 'anything worthwhile involves risk.' And look at what a coward *he's* been!"

Mickey's hand had slowly worked its way from being balled against her own chest to resting on his; she could feel his heart beating rapidly beneath it. "I know how awful it is to be lied to. I can't say I blame you for being pissed." She paused. "But. . . ."

He didn't jump on it right away, but he finally prompted. "But?"

"When do you think it would have been better to tell you? When you were little? If your parents had stayed married, it might have been best to let things be. And I can see why your mom didn't break the news as soon as you came here. Things were sort of a mess as I recall—you were in trouble already.

"I suppose it would have been better if they'd told you *before* they were married." A thought struck her that was so strong it nearly made her own heart do a double beat. "Maybe they were afraid you'd be so upset, they *couldn't*."

"Couldn't what?"

"Get married. It seems to me that your mom and Clay waited a long time to be together." Mickey knew all about waiting for someone you cared about.

He just grunted.

"And at least you know your parents—your birth

parents—loved each other. Sometimes I think my parents always hated each other. Maybe that's why my mom and I aren't . . . good together. I'm the reason she married my dad in the first place."

"We've got that in common then. Mom married Dad, I mean Peter, because of me. I guess maybe that kind of marriage never works out."

"I've always said that babies are *not* a good reason to get married. You have to be responsible for the child, but really, why compound your mistakes? I can tell you, the kid isn't any better off in the long run." She realized she sounded like she was lecturing and decided to let the subject drop there. She was actually amazed that he was handling this as well as he was. She guessed he'd done some growing up in the past months, too.

After a few minutes, he said, "I guess I don't have to worry about inheriting alcoholism any more."

She knew from the start that Riley didn't drink because he feared ending up like his dad. With that danger removed, would he start drinking like the rest of that crowd he hung with? She must have made a noise of distress, because his arm tightened around her.

"Don't worry. I don't plan on going on a bender now."

"You'd better not; I'll kick your ass."

He laughed. "As if you could."

She raised her head and looked at him. "Don't underestimate me, Riley Holt."

"I won't . . . ever again." His hand slipped behind her head and he kissed her.

As his lips touched hers, Mickey's heart skyrocketed. It felt . . . right. She *did* understand about waiting for someone. And the joy of reunion robbed her of her breath, filled her soul with light and launched long-buried hopes.

When he stopped kissing her, his thumb caressed her cheek. "How's your ankle?"

She ran her tongue along her lips, not wanting to lose the taste of him. "What ankle?"

He laughed, then pulled her head back onto his shoulder. "Try to sleep. At first light, I'll go for help."

She dutifully closed her eyes, but knew there was no way she was wasting this time sleeping. She could sleep when she was alone in her room.

After a few minutes, he startled her by speaking. "I wonder if I'll have to change my name."

She was glad there was no bitterness in the question. She cuddled closer. Then a thought occurred to her that made a chuckle bubble forth.

"What?" he asked.

"My mom's going to be so disappointed you're not a Holt."

Molly held the phone away from her ear. Lily's voice carried easily across the space. She was definitely opposed to Molly's allowing Mickey to go after Riley. And at this moment, Molly was beginning to question herself. It was almost ten o'clock and neither child had reappeared. Clay had been looking everywhere; neither car had turned up.

But Molly knew Mickey had a good head on her shoulders. And Riley—well, Riley was just frustrated, and understandably so. But he was a good kid; he'd grown up a lot in the past couple of years.

The fact that Mickey hadn't come back told Molly that

she'd found him. She was certain it was just a matter of time before they came home.

About five minutes before, Molly had called Karen and let her know what was going on. It was difficult to gauge her reaction because Karen simply hung up.

As Lily unloaded via the phone, a loud pounding sounded at Molly's front door. She let Lily continue to vent and went to the door with the cordless phone in her hand.

The second the latch was undone, Karen shoved her way inside. "What do you mean, letting Michaeline go after a boy who might be unstable? He's done something to her, I just know it! I've called the sheriff."

Molly put the phone back to her face. "Lily, I have to go; Karen's here. I'll call you back in a bit." She didn't wait for Lily to agree before she disconnected.

Karen had steamrolled on into the kitchen. The second Molly showed her face, Karen began again. "I should have known better than to let Michaeline spend time over here. You Boudreaus are nothing but trouble."

Molly had planned on calming a distraught mother, gently helping her see that there really was no danger, but this attack flipped her switch. "That sounds odd coming from the wife of the man who dealt drugs to teenagers."

"*Ex*-wife!" Karen said through gritted teeth. "Riley has kidnapped her—"

"Hold it!" Molly raised a hand. "Just hold it right there! First of all, you know that's not true. Secondly, here it is almost ten o'clock and you hadn't bothered to wonder where she was? If I hadn't called, you'd still be over there painting your fingernails."

Karen started to open her mouth.

"I'm not finished! As of yesterday, Riley Holt was a wonderful young person. You *wanted* Mickey to spend time with him—it was your own daughter you thought was odd."

"If he's hurt Michaeline—I'm going to take everything the high and mighty Holts have."

Molly wanted to slap the woman. "I was wrong about you. Earlier today I told Mickey that mothers always want what's best for their children—but I truly doubt that's the case with you. You're only thinking of yourself."

A man's voice sounded from the door between the kitchen and living room. "There seems to be a lot of that going around."

Molly spun around to see Dean filling up the doorway. "How did you get in?"

"Front door was open."

"Well, go close it—with yourself on the outside." She didn't have the patience to deal with him at this moment. What they had to discuss needed to be done as calmly and as privately as possible.

Karen hurried to Dean's side. Her tears flowed freely. "Her nephew has kidnapped my daughter!" Her hands clutched her chest. "Oh, I don't know what I'm going to do."

Dean stood unmoving, staring at Molly in a way that said he hadn't heard a word of Karen's theatrics. Everything about his posture said something was very wrong.

"Karen," Molly said, "you should go home and wait for the ransom call."

"Do you hear? Do you hear how she makes light of my baby's disappearance!"

Finally Dean's gaze moved from Molly and he looked at Karen. "Go home."

Completely undone, Karen ran out of the house. The front door slammed behind her.

Molly said, "Thank you. She's making this situation impossible. Riley got angry and went to hide someplace and Mickey thought she might know where he was and went to find him. They should have been back hours ago. Lily's beside herself. And now Karen—"

Dean took a step closer and Molly could see he was furious.

"Where's the baby?" he asked in a cold tone that whistled through her like a winter wind.

It was all Dean could do to keep from grabbing Molly and shaking her. But he needed answers, and he doubted shaking would free them. After he'd ended his conversation with Harry, he had shaken a few things—and it hadn't made him feel any better.

"Right over here in his pumpkin seat. What's the matter with you?" She put a little more space between them, stepping closer to the baby. He was glad to see she was afraid.

"What's the matter with me?" He raised a brow and put his hand on his chest, but he forced himself to stand in place and not crowd her. "I'll tell you what's the matter with me. Someone killed my sister for her baby." He raised a finger and pointed. "*That* baby right there."

Molly's hand covered her heart and she swayed slightly, looking like her knees were going to buckle. He didn't step closer to catch her. She could fall on the floor for all he cared.

She finally asked, "How do you know?"

"I know that you weren't pregnant. It was pretty easy to deduce from there."

Molly sat heavily in a kitchen chair. "Well, actually," she pressed her palms against the tabletop and licked her lips, "this is good." She paused. "Very good. I didn't know where I was going to begin." She looked at him. "I was on my way to tell you when Lily called and said Riley had disappeared."

"Forgive me if I don't believe you." He crossed his arms over his chest and remained standing.

The baby started to fuss. Molly spoke softly to him and touched his cheek, then set the seat to rocking. After that she looked at Dean and held his gaze. "Believe what you want. It doesn't matter now."

"That's all you have to say before I call the police?" He held his cell phone ready.

"I'd like to explain what happened. It's not at all what you're thinking."

"By all means, explain."

"What I told you before was true. I don't know who the father is, or why Sarah came to Boston and to my clinic—she was *not* the norm for our maternity cases, so she caught my attention right away. I didn't know she was using an assumed name, but I did get the definite feeling that she was hiding from someone. I deduced it was an abusive partner, but that was only my guess. She never said.

"She made the first gesture toward friendship. And after that, we spent a bit of time together. I really liked her; she was fragile and smart and slightly distant—but still warm and genuine. She was lonely."

He interrupted. "An easy mark."

Molly gave him a look that surprised him. She wasn't afraid, she was angry. "The more I think about it, I think *I* was the mark."

"What are you talking about?"

"I think she *picked* me, I think she groomed me for what she was going to ask me to do."

"She *asked* you to kill her."

"I didn't kill her! Do you want me to finish, or are you ready to call the cops?"

He gave a curt nod for her to continue.

"She told me she had no family. She'd made it clear that the baby's father didn't know of his existence. She said the father was dangerous. Plenty of women run from abusive men to protect their pregnancies, but those fears are usually tempered with some form of caring . . . a hope to reunite, for the impossible happily-ever-after. But Sarah was adamant the father could never, never know of this child.

"When she went into labor, she waited to come to the clinic until it was too late to transfer her for delivery. I know that was no accident. She didn't want to go to the hospital. I delivered Nicholas, and then they were transported by ambulance at my insistence. She could hardly fight four of us off. Then she and Nicholas disappeared from the hospital ER.

"Two days after the baby was born, she showed up at my apartment early in the morning. She looked frightened. She asked me to take the baby for a couple of days."

"For Christ's sake, give me some credit! You want me to believe she *gave* you her baby?"

Molly leaned across the table and jabbed a forefinger against the surface. "She *forced* me to take him!"

"What?" He couldn't believe she would take such a wild turn in her story. "By gunpoint, or some other deadly threat?"

Molly stood back up. Her chin was set at a defiant angle as she looked him square in the eye. "Your sister was scared out of her wits. She was afraid of the man who fathered her child. That morning she said she had to take care of something that would remove the threat, so she and the baby could start over. Maybe she planned on killing *him*! I don't know. All I know is that if I hadn't taken the baby, she was going to leave him at a hospital or a church. I told her she'd never get him back. Her response was, 'At least he'll be safe.'"

"Whoever this father is, he is *serious* bad news. I'm sure that's who killed Sarah—or had her killed."

"But you don't know anything about this mysterious man?"

"No." She wrapped her arms around herself. "Sarah actually called him *evil*—and it chilled my blood when she did. She was serious."

Dean had never known his pragmatic sister to dramatize. "Why didn't you go to the police?"

"I started to. I was almost out the door when I realized the danger that would pose to the baby. Sarah had extracted my promise to protect him from his father, no matter what. If I had gone to the police, all the father would have had to do was walk in and prove paternity— the baby would be his. And if he didn't, Nicholas would have been swept into the social services system—oh, the things I've seen come out of foster care. I just could not turn this tiny boy over.

"I was Sarah's friend—perhaps her only friend at the time. You cannot imagine how desperate she was to protect this child. I couldn't break my promise."

"So you packed up and left Boston, just like that? Left your own career, took the chance of being caught—for someone else's baby."

"For *Sarah's* baby. She was my friend. I coaxed this child's first breath. I made a promise to her. My God, someone *murdered* her. I had to protect him. That's all I was thinking about."

"And you passed him off as your own. Why?"

"I hadn't planned it that way. I just ran. Then when I arrived here, someone assumed he was mine. I decided that was the easiest way to keep him safe from the father, should the man start looking. And then I realized that anyone I told could be implicated if charges are brought against me. I couldn't risk that either." She turned her back and took a couple of steps away. Her voice was much quieter when she said, "She told me she didn't have any family. If I had known about you, I would have contacted you."

He huffed in disbelief. "So why didn't you tell me last night?"

When she turned to face him again, her eyes were earnest. "Because I wasn't sure why Sarah hadn't told me about you. Maybe you were some danger to Nicholas, too. I had to think before I acted."

"Or maybe you were hoping I'd limp out of town feeling like a heel for lying to you—never to show my face again. That I'd believe your well-executed lies."

"I entertained the thought."

Her candor took him off guard.

She said, "I love this baby. All I want is what's best for him. Every decision I've made, right or wrong, has been because of that."

As he stood there looking into those silver eyes, Dean had never wanted to believe a lie so much.

Chapter 18

Molly's telephone rang. The sound startled her; she'd been so immobilized by Dean's glare that she'd nearly lost track of where she was.

She glanced at the handset. "I should get this. Could be about the kids."

He continued to stare, giving away nothing of what was going on inside him.

She answered.

"Molly, the sheriff just called," Lily said. "Karen's got everyone up in arms. She wants a warrant for Riley's arrest!"

"Did you explain to him the circumstances?"

"Of course!" She sounded short tempered with frustration. "He says he has to take every complaint seriously. And since Riley and Mickey are both still missing—"

"What? Is he setting out the hounds?" She could throttle Karen for her histrionics. Things were a big enough mess without her taking center stage in this drama. "Hey, that might not be a bad idea. Send out tracking dogs. That could put this whole matter to rest rather quickly."

"Really, Molly, I thought you were concerned."

Molly rubbed her eyes. She nearly told Lily that Riley wasn't the only one in danger of being arrested. She took a deep breath. "I am. Is the sheriff's department looking for the cars?"

"Yes. Neither one has shown up."

"How about the state police? In case they really did get a wild hair and decide to take off."

"Yes."

"I really don't think they've taken off. Did anyone check the lake house?"

"Clay said there were no cars in the drive. He went inside and looked around, no one had been there."

"I have this feeling they're close. Maybe they're up in the fire tower. Or hiding in the park—there are a dozen places to hide a car if you're willing to drive across the grass. Maybe they've gone into the Hoosier National Forest. Did Clay check the old Kaleidoscope Caverns?" That tourist attraction had been closed since the sixties but kids used to trespass there all of the time; Molly figured they still might.

"No. I'd forgotten about that place. I'll have him drive out there and see if one of their cars is on the access road."

"Good idea. I just know they're fine."

"Then why haven't they come home?"

"Because Riley wants to punish you?"

When Lily didn't respond, Molly went on, "Really, how many ways does a kid have to do that? Running off, making you suffer is about the only card he has."

"Then why didn't Mickey come back and tell us he's all right, like she promised?"

There was a question Molly didn't have an answer to and it frightened her more than she wanted to admit. The late hour was making her worry. Since moving to Glens Crossing, Riley had been extremely conscious of substance abuse because of his father's addiction. Now that he knew Peter wasn't his father, would he lose himself in drugs or alcohol? Maybe he was too stoned to move and Mickey didn't trust him to stay alone.

If something did happen to those kids, Molly would never forgive herself.

Instead of giving her sister a comforting answer, a sob choked free. She quickly muffled it with her hand.

"Molly, are you crying? Oh Jesus, if you're crying it has to be bad."

She tried to pull in a draught of air quietly. "No, I'm not crying." She took another breath. "They're just somewhere talking, trying to get this sorted out. Didn't he and Mickey always use each other as sounding boards?"

"They did. But not for a long time."

"He's turning to his oldest friend here in town. They're working it through together. They'll be home soon. We should free up the line."

"Okay. Keep in touch." Lily hesitated. "And, thanks, Mol."

"Yeah."

She managed to keep herself together until she disconnected the call. The sob she'd been suppressing broke free. She wanted to bolt from the room, to hide in the bathroom away from Dean's critical gaze and cry herself out. But he was blocking the doorway.

Turning her back to him, she cried into her hands. What else could come apart today? How could she have fooled herself into thinking it was okay to send Mickey after him? *The same way you fooled yourself into thinking it was okay to keep Nicholas.*

From Dean's angry glare, she knew there would be no forgiving, no gratitude for keeping the baby safe, no becoming a "favorite aunt." She felt the life drain out of her. Her strength left along with her tears.

"I'm sorry." She turned and faced him again. "Do you want to call the police now?"

He looked at her for a long time. Then he said, "You're not really sure your nephew is all right, are you?"

Pushing her hair away from her face, she gave an unladylike sniffle. "I was—earlier. Mickey has her head on straight. I thought she'd be a good influence on him, calming. But what if something happened to them? What if they had an accident—or ran into some crazed killer?"

"You did a good job trying to calm your sister."

A sardonic laugh escaped her control. "You just said I'm a good liar."

"I won't call the police until they find your nephew." He didn't look at her when he said it, as if it was a concession that made him uncomfortable.

"Thank you." She started to get Nicholas's bottle ready. "It's time to feed him. Do you want to do it, or should I?" Those were some of the hardest words she'd ever had to say. This could well be the last feeding before Dean took him away.

"You can. I'll go sit on the porch."

"Fine." She was glad to have him out of the house so she could enjoy her last hour with Nicholas.

As she fed the baby, she studied him carefully, memorizing the curve of his ear, his tiny earlobes, his pale lashes and round blue eyes, the way his tiny fingers, with their impossibly small pink nails, grasped hers, the sweet cupid's bow of a mouth, the new downy hair over the perfect shape of his skull. *Oh, what will you look like when you're a boy? A teenager? A man?*

The magnitude of what she was losing struck her with sledgehammer force, stealing her breath, making her want to sneak out the back door and run again.

Instead, she sang to him, a soft sweet lullaby that she knew she would never sing again.

Dean had left the front door open a crack. As much as he shouldn't trust Molly, he couldn't see her sneaking out the back and taking off with Nicholas. Or maybe he was giving her the chance, just to see if she would.

He was having a difficult time getting a handle on his own motivation. Was he testing her? Or was he just hiding out here so he didn't have to watch Molly mothering a baby he was going to take away from her? He'd seen first hand the love she lavished upon Nicholas. She was as devoted as any mother he'd ever seen. Which said she was either completely committed to upholding a promise—or was a woman who wanted a child enough to kill for it.

Dean couldn't remove the memory of the bicyclist lying in the rain. Molly had acted on instinct. A person couldn't fake something like that. That act alone shouted that she wasn't a killer, that she was telling the truth about his sister.

Would Molly truly have come to him with the fact that

Nicholas was his nephew? It was certainly a convenient story. Still, try as he might, he could not see Molly Boudreau putting a bullet in anyone's brain—for any reason.

It was difficult to think of that tiny baby as his nephew, his only living relative. He tried to recall how he had felt as he held him. Had there been anything, some small voice deep inside that recognized him as family? Shouldn't that be the way of it—some intuitive affinity?

But there hadn't been. Nicholas was just a baby. Dean had felt as awkward holding him as he would have any other baby. There hadn't been the slightest spark of recognition, no hint that this child was connected to his sister. On the other hand, Molly appeared completely natural with the baby. Shouldn't there have been some telltale sign that she wasn't his mother?

That small voice deep inside did answer this time, and he didn't like what it had to say. Molly was Nicholas's mother, the only mother he'd known. The very thought made him feel disloyal to his sister.

Why, Julie? Why didn't you contact me?

He tried to think of her, the way she'd been the last time he'd seen her. Were there any clues that her life was on the fast track to trouble? It had been at Christmas; before she'd conceived this child.

As he combed through the details of that visit—they'd met in Rome for the holiday—nothing out of the ordinary came to mind. She hadn't acted like leaving New York for Christmas was upsetting any personal relationship she might have had.

He closed his eyes and remembered walking with her across the damp cobbles of the piazza at the base of the

Spanish Steps. It had been cold, but the sidewalk cafes still served coffee. They'd stopped and had strong espresso to keep them going as they spent their last day traipsing all over the ancient city like a couple of tourists. It was a very good day—the last day they would ever share.

Julie had wanted to be home by New Year's Eve. He hadn't questioned, especially since he needed to get back to Afghanistan himself. But now he had to wonder if it had something to do with seeing the father.

Dean wanted to pull out his own hair. How was he ever going to unwind this tangled mess and see the truth?

Molly's voice drifted out to the porch, a low, mellow lullaby. Dean tried to block it out; it was too bittersweet and only served to further cloud his judgment.

In those first fury-blinded moments after he'd spoken to Harry, Dean had wanted to believe he'd unearthed the truth, fully and undeniably. He had wanted to believe this was the end of the search, that justice could now be served, that dear Julie could rest in peace.

But his gut told him if he turned Molly over to the police, justice would never be done.

There were large missing pieces in this puzzle. Only Julie knew the shape of them. But Molly might know more than she was conscious of.

He thought of the large carton of unopened mail he'd left in his office. Could there be something in there? It seemed highly unlikely; he couldn't recall getting a scrap of mail from his sister any time in his life. Even birthday greetings when he was in the field were left on his voice mail. She always said it took cards too long to get there.

She wanted you to know the second she was thinking about you.

There had been no voice mails.

The police said she'd emptied her bank accounts and sold her car. She left New York in what would have been the early weeks of her pregnancy. It could only be because she didn't want people there to know about it. But why go to the extent of a false identity?

Molly was right. Julie had been hiding. Nothing else made even a shred of sense.

He had to stop riding back and forth on his emotions. He had to take a step back and look at the facts as he knew them from a journalistic point of view.

Molly stuck her head out the front door when Nicholas started fussing. She said to Dean, "You'd better come in and see this."

She didn't wait for him to get up before she turned away and headed for the bathroom. When he arrived at the bathroom door, she said, "Come in and close it."

Turning on the hot water in the shower, she explained to Dean, over Nicholas's shrieks, how to calm the baby.

He stood there looking skeptical, the steam reaching him long before it got down to Nicholas. He slipped his coat off. "Doesn't seem very scientific."

"Maybe not, but it works." She gave him a pointed look. "And you'll be thankful for it."

As Nicholas began to quiet, Dean said, "I'll be damned."

Molly had to pinch her lips together to keep from agreeing. Over and over she had to remind herself, Dean was in the right here. He had the law on his side. Still, did he think he could offer this child a better home than she could? She bet the man didn't even have a home.

After about five minutes, she got tired of him standing there wiping the sweat off his brow. "You can go on out."

"How long do you have to do this?"

She lifted a shoulder. "An hour, sometimes two."

His chin dropped and his mouth came open. "Two hours?"

"Get used to it. I use it as my time to think."

"What if you don't do it?"

"He screams."

"Every day?" There was an edge of desperation to his voice.

"Pretty much. At least for two to three more months."

"Months?"

She glared at him. "Am I not speaking clearly?" The heat was beginning to get to her, too.

The baby seemed to be the only one enjoying the sauna. His cries had dwindled to the occasional whimper accompanied by a tensing of his stomach and legs. Molly continued to rub his back.

She'd been giving this a lot of thought while Dean sat out there sulking on the porch. Now her frustration was ready to bubble over. "Do you have any idea what you're going to do with this baby?"

The look in his eyes told her he had absolutely no idea. He said, "Of course."

She said, "Well, think this through. I won't run off with him. I know he's your nephew. But good God, I will *not* hand him over without some assurance that he's going to be well cared for."

He stiffened. "He's my nephew. You think I would mistreat him?"

"Not *mistreat*. But you have to prepare yourself to take care of him. What will you do with him while you work? How about when you go back to the Middle East? Do you have a place for him to sleep—you cannot sleep in a bed with a baby; I've seen cases where an infant suffocated. Do you have any idea how often, or how much he eats? You need to select a pediatrician."

"I can change a diaper."

"I'm not saying you aren't capable of doing any of these things. I'm saying you have to address them. Prepare."

"You didn't."

She closed her eyes and huffed. "Jesus, man. Your sister gave her son to me because she could trust me *and* because I'm a pediatrician. She knew I'd know how to take care of an infant."

Now she was really getting worked up. "And just to get this straight, keep in mind she *did* choose me. Sarah—Julie—entrusted her child to *me*, not you. I'm sure she had a good reason."

He started to argue, but she held a hand up and said, "Whatever that was, I understand you've got the law on your side.

"But think! Your sister was *murdered*! I'm pretty sure the baby's father did it—a man Sarah was deathly afraid of. I had to make a decision in an instant. I worried he would come after the baby, too. Everything I've done I've done to keep Nicholas *safe*. I'm not stopping now. I need to know you can handle it."

His jaw flexed. "I can handle it." He went out the door and closed it behind him.

Even though she was tempted to hand the baby over this instant and let Dean flounder just to make her point, she hated to make the baby suffer. So once Nicholas was relaxed, she got him ready and put him to bed.

When she returned to the kitchen, Dean was sitting at the table, reading the formula can.

He looked up.

Molly lifted her hair off of her hot neck and said, "I went ahead and put him in bed. You can't leave with him until my car gets back anyway."

"Why not?" He set the can down.

"Because the car seat is in it."

"Oh. I wasn't leaving right away anyhow."

"Need to call the police first?"

He shot her a heart-stopping look. "No. I need to talk about Julie first."

"Okay. Then we talk about Nicholas." She'd meant what she said; she wasn't handing him over until she was sure he could deal with an infant.

She sat down at the table across from him. "Are you going to have me arrested?" She couldn't stop the question.

Dean had to give the woman credit. She was facing this with calm acceptance. Very uncriminal-like. "Not if you help me."

"Help you what?" she asked.

"Help me find out who this baby's father is."

"Threatening me with arrest won't make my answer any different. I don't know anything about the man. I have no idea where he lives or what he does. I can only tell you that your sister said the man was evil—oh, and he has red hair."

"She said he had red hair?"

"Actually, it was the only detail of the man she let slip—right after Nicholas was born."

Another question came to mind. "Did she name him, or did you?"

"She did. Nicholas James. But she made it clear she wasn't naming him after his father."

"No. She named him after me." He could hardly swallow around the lump of emotion in his throat.

"Your middle name is Nicholas?"

"James. My name is James Dean Coletta."

"Well, as she told me she had no family, you can see why she didn't share that with me." She leaned closer. "I really can't tell you things I don't know. You have it all."

There had to be more. Dean started back at square one. "My bet is the father is from New York. According to her work schedule and credit card statements, she hadn't been anywhere except to see me in Rome at Christmas. I'll start in New York."

"Wait just a minute! You can't be serious?"

"Of course I'm serious. The man needs to be found, and punished. I would think you'd want that for Nicholas as much as I do."

"What I want for Nicholas is for him to remain safe." She emphasized the word with a slap of her palm against the table. "If you locate the father, he can claim parental rights. Is that how you're going to honor your sister's wishes?"

"I can gain custody of Nicholas over a convicted murderer."

"Okay, back up a step. As of now, the father doesn't know of the baby's existence. What if your poking around tips him off before you can discover who he is? What if he comes for the baby? He could disappear and you'd never see him again."

"I think you're overreacting."

"Sarah said this man was very clever, that he isn't what he appears to be. Who knows what that meant? I don't like the idea of him getting away with this either, but I don't think it's worth the risk to Nicholas."

"I would think you would want to find the killer—to clear your own name." He tinged his words with just enough threat to get her attention.

"I didn't kill her." She remained unbaited. "You can have me arrested for taking the baby, but nothing more."

He raised a hand in acquiescence. "Do you really think Nicholas will ever be able to live without danger, as long as that man walks around free?"

"It's not worth the risk. I obviously didn't make myself hard to find. If the father had any suspicion that Sarah had given her son to me, he would have been here by now. He doesn't know. Why screw that up?"

His resolve settled into stone. "Because Julie deserves justice."

Molly looked at him with an equal measure of conviction. "Well, maybe that's why she gave Nicholas to me and not you. Maybe she knew you'd make that choice."

It was obvious a line had been drawn in the sand.

Well, he didn't need her permission to cross it.

Chapter 19

Molly wasn't sure if it was the missing car seat or the fact that he couldn't bring himself to dump two disasters on her in the same moment that kept Dean at her house throughout the night. Either way, it said something for his character. And for that she was thankful. *He may be ill-equipped to care for a baby, but he did have the moral fiber to do the right thing.*

They had finally exhausted themselves arguing over the validity of chasing down the baby's father. Neither one had been anywhere near conceding. Molly realized that she had very little power to control what Dean did. Her only hope was to convince him of the soundness of her argument. Maybe she'd even be able to convince him the baby was better off with her. But right now her own thoughts were growing so muddled, she didn't trust herself to convince anyone of anything.

"If you want to use my bed, go ahead," she said as they both sat yawning and rubbing their eyes at the kitchen table. "I won't be sleeping until Riley and Mickey show up."

Dean stretched his long legs in front of him. "Thanks for the offer."

"But?"

"I wouldn't feel right."

She blinked her bleary eyes at him. "Why not?"

A half-smile curved his lips and he lifted a shoulder. "Because I've been thinking about your bed for a couple of days now. It seems . . . wrong."

With her fatigue-fogged mind, it took a moment to process his meaning. "Oh." She had supposed all of those kinds of thoughts had been forever vanquished with what had been revealed this evening.

"If you want to go home, I promise not to abscond with the baby in the night. Really. I told you before, once I know the rules, I play by them. Sarah kept half of the players in this game hidden from me."

He surprised her by getting up and walking over to her chair. He laid a hand on the top of her head. The look in his eyes was unexpectedly understanding. "I know." Then he left the kitchen.

Fifteen minutes later, Molly got up and walked into the living room. It took a moment for her eyes to adjust to the darkness. When they did, she saw him lying on his back on the floor with one arm thrown across his eyes. She was cold and tired down to her very marrow. It would be so nice to lie there beside him and absorb his warmth, to pretend that her life wasn't disintegrating before her eyes.

Instead, she walked back into the kitchen and turned off the overhead light, leaving only the small light over the sink to cast the corners of the room into shadow. Then she folded her arms on the table and laid her head on them to await either a call from Lily or a cry from Nicholas.

The fire had nearly gone out. Mickey noticed the light around them changing. She could begin to make out the trunks of individual trees, now black against the graying light of early morning. Riley was asleep. He had been for a couple of hours. But Mickey wouldn't waste this time. It might be all she had. Once this was over and they were back at school, everything might go back to the way it was. It was a painful thought, but she wouldn't let herself truly hope for more.

Her ankle hurt like holy hell, but it was a small price to pay.

She heard Riley take a deep breath, then felt him move slightly beside her. She hated to see the sun rise. It was as if they'd spent the night in an enchanted forest, and the sun was going to expose it for the ugly swamp it truly was. The sun would shine, Riley would go for help, they would have to explain, she would have to go to the hospital . . . and her mother, oh, God, her mother was going to shit a brick.

Riley shifted, moving his hand from her side to the back of her head. "You awake?" he whispered.

Tilting her head so she could look into his face, she said, "Yes."

He kissed her lightly on the lips. She had to grab a fistful of his shirt to keep herself from wrapping her arms around his neck and refusing to let him go.

"You know we're in deep shit, don't you?" he asked, taking his other hand and touching her face.

"Oh, yeah. I know."

He looked around. "It's probably light enough that I can go get help now."

Her heart sank. "Probably."

"Your ankle must be killing you."

It throbbed like a son of a bitch. "Not so bad."

"Remember that first summer . . . all I wanted to do was run away from here with you. Away from Clay, away from your mom and dad. Maybe we should have."

It was an absurd statement, but she liked the sentiment behind it. "Yeah, and right now you could be working at a car wash and I could be doing the drive-through window at McDonald's. Of course, those would be our permanent careers."

He chuckled.

She forced herself to sit up.

He rose to his knees, but didn't stand. Instead he cupped her face in his hands. "I am so sorry."

"For what?" She wanted to take a mental photograph of the look in his eyes right now. That way she would be able to hold it forever in her heart.

"For being such a shit. For Codi. For you coming out here because of me and breaking your ankle."

She wanted to say a broken bone was little enough to pay to bring him back into her life. But she wasn't sure he was in her life—not permanently. Time would have to tell. Until then, she had to protect her heart.

"I'm sorry, too," she said.

Now he looked confused. "For what?"

"Actually, I'm sorry in advance . . . for the new one

my mom's going to rip you when this is all over." *Especially after she finds out you're not a Holt.*

He laughed, then he kissed her again. "I'm not afraid."

Mickey couldn't help herself. She slid her hands behind his neck and pulled him in for a kiss. After all, it could be the last time she would ever have the opportunity.

The telephone ringing right next to Molly's ear made her bolt straight up in her chair. She snatched it, realizing she must have dozed because it was getting light outside.

"Lily?"

"He's back." Lily's tone revealed she was torn between hugging Riley and kicking his ass.

"What about Mickey?"

"She found him, but Riley thinks she broke her ankle. They were someplace in the woods near the dam. He waited for first light to leave her and get help."

"Thank God." Her relief was short-lived. "Has anyone called Karen?"

"I did, before I called you."

Molly blew out a breath of relief.

"You *should* thank me—she had a full head of steam worked up before I finally told her I had to get off the phone."

"Is Mickey at the hospital?"

"Not yet. The rescue crew for the fire department is going in with a stretcher to bring her out."

"Is Karen meeting them at the hospital?" Molly tried to massage some of the stiffness out of her neck.

Lily's voice was cold. "Probably, right after she talks to her lawyer."

"Jesus. She can't be serious."

"As a heart attack."

"I wish I could come out—but Nicholas . . ."

"Don't worry about us. When the guys get back we're going to take a long nap, then have another family talk. I really think whatever happened in the woods last night was good for Riley."

Molly bit her lip before she could outwardly speculate just what that might have been. Surely with Mickey's injury they'd behaved themselves. She closed her eyes and sent a quick prayer that Karen would behave reasonably—not that her prayers had been answered much of late.

She said to Lily, "Call me later."

"I will."

"Oh, Lily!"

"Yes?"

"Do you know where my car is?"

"Um, no. Riley didn't say. I'll have Clay bring it by. He's out with the fire department and Riley."

"Thanks."

When Molly disconnected the call, she looked up and saw Dean standing in the doorway.

"Everything all right?" he asked in a tone that said he actually cared.

She nodded. "Mickey found him, but she hurt her ankle. He wouldn't leave her in the woods in the dark. The fire rescue squad is going after her now."

Dean's gaze flicked to the house next door. "I'm sure Ms. Kimball is in rare form."

"As always." Molly didn't want to think about Karen Kimball. She didn't want to think about anything. Her head ached and the baby was going to be up any minute.

"I guess I'll go on out to the cottage. We both need some sleep."

She looked at him in confusion.

He gently caressed her hair and said, "I didn't stay because I thought you were going to sneak off with the baby. I stayed in case there was bad news about your nephew."

Molly was pretty sure she was moving her lips, but no sound was coming out.

"I'll be back later today. We'll talk more then."

She couldn't believe it. He actually left—without Nicholas.

Although a small, desperate part of her wanted to take advantage and pack up and leave, she just couldn't do it. Anyone who honored her with that much trust might just be persuaded to see the advantages to allowing her to keep Nicholas. Plus, this was a man who made a profession out of divining secrets; he would find her. A life on the run, in constant hiding wouldn't be any better than a life with a single man who spent all of his time in war zones.

But Dean might be reasoned with.

There was hope.

She stumbled into her bedroom and fell face first onto the bed. She could not think any more without sleep. She had no more than taken a deep breath when she heard Nicholas begin to stir in his crib.

*   *   *

Mickey closed her eyes and held her breath when the ambulance doors opened and she saw her mother standing at the hospital entrance. When she heard her mother shriek, she knew it was going to be worse than she had imagined.

"Michaeline, sweetheart! I've been frantic. What has that boy done to you?" Her mother got in the way as they tried to unload the gurney.

Mickey thanked God that she'd been able to convince Riley and Mr. Winters to go on home. It would be horrible to endure this with Riley watching.

That relief lasted about three more seconds, when Mr. Winters and Riley walked up. Mickey wanted to crawl inside herself with embarrassment. Instead she stood up to her mother. "I just twisted my ankle. I'm fine."

Riley was behind her mother now. Mother hadn't seen him yet.

"You don't look fine. You were gone *all night*."

"Excuse me, ma'am," one of the ambulance technicians said, "we need to get her inside."

That's when her mother turned and saw Riley. She took three jerky steps toward him, stopping right in front of him and jabbing a finger in his face. "You, young man, are in serious trouble!"

"Mom!" Mickey yelled.

Her mother spun and glared at her as the gurney went through the automatic doors. "That's enough out of you! I'll deal with you later."

As Mickey was wheeled into the emergency room, she heard her mother's voice escalate with anger. Somewhere beneath the yelling, she heard Mr. Winters speaking. Then she heard a "yes, ma'am" from Riley.

Oh, God, she wanted to jump off this gurney and grab her mother by the hair. She was going to ruin everything.

Then she got an idea. She started crying—hysterically. "Where's my mom? My leg hurts! I want my mother!"

Out of the corner of her eye, she saw one of the pink-garbed hospital volunteer ladies scurry out the door. In four seconds her mother was hovering over her.

"There, there, baby."

Mickey nearly barfed. Her mom hadn't called her "baby" since her brother was born.

She put a comforting hand on Mickey's brow for a millisecond, before she turned to the nurse and began making ridiculous accusations that Mickey had been abducted by an old boyfriend.

"Mom! Stop! I went out there myself and twisted my ankle. Riley found me and wouldn't leave me alone in the dark to get help. Stop sounding like a crazy woman."

Karen spun and glared at her. "What did you call me?"

The ER doctor saved her. "Hello, Michaeline. Anything hurt besides your ankle?" He laid down a clipboard and walked to examine her leg.

"No. I twisted it on a rock or something. My foot rolled all the way on its side." The memory made her stomach lurch.

Her mother stepped close to the doctor. He didn't look as old as Dr. Boudreau—and Mickey had thought *she* looked too young to be a doctor. But he held his ground with her mother's crowding.

"I think she should be examined for sexual assault,"

Mother said quietly, but not so quietly that Mickey couldn't hear.

"Mother!"

The doctor looked at her mother and said, "Nurse Williams will show you to the waiting area and get you something to drink. I'll be out shortly to discuss my findings."

For a moment, her mom looked like she was going to explode. Then she turned around and left the cubicle with the nurse.

"Okay, Michaeline—"

"Mickey. I like to be called Mickey."

"Mickey, I'm going to cut this sock off. You've got a lot of swelling here, the increased pressure might be a little uncomfortable."

"It's been hurting like hell for hours. A little pressure isn't going to kill me."

He grinned. "I like a patient with spunk."

Mickey tried to grin back. "But it's their crazy mothers you could do without?"

He winked at her. Then he cut the sock and Mickey stiffened with the pain, but kept her lips pressed together.

"There, done." He gently examined her ankle. "Pretty hard to see much with all of this swelling. I'm going to send you up to X ray." He picked up the clipboard and wrote something. As he did, he asked, as evenly as if he was asking if she liked ice cream, "Are you sexually active?"

She closed her eyes and tried to keep her face from turning red. "No. And I haven't been assaulted either. My mother is . . . dramatic."

"So there's no chance that you're pregnant—we're taking X rays and need to know."

"*Absolutely* no chance."

"All right then. I'm going to have Marcia give you something for pain before transporting you to radiology."

"Thank you." She was curious but too embarrassed to ask if he was going to do any . . . other . . . kind of exam. She'd fight that battle when it came. If that was what it was going to take to get her mom off this assault thing, she guessed she had to do it—for Riley's sake.

Marcia arrived with a syringe and gave Mickey a shot in the butt. Mickey closed her eyes and let it go to work. She barely felt the movement when they started to wheel her to radiology.

By the time the X rays confirmed her ankle was indeed broken and her mother was allowed to come back in, the pain medication reduced her mother's words to a muffled garble. She wondered briefly if the doctor could give her mother something to calm her down—and shut her up.

She drifted off to sleep, the pain in her leg reduced to a dull ache and her heart full of fear that all of this was going to drive Riley away again.

As soon as Dean got back to the cottage, he went through the notebook he had begun the day he discovered his sister was missing. He found the phone number he was looking for and dialed.

"Detective McMurray, here."

"This is Dean Coletta, Julie Coletta's brother."

"Yes, Mr. Coletta, what can I do for you?" There was a slight edge to her voice.

"I might be able to do something for you. I'm fairly certain I know who killed my sister."

"Yes?" Now he had her full attention.

"I have reason to believe that the father of her child murdered her."

There was a small stifled sigh, then McMurray said, "I'm sorry. I know you want the murderer caught, but there was absolutely nothing that said this was a crime of passion, or a domestic disturbance. This was a clinical, unemotional taking of life."

"I didn't mean like that. I think she was involved with someone who, underneath a respectable veneer, was involved in something so abhorrent that she felt like she had to hide from him once she discovered she was pregnant—to protect her baby."

"Do you have a name for this man—or what he was involved in?"

Dean recognized the shift in tone; he'd hit on something. "No. But I intend to find out. I'm fairly certain she was involved with him in New York City. For some reason, she'd been keeping the relationship quiet, or it was relatively new."

"New York. Why are you thinking that?"

"She hadn't been anywhere else. She met me in Rome last Christmas. Other than that she hadn't left the city— I've traced credit cards, interviewed co-workers and friends. I'm certain he was in the city."

There was a prolonged silence on the line.

"Detective McMurray?"

"Yes, I'm here." After a pause, she said, "Have you

considered the possibility that it was someone she met
while in Rome?"

His investigative antenna quivered, then snapped to
attention. "Why?"

"Just thinking out loud. Perhaps . . . someone on the
plane?"

Police detectives didn't "think out loud" to bereaved
kin. McMurray obviously wasn't in a position to share
what *she* knew, but once she understood that Dean
was onto something, she must have decided to prod him
in the right direction. He mentally reshuffled his
perspective.

"I suppose she could have met someone there, but it's
not very likely. We stayed in the same hotel, spent every
day together. I can't say about the plane or the airport. I
departed six hours before she did."

"Hmm."

"What do you know, detective?"

"That's just the problem, Mr. Coletta. I don't *know*
anything. You understand the constraints of our system.
I'm operating under certain . . . handicaps." She paused
just a beat. "I want to tell you how impressed I am with
your investigative reporting."

Now Dean sat quietly for a moment, digesting the
oddly placed compliment. "Thank you."

"I find the Middle East very interesting these days.
The politics are always so volatile."

Dean's stomach turned over slowly. "Has there been
federal agency interest around my sister's death?"

"Why yes, now that you mention it." She sounded as
if he'd just asked if she liked roses.

"Can we meet to discuss it?"

"Oh, absolutely not." Her tone was impersonal, professional. "But I will keep you apprised of any advancements our department makes in this case. Good-bye, Mr. Coletta."

Dean disconnected. His guts were writhing. Federal interest. That opened up a whole horrific world of possibilities.

Chapter 20

Dean knocked on Molly's door at three-thirty in the afternoon. He was more than surprised when Brian Mitchell answered holding Nicholas.

Dean's heart jumped. "Is something wrong?" He suddenly realized that if there was some connection between international crime and Nicholas's father, the potential for danger was limitless. Molly had been right to fear for the boy's safety. He felt that fear now, too.

Brian opened the door wider, but whispered when he said, "I heard about the horrible night Molly's family had, so I came to take care of the baby while she gets some sleep."

Dean's fear evaporated, replaced by bristling irritation; he couldn't help feeling Brian was walking on his turf. "Well, I'm here now, so you can go."

"Oh, I don't mind staying. I thought I'd take Molly out to dinner when she gets up."

"Molly and I already have a date." He was almost

embarrassed by his cutting tone. Brian was a nice enough guy.

"Really? She didn't mention it."

"She was pretty tired when I left here this morning."

His comment had the desired effect. Brian looked dejected. Dean knew he shouldn't let the man leave with the wrong impression, but decided to anyway. The thought of Molly dating Brian set his teeth on edge.

A much less happy Brian handed Nicholas over to Dean, then went into the kitchen to retrieve his sport coat. "Nicholas was fed at two-thirty. I just changed his diaper. He should be ready to go down for a nap any time now." He glanced toward Molly's closed bedroom door. "Tell her . . . tell her I'll give her a call tomorrow." There was just enough challenge in his voice to tell Dean he hadn't given up.

Dean just nodded and opened the front door, shocked by the strength of the jealousy that slithered around his insides. He didn't know how he and Molly would be able to overcome the gulf between them, but he now realized he wanted to try.

After he watched Brian get in his car, which was parked on the far side of the street, Dean studied the baby. This was the first opportunity he'd had to really examine Nicholas closely since he'd discovered this was his sister's child.

He searched the tiny features for some trace of Julie. But all he could see was a baby—they all looked so much alike. Perhaps the blue of his eyes was near the shade of hers. As he walked around the living room, the light shifted on Nicholas's face, revealing a tiny, shallow dimple in the middle of his chin that Dean had not noticed earlier. A dimple much like his own.

As he studied the baby, Dean started to talk to him. He felt funny about it at first; there was no way this infant could understand what he said. But he kept talking, telling him things about his mother.

Then Nicholas smiled. That affinity Dean had been searching for struck his heart like a steel blade. *My flesh and blood.* A lilting feeling of joy graced his soul.

By the time Dean had given Nicholas an overview of Julie's best qualities and most significant achievements, the baby's eyes were drifting closed. With care, he opened Molly's bedroom door. Quietly, he placed Nicholas in his crib and covered him with a blanket. He laid him propped on his side, the way he'd seen Molly do. Then he lingered next to the crib and watched him sleep for a few minutes. The child was at such utter and complete peace. *Why do we have to lose that as we grow up?*

Dean turned and looked at Molly asleep on her bed. She was on top of the yellow comforter, still wearing the clothes she'd had on when he'd left this morning. Her dark hair covered half her face, making him want to reach over and lift it away. That lightness he'd felt holding his nephew bloomed again in his chest. She was extraordinary in every way. The things she'd sacrificed to protect Nicholas attested to her selfless devotion to him. Dean's conversation with Detective McMurray had cast that bravery into new light.

"Brian?" Molly said sleepily as she turned toward the crib.

"No, it's Dean. I sent Brian home," he said softly.

Pushing her hair away from her face, she asked, "What time is it?"

"Nearly four. Nicholas just went to sleep. You should go back to sleep yourself. We can talk later."

Lifting herself up on one elbow, she said, "You look like hell. Didn't you sleep?"

He shook his head. He should have at least shaved before he came, but with his preoccupation with Molly and Nicholas, it hadn't crossed his mind until now. "Too much on my mind."

She blew out a long breath and lay back down. "I just can't drag myself up yet."

"I'll just hang in the kitchen in case the baby wakes."

"Don't be ridiculous. Come over here and lie down before you fall down."

He gave her a cautious look.

"I don't have a couch, or I'd send you there. Just lie down and take a nap. We both need to be clear headed when we . . . make decisions."

He didn't miss the fact that she included herself in the decision making, as if he didn't hold all of the cards. The arguing could wait. For some reason, now that he was back here, his restlessness began to unwind. He did feel sleepy. And half of her bed was certainly preferable to the living room floor.

She turned on her side, facing away from him.

He slipped his shoes off and lay down on the bed beside her as slowly and carefully as if the bed were made of eggshells. In his effort not to crowd her, he was nearly hanging off the side of the mattress.

He felt her moving beside him, but kept his gaze respectfully on the ceiling. He'd been thinking about getting in her bed for days, but this was far from what he'd had in mind. Unbidden, the memory of her on the living room floor loomed large in his mind; the moment in which she'd let herself respond to his kiss had ignited something in them both—something he really shouldn't be thinking about right now.

She started to laugh.

He turned his head to look at her.

"You're lying there like an unwilling virgin bride," she said, the words riding on suppressed laughter. "You can relax and make yourself comfortable. I promise not to take advantage of you."

He inched over to a more restful position on the bed. "It's not *you* misbehaving that I'm worried about."

Her eyes grew serious. "You don't hate me then?"

"Jesus, Molly." He rolled on his side to face her. "How could you think that?"

"Just a few hours ago you thought I murdered your sister and kidnapped your nephew. It's an easy assumption."

"A few hours ago, I didn't know the whole story." He paused. "You could have made it easier if you'd just told me when I admitted I was Julie's brother."

"I explained why I couldn't do that. If I had to do it over, I'd do it the same way again. I had to be sure, to think things through; the truth wasn't going to change overnight just because I didn't tell you right away."

"And that's why I can't hate you." He touched her cheek. "I do believe you have tried to do everything in your power to keep Nicholas safe."

"At least there's one thing we can agree on. We'd better leave it at that until we've had some sleep. Nicholas will be up again in a couple of hours."

"Right."

With amazing swiftness, Dean felt himself sliding into sleep. The gentle sound of Molly and Nicholas breathing in the same room with him acted like a sedative. His last conscious thought was of how tenuous this feeling was. Even without their disagreement about going after the baby's father—which was bound to be more volatile if he was honest with Molly and told her of his conversation with McMurray—Molly was still going to hate him when he left here with Nicholas.

Riley rolled over and looked at the clock. Six. He was supposed to be sleeping. He'd avoided a long explanation to his mom by saying he was too tired to talk. But all he'd been doing was flopping from one position to another on the bed. If only he'd been able to speak to Mickey before Clay made him leave the hospital. Mickey's mother was nuts. She couldn't be serious about pressing charges against him.

A knock sounded at his bedroom door. He thought about pretending to be asleep, but that was just going to postpone the inevitable. He was going to have to talk to his . . . parents—he decided the first step was to start thinking of Clay as one of them—about this whole mess. He might as well get it over with.

"Yeah."

He was surprised when it was Clay, not his mom who came in the room. He wasn't sure if he was relieved or pissed.

"Get any sleep?" Clay asked as he sat at the foot of the bed.

"Not much."

"Me either." Clay rubbed his palms together between his knees. "I guess we should start with the hard question."

Riley swallowed hard. He was prepared to face the fact that Clay was his father, to have that "discussion" his mother had wanted when he'd stormed off to his room yesterday. But what "question" could there be?

Clay must have seen his confusion. He cleared his throat and asked, "Is there anything that happened between you and Mickey last night that could be, ah, . . . construed as a sexual assault?"

Riley bolted upright on the bed. His body flashed as hot as his temper. "You think I raped her? Jesus! I thought you were on my side."

Clay raised a palm in the air. "Hold on. I didn't say any such thing. It's just that, if Mickey's mother requests an examination," he paused, "any evidence of intercourse could be interpreted as assault. The burden of proof that it was consensual will be on you—and with Mickey being a minor, it might just not matter."

This was too much. "You think just because you knocked up my mom, I'd do the same thing to Mickey?"

Anger flashed across Clay's face. He took a couple of deep breaths that flared his nostrils. For a second, Riley thought Clay might just punch him. He watched as Clay's fists clenched, then opened.

"I loved your mother then as much as I do now. We had planned to marry." Then he pushed the air between them, as if to move the comments aside. "But let's keep these two discussions separate for the moment. Is there any need to worry about Mickey's mother's accusations finding solid evidence?"

Riley didn't want to answer. He wanted to get up and walk away. But he owed it to Mickey to face this head on. "No."

God, what was Mickey enduring at the hands of her nutcase mother right now?

"All right, then." He got up. "Why don't you come down for supper and we'll have that other discussion."

Riley got up and followed Clay downstairs, anxious to get this out of the way so he could go to the hospital and see Mickey.

Two hours later, after listening to the *entire* story of how his mother came to be married to his dad again, Riley was finally free. With all of the trouble for Mickey, suddenly Clay being his real father didn't seem nearly as big of a deal. He was still pissed that they didn't tell him before, but Mickey had made him see things so much more clearly. It was sort of scary really, to realize your parents—all three of them—were just as screwed up as everybody else.

He picked up his car keys and started out the door.

"Where are you going?" his mom asked.

"I'm going to the hospital to see Mickey. I won't be long."

His mom looked at Clay. He said, "Um, Riley, I don't think that's a good idea right now. Not until Mickey's mother calms down. There's no need to ask for more trouble."

"How can going to see how she is be asking for trouble? She broke her ankle looking for me! If I don't go to the hospital . . . well, that's just wrong."

"You can't go," his mother said, as if there would be no further debate.

Riley shouted, "What's all of this bullshit Clay's been giving me about standing up and taking responsibility? You should only do it if it won't cause you more trouble? That's a bunch of crap! It's my fault she's in there, it's my fault her mother's having a shit fit." He turned around and shoved out the door. "I'm going to see her."

He half-expected to see his mother running out the door after him as he got in his car. But when he looked back, he saw her standing in the doorway with Clay holding her shoulders to keep her inside.

After driving past Mickey's house to make sure her mom's car was home, he went to the hospital. It was after visiting hours, so the lot was nearly empty. He called the desk from his cell phone to see what room Mickey was in. Then he walked in the front door and got on the elevator as if he had every right to be walking the halls. That was usually the trick, just act like you were in the right. Hardly anyone will stop you then.

The door to Mickey's room was closed. He inched it open slowly, just in case there was a nurse in there that would run him off. But Mickey was alone, lying in bed with the lights off and the TV on. Her eyes were closed. Her leg was elevated on a couple of pillows and there was a huge cast that went all the way over her knee. An IV bag hung on a hook at the head of the bed. She looked much more severely injured than she had lying on the ground in the woods.

He slipped inside and closed the door behind him. Mickey didn't stir. Standing at the side of her bed, he slowly reached for her hand. When he held it, her eyes opened.

"Hey," she said, sleepily.

"Hey." He glanced at the cast. "Looks bad."

She smiled weakly. "They said they had to immobilize my knee because of where the break is. It's not really that bad."

"Hurt?" His thumb rubbed the back of her hand.

"Not so much. Thanks to the wonder drugs."

"How long are they keeping you here?"

"They probably would have sent me home tonight, but my mom was all, 'I have to make preparations for an invalid,' so they'll keep me for twenty-three hours without actually admitting me."

She must have seen the anger build up in his face, because she was quick to say, "I was glad not to have to go home tonight."

As long as they were talking about her mother, Riley forced himself to say, "What about the . . . other thing?"

It took a fraction of a second before her face registered comprehension. Then she put on a cocky smile and said, "Oh . . . I'm officially a virgin."

Riley felt like throwing something. "Goddammit! Why did she have to do that to you!"

"It's not a b-big de—" Suddenly her words crumpled into tears.

"Aw, shit." For a second, Riley turned his back on her looking for something to punch. He ended up just slamming his fist into his palm.

Mickey fanned the air in front of her face with her hands. "I'm okay."

"I'm not." He might be, once he strangled her mom. "You shouldn't have let them do it."

"It was the only way—" she cut herself off. Tears still slid down her face; he didn't think she was aware of them.

"What?" he prompted.

She shook her head.

"The only way to keep your mom from coming after me?"

Mickey covered her face with her hands, unable to hold back her sobs.

In that moment, Riley felt the same urge to take her away from here that he had after her dad had put bruises on her years ago. Dammit, how could she have such shits for parents? It wasn't fair.

He lowered the side rail on the bed and leaned back next to her. Wrapping her in his arms, he let Mickey cry herself out. He imagined she'd been holding it in all day long. And it was all his fault.

Molly awakened to find herself pressed against Dean's side with his arm around her. Strangely enough, she didn't feel in the least awkward or surprised this time. Sleeping next to Dean, even though they had issues, felt natural. In some ways their conflicts bound them even more tightly to one another.

It was completely dark. She lifted her head and looked at the clock. It was nearly six-thirty and the baby continued to snooze in his crib. From the sound of Dean's regular deep breathing, he was asleep too.

Gently she put her head back on his shoulder, happy to bask in a false sense of togetherness. Her, Dean, and

Nicholas. Deep inside there was a whisper of hope that it actually could be.

As she lay there, she tried to sort out her emotions. Was her love for Nicholas coloring the way she looked at Dean—a complete family package? Was she only thinking of Dean this way in order to hang onto Nicholas?

She tried to tell herself they were separate feelings; she had been strongly attracted to Dean *before* she knew he was Sarah's brother. Those kisses she'd accepted in ignorance of his identity had been unlike any she'd ever shared with anyone. If anything, his relationship to the baby should dash her ardor, not fan the flames. And, with his body beside hers, she couldn't deny the smoldering embers that remained from their last encounter.

He stirred beside her and she looked at his face.

In the darkness, she could make out his eyes and the fact that he was smiling. Could he tell what was going through her mind?

Without a word, she eased closer and brushed her lips lightly against his, teasing, testing. She rubbed her forehead against his chin, breathing in the mingling of their sleep scents. He'd said the two of them together were a dangerous mix and she couldn't deny it. There was something about their chemistry when they came close that defied logic and thwarted control. Something that drew them together like oppositely charged particles.

Seeking more of him, she kissed his throat. He hadn't shaved; she liked the rough play of his skin against hers.

For a moment he didn't react, but she realized he was holding his breath.

Her tongue dipped into the hollow at the base of his throat and he sucked in a breath that could easily have been either surprise or arousal. It became blindingly clear which one as he slid a hand into her hair and cascaded kisses along her forehead, her temples, her neck.

His breath against her ear sent shivers coursing through her like earthquake tremors; erasing all doubt that this had *anything* to do with Nicholas. When he did these things to her, there was nothing in the universe except the two of them.

His lips found hers. For a moment he teased gently, then it was as if something inside him gave way and his mouth possessed hers completely, with an intense desire that rocked her to her very soul. A muffled sound came from deep in his throat, as if in surrender.

Molly could hardly draw in air as her body responded, fast, hot and explosive. My God, if they set this kind of fire when they were at odds with one another, what would it be like if they were in complete agreement?

He shifted onto his side, never breaking the kiss. His hand slid underneath her shirt and she thought she'd burst into flame. She finally understood: this was what drove sane people to irrational acts. She'd never experienced anything so volatile, so completely beyond her control, so amazing.

Without thought, she worked the buttons of his shirt. The need to feel his skin against hers eclipsed all else.

When she felt him unfasten her bra, her mind and body tumbled into a dark place where only physical sensations registered.

Suddenly his hands stilled and his lips left her wanting.

He whispered, "I promised not to take advantage." His voice was strained.

She didn't want to talk. She wanted to *feel*.

Her body was so prepossessed with desire, she couldn't form words. She sat up and in one quick motion stripped to the waist. Then she rolled him onto his back and straddled him, spreading his shirt open by running her palms over his chest. It was as if she'd never laid her hands on another man before, the exploration of muscle and skin totally new and electrifying.

While she enjoyed the feel of his flesh, his hands knotted in the comforter beside them as he struggled to keep his word.

Holding his gaze, she reached down and untangled his fingers from the fabric. Interlacing their fingers, she picked up his hand and brought it to her lips. After kissing it suggestively, she placed it on her breast.

Leaning close, her mouth captured the low moan that he couldn't contain. Then she whispered, her lips brushing his as she did, "I'm the one taking advantage."

He wrapped his arms around her, crushing her to his chest and kissing her with a passion that took both her breath and her strength away. At last they were skin against skin and Molly trembled from her skin to the marrow of her bones. She felt as if she flowed into him, that their sensations became one.

There was nothing left to her but a driving need, an urgency to meld closer to him in body and soul. It was startling and new and frightening—and inescapable.

The feel of his hands on her was like a dream, something she'd been yearning for all of her life and yet could never define. They were strong and capable and protective. She'd never wanted to surrender herself so totally.

In an instant, he switched their positions. She lay beneath him, his mouth exploring her throat, her collar bone. Arching her back, she urged him where she longed for him to go.

Instead of her breast, he returned his attention to her lips. Bracing himself on his elbows, he used both of his hands to push her hair away from her face. Then he looked into her eyes and said, "You're killing me."

"Then do something about it." She wasn't sure where she found the air to speak.

His forehead touched hers. "I can't."

Molly stifled a low laugh as she moved her thigh against his jeans. "It doesn't feel that way to me."

He sighed. It was a mix of exasperation and unfulfilled need.

"I take full responsibility," she said. "You're not taking advantage—although I do admit, my brain is definitely disengaged."

"Obviously." He kissed her again. "But I don't have anything. . . ." Then he lifted his head and looked at her again. "I don't suppose you—"

Molly gritted her teeth and groaned. "Hardly. I hadn't planned on . . . ." She hadn't planned on *him*. Never in a million years had she thought she'd feel like this. She blew a breath through her teeth. "Shit."

Raising up, he nibbled her neck.

"Stop teasing!" She squirmed. "That's just mean."

"I don't have a mean bone in my body. In fact, I'm a very generous man." His mouth moved slowly down her body and he proceeded to show her exactly how generous he could be.

* * *

They managed to ignore the reality of their situation until after they'd eaten a pizza; had fed and bathed Nicholas; had spent twenty minutes marveling at his tiny perfection as the three of them lay on the bed; and a full hour of bathroom sauna when he began acting colicky. This time Dean insisted on relieving Molly and took a thirty minute turn in the steamy bathroom.

Once the baby was down for the night, a somber silence fell over them. For a long while, neither one seemed inclined to break it.

"Maybe I should borrow some more firewood and make a fire," Dean said.

"I don't think that's a good idea." Molly said, even as she calculated how long that activity could put off having to deal with the real issue. "Not tonight, anyway. We've got too much to discuss."

He nodded and sat back down at the kitchen table. Since he remained silent, she assumed he thought she should go first.

"Have you given thought to how you're going to handle a baby?" she asked.

"Except when I was in bed with you, I haven't thought of anything else."

Molly felt her ears burn, quickly tucking that particular memory away for when she could relive it in private. "Have you come up with a plan?" She thought she'd let him reveal how completely unprepared he was before she presented her case.

He looked at her as if he could see the inner workings of her mind. For a long moment, he fiddled with the salt shaker, rotating it on the table but keeping his gaze on her. She shifted her own gaze to a place she felt would be safer, his fingers. It turned out to be as dangerous as looking in his eyes. Their time in bed together slid underneath the crack in the door she'd closed on it. She'd always thought he had nice hands; now she knew they were incredible.

He finally said, "I thought I'd leave him with you."

Molly blinked twice before she allowed herself to believe her ears. All of her mental organization flew out the window. She wasn't going to have to strong arm him after all.

"That's wonderful!" Her heart danced on air. "I know it's hard for you. But really, he'll be so much better off here in the long run." Her words were coming in a rush of happiness. "Of course, you'll come often. And I promise to keep you informed of his every development."

Dean silently cursed his lack of forethought. Of course she was thinking he meant forever. "Molly." He reached across the table and took her hand. "I meant for a few days. I need to go back east and make some arrangements."

She looked as if he'd taken a two-by-four to the back of her head. For a moment, she was frozen. Then she blinked. Her mouth opened slightly and closed.

Then he saw the storm gathering in her eyes.

Chapter 21

Molly jerked her hand free of his and jumped to her feet. She opened her mouth, but didn't speak. Instead she spun around, leaving Dean to stare at her shoulders rising and falling on her rapid breaths.

He got up and stood behind her, wanting to put his hands on her shoulders, but knowing she would just pull away. "I'm sorry. I didn't think . . . I should have made myself clear—"

She turned to face him, her movement jerky with agitation. Her voice quivered with fury when she said, "Do these 'arrangements' have to do with preparing a home for Nicholas? Or are you hunting down his father?"

Dean had braced himself for an attack, but not of this nature. He was quickly formulating words for the argument of why he could not give up his nephew, his only family. Not this.

For a moment, he nearly weakened and told her of his conversation with Detective McMurray. But he knew she would not view it in the vein of a breakthrough in the case as he did. She would think it added credence to her argument that the murderer should be left untouched.

He looked into her eyes, trying not to see the fear there. "I need to go through Julie's things; her super has them in storage."

"Looking for clues?" The challenge in her voice was cutting.

He scrubbed his hands over his face. This was a damned difficult situation. He spun around, hiding himself from her scrutinizing glare. "There are a hundred things I have to do to get things cleared up and a place for Nicholas. I live in a single rented room."

She took a step closer and launched her assault. "What are you going to do about working? Are you going back to the Middle East? You can't seriously think you should take a baby there. Don't you think he'd be better with me than some nanny you hire? He *needs* a family—I can give him that! What if you get yourself killed? You've already been shot once! Who will take care of him then? With no relatives, he'll become a ward of the state—believe me, you don't want that to happen. Have you really thought these things all the way through? And what do you mean, 'cleared up'? Don't you know how dangerous it will be for Nicholas if you try to hunt down this man?"

"Do you want the answers in the same order as the questions?" he asked in as calm a tone as he could manage.

Molly set her jaw; Dean could see it was to keep her chin from quivering. There were unspilled tears in her eyes. He was sure nothing more than her iron determination kept them from falling. He felt like a jerk, but he knew he could not rest until this killer had been punished.

The baby would be safe here with her until he got that job done.

He said, "I'm going to do my best to take care of him. I swear it." He paused and cast a glance at the ceiling. He wanted to hold her in his arms while he explained. But he could tell by the set of her shoulders that was not going to happen. "I know both Julie and I are indebted to you beyond repayment. And I don't want to hurt you. But can't you see? Nicholas is all I have. I can't just walk away from him." He looked deep in her eyes. "I need a family, too."

Why did it have to be that to get what he needed, he was going to have to hurt the only woman he'd cared about in a very long time? He hated the pain in her eyes. But he couldn't see a way around it.

She didn't say anything.

"Will you help me?" he asked. "Will you keep him for a few more days?"

A single tear slid down her face. "I'll keep him as long as you'll let me."

Riley held Mickey until she went to sleep. With the falling of every one of her tears, his resolve to protect her had become stronger. He just had to figure out a way to do it. A part of his anger was directed at himself. He had hurt her and tried to make himself think it didn't matter. He'd let her go because it had been easier for him.

After slipping carefully from the bed, he paused before he left the room. Mickey was strong because she had to be. No one *ever* put her first—and she knew it. Today had only proved that to her again. She had tried to do something for Riley and ended up not only with a broken ankle, but humiliated at the hands of her own mother.

Something deep in his chest felt tight as he looked at her and he found it hard to swallow.

As he left her room, he vowed he would never take the easy road again.

Dean spent Thursday night in Indianapolis. His flight left for New York at seven-thirty on Friday morning. As he sat on the plane watching the clouds pass beneath him, he once again mulled over Detective McMurray's leading questions. Which federal agency had shown an interest in Julie's death? CIA? The detective suggested someone in Rome, or the airport. Someone international?

When he landed at LaGuardia, he called Harry. The investigator was supposed to have arrived in New York yesterday.

Amazingly, Harry actually picked up.

"Dean. I was just about to call you."

"Making headway already?" Dean had mixed emotions; he wanted answers, but if Harry got them in twenty-four hours and Dean had missed them himself . . .

Harry said, "Your sister cancelled her New Year's Eve plans at the last minute."

"She made a point of being home by New Year's Eve."

"Yeah, apparently she and her friend, Annie from college, have spent New Year's Eve together for the past few years. Seems Annie got married last year. She said Julie called and cancelled that morning. Annie said she thought it was because of her marriage—Julie felt like a fifth wheel or some girl crap like that. But the more we talked, she said that just didn't seem right. Inevitably, someone was single in that group every year and Julie had come alone at least once."

Again, Dean felt negligent. Shouldn't he have known about something like a long-standing New Year's Eve tradition? Then he said, "I talked to Annie. She said she didn't have a clue why Julie left—said she didn't think Julie was dating anyone."

"You weren't asking the right questions, my man. New Year's Eve was over two months *before* Julie disappeared. Annie wasn't thinking of New Year's Eve when you spoke to her; in fact I had to probe around a little before it shook loose."

"All right. Julie cancelled. Do you have any leads as to why?"

"Not yet. Hey, I've only been here a day. Her work turned out to be a dead end."

Dean decided to offer Harry his own newest development. "I had an interesting conversation with a detective at BPD. She's making noises like there's federal interest in this case."

Harry whistled. "Now that opens up some possibilities. Let me work on that. She say FBI?"

"No. She didn't *say* anything. She brought up Julie's trip to Rome at Christmas, though."

"CIA . . . that might take a little longer. Things have gotten more complicated since 9/11."

"She made a point of mentioning my work in the Middle East."

Harry moaned. "Even more complicated. I'll poke around and be in touch tomorrow. I know some people who know some people."

"That's why I hire you, Harry. You're a man of many

acquaintances. I'm going to the office and see if there are any leads I missed—plus I happen to know some people, too. With this information, I think it's time to use them."

"Tomorrow then."

Dean disconnected the call. For the first time since he'd identified Julie's body in Boston, he felt like he had a direction, even if the destination was still obscured by a thick bank of fog. Unfortunately that compass pointed east, across the Atlantic.

Molly took Nicholas for a long walk in his stroller on Friday morning. She was still tussling with her conscience. She wanted to do everything in her power to fight for this baby. And yet, the sad truth was, she had no power. If she made it too difficult for Dean, all he had to do was call the police and it was bye-bye medical license, hello jail.

Her heart told her he would never do that to her. But she had to think, if she held that power, would she use it to gain guardianship of this child? Would she sacrifice Dean's career to keep Nicholas with her?

The fact that she couldn't answer that question immediately and unequivocally told her she could be in trouble. She hoped he took her questions to heart and perhaps would return with a revised view of taking the baby with him. Surely he could see how much better it would be for Nicholas to be with a parent who was going to live on a single continent.

As she lowered the stroller down a curb to cross the street, she realized she was dreaming. Dean had made his case. Nicholas was his only living relative. He wasn't going to walk away.

For a moment panic seized her and the irrational urge to run burst forth. And she might have actually given in to it, gone home and packed her car and driven away from here just like she'd driven away from Boston. But that would be as selfish as Dean taking Nicholas to the Middle East. Living on the run was no life to offer this child. There would never be a day's peace, never a restful night, knowing that at any time someone could come forth and take Nicholas away. And how could she support him?

Even as she saw it for the ridiculous action that it would be, the temptation remained.

Molly stopped on the sidewalk in front of the grade school. Children were at recess, swinging, shooting baskets, and playing dodgeball. Just days ago, she had envisioned Nicholas playing on this playground, growing up in this quiet town. In her mind's eye, she had seen his blond head bobbing with the other children at play.

She reached down and touched his cheek to make certain he wasn't getting too cold. He smiled, then moved his mouth and waved his arms as if he was trying to say something. Grabbing him up blanket and all, she hugged him against her, pressing her cheek against his knitted hat. At one time, she had thought she would never be a mother. And now, even if she was physically unable to bear a child, she would at least know the joy of motherhood. As she held Nicholas next to her heart, she understood with startling clarity, even if she bore a dozen children, there would never be one that could replace him.

*   *   *

Riley was late coming home from school. In light of recent events, Lily's mind quickly leapt to disastrous conclusions. He had seemed all right when he left this morning. For the past few days he'd been quiet, his moods deeper and more veiled than usual. And his focus didn't seem to be the recent revelation that Clay was his father. Which caused her to be more concerned. She had expected an angry haze to linger, but all indications said he was preoccupied with something else.

She only hoped her own father would take the news in the same stride. She had managed not to give a full explanation to him just yet.

Keeping a steady gaze through the glass-paned door that faced the driveway, she paced the kitchen.

The hiss of a pot boiling over on the stove drew her back across the room. She turned down the heat and stirred the chili, then she checked on the cake in the oven. Finding it done, she pulled it out and breathed in its sweet aroma. It was lemon, Mickey's favorite. She was planning on sending Riley to the Fultons' with it this evening—if he ever showed up.

The back door opened.

Spinning around, she was relieved to see Riley. She quickly calmed herself before she spoke to him. Clay said she was smothering him; that she had to give him more space and wait for him to come to her to talk about what was bothering him. But it was so hard; all she wanted was for him to be happy and safe.

One look at his face told her something was very wrong.

"Hi," she said with a question in her voice and fear in her heart.

He walked over to the upholstered chair next to the fireplace and flopped down.

"Something wrong?" she asked, keeping to her side of the room by sheer will.

"I went to see Mickey and her mom wouldn't let me in the house."

"Oh. I thought Mrs. Fulton finally agreed you hadn't done anything wrong. She seemed much better when I spoke to her yesterday. Maybe Mickey was sleeping."

"Ha! I heard her crying in the background. Mickey's not allowed to see me *ever*."

"I thought Karen was letting this pressing charges thing go."

"It's not that. Besides, I don't know how she could anyhow; she made Mickey get examined by a doctor just to prove that I didn't . . . ."

Lily felt sick. As if Mickey wasn't under enough stress. She huffed, then held onto her indignant thoughts. "Maybe she'll cool off, now that things are settling back down. She always seemed to like you—"

He set his angry gaze on her. "That's when she thought I was a Holt."

Her stomach lurched. "How does she know that you aren't?"

He shrugged. "I told Mickey, she must have said something."

Lily wanted to say that just showed what a vile and shallow woman Karen was, but held her tongue. "And Mrs. Fulton said something to you?"

Looking away, he didn't answer.

"Riley?"

"It doesn't matter. She says stupid stuff all of the time. It's just that I really need to see Mickey, Mom."

Lily looked at the cake. "Do you know when Mickey is coming back to school?"

"I guess Monday. When I talked to her on the phone yesterday, she said she'd be there today. I'm worried about her."

"I have a gift for Mickey. Maybe we'll deliver it in the morning."

Riley looked at her with panic and gratitude in his conflicted eyes. "Mrs. Fulton doesn't like you any more than she likes me."

"I know. But it's a lot harder to look an adult in the eye and use an irrational argument than it is to push teenagers around. Maybe she'll be in a better mood tomorrow. At least I think I can get us in the door to make sure Mickey's all right."

He nodded, clearly relieved. "Thanks, Mom." When he stood and kissed her forehead, she saw him for the man he was becoming. He had ten times the character of any Holt she'd ever met. Damn Karen Fulton.

"Lucky for you, criminals work at night and so do the guys trying to catch them," Harry said as soon as Dean answered his cell phone early the next morning.

"What do you have?" His taxi was stuck creeping along behind a garbage truck.

"I checked the manifest for your sister's flight back from Rome and ran a cross-check with my people who know people. One name in particular caught my people's attention."

"Does he live in New York?"

"Yes. Seems the man keeps leaving the feds holding nothing more than a fistful of suspicion."

"So tell me."

"Not on the cell. I'll meet you at eleven at my hotel."

"I'm headed to Julie's apartment now. See you at eleven."

Julie had lived in a five-story building near midtown. It was on an impossibly narrow and quiet street—which was why the garbage truck caused such a problem. When they were within a couple of blocks, Dean paid the driver and walked the rest of the way.

He knocked on the superintendent's apartment door. A tiny, white-haired woman answered, leaving the security chain in place.

Dean offered her his most reassuring smile. He held up his press ID. "I'm Dean Coletta, Julie's brother. Mr. Fiore let me check on my sister's things a few weeks ago. I'd like to have access to them again."

One wrinkled eye narrowed through the crack in the door. "My son is in the basement working on the boiler." She closed the door.

Dean heard three locks snap into place.

"Thank you, ma'am," he called through the closed door.

He got a thump in response from the other side.

The door to the basement was ajar. Dean pushed it open. The stairwell was narrow and flanked by exposed brick walls. The tiny fluorescent light at the top faded long before the bottom step. At the base, there was a long hallway with a gray painted floor and another inadequate light fixture. He shuddered to think of his sister coming down here late at night to do her laundry. He stopped at a door marked "MECHANICAL" and knocked loudly.

"Mr. Fiore?" he called as he opened the door.

Fiore was on his knees with his face near the floor, peering under the boiler.

"Excuse me, Mr. Fiore?"

Fiore looked up. Although Dean had seen him before, he was still taken aback by the burn scar that covered half of the young man's face.

Fiore wiped his hands on a rag and said, "Damn thing should have been replaced fifteen years ago—but the old tightass who owns the building seems to think it'll last forever."

Dean gave a sympathetic nod. "You must be good at keeping it going."

"Too good. I should have taken a sledgehammer to it this time."

Dean extended his hand. "Dean Coletta, Julie's brother. I was here a few weeks ago."

"I remember." He shook Dean's hand and smiled, but only with the right side of his face. The left side remained as stationary as if it were made of plastic. "Again, sorry to hear about your sister. I really thought she'd come back. That's why I didn't set her stuff out for the trash like the landlord said to. He doesn't know it's all down here."

"I appreciate your consideration. I promise to make arrangements for having it moved soon. But right now I need to look through her things again . . . do you mind unlocking for me?"

"No problem." As they walked out of the boiler room,

Fiore said, "Sometimes this world just makes me sick. Who would want to hurt a nice woman like her?"

"That's what I intend to find out."

Fiore gave a somber nod of approval. "Like I told you before, she always paid her rent on time. When she was late, I got worried. I called her work and they said she hadn't been there in two weeks. That's when I called the police—for all the good it did."

This was ground Dean had already covered, but he was having to go over everything again in light of his new information. "How thoroughly did they search her apartment?"

"Checked for a body is about all." He looked embarrassed. "Sorry, didn't mean to sound crude. But that's about all they did. I think they used one of those lights that looks for blood. They said it looked like she just up and left—skipped town. I didn't believe it. She had too much class for that."

"Anyone else ask to search the apartment—other than NYPD?"

"Nope. Ma swore she heard someone up there one day while I was out. But I checked and everything was fine, the door was locked and all. Sometimes Ma gets a little . . . overanxious. The neighborhood is changing.

"She liked Julie," he kept talking as they walked to the storage room. "She and Ma shared a birthday, you know. Your sister always remembered Ma with little candies at the holid—" He stopped cold as he opened the door and flipped on the light.

Dean nearly ran into the back of him. He looked over Fiore's shoulder. The contents of the room had been searched, and none too delicately.

"I was in here yesterday to check the mouse traps. It wasn't like this."

Wordlessly, Dean stepped around him. He shifted some of the stuff on the floor and saw a small framed photograph of Julie and Big Bird that had been taken at an ice show when she was four. He picked it up and thought of Molly's Tinkerbell clock. He slipped the photo into his pocket.

Harry's questions had obviously poked at someone's hornet's nest. It was pointless to look for clues in her possessions. If evidence had been here, it was gone now.

Somebody was worried.

Chapter 22

At ten-forty, Dean began to pace the lobby of Harry's hotel like a caged animal. He felt as if he had a rash deep beneath his skin and nothing would relieve it. Those rifled boxes and ripped upholstery said someone feared they'd overlooked something when they killed Julie. No doubt this had been triggered by renewed interest in her disappearance. But what was the conduit that let the murderer know it was happening?

Dean had tried Harry's phone after he left Julie's apartment; but true to form, Harry didn't pick up. Why hadn't Dean insisted they meet earlier? The seconds dragged by as panic inched closer to the surface. The kind of bad guys who could elude the hands of the feds kept on top of things; their quick reaction in searching Julie's belongings confirmed it. They would soon figure out that Dean was behind this renewed investigation—if they hadn't already. And Dean had left an easy trail straight back to Molly's front door.

He'd already called her six times and gotten no answer. Damn, why didn't the woman at least get voice mail?

A two-thirty airline reservation awaited Dean at La-Guardia. He would meet with Harry, then head back to Indiana. Harry could finish here. Dean had to stay with Molly. She might have been vigilant those first few days in Indiana, but now her guard was down. Even if she thought his questioning could lead the father to Nicholas, she wouldn't have any idea it would be happening so blindingly fast.

Maybe he should call the Glens Crossing police.

No, not until he spoke to Harry and had some idea what was going on.

Where was that damn man?

He called his office and asked Smitty to pack up his boxes of mail so he could pick them up on his way to the airport. Dean would take all of it back to Indiana and comb through it piece by piece. He'd made a cursory pass through the whole mess yesterday, but he'd been looking for something from Julie. If she *had* sent him evidence, maybe she covered her tracks with a bogus return address.

Then he tried Molly again. He gave up after the ninth ring.

Harry finally showed his lanky hound-dog face. Dean had never been so glad to see anyone.

Harry grinned like this was a social meeting and said, "Hey, buddy, let's sit in the bar."

"I don't have time. I'm going back to Indiana. Just tell me."

Harry laughed loudly and hugged Dean, patting him roughly on the back. Then he took Dean's elbow and moved him in the direction of the bar. "Let's have a drink." His voice was even more insistent and the biting pressure on Dean's arm said not to resist.

Once they were seated at a table in the back, Dean said, "Christ, you're acting like someone's tailing you."

"Someone is."

Dean resisted the urge to look around. "Good guy or bad guy?"

"My guess is fed. Don't know which category."

"Dirty fed?"

"I think there's someone buttering his bread on both sides." Harry lit a cigarette. "Your sister was supposed to meet with someone from the CIA at the train station the day she was killed. It's just too coincidental that this boyfriend of hers couldn't locate her for six months and the very day she was to meet with the feds, he takes her out. Either someone is tailing the CIA—which I'm not putting out of the realm of possibility—or someone on the inside told him where she was."

"Who is 'him'? And how do you know she was meeting with someone? My God, CIA. . . ."

"I don't have it in stone yet, but all signs point to Stephen VanGraff. He was on her flight from Rome. For the past four years, the feds have been watching him and he's been watching the feds. It's a real tango. He heads a not-for-profit relief organization, but there's heavy suspicion that it's a cover for arms dealing. If it's him, he wouldn't have done the hit himself. He hires that kind of work done."

Dean's stomach turned sour. Arms dealing. Terrorists. "That's why McMurray laid it on heavy about my Middle East experience."

"I haven't been able to put VanGraff and Julie in the same place at the same time yet, other than they were seated in the same row on that flight."

Something Molly said bounced back in Dean's brain. "What does VanGraff look like?"

"Innocent. Boy-next-door. Tall, handsome, blue eyes, reddish hair and just enough freckles to seal the deal."

"How reddish—like auburn . . . carrot top?"

"Like Opie. You know, sandy."

"Shit." After a moment he asked, "Why didn't I call you in the first place?"

"Cause you think you're smarter than me—and you are." He took a drag on his cigarette and blew out a long puff of blue smoke. "I just happened to have the right connections this time." He knocked off the ash and asked, "If Julie had something on this guy, why didn't she go to the feds right away?"

"Because she was protecting her baby." Dean closed his eyes and tried to quell his rolling stomach. She *had* set Molly up. In her very practical, methodical way, Julie was taking care of business. She had waited for the birth, then separated herself from the baby to deliver whatever information she had to the government. And she had made sure that he knew nothing about it, because she knew that if he knew, he would come after the bastard. And that would put Nicholas at risk.

Oh, God, I'm sorry, Julie. But I'll protect him. I swear I will.

"Stay on this and keep me posted. I'll see if Van-Graff's name pops up with any of my people." Dean got up. "I have to go."

"Are you sure? You can help more here."

"The only thing that matters is in Indiana. That's where I have to be." He hurried out of the bar and onto the street to get a taxi.

"Stop looking so confrontational," Lily said to Riley as they waited for someone to answer the door at the Fultons'.

"I'm not."

"You are too. You look like you want to punch someone in the face." Not that she could blame him, she felt that way herself. But that was definitely not the way to handle Karen. She shoved the cake into Riley's hands. "Here, at least you'll be bearing gifts."

It was taking an awfully long time for someone to get the door.

Finally, it opened slowly. Mickey stood there on her crutches in a T-shirt and boxers.

Lily glanced at Riley, who was now wearing a broad grin. She said, "Hi, Mickey."

"Hi." But Mickey wasn't looking at her, she was looking only at Riley.

"We brought you a surprise," Riley said, lifting the cake like an offering.

After a quick look over her shoulder, Mickey said, "Come on in."

They followed her as she thumped her crutches into the living room. The television was tuned to MTV and the sofa was piled with pillows to support her casted leg. She eased herself onto the couch and propped her leg up, then muted the TV with the remote.

Lily sat on the love seat placed at a right angle to the couch. Riley just stood there with the cake in his hands.

Lily said, "It's lemon. Maybe Riley should put it in the kitchen?"

"That would be good. And thanks so much; I love lemon cake."

"I know." Lily smiled.

Riley disappeared for a couple of seconds. When he came back in, he sat on the floor beside Mickey.

Lily asked Mickey about her leg. While Mickey was answering, Lily noticed Riley looking at her with more than friendship shining in his eyes. There was the answer to his mood, she thought—and the reason the news that Clay was his father wasn't overwhelming him.

"Well, hello," Karen said as she came down the stairs into the living room.

Lily stood, unable to read the mood in either Karen's voice or her expression. Might as well present an innocent and happy front. "Hi, Karen. We just brought by a cake to cheer Mickey up. The pottery plate it's on is a gift, so don't worry about returning it."

Karen's gaze cut to Riley and back again. "How nice."

Both Riley and Mickey seemed to be holding their breath.

When Karen didn't seem inclined to further the conversation, Lily said, "I know you have your hands full here." She forced a smile, thinking of how Mickey had to answer the door on her crutches. "Do you need anything—something from the grocery or drugstore?"

"Thank you, no."

"Well," Lily sighed lightly, "I guess we should be going then." She turned to Mickey. "Would you like Riley to pick you up for school on Monday?" She turned a false but bright smile on Karen then. "I know how hard it'll be driving her to and from school with your work schedule."

For a second, it looked like Karen was going to refuse, then she seemed to reconsider. "That would be a help. I have to be at the bank early on Monday for a tellers' meeting."

"Great, then." She looked at Mickey again. "You take care of yourself. If any of you need anything, just call."

Riley got to his feet. Lily noticed he touched Mickey's hand briefly. When her worried gaze moved back to Karen, it appeared she hadn't noticed.

As they left the room, Riley said, "See ya, Mickey." Then he stopped in front of Karen. "Good-bye, Ms. Kimball."

Karen's tight-lipped expression softened slightly. "Bye."

Lily wanted to give the kid a big pat on the back, but she waited until they were outside. "Well done."

He looked at her with surprise. "What?"

"You faced her and said a respectful good-bye—and you remembered she likes to be called Ms. Kimball and not Mrs. Fulton."

He quirked his mouth and shrugged. As he went down the porch steps, he said, "Thanks, Mom. I feel better after seeing her. It's just sometimes . . . her mom can be so mean to her."

"I know. You're a good friend." Lily left it at that. She wasn't sure that Riley even knew he was in love yet. Then she said, "Let's see if Molly and Nicholas want to go to the park and to lunch."

Much to her surprise, he agreed. The strong glimpses

of maturity she was seeing in her son continued to catch her off guard.

He surprised her further when he asked, "Why do you suppose Aunt Molly didn't marry Nicholas's father?"

Lily paused on the sidewalk, wanting to get this answer right. She had the feeling this was one of those few moments in a parent's life that they have a chance to say something that will stick.

"I don't know, really. She doesn't like to talk about him. Sometimes things don't work out between two people. She has a career and can care for a baby on her own, so I guess she decided that was best."

"Mickey says babies aren't a good reason to get married."

She had to bite her tongue to keep from asking how that happened to come up in conversation between them. "I suppose that's right in a sense. Sometimes getting married because there's a baby on the way only compounds one mistake with two."

"Would you have married dad if you hadn't been pregnant?" He cast his gaze down the street when he asked.

She drew a fortifying breath. "Probably not *when* I did, but I did love your dad, so we probably would have ended up together if. . . ."

"If Clay didn't come back?" Now he was looking at her.

It seemed impossible that they were having this conversation standing on the street. "I've always been in love with Clay. I won't lie to you. If he had been around, Peter and I would never have married." She thought of that look she'd seen in her son's eye as he looked at Mickey. "Keep in mind, there is a lot of responsibility that goes along with . . . making a baby. Even if you don't marry the other parent, you'll still be tied to them for the rest of your life."

He looked at her for a long minute. Then he smiled and said, "Don't worry about me, I'm not planning on . . . you know."

"Riley, sometimes plans have absolutely nothing to do with it."

He looked at his shoes for a second, then said, "Mickey's mom always made Mickey feel responsible for her having to marry Mr. Fulton."

Lily put an arm around her son. "You said it yourself, Mrs. Fulton says a lot of stupid things. Let that be a lesson—don't look for other people to blame for *your* choices. It's very hurtful."

He nodded, then started walking toward Molly's porch steps. "Hey, here comes Aunt Molly." He pointed down the street to where Molly pushed the stroller in their direction.

Lily paused for a moment and said a little prayer that Riley and Mickey would have better sense—and if not that, better luck—than she or Molly did.

Molly rolled the shopping cart across Kingston's lot. It clattered loudly on the rough, pitted pavement. She figured Nicholas was getting his evening jostle early as he rode along in the cart's infant seat. Leaning close, she asked him, "So, you like it? Maybe we should do this instead of sitting around the bathroom."

His little face broke into a grin and his eyes lit up.

Molly's heart broke. How was she going to live without him?

It was still early evening, but it was as dark as the middle of the night. For some reason, the shortening days bothered her this year. The early onset of night seemed much more depressing than she ever remembered. It used to be the herald of the holiday season, a sign that it was time to start thinking about turkey and mistletoe and Christmas shopping. Now it just felt . . . dark.

She put her groceries in the trunk and then put Nicholas in his car seat. Giving him a quick kiss on the cheek, she got out and closed the door. As she opened the driver's door, she paused with her hand on the latch. She saw the cloud of her breath in the dim light of the parking lot. On the other side of the lot a father tried to corral three young children into seat belts. She watched for a moment, imagining Dean with Nicholas doing ordinary everyday things—like running to the store for ice cream after dinner. It would have been a heartwarming picture, if only she were in it, too.

Listening intently, Molly strained to hear the violin that she had heard on her previous two nighttime trips here. The night was damp and quiet, much more quiet than the last time she'd heard the mysterious music. After a moment, she gave up in disappointment and got in the car and drove home.

As she pulled in the driveway, she realized she'd forgotten to leave on the kitchen and porch lights. She parked the car near the kitchen door and leaned over the back of her seat to see if Nicholas was awake. As always with the shortest car ride, he was snoozing.

She decided to take the groceries in first. She'd rather stumble in the dark with groceries than with Nicholas.

There were only two brown bags in the trunk. She

hefted one in each arm, with her keys ready in her right hand. Her load blocked any visual of the ground she might have managed in the dark. She stubbed her toe just as she reached the back walk that led to the alley. Unable to maintain her balance, she pitched forward with a gasp, bracing herself for the sharp pain as she hit the ground.

Instead, a pair of arms grabbed her. The grocery bags tumbled free of her grasp as fear made an icy stab at her heart. She heard her keys hit the concrete.

She tried to scream, but only a long breathy whine came out. She thrashed against her assailant, whose hold tightened with every move she made.

"Stop! Molly, it's me!"

She kicked his shin before the voice registered.

"Dammit! Stop!"

The arms released her and she stumbled backward two steps, then tripped over a jar of spaghetti sauce and landed on her rear end in a huff of breath.

"What in the hell are you doing back here in the dark! You're supposed to be in New York."

Dean limped over to her and offered her a hand up.

When he pulled her to her feet, he yanked her against him and held her tightly against his chest. "Thank God you're all right." He let her go. Framing her face with his hands, he covered her forehead and then her lips with desperate, frantic kisses.

"What's the matter? What happened in New York?" Even as she said the words, cold, clammy fingers of dread settled on the back of her neck. Her worst fears were about to be realized. "His father?"

"I've been trying to reach you all day. Where have you been?"

"We were out, doing stuff. Now tell me what's happened."

"Where's the baby?"

"In the car."

His hands finally released her. "I'll get him. You open the house."

By the time she had the door open and the lights on, Dean was there with the baby. He handed the pumpkin seat over to her and went back outside to retrieve the groceries. Molly forced herself to take care of the tasks at hand while he did that, changing Nicholas's diaper and warming his bottle. It took Dean four trips to shuttle in the groceries because one of the bags had split. Then he made another trip and hauled in a nylon duffle bag.

Finally, he was inside and had locked the door behind him.

Sitting down at the kitchen table to feed Nicholas, she said, "Now tell me what's going on."

Before Dean could open his mouth, the telephone rang.

Frustrated by the interruption, Molly shifted the baby so she could answer it. "Hello?"

The hollow quality of the silence told her the line remained open, although there was no human sound on the other end. "Is anyone there?"

The line clicked, then went dead.

She sighed in irritation, punched the off button, and tossed the phone on the table. Returning her gaze to Dean, she said, "You were saying?"

He was frowning. "Who was that?"

"Probably a wrong number. I'm not in the book."

"They didn't say anything?"

"No." A lump of ice formed in her stomach. "Maybe it was kids messing around."

"Maybe. And maybe it was trouble."

"Him?" Could it have been Nicholas's father?

"Probably not. Too amateurish."

"Now you're scaring me. Tell me what's going on."

"First I'm making a call." He picked up the phone and dialed 9-1-1.

As she opened her mouth to question him, he raised a finger to silence her.

"I'm calling from Dr. Boudreau's residence. 1544 Grant Street. The doctor thinks someone has been prowling around her house. We'd like to have extra patrols throughout the night." He paused. "Yes . . . Dean Coletta . . . Thank you." He disconnected and put the phone down.

"You think that's going to help?"

"It can't hurt."

"You really think he's coming here."

"That call was most likely a wrong number. These guys don't operate like that."

She hadn't been truly frightened for weeks. The cold clutches of fear settled around her heart. She forced herself to say, "Explain to me what happened in New York."

"Before I left for New York, I hired an investigator—"

"So all of that talk was just to placate me—you already had someone looking for Nicholas's father?"

He rubbed the back of his neck. "You know as well as I do, if this man is dangerous, he needs to be stopped now. That danger won't go away just because you ignore it!" Then he gave her a cold hard look that sent a shiver over her. "And believe me, this man is dangerous."

"That's why you were so panicked outside—you thought he'd beat you to us?" Holding the baby, she got up and took a step toward him. "This is exactly why I didn't want you to do this!"

Putting his hands on her shoulders, he said, "I understand how you feel. Jesus, I was so afraid I wouldn't . . . this has made me see, keeping you and Nicholas safe is far more important to me than punishing Julie's killer. And the only way to truly keep you safe is to eliminate him."

"You can't kill him!"

"I will if he tries to harm you." He clasped her face in his hands again. "I swear I will. No one will hurt you or Nicholas. I'd die to protect you."

She could feel him trembling. Looking in his eyes, she saw something so startling that it took her breath away.

He leaned across Nicholas and kissed her lips; she tasted the promise he'd just made and knew he'd meant every word of it.

His lips caressed the corners of her mouth, her nose, her eyes. His hands ran into her hair and he pulled her forehead against his.

They stood there for a long moment, his hands in her hair, heads together with the baby between them. Molly's heart felt like it was going to force itself through her ribs. Fear mingled with something stronger, something much more powerful, and she was as afraid for her heart as she was for Nicholas's life.

She was in love with Dean. It was suddenly as blazingly clear as the rising sun. And it only screwed things up worse; if she told him now, he'd think it was a ploy to keep Nicholas with her.

So she kept her love locked safely in her heart.

Finally she whispered, "What are we going to do?"

Lifting his head slightly, he looked in her eyes and she feared he could see her feelings lying naked there. She lowered her lashes, but worried it was too late.

Instead of answering, he kissed her again.

Had he been thinking similar thoughts?

"What do you think we should do?" he whispered an echo.

The bottle squeaked empty and Nicholas began to squirm between them.

Dean looked down, placing one hand gently on the baby's head.

Molly needed to blow away the sensual fog that had suddenly surrounded them. She shifted slightly away and lifted Nicholas to her shoulder for a burp. She said, "I meant, what are we going to do about his father?"

Dean blew out a breath, then said, "He won't come here himself. He'll send someone else. The only way to get him is the way I believe Julie was trying to get him— through the federal government."

She tried to absorb what he'd just said. "Federal government? I think I need you to back up. Who is this guy?"

Dean explained what Harry had told him. After much deliberation, he decided to tell her about someone going through Julie's stuff sometime overnight.

He finished, "They had to be looking for something incriminating that they think she had. I brought all of the mail from my office, maybe she sent something to me."

By this time, Nicholas was asleep in Molly's arms.

She went to put him down. When she came back in the room, he was starting to go through the mail. He asked, "Did she give you anything—a note, a computer disk, a safe deposit key?"

She shook her head.

"What all did she leave with the baby? Stuffed animal? Diaper bag?"

"The diaper bag. That was it." Then light dawned in her eyes. "You can't think she hid the evidence in something of the baby's! She would never have put him at risk like that—not after everything she did to protect him."

He tore open another envelope. "You're probably right."

"I'm definitely right." She started to put the groceries in the refrigerator. "Are you hungry?"

"No."

"When was the last time you ate?"

With a shrug he said, "I don't know . . . seven this morning, I guess."

"It looks like we have a long night ahead of us going through all of that mail. I'll make us a sandwich. You can't concentrate with low blood sugar."

As Dean dumped the contents of the bag onto the table, he hoped against hope that Julie had sent him something, if not incriminating evidence, at least a clue that would put an end to this. He looked at Molly working at the counter.

And then what? The man who murdered his sister was only one of the demons Dean was going to have to wrestle.

Chapter 23

Dean and Molly worked together on the mail. In order not to miss something that might be a cryptic message from Julie, every piece had to be read thoroughly. With each envelope, Molly asked if he knew the person on the return, then opened it and combed through the contents. She asked several sharp-witted questions as she searched for clues. Even tired and dealing with something she was totally unfamiliar with, her intelligence shone through like a beacon in the dark.

At twelve-thirty, Dean raised his fatigue-scratchy eyes and looked across the table at her. Dark circles showed under her eyes in the overhead lighting. Her brow was creased with concentration. She was looking down, inspecting another letter. Her dark hair kept falling over her shoulder, getting in her way. Absently, she set down the paper she was studying, keeping her eyes on it, and worked her hair into a single braid in the back. Her action was so automated, he didn't think she realized she was doing it.

He watched transfixed as her fingers twisted the hair, exposing her slender neck. Her shirt rode up and bared a narrow swatch of skin at her waist, making him want to touch her.

But there was more than the need to touch. And that's where the problem lay. It had become startlingly clear to him today. His fear had taken his feelings for Molly and put them under pressure and, like coal into a diamond, what emerged was something precious. And yet, conversely, it seemed much too fragile to handle.

The fact was they barely knew one another. Still, he saw her brilliance, her insight, her humanity, and her love more clearly than he'd ever seen inside another human being. It was more than a little frightening. Could he trust it? With Nicholas involved, there was so much more at stake.

"Why don't you go to bed," he suggested. "The baby will be up early."

Seemingly startled by his voice, she looked up at him with those smoky eyes and the urge to touch her was stronger than before.

She gestured toward the large pile of unopened mail. "Are you working without sleep until this is done?"

He got up and stood behind her chair. Massaging her shoulders, he said, "I don't think we have a lot of time. That phone call . . . it *probably* wasn't . . . still . . ."

She stretched her neck and moaned softly. "I'll work until it's done. I'm used to going without sleep. I can nap when Nicholas does tomorrow." She leaned her head back and looked up at him.

He bent down and kissed her chin. "How about some coffee, then?"

"Sure." She started to get up, but he held her in place. "I know where the coffee is; keep reading."

A few minutes later, when he set a mug down beside her, she looked at him with serious eyes. "Do you get many of these?" She held up a single folded sheet of paper that looked like it came out of a TV crime drama. All of the wording had been cut out of publications and glued onto plain white copier paper. It threatened his life, cursing him for bringing his Western ways onto sacred Muslim soil, committing sins against Allah.

He gave her a self-assured cocky grin in an effort to erase that look of disquiet in her eyes. "Sometimes there's actually a rock attached and it's hurled at my head. When they come through the mail they're not nearly as dangerous."

He saw her shiver.

"Why do you keep going back?" she asked.

"Because it's completely foreign to the Western world and everything that happens there affects us. If there's ever to be any common ground, someone has to forge it. We *need* to understand them. And I've been there long enough that I can ask some of the right questions. So I stay." As he said it, dread crept through his veins. Seeing Clifford die and leave children behind . . . Nicholas needed him. Everything had changed.

He made a circuit of the house, checking out all of the windows before he sat down and went back to work. He pushed away the most important thing that had changed—his feelings for Molly. He couldn't climb that mountain until he finished scaling this one. First and foremost, he had to keep her safe.

Three hours later, he threw the last scrap of paper onto

the "read" pile. "That's it. Nothing." He put his elbows on the table and ran his hands through his hair.

Molly said, "You really thought she would have sent you evidence, something that pointed to the man who killed her and why?"

He couldn't believe she'd just asked that. "Of course. Why else would we have spent most of the night doing this?"

"Because it's better than doing nothing?"

"This is too serious to be wasting time."

"I know it's serious. Julie knew it was serious. That's why I didn't think you would find anything in there."

"But if she knew this guy was bad—evil, as she said—I have to think she would have done something. It's not like her to not cover all the bases."

"Dean," Molly looked in his eyes. "She didn't tell you she was pregnant. She didn't send you evidence, just like she didn't send evidence to the police or the federal government. She told me what she was going to do would allow her and Nicholas to start over safe. She knew that if she left a trail for someone else to follow if she was killed, the father would find out about the baby." She paused and took his hand. "Julie was going to deliver her evidence to the authorities in person or not at all. And remember, she was careful to do it without Nicholas. None of what she did was accidental, or unplanned— including befriending me. She had one goal and only one: to protect her child.

"If she failed, she wanted this to die with her. She wanted it to end. She did everything she could to insure that. She would not risk Nicholas, not even to punish the man who killed her."

Dean wanted to tell Molly she was wrong. Julie's sense of justice, of right and wrong, had always been strong.

Then a little voice deep inside, one that had been fed by watching Molly with Nicholas, by seeing the sacrifices she herself had made for a child she hadn't given birth to, grew in intensity until it shouted: *Nothing mattered more to Julie than her child—not justice or conscience or ethics.* He realized that a mother's fierce protectiveness had, up until now, been as foreign to him as Islamic culture had once been.

He squeezed Molly's hand. Looking into her gray eyes, he saw the same ferocious drive to protect Nicholas. Molly could be angry, bitter that his sister had used her in this way, that Julie had set upon her a life she did not have a hand in choosing. But there was none of that in Molly's eyes. All he saw there was love.

Why hadn't he seen this before he set these wheels in motion? Now there was a killer as determined to protect himself as Julie had been to protect Nicholas. If he'd listened to Molly, maybe the baby would have remained undetected and things could have moved along as his sister had planned.

Too late now. Now he had to see this through to the end. He had to eliminate this threat, and keep Molly and Nicholas safe in the process.

As if she read his mind, she said, "Can you call off your investigator? Maybe if we stop looking for the father, he'll realize we've given up."

He closed his eyes for a moment. "It's too late. He thinks Julie hid evidence. He won't stop. It's just a matter of time before he connects the dots and realizes you have Julie's baby—he'll assume, as I did, that the evidence could be with you, too."

Molly sighed, sounding as tired as he felt. "Let's get some sleep," she said.

Sleep seemed as impossible as turning back time. But he could see she was exhausted, so he said, "Good idea. I'll just crash in the living room."

Still holding his hand, she rose. "Don't be ridiculous. Come to bed with me."

He stood and wrapped her in his arms. He held her tightly for a long while. He shouldn't do it. He was going to hurt her; sleeping with her knowing that seemed unconscionable. But when she stepped away and said, "Come on," his will deserted him. All he wanted to do was hold her next to him, feel the silk of her skin against his, breathe in her exhaled breath.

Exhaustion precluded a long, languorous undressing. Instead they both stripped off their clothes and slid under the sheets from opposite sides of the bed. When they came together, it was with passion fueled by high emotion, fear and loss mingled with desire and devotion. The fact that danger could be lurking outside their door heightened every sensation, made each touch brilliant with meaning.

At the moment their bodies joined, Dean looked into her eyes and saw that he was home. For the first time in years, complete peace flowed over him. And the most amazing thing was that he saw the same emotions reflected from her own gaze.

He held her close long after she'd fallen asleep. It seemed impossible that fate, as cruel as it had been to his sister, could deliver this woman to him by the same tragedy. And now he had to prevent that tragedy from compounding itself. Tomorrow, he'd contact the authorities and try to come up with a plan to take Stephen Van-Graff out of the picture. He didn't know where else to turn. He ignored the reporter's logic that told him if they had enough evidence to get VanGraff, they'd have him by now. And, at this point, Dean had nothing new to add to their arsenal.

At some point Dean must have dozed, because the scraping on the outside wall of the house brought him straight up in bed. He listened intently.

Molly roused next to him. "What?" she whispered.

"Shh."

It sounded again.

"There's a tree that scrapes on the house when it's windy," she said sleepily.

Dean got up and moved the curtain aside to look out the window. The wind had picked up, bending tree branches that looked like an audience of gray skeletal fingers applauding against the pre-dawn sky. Still he wasn't satisfied until he went through the house, checking the locks and peering out each window.

When he returned to the bedroom, Molly was sound asleep, but Nicholas was beginning to make those tiny noises Dean had grown to recognize as precursors to waking.

He slipped on his clothes, then picked up a fresh diaper and the baby before Molly awakened. With Nicholas in the crook of one arm, he set a bottle to warm. Then he changed the diaper quickly, before Nicholas could get himself worked into a real cry.

As he sat feeding the baby, barefooted in the gray of

early morning, he listened to the increasing wind. To Nicholas he said, "Well, little guy. You and I have a real problem. What are we going to do about your mommy?"

Looking into those tiny blue eyes, watching the little fists clutch in front of Nicholas's chest as he took the bottle, Dean realized there was only one answer to that question.

As soon as Dean finished feeding the baby, he set him in his pumpkin seat and made a call to Harry. They had to contact the feds. If nothing else, perhaps they could put an alert out for VanGraff's known contacts and look for anyone flying to Indianapolis or Louisville. It wasn't much, but it was better than nothing.

Harry's voice sounded groggy when he answered.

"You think I'm paying you to lie in bed all morning?" Dean said.

Harry groaned. "What time is it?"

"It's eight where you are."

With a deep breath, Harry said, "Well, that means thanks to your stinkin' case, I've been asleep a grand total of fifty-six minutes."

"What's going on?" Even as he asked, his skin prickled with anticipation.

Dean listened with disbelief as Harry told the tale of his night. When he finished the call, he picked up the baby and carried him back into the bedroom. He put the child between himself and Molly in the bed. He wasn't in the least worried about falling asleep and suffocating the baby—not after what Harry had told him.

Even though he tried to be quiet and careful not to jostle the bed too much, Molly's eyes came open. She smiled sleepily at him, then inched closer to the baby. When she held Nicholas's impossibly tiny hand between her thumb and forefinger and kissed it, Dean's heart nearly stopped beating. There was going to be no more excuse for delay. Everything was about to change— again.

When Molly's eyes fully focused, she saw something on Dean's face that made her skin crawl with apprehension. "What's wrong?"

"I just spoke to Harry. Seems the CIA rousted him in the night, asking what he had on VanGraff, accusing him of upsetting the delicate balance of their investigation."

"That should be good, right? They're keeping an eye on VanGraff."

"It seems that the CIA weren't the only players on the move last night. VanGraff left a nightclub around three A.M. and someone shot him as he was getting into his limo."

"Dead?" It was almost too much to hope for.

"Dead. CIA's pissed. VanGraff is just a link in a chain to them; they wanted the whole chain. They think he was killed because they were getting so near to springing their trap. Harry's digging around made his 'associates' additionally nervous. They didn't trust VanGraff not to turn on them once in custody."

"No honor among thieves," she said quietly.

"Very much like that."

"Why are you so unhappy?" This had been the answer to her prayer. Nicholas was safe forever and Dean didn't risk his own life getting it done. What more could he want?

"I'm not." He leaned across the baby and kissed her. "Try to go back to sleep."

She rolled onto her back and stretched. "I can't. I promised Lily I'd come to brunch at her house this morning. She says she's worried Dad and I won't get completely made up on our own. But I think it's really because she wants someone more scandalous than herself there when she tells Dad that Clay is Riley's father."

As she started to get out of bed, he grabbed her hand. "Wait."

She lay back against her pillow with her heart hammering. She knew there was more that he'd been holding back. With great effort, she looked him in the eye.

He appeared uncomfortable, yet held her gaze. "You've been a wonderful mother to Nicholas. I don't want to hurt you—"

"Stop!" She raised her hand in the air between them. "I don't want to hear it—not yet. Please, give me that." Without waiting for any kind of response, she got up and went into the shower where she cried for a solid thirty minutes.

Molly was surprised when Dean asked if he could go to Lily's with her. She allowed herself this one weakness. At least when she told her family of her great big lie she'd have Dean there with her. Maybe he could shed a noble light on it in her father's eyes. Surely Dean would do that for her.

When they arrived at Lily's farm, Dean made a point of carrying Nicholas inside. It rankled, as if he was staking his territory, but she decided she'd better get used to it. She'd come to the conclusion that she would not beg to keep the baby; it would be pointless and might just cause Dean to alienate her altogether. He felt strongly about family—and Nicholas was all he had. But she wasn't going down without a fight to remain in the child's life. So she put a smile on her face and followed him up the front porch steps.

Lily let them in and snatched Nicholas for some baby kisses, while Dean apologized for barging in on their family meal.

Lily dismissed his apology and graciously welcomed him.

When they entered the big kitchen at the rear of the house, Dean made all of the appropriate noises of appreciation and said, "Something smells good."

"Help yourself to coffee. Everything will be ready in a minute." Lily handed Nicholas back to Dean and started pulling things out of the refrigerator.

Benny was in the overstuffed chair beside the fireplace and Faye was perched on the hearth. With her red hair, she reminded Molly of a parrot hovering near her burly pirate.

Molly introduced Dean, unnecessarily as it turned out, to Faye and then kissed her dad on the cheek. "Hi, Dad."

"Hi, baby." He still looked a little edgy, so she moved away from him and helped Lily shuttle food to the dining room table.

As they sat down to brunch, a quality that reminded Molly of static electricity buildup hung in the air. While they ate, everyone was careful to avoid the topic of Riley's disappearance. But when Lily served dessert, their dad said, "So young man, you gave everyone quite an upset the other night."

Riley cast a quick glance first at Lily, then Clay. "Yes, sir."

Benny said, "That's all you have to say? That little girl broke her leg. Your mother was frantic. And poor Faye didn't sleep a wink until she knew you were safe."

For a moment, Molly thought Lily was going to let Riley go it alone. She was just about to speak up herself, when Lily said, "Dad, Riley had a very good reason to need to spend time alone. But when Mickey hurt her leg, he did the right thing and stayed with her until daylight." She swallowed dryly.

Clay reached over and held her hand. He then looked his father-in-law in the eye and said, "Benny, the reason Riley was so upset is that Lily and I had just told him that I'm his father."

Molly watched her dad's brown eyes cut quickly from one of them to the other. She held her breath. Poor Dad, this was going to be a day filled with shockers.

Benny said, "Well." He cleared his throat. "This is certainly a surprise." Then he looked at Riley. "I understand you were upset. But running away is no way to handle something like this. It did nothing but put your mother in a state and cause that little girl to get hurt."

Molly nearly blurted out that at least his reaction got things aired out better than just shutting the door on someone. But this wasn't about her and her dad, it was about Riley and Lily.

"I know, Gramps. I'm sorry I worried everyone."

Wow, no excuses? No blaming Lily and Clay? Now it was Molly's turn to absorb her surprise. Riley had become a man before her eyes and she hadn't noticed until now.

Lily tearfully explained how she ended up married to Peter and Benny listened in tight-lipped silence.

When she was finished, Benny remained still, his expression unreadable.

Molly knew this was particularly difficult for him to swallow. Their dad had raised them on two basic principles: truth and responsibility. Any transgression in these areas was serious trouble. Most all other sins could be eventually pardoned. Molly always suspected he felt so strongly about this because of their mother—who in the end was neither truthful nor responsible.

Now, in one afternoon, the poor guy was going to discover both of his daughters had lied to him.

She tried to relax while Lily's revelation soaked in before she admitted her own duplicity. Somehow, she thought, all of the good intentions in the world were not going to make a difference here today.

"Well, now, see how things had a way of working out." Faye spoke up, apparently trying to soften Dad's lack of response. "The three of you are together, just like you should be."

Molly knew this must have been for Riley's benefit, because Faye never went out of her way to make things easier for Lily. Theirs had been a battle of wills from the start; three years ago they had squared off at odds over what was best for Benny. Molly knew her dad would never be swayed by *anyone* to do something he didn't want to do, so she didn't understand the purpose of the whole conflict. Their truce was always tenuous at best.

Clay said, "Riley, if you'd like to be excused, you may."

Riley looked grateful and left the table.

For that, *Molly* was grateful. She hated to deliver her bombshell in front of him, especially since she wasn't sure she'd hold up under her father's reproach as admirably as Riley had. Her weakness wouldn't be triggered because she was afraid of her father, but because once the fact that Nicholas wasn't really hers was out there, it would become reality. Just looking across the table at Riley made her long for the boy that Nicholas would someday grow to be. Already a lump was gathering in her throat. Would she be able to get the words out at all?

"Dad, aren't you going to say something?" Lily asked.

Benny shifted in his seat, then put his napkin on the table beside his uneaten cake. "What do you want me to say? That I'm glad you were so afraid to tell me you were in trouble that you'd marry a man you didn't love to avoid it?"

"Dad, I—"

"What kind of father was I—that you couldn't come to me?"

Lily got up and walked around the table and put her hands on his shoulders. "I did love Peter, Dad. It wasn't the right kind of love, but I didn't know that then. I made a choice that I thought was best for everyone. I would have come to you if I didn't think Peter and I had a chance. I really would."

Benny's chin puckered and his hand covered Lily's where it lay on his shoulder. Lily sat in the chair that Riley had just vacated, next to their dad. She left her arm around him and rested her head on his big shoulder.

Molly decided it was best not to wait for this forgiving atmosphere to pass. "Um, Dad. I'm afraid I have something to tell you, too." Suddenly she felt light-headed. Giving voice to the fact that Nicholas was going to leave forever robbed her of breath.

As she made a conscious effort to fill her lungs, her Dad's hand slammed against the table, stopping her mid-breath.

"I knew it! I knew it!" he said brusquely. "Coletta denied it, but I knew there was more going on."

Molly swallowed her surprise. "What—?"

Dean put his hand on her leg and squeezed, cutting off her words.

"By God," Benny said, "I knew you were the father of that baby. He's got your chin." He pointed to where Nicholas was lying on a quilt on the floor looking at a portable mobile and kicking his legs.

Dean stood. "I'm sorry we didn't tell you sooner. But Molly and I had some things to work out."

A little gasp came from Lily.

Dad looked surprisingly proud when he said, "I knew there was no way they'd waste you on some pansy-assed story about small towns." Then he turned his gaze on Molly and that pride disappeared in a wisp of ill-tempered smoke. "So, what's your excuse?"

Molly blinked as she tried to assemble her words. Where had her dad gotten the idea that Dean was Nicholas's father? Did Dean know this was coming, is that why he'd silenced her? Did he want to leave her family believing this? As tempting as it was, she would tell no more lies. "This is an even longer story than the one that preceded Lily's marriage to Peter." She gulped a huge gasp of air. "Nicholas isn't Dean's son—and he's not mine either."

"What!" Dad's voice overrode all of the other sounds of surprise from around the table.

Molly straightened her back and looked her father in the eye. "Nicholas is the son of Dean's sister. She was a friend and patient of mine in Boston."

Dean stepped behind Molly and put his hands on her shoulders. She was grateful for the warmth of his touch because she was suddenly chilled to the bone.

"Why did you tell us he's yours? This doesn't make a scrap of sense," her Dad said gruffly.

"Molly, why?" Lily's softer voice asked.

"Nicholas's mother was murdered; she left him with me. I promised her I would protect him."

"You hardly had to lie to your family to protect him!" Dad said.

"But I did—and to protect you, too. It's complicated, let me tell you the whole story, then you can ask questions, okay?"

Benny looked impatient but nodded tersely.

Lily looked at her with questioning eyes.

Clay's gaze offered sympathy, a place Molly could hide while she recounted the past months. So she looked at him while she told her family the entire thing, from her first meeting with Sarah until the phone call this morning saying Nicholas's father was dead. She did not mention the father's name—she would never reveal that to anyone.

When she was done, no one said a word. Lily sniffled and wiped her eyes and nose on a napkin.

Molly was suddenly tired, the emotions over the past two months finally weighing her down. She hated to see disappointment in her father's eyes, and yet, nothing seemed to matter much now. Nicholas was lost to her. The feelings for Dean that had begun to gain substance like the layers of a watercolor painting were no more than that, colors that would run and blur and wash away when exposed to the weather of time and distance.

It startled her to realize the loss of that growing love was nearly as painful as losing Nicholas. Dean had carved himself a place deep in her soul. There was going to be a huge aching void when he left.

Finally, her dad broke the heavy silence. "So you didn't trust us with the truth?"

"Dad, I had no idea who the murderer was, or how much he knew. I couldn't tell *anyone*—but that wasn't the reason I didn't tell you. I broke the law when I kept Nicholas and left Boston with him. If I had been caught and charged, anyone who knew could have been charged, too. I could risk my career and my freedom, but I had no right to risk anyone else's."

Her dad's eyes cut over her head to Dean. "Are you going to have my daughter arrested?"

Molly felt Dean's hands tighten on her shoulders. "Molly acted selflessly to protect my nephew. Of course I'm not."

Lily's voice was shaking when she said, "But you're going to take Nicholas away from her."

A tiny stifled sob broke loose from Molly's chest. She swallowed it, but her tears couldn't be stopped. She felt their burning tracks on her cheeks. Her ears started ringing and, although she was seated on a sturdy oak chair, it felt as if she were on the deck of a pitching ship. She grabbed the edge of the table with both hands to steady herself and the bow of that ship plunged into another trough between giant waves.

It'll be all right, Dean will let me visit. Oh please God, don't let him cut me completely out.

She must have swayed in her chair, because Dean slid his hands down, wrapping them around her upper arms, and held tight.

"No. I'm not taking Nicholas away from her." Dean's voice sounded as if he was speaking at the far end of a long tube.

Could she trust her ringing ears?

Molly jumped up and turned, her balance completely off, and would have toppled to the side, if Dean hadn't wrapped his arms around her. As if he knew she needed to hear it again, he said into her ear, "I'm not taking him away from you." His arms held her tightly against his chest. She could hear the emotion in his voice. "I couldn't do that to you—or to Nicholas."

Chapter 24

Molly and Dean didn't talk the whole way home from Lily's. The air between them seemed as fragile and cold as thin strands of crystal glass. Molly was afraid to question his decision, for fear he'd change it. And he looked pensive and distracted as he drove her car back to the little house on Grant Street.

When Molly came out of the bedroom after putting Nicholas down for a nap, she saw that Dean had stolen more firewood. The crackling fire lent a false sense of cheerfulness to the room. The gathering dark clouds outside and increasingly cold wind suited the look on Dean's face much better.

He was standing with his elbow propped on the mantel, looking at her Tinkerbell clock. His forehead was creased and his mouth held a stony line.

She forced herself to ask the question that had been burning her tongue for the past hour. "Why? Why are you letting me keep him?"

When he looked at her, there was such pain his eyes—

normally the blue-green of a warm Caribbean sea, now the flat color of stormy waves—she nearly shied away. But she stood strong and held his gaze.

He straightened. "Because fate stole one mother from Nicholas; I can't take another."

She saw how difficult this choice was for him, how much he denied himself in giving Nicholas this—giving her this. Her hand went to his cheek. She held it there, love growing in her heart.

A single tear slipped from the corner of his eye and touched her fingertips.

He leaned into her touch, then wrapped his long fingers around her wrist. Turning his head, he kissed her palm. "I want him. But you're good for him in ways I can never be."

She moved her hand to rest over the scar on his neck, then brushed her lips lightly against his. "He's ours. Yours and mine, as surely as if we had made him."

He crushed her to him, burying his face in her hair. His breathing was uneven, but she didn't think he was crying; he was . . . accepting. Her own tears were flowing freely.

She'd asked herself this question a hundred times in her life, and she asked it again: did someone always have to suffer for another to find happiness? It certainly seemed so today.

In a moment of desperate wanting, she nearly asked him to stay; the words were ready on her lips. But that would only be asking him to sacrifice something else he loved to stay here and . . . what, what would he do in a place like Glens Crossing?

When he released her, he put his hands on her neck,

his thumbs along her jaw line. "There's also a very selfish reason I'm leaving him with you."

Looking as deeply as she could, she could see nothing selfish in his choice. It must have shown in her eyes.

"Leaving Nicholas here is one sure way to keep distance from tearing apart what you and I have started."

An unnatural lightness overtook her body. He felt they'd started something worthwhile, too.

He lowered his lips to hers, gently teasing the corners of her mouth, tracing the borders of her lips, before he engaged them fully in a kiss. The sweetness of it flowed the length of her body. The possibilities for their future sang in her veins. And she knew in that moment, that until they were together again, she would not be whole.

"How soon?" she asked, her gaze fixed on their clasped hands.

"Tomorrow. I have to get back to New York. The magazine. . . ."

She shook her head. "You don't need to explain."

After a deep breath, he said, "I'll come back as soon as I can. But I'm not sure when that'll be." After a pause, he added, "I may have to go back to the Middle East."

Molly's heart seized with panic. She bit her lip to keep from saying what was on her mind. The Middle East— where people shot at him. Could they have come this far, only to lose one another? Nicholas needed him. She needed him.

Kissing her forehead, he said, "I'll call as soon as I know something." He paused. "I'll call tomorrow. And the next day. And the next."

She laughed tearfully. "Stay with me tonight?"

"You won't be able to get me out of here tonight with a crowbar."

Dean was ready to leave the next morning before the sun edged over the horizon. A sleety drizzle was falling that reminded Molly of the first hours of the storm that brought Nicholas into the world. The temperature was hovering just above freezing and was supposed to remain there throughout the day, so she didn't fear for Dean's safety on icy roads.

She stood at her front door wearing nothing but her flannel robe. Dean had picked up his things from Brian's cottage yesterday afternoon, so he was ready to go. He hadn't bothered to shave this morning after his shower and was looking ruggedly handsome and heartbreakingly gentle as he stood there holding the baby.

He kissed Nicholas, then held him slightly away so he could look into his tiny face. "You take care of your mother." Then he kissed him on the cheek again and handed him to Molly.

"And you take care of yourself," she said, grabbing the back of his neck with her free hand and pulling his head close to hers.

His hands settled on her waist and held her gently. His kiss was laced with all of the passion they'd shared and all of the uncertainty of their future. He broke off quickly, picked up his bag and left without another word. They'd said it all last night. Their feelings for one another were strong, had been tempered by the fire of tragedy, but were they enough to weather the test of time and distance? She wanted it to work—and not just because of Nicholas. But all they could do was feel their way along and hope their hearts were speaking true.

She watched through tears that blurred his figure as he got in his rental car. She remained standing in the chilly air of the open doorway, Nicholas wrapped warmly in a blanket in her arms, until long after Dean's taillights had disappeared down the street.

Even with this baby in her arms, Molly had never felt so lonely. Her empty house echoed the starkness in her soul. But beneath all of the sorrow, there burned a tiny flame—not strong and steady, but still hot and bright— that Dean Coletta had ignited. She would not let it die.

She would fill this house with comfort and love and laughter, for Nicholas, and for Dean when he returned— whether for a visit, or, could she hope . . . longer.

The rest was in his hands.

Riley's Mustang was low and hard to get in and out of with a heavy cast. They'd managed to get Mickey in with no problem with the seat all of the way back. Now, in the school parking lot, he took her crutches out of the back and had her turn sideways in the seat, with her legs out the door.

He faced her, putting his hands on her elbows, ready to pull her up.

Her cheeks turned pink with embarrassment. "Really, if you just hand me the crutches, I think I can get out myself."

"I don't want you to fall. This is your first time. Shut up and hold on to me."

She flashed him a grin that said she knew she should be defiant, but she held his forearms and he pulled her to a standing position. Once she was up, their faces were inches apart.

He just stood there for a second with her clinging to him.

"My crutches?" she said.

Instead of handing them to her, he leaned down and kissed her quickly.

She glanced around with burning cheeks to see if anyone was watching. She thought she was probably the only one in high school not used to kissing in the parking lot.

Riley handed her crutches to her, then he got both of their backpacks out of the car. He let her set the pace as they walked inside. He tried to act like he wasn't slowing down for her sake. Just before they went inside, he stopped.

"Wait a minute," he said, stepping out of the flow of students entering the building.

She followed him. "What?"

It made him feel like a heel when he saw a flash of fear in her eyes.

She said quickly, "You can go on in. Just put my backpack on my shoulder."

Now he felt like an even bigger bastard. Is that what she thought? That he was embarrassed to be seen with her?

With a shake of his head, he said, "I just want to warn you, there are some . . . rumors going around." There'd been plenty of talk on Friday; he'd heard whispered comments. The rumors were varied and many—and all of them wrong.

She pursed her lips knowingly. "Let's see . . . in each

of them I'm sure you scored in the woods the other night."

He glanced down, then looked in her eyes. "I've told everyone the truth."

"Who wants to hear that?" she asked flippantly and turned around to walk—well, hobble—into school.

He had to run to catch up and open the door for her.

They stopped at her locker first, then his. Then he walked her to her first class.

"Listen, you don't have to babysit me," she said as he set her books on her desk. "I can get around fine with the stuff for one class at a time."

He heard a little ripple of speculation in the voices in the background. He looked around the room and everyone tried to look like they were doing something else.

"I'll be back at the end of first period. Mrs. Beaver gave me a pass to get out of each class a couple of minutes early as long as you're on crutches."

There was an odd look in Mickey's eyes—wary, vulnerable.

He said goodbye, then left for his own class. As he walked down the hall, he wondered how long it would be before she trusted him again—how long before that look went away.

At the end of the last period class on Wednesday, Mickey waited for Riley until everyone else in the room had left. He was always at the door before the bell rang.

She finally got up on her crutches, picked up her notebook and purse and headed to her locker on her own. She'd been hearing people talk all day long about how he and Codi were getting back together. She should have known this would happen. Why did she let herself think things were going to be different? After three days of schlepping her junk from place to place, Riley was tired of it. She couldn't really blame him. He'd been spending all of his time babysitting her and not hanging with his friends.

As she opened her locker, she tamped down her disappointment. After all, she knew this would happen.

Her notebook slipped out of her hand. It hit the tile floor with a snap. It wasn't going to be a pretty sight, her picking up that notebook with this damn cast on her leg. Maybe she'd just leave it. It was for a lit class, she didn't really need her notes, she'd read everything they were studying at least three times.

She was careful not to drop anything else as she loaded her backpack.

Then she realized she didn't have a way home from school. It was pretty far to walk on crutches, especially with the load in her backpack; she had two tests tomorrow and couldn't leave this stuff here. She'd just have to wait until five and have her mom come and pick her up. She supposed she could study on one of the benches outside the main office until then.

Just as she slammed her locker closed, feeling pretty sorry for herself—another thing that made her mad, she hated feeling sorry for herself—she heard someone running down the hall.

"Mickey!" Riley called.

She looked up but didn't say anything. She couldn't open her mouth without her chin quivering. Damn self-pity.

"Sorry I'm late!" He reached for her backpack, then saw the notebook on the floor. "This yours?"

She nodded.

He scooped it up and put it in her pack. "We had this group project in history. It took longer than the class time." He looked miffed. "Because some people are too lazy to do their part."

A voice called down the hall. "Riley! I'll see you at six."

He closed his eyes for just a second, his jaw tight. "Okay." But he didn't turn around and look at Codi.

Mickey said, "My mom's coming to get me after work. You can go on."

"Bullshit." He started walking toward the doors to the student parking lot.

He had her bag, so she had to follow. He waited for her at the door.

"This group project—it's due tomorrow. It's Codi, Jen, and Jeff and me. We signed up for groups two weeks ago. I have to finish it."

Mickey looked into his eyes. "You don't have to explain to me." She turned around and pushed open the door with her backside, then started down the walk. She heard him swear behind her.

They didn't talk as they got in the car. When he climbed in the driver's seat, he didn't put the keys in the ignition and start it. They both sat there staring out the windshield.

He turned in his seat, the leather upholstery creaking in the cold. "Come with me."

"What?"

"Come with me to Codi's. You're a brain when it

comes to history—and everything else. That way we can get this done fast and I can get out of there."

She screwed her mouth to the side. "I don't think so."

"Please. Codi's being a real pain in the ass. She's already hooked up with Nathan Pryor. She just wants to hurt your feelings."

Mickey couldn't help herself. She looked at him coolly. "I heard she dumped Nathan and was getting back with you."

He reached over and grabbed her hand, which was fisted on her thigh. "You heard wrong. Probably from those same people who said I scored last week."

She couldn't suppress a small smile.

"Listen. Codi Craig can say or do whatever she wants. She's a nasty, hateful person. Nothing will change my mind about that."

Mickey looked down at their hands; his were so much bigger than hers. She liked that. And she wanted him to touch her in ways she probably shouldn't. Sometimes at night when she was lying in bed, she thought about how his hands would feel touching her. But it made her so scared.

As if he could read her mind, he leaned close and kissed her, putting his hand on her neck. His tongue traced her lips, then gently slid inside her mouth. After a moment, his hand slid down her chest on the inside of her open jacket until it rested lightly on her breast. He didn't get rough and grabby, he just let his hand lie there over her heart.

It started beating so fast, she was afraid he would feel it. Her body tingled—everywhere. A heat started where his hand rested and shot straight to the pit of her stomach.

This was so much more powerful than any of her imaginings—and it was through her sweater. She trembled to think of what it might be like skin on skin.

When he stopped kissing her, he put his hand back on her cheek. "I love you, Mickey. I think I always have."

She drew in a trembling breath. "Oh, I want to believe that's true." There was no way she could say the words to him that she'd been keeping locked away for so long. That just left her too vulnerable.

He leaned back into his seat and started the car. "I know I've been a jerk." Then he smiled in a way that set her heart on fire. "But just give me some time—I'll prove it to you."

As they left the school parking lot, Mickey tried to absorb this moment, the skyrocketing joy that was in her heart. And spitefully, yet unashamed of it, she wished Codi was around so she could flip her off one more time.

Molly went home at the end of her second four-day rotation in the emergency room at Henderson County Hospital exhausted, but very happy to be back to doctoring. Coming in the back door, she smelled the tantalizing aroma of the stew Hattie had bubbling on the stove.

As always upon her return, Hattie and Nicholas were in the rocker that Hattie herself had carried in from the farm. Nicholas was freshly bathed and fed.

She never would have believed she could be so comfortable leaving Nicholas with anyone for twelve straight hours. But Hattie was like the mother Molly never had. Quickly seeing things that needed doing, Hattie handled them. She was like a guardian angel with Nicholas—

Molly had seen that the first time she'd stayed with him while she'd had dinner with Brian.

He had called and, as time had been fast rushing toward her first day of work, Molly had agreed it was time for their dry run with Hattie. It was also a good time for her to explain things to Brian before the rumor mill had ground her story into a tawdry dust. She had ended the tale with the fact that she and Dean were trying to work out a long-distance relationship.

At first his eyes had clouded, then he smiled, sadly but sweetly, and wished them well. As they had parted ways at their cars, he told her if Dean proved unworthy, she should give him a call. He kept the mood light and kissed her on the cheek. He really was a nice guy—he just wasn't Dean.

"Hello, you two." Molly put down her purse and took off her coat and gloves. Then she took Nicholas from Hattie.

"How was your day?" she asked, nuzzling Nicholas's soft warm cheek.

"He's a reg'lar piglet today. Prob'ly time to add some cereal," Hattie said as she got up and went to the kitchen to put their late supper on the table.

Molly liked it that Hattie completely ignored the fact that Molly was a pediatrician and therefore might just have some ideas of her own on what a baby should be eating, or when it should be doing certain things. It was good to have a practical hand helping her with the rudder. Both she and Nicholas benefited from Hattie's no-nonsense hands-on wisdom.

It was also good to have someone to eat supper with at the end of a twelve-hour day. Molly had made another visit to McDougall's Furniture and outfitted the second bedroom with a twin bed for Hattie, in case she wanted to stay over. Which, so far, she never did; always saying her chickens needed to be tended. The woman had the energy of three twenty-year-olds.

Molly also moved Nicholas's crib into that room—*his* room. Someday, probably long before she was ready, he would be sleeping in that twin bed.

After the dishes were done, she saw Hattie to the door. Then she rocked and sang to Nicholas until it was time to put him down for the night. His bouts with colic had become more sporadic, making her spend fewer evenings in the steamy bathroom.

Dean didn't call every day, but rarely let two days pass without. He never called before eleven, just in case Nicholas was having a bad evening. And he was always careful not to keep her too long on her work nights.

Just as Molly was slipping into her jammies, the phone rang. As always, she answered with excitement buzzing in her veins. Even in their briefest conversations, she felt his caring. Whenever she hung up, however, a hollow ache settled in her chest. No matter how much she told herself she was being foolish, she could not vanquish it.

"Hello," she answered, her fatigue of four long days melting away in anticipation of hearing his voice.

"Is he asleep?"

"Yes. No colic tonight. Good thing too, I'm beat."

"Hattie's still doing fine?"

"Oh my gosh, the woman is a walking miracle. I could not do this without her."

"You don't have to, you know," he said gently.

"What?" Maybe that fatigue was sticking with her; it felt like she was missing a cog in this conversation.

"You don't have to do it—work. I'll take care of you and Nicholas as long as you want to stay home with him."

This suggestion took her completely off guard. She knew he offered with good intentions, but it made her feel . . . like a mistress.

"I like being a doctor. I'm only working about 15 days a month. Hattie's working out great. I want to stay with it—unless it proves to be detrimental to Nicholas, which I can't foresee right now."

"Okay. I just . . . I feel so . . . cut off. I need to be doing something."

"You've already sent enough money to keep him for six months. Just come and spend time with him as often as you can. That's the most valuable thing you can give him."

"What about you?" he asked with the now familiar longing in his voice.

She smiled and felt warm all over. "Oh, that's what I want, too—your time . . . and your body."

He chuckled and she missed him terribly.

"God, I miss you," he said, echoing her own thoughts.

"I miss you, too. Do you have any idea yet where you'll be assigned?"

"Smitty's being an ass. I'm still being punished and chained to my desk. I should know something next week."

"Oh." The thought of him seven hundred miles away was hard enough. Dean on the far side of the world was unbearable.

He tried to lighten her mood with a couple of bawdy jokes and a story about one of their Jewish reporters who got stuck in an elevator in Rome with three Cardinals for five hours.

Finally he said, "I should let you go. You've had a long day and the baby will be up early."

She wanted to ask him to talk to her until she fell asleep, but he had to go to work in the morning, too.

"Okay. Nicholas says he loves you." She hesitated. "And I do too."

She heard his intake of breath.

"I've been waiting for you to say that," he said cheerfully. "I didn't want to scare you off, thinking I was jumping the gun. But, damn woman, I've loved you for over three weeks now."

"Well, not to be outdone, I'm going on four."

"What are we going to do about it?" his voice was just a little husky when he asked.

"Let it run its course?"

"I told you the first time I kissed you, we're a dangerous mix. There's no 'running its course' with us."

She felt like jumping up and down. But she kept her voice calm and said, "We'll see, Mr. Coletta."

"Damn right, Dr. Boudreau." And he hung up the phone.

Chapter 25

As it turned out, it was nearly two weeks before Dean called with the news Molly had been dreading. His scheduled visit to Glens Crossing the previous weekend had been cancelled because he had been sent to Switzerland at the last minute to cover peace talks. Of course, there was no peace agreement, just more finger pointing. But the fact that Dean's boss sent him there was a bad sign to Molly—a very bad sign.

"They're sending me back to the Middle East," he said in a flat voice that Molly couldn't read.

"When?" It was little more than a squeak.

"That's the thing about the Middle East. If you're going to catch something before the buzz dies down, you needed to be there yesterday. I leave tomorrow."

"Can't they give you a day or two to see Nicholas?" She was slightly ashamed of the childish pleading tone in her voice, but she couldn't help it.

He sighed heavily. "As much as I want to see the little booger, it's you that's keeping me awake at night."

Something just short of a hiccup came out of her mouth. She swallowed and tried to speak again. "How long?"

"I don't know. Depends on the situation over there."

"You'll miss Nicholas's first Christmas."

"I know. I'm sorry—but short of quitting, I'm stuck."

She wanted with all of her heart to tell him to quit. Quit and come to Indiana and write the great American novel, start a newspaper, be a ghost writer, anything he wanted. She could support them.

Instead, she tried to smile, hoping it carried in her voice. "He won't remember this one anyway. But next year. . . ." A man like Dean would die of boredom in Glens Crossing. She couldn't ask it of him, no matter how desperately she wanted to.

"Yeah," he said softly, "next year." Someone said something to him in the background. "Listen, I have to go. I'll call you again before I leave."

She closed her eyes and pressed her lips together to keep from crying. "Bye."

"I love you, Mol. Kiss Nicholas for me."

Then he was gone. Gone to prepare to fly to the other side of the globe—where people would shoot at him. To-morrow. Oh, God, she might never see him again.

Molly stood there with the phone in her hand for a long moment. A place deep inside her called out, only to be met with lonely silence. She should have said more. There was so much in her heart that defied words. He knew she loved him; but did he know the depth of that love, that she'd never given her love to anyone before?

He said he'd call again. It would be hard over the phone, but she swore to herself she would find a way to convey the frightening power of her feelings. Maybe that would be enough to keep him safe, to bring him home to her when his work was finally done.

But Dean didn't call. She waited until one A.M. before she gave up and went to bed. She took the cordless handset to bed with her and fell asleep with it clutched against her heart, like a child's beloved bear.

Nicholas awakened early and fussy with a runny nose and a low grade fever. The mother in her suddenly outweighed the doctor and she began checking his temperature much more often than necessary, fretting over all sorts of improbable illnesses. Of course, it was just a cold.

She dosed him with Tylenol and sat in the steamy bathroom with him to help clear his stuffy nose. That soothed his fussiness and allowed him to go back to sleep.

After putting the baby down, she paced the floor with the phone in hand. Finally, at one o'clock, she broke down and dialed Dean's cell phone. It went to voice mail on the second ring.

He wouldn't just leave, would he? What if his schedule had been bumped up? *Then he'll call when he lands.*

Why hadn't she gone ahead and spoken her heart yesterday?

When Nicholas awakened, nothing would soothe him, not even the steamy bathroom. Molly walked the floor, cleaned his nose and gave more Tylenol. She'd never understood that helpless plea she'd seen in mothers' eyes when they brought their children to the clinic with just a simple cold. Now she did.

At five, she finally got him back to sleep. She was exhausted and heartsick. It was obvious Dean wasn't calling before he left the country. She made herself a cup of tea, then went to lie on her bed and sip it while she looked at the newspaper.

It seemed every article she read depressed her. A child molester was busy in Indianapolis. A teenager shot and killed his girlfriend in Bloomington. The trial for the murder of a child starved to death in foster care was granted a continuance. Then there was the national news, which spoke of nothing but terrorist attacks around the world and warfare in the Middle East. She finally threw the paper down in disgust and curled on her side to stare out the window.

Snow was beginning to fall—fat, fluffy flakes that normally made her childishly giddy. Today they just looked cold. She closed her eyes so she didn't have to look at them.

As she drifted into a doze, a single strand of music flowed over her, distant, yet distinct. She was torn between wanting to open her eyes and prove it was not real and allowing herself to ride on its melody to see where it took her. Her eyes remained closed. The melancholy violin escorted her deeper and deeper into sleep, until she heard it no more.

Seemingly an instant later she heard Dean whisper her name in a dream, his hand settling on her shoulder. It was so vividly real, it startled her to near waking, but she determinedly buried herself in sleep to hold him with her.

"Molly." His lips rested on her cheek.

Her eyes opened. He didn't vanish in the clash with reality.

She gasped and touched his face. Once convinced he was flesh and blood, not imagination and wishes, she threw her arms around his neck. His shoulders were damp with melting snow and he smelled of fresh outdoors.

"I didn't mean to frighten you." He held her in a crushing embrace.

After a moment, her heartbeat began to settle back to a normal rate. She leaned back. "You're supposed to be on a plane heading east."

"I came west instead."

"You quit?" She could hardly believe it. She felt like pinching herself to make certain she wasn't still dreaming.

He cradled the back of her head with both of his hands. "It's time for someone else to write those stories. I have other responsibilities now.

"And," he said, "I couldn't imagine living with an ocean between you and me. I don't want to rush you, but Molly, we belong together. It's stupid to deny it. Fate had a plan when it took Julie. Nicholas was born to bring us together. We can't ignore something like that."

She threw herself against him and kissed him, her body light, her heart on fire. "I love you."

He rolled onto the bed with her, kissing her with a passion that burned brightly, but not so hot that it would consume quickly and soon be exhausted. She could taste the promise on his lips.

He said, "However much time you need, I'll wait. But I'm not going away."

Her lips felt swollen from his ardent kisses. She ran

her tongue over them. Then she smiled and said, "*Red* raspberries."

At first he looked confused, then a light gleamed in his eye. "You do know the consequences of that statement, don't you? No one outside the Coletta family can know the secret ingredient in Grandma's mulled cider. You leave me no choice but to marry you."

"I accept the consequences—gladly."

After they sealed their pledge with their bodies as well as their souls, Molly lay wrapped in Dean's arms watching snow accumulate against the window glass, and childish giddiness didn't begin to describe what was in her heart.

About the Author

Hoosier native, **Susan Crandall** grew up in a small town, loving the fact that if you didn't know everyone, you at least knew of them—or their aunt, or their cousin, or the person who cuts their hair. She's taken the warmth and emotion of that sense of community and flavored her books, drawing fond memories from those who've lived in a small town and a quiet yearning from those who have not.

After a few years in the big city (Chicago), she returned to her Indiana hometown where she lives with her husband, two college-age children, a menagerie of pets, and a rock band in the basement.

Susan loves to hear from her readers. Contact her at:

P.O. Box 1092, Noblesville, IN 46060.
E-mail: susan@susancrandall.net.
Or visit her web site at www.susancrandall.net.

More
Susan Crandall!

Please turn this page
for a preview of

At Blue Pond Falls

a new Warner Book
available soon in paperback.

G ranny Tula insisted with all of her Jesus-loving heart
that God's hand was in everything. She held the deep
conviction that, although it might not be easily or readily
seen, there was a divine reason for all that transpired in His
earthly kingdom; even the terrible derailment of Glory's life.
But Glory Harrison didn't possess her grandmother's unwa-
vering faith. Glory had spent the past eighteen months on
the run and had never once seen a glimmer of God's hand in
any of it.

Tragedy, a dark and unexpected assailant, had robbed
her of her home, her husband, and her child. Drowning in
grief, Glory had fled Tennessee. Small towns could be a
comfort during times of disaster and misery—but they
could also hold your heart forever in that place of loss.
The piteous looks and the well-meant platitudes were
going to do just that, keep her heart a bloody mess that
would never heal.

Granny had never understood Glory's need to leave.
Luckily, Granny did not hold that incomprehensible need

against her. She might not understand Glory's choice, but kin was kin—and that meant she would hold onto you no matter how far from the hollow you roamed. More than once, Gran had said this family tree was oak, not poplar; and its roots went deep into the bedrock of eastern Tennessee soil. She lived her life by a simple rule: In the face of adversity you raised your chin, stiffened your back, held on to your faith and marched forward on the very path that had become littered with your broken dreams. Certainly, Granny had trod on the splinters of her own life often enough. But Glory had not been able to force her feet to crush the fragile remains of who she used to be. So she left it all behind and tried to reinvent herself.

Unfortunately, new Glory bore the same heavy sadness as old Glory, just in different climates. It had become clear that no matter how far she ran, the pain, deep and cold and fathomless, would follow her like a shadow. Sooner or later, she realized, you have to either accustom yourself to its presence, or stay forever hiding in the dark.

The time was fast coming to step into the light.

Chapter 1

Glory's key stuck in the old lock on her apartment door, refusing to turn; refusing to slide back out. She gritted her teeth, gripped the doorknob, and shook until the door rattled on its hinges, fully aware that her response was overreaction in the extreme. This lock had recently become an unwelcome symbol of her life: stymied in a dull and disconnected present, unable to move toward her future. She knew it was wrong, this hiding, this pretense of living. But she'd buried herself here and couldn't find a way to claw back out.

Taking a deep breath, she tried to use more delicate force against the lock. Her nerves had been raw and on-edge all day long. Her job at the veterinary clinic normally had a soothing effect upon her, allowing her to focus on something outside her own aching hollowness. But today she couldn't shake a nagging feeling that something was wrong. It was an insidious awareness that she just couldn't quell. Maybe it was simply her own growing understanding that she was running from the inescapable. But it seemed heavier than that; she was anxious to get inside and call Granny, just to ease her mind that the feeling had nothing to do with her.

For all of her life, Glory had had an inexplicable connection to her grandmother. Time and again she'd call and Gran would say, "I was just about to call you." It worked the other way around, too. Glory didn't share that mysterious connection with anyone else. When she was young, Granny would wink and lean close saying they came from a long line of spooky women. Back then it had made Glory think of witches and spells. But now she understood; there were some people who were knit more tightly together than by just family genetics.

The telephone began to ring inside the apartment.

Glory juggled the key with renewed vigor. Finally, on the telephone's fourth ring, the key turned and she hurried inside.

"Hello," she said breathlessly as she snatched up the phone.

"Glory, darlin', are you all right?"

Granny's slow Tennessee drawl immediately soothed Glory's nerves.

"Fine, I was just coming in and had trouble with the lock." She pushed her hair away from her face. "You've been on my mind today, Gran. How are you?"

There was a half-beat pause that set the back of Glory's neck to tingling before Granny said, "Fine. Busy. Had Charlie's boys here for the weekend."

"All of them?" Glory's cousin Charlie was getting a divorce, and had taken to foisting his five little hellions off on Granny when it was "his weekend." It really burned Glory, his taking advantage like that. Granny was nearing eighty, five boys under the age of thirteen was just too much.

"Of course. We had a great time. Hiked back to the falls. They can't get enough swimming. Travis caught a snake."

Glory closed her eyes and drew a breath. The very idea of Granny alone with five rambunctious little boys—swimming, no less—a two-mile hike from help made her stomach turn. Blue Pond Falls could have a wicked pull at the base. What if something happened? That tingling grew stronger; maybe something did. The horrors that passed through Glory's mind were endless.

"Everyone all right?" Glory tempered her question. Granny's feathers got ruffled if you treated her like an old person—overprotection was a sin not to be forgiven. Any allusion to age infirmity quickly drew pursed lips and narrowed eyes.

"'Course. Them boys all swim like fish."

"Charlie shouldn't expect you to take the boys all of the time." *Careful, don't make it sound like it's because of her age.* "They need to spend time with their father."

Granny made a scoffing sound. "Keeps me young. It's only a couple of times a month. Charlie sees plenty of them."

Glory sat on the rest of her argument. She'd be wasting her breath.

After a tiny pause too short for thought, she said, "I'm thinking about moving again." Even as the words tumbled out, she surprised herself. She'd been skirting around the idea for a few weeks now, but didn't have any solid plan laid out.

A knowing *hmmm* came over the line. "Where?"

"I don't know yet. I can't imagine staying in St. Paul through winter. The snow was fun for a while—but the thought of a whole winter here makes me depressed."

She heard Granny take a deep breath on the other end of the line. It was a tell-tale sign of trouble.

"What? Is something wrong?" Glory couldn't keep an edge of fear from her voice. She'd known something was happening.

"Not wrong. It's just . . . I had a little episode with my eye—"

"Why didn't you call me?" Glory's heart leapt into her throat. Her foreboding all day now honed in on its source.

"I just told you."

"So have you seen a doctor? What happened? Is someone there with you?"

"Calm down. I'm fine enough. I saw the doctor this morning and he said it should clear up this time."

"This time? Have you had other episodes?" Years ago Granny had been diagnosed with macular degeneration, a disease that would most likely rob her of her central vision, altering her life immeasurably. But so far Granny had been lucky. This was the first time Glory had heard a hint of a problem.

"It was a little broken blood vessel. He wants to see me again next week after the blood clears and he can see more."

Glory asked herself to ask, "Can you see?"

"Right eye's fine."

"But the left?"

"Eh." Glory could see her grandmother dismissing it with the lift of a sharp-boned shoulder. "It should be better tomorrow."

"So the condition is getting worse."

"Not necessarily. But, darlin', you know it's been just a matter of time. I've been luckier than most. It's time to take note."

Glory couldn't swallow; emotion had closed off her throat.

Granny went on. "I was wondering . . . could you . . . could you come home?" She rushed on, "Not permanently. I just want to be sure I get the chance to see your face clearly one more time."

This was the first time in Glory's memory that Tula Baker had asked *anything* of another human being. A cold sweat covered Glory from head to foot. "I'm on my way."

Twelve hours later, Glory had her car packed with her few belongings and was headed south. The miles and the hours passed barely noticed as she wrestled with emotions that were quickly becoming a two-headed monster. It certainly wasn't difficult leaving St. Paul, she'd been inching closer to that decision every day.

For the past eighteen months she thought of herself as "trying on" different places, like one would when searching for a new winter coat. She'd left Dawson with the firm conviction that there was a place out there that would act as a balm, a salve to her soul; and she could bask in it like a healing Caribbean sun. But the climates changed, population fluctuated, and Glory still felt as if she was an empty vessel, insides echoing her barren life like a bass drum. East, west, cities, rural towns, suburbia . . . nothing brought peace.

No, leaving Minnesota was easy—but the very

thought of returning to Tennessee brought beads of sweat to her upper lip and a sickness deep in her belly.

What if Granny's sight didn't return? What if this truly was the beginning of the end of her independence? Glory's heart ached for lost time and uncertain futures. A part of her could barely force herself to press the accelerator for the dread of seeing her hometown of Dawson again; yet another part of her could not reach her grandmother's wiry embrace fast enough.

Suddenly she realized she was a mere handful of miles from the Tennessee state line, less than two hours from Dawson. Her grandmother lived a few miles beyond that, deep in Cold Spring Hollow, nestled in the verdant, misty foot of the Smoky Mountains.

The rolling lay of the land in Kentucky seemed to be priming her for that inevitable moment when she crossed into the lush hill country that had nurtured her for her first twenty-six years. As her car chewed up the rapidly decreasing miles, Glory prepared. She assured herself that there would not be a great crashing wall of memory that would overcome her at the state line. Months of therapy had suggested perhaps there would be no memories—ever.

Still, Glory doubted the professionals' opinions. True, she had no "memory" of that night. But she did possess an indefinable sense of gut-deep terror when she turned her mind toward trying to recall. Which told her those memories were there, lying in the darkness, waiting to swallow her whole.

She rolled down her driver's side window. The roar of the wind at seventy filled her head. She glanced at the graceful rise and fall of the green pastures beside the interstate. She drew deep breaths, as if to lessen the shock by easing herself home, by reacquainting her senses gradually to the sights and smells of hill country.

As a child, Glory had loved visiting the wild of the deep hollow where Granny Tula had lived since the day she was born. Life in the hollow was hard, but straightforward—understandable. People of her grandmother's ilk had no time or patience for dwelling on the superficial. They accepted whatever life handed them with a nod of stoicism and another step toward their future.

Hillbillies. That's what her in-laws called folks like Tula Baker. Of course, they would never say anything like that directly about Granny—but the thought was there, burning brightly behind their sophisticated oldmoney eyes. What they had never understood was that neither Glory nor her grandmother would have been insulted by the term. Glory's mother, Clarice, on the other hand, would have been mortified. Clarice, the youngest of Tula Baker's seven children, had struggled to separate herself from the hollow and all it implied.

As Glory watched the terrain grow rougher and the woodlands become increasingly dense, she didn't feel the tide of panic that she'd anticipated.

I'm going to make it. The thought grew stronger with each breath that drew the mingling of horse manure, damp earth and fresh grass. *I'm going to make it. . . .*

The instant she saw the large sign that said, "Welcome to Tennessee," Glory's lungs seized. Seeing the words caused all of her mental preparation to disappear on the wind rushing by her open window.

Suddenly lightheaded, she pulled onto the emergency stopping lane of the interstate. As soon as her car stopped moving, she put it in park, fearing that she might pass out and start rolling again.

The car rocked, sucked back toward the racing traffic when an eighteen-wheeler whizzed by going eighty. Miraculously, the truck was gone in no more than a blur and a shudder, and Glory's four tires remained stuck to the paved shoulder out of harm's way.

She concentrated on her hands gripping the steering wheel—hands that could no more deny her heritage than her green eyes and thick, auburn hair. Sturdy, big-boned hands that somehow remained unsoftened by the cultured life she'd led. Hands that reminded her of Granny Tula's. That thought gave her strength.

After a few minutes, the cold sweat evaporated, the trembling in her limbs subsided, and her head cleared. She put the car in drive and rejoined the breakneck pace of traffic headed south.

Eric Wilson left the fire station in the middle of his shift—something he would have taken any of his firefighters to task for. But he was Chief, and as such frequently had business away from the firehouse. No one questioned when he got into his department-owned Explorer and drove away.

But this was far from official business. This was personal—very personal. He and his ex-wife, Jill, shared amicable custody of their two-and-a-half-year-old son, Scott. But Scott's increasingly obvious problems were something that the two of them were currently butting heads over. In Eric's estimation, Jill was in denial, plain and simple. And lately, it seemed she was doing as much as she could to prove Scott was just like any other boy.

Part of that strategy was *not* hovering by the telephone worrying if today was going to be the day for trouble.

Whenever he mentioned the idea that she should get a cell phone, she took the opportunity to remind him that she couldn't afford one. Which was a load of bull. She worked as a medical secretary and made decent money—comparable to Eric's fire department salary. It was always more convenient for Jill to be unavailable—especially on Wednesdays, her day off.

This was the third time in a month that the preschool had called Eric at work because they couldn't locate her. It had been a familiar message; Scott was having a "behavior problem," causing such disruption that the teachers requested he be taken home.

The staff at the church-housed preschool were sympathetic, had made every effort to help assimilate him into classroom activities; but, they explained, as they frequently did, they had to consider the other twelve children in the class.

As Eric pulled into the rear parking lot of the Methodist church, his stomach tightened with frustration. This summer preschool program was intended for children who were going to need extra time and attention to catch up; children who would benefit from not having an interruption in the development of their social skills by a long summer break. Even so, it seemed Scott was on a rapid slide backward. Eric couldn't help the feeling of terror that had begun to build deep in his heart; he felt like he was locked high in a tower, watching his son drown in the moat outside his window—close enough to witness, yet too far away to save him.

For a long moment, he sat in the car, staring toward the

forested mountains shrouded in their ever-present blue mist. In a way, Scott's mind was concealed from him much the same as was the detailed contour of those mountains. He wished with all of his soul that he could divine the right course to lead his son out of the mysterious fog. Lately they'd been making the "doctor circuit," visiting clinics in ever widening geographic circles, reaching larger and more prestigious facilities. It seemed the greater the number of professionals they consulted, the more diverse the suggestions for dealing with Scott became. Even the diagnosis varied from Asperger's Syndrome, to mild autism, to he'll-grow-out-of-it, to it's-too-early-to-tell.

Eric was willing to do whatever it took to help his son—if only there was a definite answer as to what that was. Why couldn't *someone* give him that answer?

He slammed the steering wheel with the heel of his hand. Then he took a deep breath and tried to exhale his frustration. He would need all of the calm he could muster to deal with what awaited inside.

When he entered the hall that led to the basement classroom, he could hear Scott crying—screaming. A feeling of blind helplessness *whooshed* over him like a backdraft in a fire. He quickened his pace.

With his hand on the doorknob, he paused, heartsick as he looked through the narrow glass window situated beside the door. His son stood stiffly in the corner, blue paint streaked through his blond hair and on his face. Mrs. Parks, one of the teachers, knelt beside him, careful not to touch him, talking softly. Scott really didn't like anyone outside of his parents to touch him.

Scott ignored his teacher, his little body rigid with

frustration. It was a picture Eric had seen before. Still, it grabbed his gut and twisted with brutal ferocity every time.

When he went into the room and knelt beside his son, there was no reaction of joy, no sense of salvation; no throwing himself into Eric's arms with relief. Scott's cries continued unabated.

Was this behavior an offshoot of the divorce, as Jill insisted? It seemed implausible, as he and Jill hadn't lived together since Scott was ten months old. Still, that nagging of conscience couldn't be silenced. What if that was all Scott needed; his two parents together?

Mrs. Parks, a woman whose patience continually astounded Eric, said, "I'm sorry. I didn't know what else to do but call you." She pursed her lips thoughtfully and looked back at Scott. "I think he wanted the caps put back on the finger paints. Although, I can't say for sure." In her hand she held a wet paper towel. She handed it to Eric and got up and walked away. "Maybe he'll let you wipe his hands."

Eric took the towel. Scott had become increasingly obsessed with closing things—cabinets, windows, doors, containers—with an unnatural intensity. Anything that he wasn't allowed to close sent him into an inconsolable tantrum, as if his entire world had been shaken off its foundation.

Jill's mother said the child was overindulged, spoiled because his divorced parents were vying for his love. Jill's family *did not* divorce. At first Eric had bought into the theory. But he'd been careful, studied to make sure they weren't acquiescing to Scott's every demand. The tantrums, when he tried to make a more scientific study of them, were not random. Lately, the trigger had been his need to close things.

"Okay, buddy, can I wipe your hands?" Eric asked, holding out the towel.

Scott's cries didn't escalate; Eric took that as permission. He got the worst of the blue off his son's hands, then scooped him up in his arms and carried him, still stiff and crying, out of the classroom.

Scott wiggled and squirmed, but Eric managed to get him strapped in his car seat. By the time he was finished, Eric had almost as much blue paint smeared on him as Scott did. Before he climbed in the driver's seat, Eric tried to call Jill again. No answer.

Eric then called the station. When the dispatcher picked up, he said, "Donna, I'm going to have to take the rest of the afternoon off; I had to pick Scott up at school, he's . . . sick."

Eric hadn't discussed his son's possible condition with anyone. It was still too new, too baffling. How could he explain something that was currently such a mystery to his own mind?

In many ways the trying to get confirmation that Scott *had* a problem caused as much confusion as his son's behavior did. The professionals couldn't seem to agree on anything. Specific diagnosis, treatment and prognosis were as varied as falling snowflakes.

Donna made a tiny noise of understanding. "No problem," she said with overkill on lightheartedness. "Hope he feels better soon."

Eric realized he hadn't been fooling anyone—Scott's problems were becoming evident even to those outside the family.

By the time Jill called forty minutes later, Scott was sitting quietly on the floor of Eric's living room, playing with his current favorite toy, a plastic pirate ship.

"What happened?" she asked. "I went to pick him up and they said you'd taken him home early."

"More of the same. A tantrum that wouldn't stop." Eric rubbed his eyes with his forefinger and thumb.

"You would think a preschool teacher could handle a two-year-old's tantrum without calling parents."

"Jill —" he took a deep breath "— you know it's more than that. Dr. Martin—"

"Stop! What if *Dr. Martin* is wrong? Dr. Templeton saw nothing out of the ordinary in Scott. Why do you insist upon thinking the worst?" Thankfully, she caught herself before she pushed them into their normal angry confrontation on the subject. Her voice became pleading. "Eric, I don't want him to be labeled. If they treat him like he's disabled, he's *going to be* disabled. He's just slow to mature. Lots of kids are. He's just a baby! A friend of Angela's said she knew a boy who didn't talk until he was four and he turned out just fine. And Stephanie's daughter has tantrums all of the time. A few more weeks in school and—"

"And what?" Sometimes Eric felt he was fighting the battle for his son on two fronts—against both an as-yet-unnamed developmental disorder and Scott's mother's refusal to face facts. "They'll probably ask us not to bring him back. We need to find a better solution for him. It's not just the fact that he's not talking. He doesn't interact with the other kids. Maybe he needs more structure, like Dr. Martin said."

"And Dr. Blanton said it's too early to be sure. None

of the experts can even agree! And you want him locked up in an institution!"

"Stop over-reacting. You know that's not what I meant." He closed his eyes and willed his anger to subside. "We need to find a better way to help him learn, help him cope."

She sighed heavily. "Let's give this school a couple more months. Please. Then we'll decide."

"I just feel that time is slipping away. The sooner we start, the better his chances."

"I *do not* want this whole town talking about Scott as if he's retarded. He's not."

"Of course he's not! But he's going to need more help."

"Maybe. Maybe not. I won't take the risk for nothing. I agreed to send him to school over the summer, isn't that enough for now?"

"All right." It was all Eric could do to hold his argument. It was going to take time to get Jill turned around. "We'll leave things as they are for a few more weeks. But I think it's time to start at least looking for options."

She let it drop, apparently satisfied with her temporary victory. "Since tomorrow is your day, why don't you just keep Scottie tonight? I have a ton of things to get done. It'd really help me out. I'll just pick him up out at Tula's on Friday after work."

This was yet another tool in Jill's arsenal of denial— spend less time with Scott so she didn't have to see what was becoming progressively more obvious. But that worked out just fine as far as Eric was concerned. He'd been spending every minute he could with his son, studying him, trying to decipher what was happening inside the child's mind.

"Sure. Do you want to say hi to him before I hang up?" Eric spoke to his son every day on the phone, regardless of the empty silence on the other end of the line.

"Sure."

After holding the phone next to Scott's ear for a moment while Jill held a one-sided conversation, Eric got back on the line. "I'll tell Tula you'll be there at five-thirty on Friday."

"Okay. You boys have fun." She hung up.

You boys have fun. As if he and Scott were going to a baseball game and sharing hot dogs and popcorn. Would Jill ever be convinced their son wasn't like other children?

Eric hung up the phone and stretched out on the floor next to Scott. He'd taken to only setting out one activity at a time for Scott and keeping the background noise to a minimum, as Dr. Martin had suggested. It did seem that Scott was less agitated.

There was still blue paint in Scott's hair. Eric decided to leave that until bath time—which would develop into a battle of its own; Scott didn't like to be taken away from whatever he was doing. Changing activities seemed to trigger more than just normal two-year-old frustration.

For now, he tried some of the repetitive exercises he'd read about, just to see if it seemed to make a connection. Dr. Martin said sometimes these children need to find alternative ways of communication—it was just a matter of searching and working with repetition until you found the right one.

As Eric worked with Scott, the light in the room turned

orange with sunset. Scott's pudgy toddler fingers spun the pirate boat in tireless circles. With a lump in his throat, Eric wondered if he would ever understand what was going on inside his son's mind.

It was sunset as Glory wound her way into Cold Spring Hollow. She'd driven twenty-five miles out of her way to avoid passing through Dawson; approaching the road to the hollow from the north instead of the west. It was foolish, but she somehow felt she'd be better fortified to face the town after spending the night with Granny.

In the shadows of the wooded hollow it was dark enough that her headlights came on. Glory slowed for a hairpin curve. After the road straightened back out, she saw three deer standing nearly close enough to reach out and touch. They held their bodies poised for flight, their dark eyes wide and their ears twitching. But they remained in place, studying her as closely as she studied them.

She felt a peculiar kinship to them, with their wary eyes and nervous posture. She imagined she had a similar air about herself at the moment. They remained watching her bravely as she drove on.

The narrow gravel road that led to Granny's house cut off to the right. Glory made the turn and felt more settled already. Normally, Granny would be on her porch with a cup of tea about now, impervious to the swarming mosquitoes as she sat on her beloved swing. Before Granddad died, the two of them used to sit on the porch every evening, at least for a short while, even in the winter. Glory remembered spending the night, lying in her bed and listening to their quiet voices drift up to her bedroom window. There was something about listening to them, to Granny's soft laugh and Granddad's gruff chuckle, that soaked contentment deep into Glory's bones.

Granny's house came into sight. Glory's heart skittered through a beat when she saw it sitting dark and silent under the canopy of trees. It looked deserted.

Finally, in the deep shadow of the L-shaped front porch, Glory saw movement of the swing and drew a breath of relief.

By the time she'd put the car in park and gotten out, Granny had moved to the top of the front steps, leaving the swing to jiggle a jerky dance after her departure.

She stood there, her silhouette in the twilight tall and wiry, looking as strong as the ancient willow down by the old mill pond.

Glory got out of the car quickly and ran up the steps. She paused on the tread before the top, ready to give her grandmother the greeting she deserved. But the instant Glory opened her mouth the tears that she'd thought were spent spilled forth.

Granny opened her arms and pulled Glory's head against her chest. "It's all right, darlin', you're safe in the holler now. You're home."

As Glory cried in the comfort of her grandmother's arms, she knew coming home was going to be even more painful than she'd imagined.

THE EDITOR'S DIARY

Dear Reader,

Like a breath of fresh air, love has a funny way of putting a little extra spring in your step and sparkle in your eyes. And, oh what a difference it is when you've just been through a bad patch. Need a little help keeping your faith in love? Try our two Warner Forever titles this March.

Booklist has called **Wendy Markham's** work "breezy, scrumptious fun" while *Romantic Times BOOKClub* raves it's "wonderfully touching romance with a good sense of humor." Check out her latest, **HELLO, IT'S ME**, and don't forget the tissues! It's been almost a year since Annie Harlowe's beloved husband died, leaving her to raise their two children. But she has a secret: she's been paying his cell phone bills just so she can hear his voice. Yet with funds stretched so tight she fears they'll never dig out of debt, Annie has to face the facts. Her late husband will never answer...until one night when the impossible happens and he does. Thomas Brannock IV has had his life mapped out from birth. But he never counted on Annie, a free-spirited woman with sun-kissed cheeks to blow into his life. When they literally crash into one another, it feels like a heavenly accident. But is an angel with cell phone reception playing matchmaker?

Have you ever worked for something your entire life only to find it just isn't enough? That's exactly how Molly Boudreau from **Susan Crandall's PROMISES TO KEEP** feels. After years of work and sacrifice, she's finally a doctor. But she yearns for a soul-stirring connection and she'll soon find it in her own ER. Molly has befriended a young pregnant woman who refuses to speak of her past. Her only request: that Molly protects the baby from his dangerous father. So when the woman is murdered after giving birth, Molly must keep her promise. Fearing for their safety, she returns home where she passes him off as her son. But before long, Dean Coletta, a reporter with smoldering eyes and probing questions, starts digging for the truth. With each explosive fact he uncovers about Molly and her "son," Dean's desire to protect them grows stronger. But can they build a life together with the secrets of their pasts tearing them apart? *Romantic Times BOOKClub* raves that she "weaves a tale that is both creative and enthralling" so prepare to be dazzled.

To find out more about Warner Forever, these March titles and the authors, visit us at www.warnerforever.com.

With warmest wishes,

Karen Kosztolnyik

Karen Kosztolnyik, Senior Editor

P.S. Next month, check out these two spicy little treats: Sandra Hill delivers more laughter and even more hot Cajun love when a confirmed bachelor looking to escape it all winds up in the middle of a kidnapping plot with a tantalizing celebrity in THE RED-HOT CAJUN: and Julie Anne Long debuts her latest witty and heartfelt tale of a barrister who rescues a feisty pickpocket and passes her off as a lady to win another woman's hand in TO LOVE A THIEF.